THE MAN WITH MY FACE

What do you do when you come ho.
chops in hand, ready for dinner, only to find another man in
your home who looks exactly like you? Who, in fact, claims to
be you? Not only that, but your wife and two best friends
agree with him. Even your dog doesn't recognize you. And
when you call in a cop, you can't find one bit of identification
to back up your claim. If you're Chick Graham, you get the
hell out of there and try to figure out what's going on. But
whoever this guy is who has taken your place, he's done an
excellent job. And not only that, he's robbed a million dollars
in bonds, and gotten away with it. And now everyone thinks
that you are him!

THE GRINNING GISMO

The letter from Jim asks Hank to come out west to San
Francisco and "get close to Clara" but not to let Clara knew
who he is. Which is weird enough since Jim is supposed to be
dead. But Hank knows the letter had come from Jim because
he recognizes the distinctive *E*'s of his old Corona. Then he
receives a phone call from a Mr. Smith warning him to stay
home or he'll be murdered. Hank decides he has to go. It is
soon obvious that he is being followed by a strange couple.
Once in San Francisco, he finds Clara, who works for a
dentist—she recognizes him immediately. And now he is
plagued by blinding headaches, for which the dentist
recommends immediate surgery. Something about this whole
situation is terribly wrong. If Jim is really still alive…. where
the hell is he? And why does he seem to want Hank dead?

Samuel W. Taylor Bibliography
(1907-1997)

Novels:
Heaven Knows Why (1948)
The Man With My Face (1948)
The Grinning Gismo (1951)
Uranium Fever (with Raymond Taylor, 1970)
Take My Advice, Mr. President (1996)

THE MAN WITH MY FACE

- - - - - - -

THE GRINNING GISMO

- - - - - - -

Samuel W. Taylor

Introduction by
Nicholas Litchfield

Stark House Press • Eureka California

THE MAN WITH MY FACE / THE GRINNING GISMO

Published by Stark House Press
1315 H Street
Eureka, CA 95501, USA
griffinskye3@sbcglobal.net
www.starkhousepress.com

THE MAN WITH MY FACE
Originally published by A. A. Wyn, Inc., New York, and copyright ©
1948 by Samuel W. Taylor. Reprinted in paperback by Pocket Books,
New York, 1950.

THE GRINNING GISMO
Originally published by A. A. Wyn, Inc., New York, and copyright ©
1951 by Samuel W. Taylor. Reprinted in paperback by Ace Books, New
York, 1952.

ISBN: 979-8-88601-086-2

Cover design by Jeff Vorzimmer, ¡caliente!design, Austin, Texas
Text design by Mark Shepard, shepgraphics.com
Proofreading by Bill Kelly

First Stark House Press Edition: July 2024

"The Doppelgänger Fiend and the Teeth Worth Dying For"

by Nicholas Litchfield

Bestselling author, playwright, screenwriter, and historian Samuel W. Taylor (1907—1997), grandson of President John Taylor of the Church of Jesus Christ of Latter Day Saints, and the son of the late apostle John W. Taylor, was one of Utah's most famous residents. He was the most successful writer ever to come out of Provo and "one of the most successful ever produced by Utah" (The Daily Herald, 1951), and he was well-known on the San Francisco Peninsula, the region where he spent much of his adult life. Family connections didn't benefit him, though; growing up, they were undeniably a hindrance, but his imaginative flair for storytelling and his dedication, discipline, and persistence in getting his words into print established him as a notable figure.

By his mid-fifties, he had published millions of words, placing novelettes, serials, and hundreds of articles and short stories in national publications like *Saturday Evening Post*, *Collier's*, *Liberty*, *American*, *Country Gentleman*, *Woman's Home Companion*, *Esquire*, *True*, *Argosy*, *Bluebook*, *Country Home*, *Reader's Digest*, *Holiday*, and *Family Circle*. (Cracroft, 2001). Early on, he became mindful of the many rights of a piece of literature, often making more money from screen and radio rights than the original publication (Redwood City Tribune, 1950). A number of his stories were optioned for film, and he wrote scripts for Disney, Columbia, MGM, Warner Brothers, and independent producers (Spencer, 1968). He even received royalties for The Flying Car concept, filmed as *Chitty-Chitty Bang Bang,* the screenplay by another writer. His best-known story, "The Absent-Minded Professor," published by *Liberty* magazine during wartime, based on rubber shortages and experimentation to find a substitute, eventually became an Oscar-nominated Disney movie starring Fred MacMurray, directed by Robert Stevenson, who was responsible for the movie versions of *Mary Poppins*, *The Love Bug*, *Herbie Rides Again*, and *Bedknobs and Broomsticks*. Taylor did the screen treatment for the story, and unlike much of his other movie work, he didn't mind the finished product, saying that "from a writer's point of view they didn't hurt it" (Kernan, 1961).

Though he excelled at fiction, forging a lucrative career out of novels and adapting stories for stage and screen, his fact-based literature also brought him notice. His nonfiction works include *Fighters Up,* a history of the U.S. Air Force in Europe during World War II (The Herald-Journal, 1951), and the eye-opening *Family Kingdom*, which began as an article in *Holiday*. He spent more than a year adapting it into a book, tentatively called "The Principle," the term applied by the Mormons to the tenet of plural marriage, by which a man was able to attain a higher glory in heaven (Bell, 1950). The biographical book was based on the life of his father, "an Apostle of the Mormon Church who insisted on maintaining polygamy despite the laws against plural marriage and was thrown out of the church" (Citizen-News, 1951). Apparently, John Whittaker Taylor (1858-1916), who was neither discreet nor low profile, had six wives and thirty-six children and was unwilling to recant or renounce his wives (Cracroft, 2001). Sam's mother, who was "wife number three," would herd her eight children out into the canyon to hide when federal government agents came to their home pursuing the boy's fugitive father (Mavity, 1951a). Under U.S. federal law, they could confiscate Mormon property and imprison polygamists, male and female, on charges of unlawful cohabitation. Sam and his siblings were direct evidence of John W. Taylor's wrongdoings, so to speak.

His fascinating childhood was full of the sort of drama that fuels great literature, so it's fitting he devoted his life to writing. As a student at Brigham Young University, he contributed a weekly column, "Taylored Topics," to the semi-weekly student newspaper, *Y News* (Cracroft, 2001). He sold his first article to a psychology magazine, then started writing western stories for "pulp" magazines before switching to "slick" magazines, selling many stories and articles to national weeklies and monthlies (The Press Democrat, 1954). He continued writing stories while in the Army and the Air Force during World War II.

In February and March of 1948, *Collier's* featured "The Mysterious Way," a Mormon comedy serialized in six parts. Pulp magazine publisher A.A. Wyn (later rebranded as Ace Books) retitled the work *Heaven Knows Why!* and released it as a novel in May of that year. Sam's second novel, a crime yarn titled *The Man With My Face*, which serves as the opener to this Stark House collection, was also serialized in 1948, appearing in six monthly installments from February to July 1948, this time in *Liberty* magazine. A.A. Wyn published it as a novel in September 1948.

It's a rather fantastical tale, set in Taylor's hometown of Redwood City, in which a regular guy named Charles "Chick" Graham comes home from work one day to find an imposter in his home pretending to be him. The man is wearing Chick's clothes and has an identical face to his, and most alarmingly, Chick's wife and business partner (even his dog) appear to believe that this shady doppelganger is the genuine product. It's no use looking to the police for help—astoundingly, Chick's fingerprints don't match those on file.

Rapidly, others soon question the authenticity of the real Chick Graham, hoodwinked into believing he's actually Albert Rand, a bank messenger who murdered a guard and disappeared with two million dollars in Government bonds. Unable to prove to people that he *isn't* Albert Rand, Chick becomes a fugitive, on the run from the police and frightened to show his face in public as there's a sizable reward out for his arrest. His only hope is to outthink the devious gang of crooks who have spent years preparing a remarkable web of lies to trap the war hero and reap their fortune.

What seems, at first, laughably preposterous steadily becomes entirely rational as Taylor uncoils the heavily layered plot and begins an extensive explanation of how such a strange crime can be committed. So convincing is he that many reviewers couldn't discount the logic behind the crime—*Valley Times Today* said the chilling story was "made more chilling by the thought that it could happen!" (J.A.B., 1962), and Anthony Boucher wrote, "Once you assume that such an impersonation could be successful, even for a few hours, you will find the rest of the story as logical as it is fast and furious" (Boucher, 1948).

Plot aside, the author's dry wit and flair for good character descriptions and thrilling action make this a pleasant reading experience. It's little wonder the novel became a bestseller and spawned a profitable motion picture a few years later.

Actor Ed Gardner, who made his name churning out radio shows in New York and Hollywood, wanted to branch out into the movie world. Having settled in Puerto Rico, he continued to record his long-running comedy radio program "Duffy's Tavern" from a studio in San Juan. He planned to produce several motion pictures, including a comedy titled "Pigsfeet in Paris," in which he would star (Barron, 1951; Shamokin News-Dispatch, 1952). *The Man With My Face*, ultimately the only project he managed to produce, became the first motion picture made entirely in Puerto Rico. Emmy Award-winning writer Vincent Bogert, as well as Sam Taylor, Tom McGowan, and the director Edward Montagne, had a hand in adapting the screenplay. The movie was a hit, although reviews were mixed: *The New York Times* described it as "a tepid tale more concerned with dialogue than excitement" (The New York Times, 1951) and the short-lived Los Angeles newspaper *The Mirror* called it "a weird, thrill-packed melodrama" that was "one of the best jobs turned out by the movies in a long time" (Fox, 1951). Others drew attention to the solid performance by the lead actor and the colorful scenery (The Knoxville News Sentinel, 1954). With the exception of *The Absent-Minded Professor*, it was the only movie version of his work that Taylor could ever bring himself to watch (Kernan, 1961).

The movie's release coincided with one of the busiest times in Taylor's life. On March 27, 1951, McGraw-Hill published *Family Kingdom*. It was a critical success, with interviews and publicity keeping his name in the news while other projects unfolded. The *Saturday Evening Post* had previously published his story "Last Man in London," based on his Air Force experiences (The Press Democrat, 1954). He later converted it into a satirical play about the pre-war experiences of three former news commentators working in the United States Air Force public relations office following the German surrender in World War II (Redwood City Tribune, May 10, 1951). He titled it *The Square Needle*, which opened at the little Las Palmas Theater at the end of February (The Los Angeles Times, 1951). Well-known screen actress Marjorie Lord was among the Hollywood cast, and Academy Award-winner Ernst Fegte was the production designer (Redwood City Tribune, February 14, 1951). It "had an extensive run" and "received excellent reviews" (The Wasatch Wave, 1951). It began a second run at San Francisco's Downtown Theater on May 10, with Victor Joy (from *Gone with the Wind*) the prime name among the experienced cast of film actors. Writer Tom McGowan (who collaborated with Taylor on *The Man With My Face* and later worked on Disney's animated romantic musical comedy film *The Aristocats* and the bawdy Russ Meyer exploitation film *Cherry, Harry & Raquel!*) was one of the producers.

While all these projects unfolded, Taylor was busy with another literary assignment—promoting his new novel, *The Grinning Gizmo*. It was another action-packed pulp yarn, engagingly narrated and with measured humor and gritty action. It begins with a letter penned by a man believed to be dead and a veiled threat to expose a family scandal. The recipient, the pampered Henry Chatworth Oates III, is lured to San Francisco on a mysterious mission to somehow help his old wartime buddy Jim Daniels. Henry is the heir to the founder of a world-famous breakfast cereal, and he's keen to neither jeopardize his large inheritance nor tarnish his family name. Years earlier, he reneged on a business deal with Jim and jilted the man's sister, Trudy. They haven't spoken since.

However, according to news clippings, Jim committed suicide three months ago, jumping off the Golden Gate Bridge, and yet, a freshly mailed letter to Henry suggests otherwise. The subsequent anonymous telephone call, warning Henry not to get involved, compels Henry to investigate Jim's phony suicide and the murderous plot against his old friend.

What unfolds is a rather complex insurance scam plot with the rather naïve and trusting Henry, manipulated by just about everyone he meets, perpetually hoping that he can get to the bottom of Jim's situation without sacrificing his own life. The problem is that everyone seems to either want to kill poor Henry or set him up as the fall guy to murder. He can't trust anybody, not even the man he once thought of as his best friend.

Once again, the central character is full of regret and dwelling on the past and missed opportunities. His general curiosity and need for atonement are ultimately his undoing. Focused on rekindling bygone friendships, he doesn't want to escape danger, and shame over the snobbish way he behaved years earlier anchors him to the people who almost became his family. Is it too late to return to how things once were between him and Trudy? It's a question that nags him like a toothache, and his desperation to rewind the clock and redeem himself snares him in a world of peril, surrounded by murderers and manipulators.

Although Anthony Boucher wasn't enamored with the novel, complaining about the unsound plot and character motivation (Boucher, 1951), journalist and mystery author Nancy Barr Mavity rightly points out the book's intrinsic qualities: "Taylor's agility in double aerial somersaulting his characters so that the villain posited in one chapter is the beguiled innocent and possible victim in the next keeps everybody, including the reader, in quite a whirl" (Mavity, 1951b). Through suspenseful prose and misdirection, Taylor disguises plot faults and inconsistencies, maintaining the reader's interest through relentless action and absorbing mystery, a device that works rather nicely.

"Those who have read *The Man With My Face* know the ability of this author to tie your stomach in knots with suspense and to hold the reader to the bitter end," wrote critic Alice Pardoe West about *The Grinning Gizmo*. "He does just that in his new book" (West, 1951).

Though the similarities between the two books are clear, the tone is markedly darker in *The Grinning Gizmo*, and the players are crueler and more sinister. Taylor baits the reader with an intriguing hook, dangling a complex mystery that promises unpredictable twists and plenty of deception, and few will be able to look at a dentist's chair the same way again.

—March 2024
Rochester, NY

Nicholas Litchfield is the founder of the literary magazine *Lowestoft Chronicle* and editor of eleven literary anthologies. His stories, essays, and book reviews appear in many magazines and newspapers, including *BULL*, *Colorado Review*, *Daily Press*, *Mobius Blvd*, *Pennsylvania Literary Journal*, *Shotgun Honey*, *The Adroit Journal*, *The MacGuffin*, and *The Virginian-Pilot*. He has also contributed introductions to numerous books, including twenty-one Stark House Press reprints of long-forgotten noir and mystery novels. Formerly a book critic for the *Lancashire Post*, syndicated to twenty-five newspapers across the U.K., he now writes for *Publishers Weekly*. You can find him online at nicholaslitchfield.com.

Works cited:

Barr Mavity, Nancy (April 15, 1951a). "Frenetic family Background Leaves Writer With Muse of Many Facets." *Oakland Tribune*, p. 64.

Barr Mavity, Nancy (April 15, 1051b). "Crime of the Week." *Oakland Tribune*, p. 64.

Barron, Mark (June 7, 1951). "Broadway." *Corsicana Daily Sun*, p. 8.

Boucher, Anthony (Apr 15, 1951). "Criminals At Large: In the Chair Freudian Caper Teacher-Sleuth." *New York Times*, p. 208.

Boucher, Anthony (Nov 21, 1948). "Reports on Criminals at Large: The Man With My Face." *New York Times*, p. BR48.

Citizen-News (February 16, 1951). "Book Briefs: Taylor's Latest." *Citizen-News*, p. 15.

Cracroft, Richard H. (Fall 2001). "Samuel Woolley Taylor: Maverick Mormon Historian." *Journal of Mormon History*, Vol. 27, No. 2, pp. 64-91. URL: https://www.jstor.org/stable/23288259

J.A.B. (Sep 20, 1962). "Paperback Rack." *Valley Times Today*, p. 38.

Kernan, Michael J. (April 28, 1961). "RC Author Penned Current Movie Hit." *Redwood City Tribune*, p. 3.

New York Times (Jun 15, 1951). "The Screen in Review." *The New York Times*, p. 27.

Redwood City Tribune (February 14, 1951). "Samuel Taylor's Play to Open In Los Angeles This Month." *Redwood City Tribune*, p. 2.

Redwood City Tribune (July 6, 1950). "RC Kiwanians Hear Writer." *Redwood City Tribune*, p. 17.

Spencer, Betty G. (August 4, 1968). "Top Authors To Address League Of Utah Writers Roundup Sept. 6-8." *The Daily Herald*, p. 24.

The Daily Herald (October 22, 1951). "Drama By Provo Writer Appears On Screen Here." *The Daily Herald*, p. 5.

The Herald-Journal (April 21, 1951). "Sam Taylor Here Tuesday: Western Author To Address Logan Writers' Unit." *The Herald-Journal*, p. 1.

Los Angeles Times (February 24, 1951). *Los Angeles Times*, p. 10.

The Press Democrat (April 26, 1954). "Redwood City Writer And Thompson Panel Members." *The Press Democrat*, p. 1.

The Wasatch Wave, 1951 (April 20, 1951). "New Book About Mormons." *The Wasatch Wave*, p. 5.

West, Alice Pardoe (Mar 25, 1951). "Provoan Pens Best Seller." *The Ogden Standard-Examiner*, p. 20.

THE MAN WITH MY FACE

MY FACE

- - - - - - -

Samuel W. Taylor

1

Wednesday was just another day. The alarm went off at six, Cora and I got up, and she fixed breakfast while I shaved. We ate. She drove me to the station for the 7:12. In San Francisco, I walked from the station to the office for exercise, did the usual day's work, and that afternoon caught the 5:29 back to Redwood City, Climate Best by Government Test.

And that day could have melted into the other days just like it, except that it was the last of its kind.

I swung off the S. P. that afternoon at 6:06 with a swarm of other commuters. There was the usual bustle and confusion, horns honking, white arms waving from car windows, kiddies scampering for daddy, wives calling, "Jim—over here!" And I was one of them, craning my neck, looking for my tan Nash with Cora in it.

I was Charles Graham, doing okay, a partner in my own business, a GI house on a quarter acre out of town, a beautiful wife, a dog— that was me, the *News* in one pocket of my topcoat, a pound of butter in the other, a package of pork chops in my hand, listening for Cora's special *beep-beep-be-beep-beep*, watching through the gathering darkness for the Nash, for Cora's waving arm and the lush blondness of her hair, listening for her call, "Chick—over here!"

That was me. A man doesn't even think about it. Why should he?

But pretty soon the others had made connections and I was standing alone. I didn't think too much about it; Cora had been late before. The 6:18 came in, then the 6:33. I wondered if the car wouldn't start, or if Cora had had an accident on the way, or had run out of gas. I went inside the station and dialed my home number.

"Hello," Cora's voice said.

"Hi, honey. I'm at the station."

"What was that, please?"

"I'm waiting at the station. Car okay, or what?"

"I don't understand," she said. "Who is speaking, please?"

"This is the Green Hornet."

"I'm sorry. Do you have the right number? Horner, did you say?"

"Remember Chick Graham?"

"Yes. He's my husband."

"A terrible meathead. He's always wondered what a girl like you saw in him."

"Do you know my husband? Are you a friend of his?"

"I have a nodding acquaintance," I admitted. "And your devoted husband is now at the station, waiting patiently for a ride home. He's hungry, to boot."

"What station?"

"By mere chance it happens to be Redwood City. Climate Best by Government Test. Isn't that a coincidence?"

"And who is the person, Mr. Horner, who is waiting at the station?"

"Okay, Cora," I said. "Buzz down here and pick me up or I'll spank your pretty bottom."

She hung up. I waited around. The 6:45 came in. No Cora. My temper is none too good when I'm hungry. Whose is? When she hadn't showed up by seven o'clock, I phoned home again.

"Hello," Cora's voice said.

"Now look, beautiful. What the hell's the gag? I'm waiting for you. If the car's broke down or something, let me know and I'll grab a taxi or something."

"Who is speaking, please?"

"Cut it out, will you? Enough's enough."

"I don't believe I understand."

"Damn it, neither do I. How about getting down here?"

"Is this Mr. Horner again?"

"Look, I can take a gag as well as the next one. Go ahead, spring it. I'm all ready to laugh."

"Are you sure you have the right number?"

"After supper, yes. I'll play games. But let's get me home and a little chow under the belt, huh?"

"Just a moment, please." And I heard her voice faintly, as she turned from the phone. "I think it's the same guy."

"What does he want?" a man's voice said.

"He wants me to come down and pick him up."

"Is he drunk?"

"How do I know?"

"Let me talk to him," the man's voice said. It came directly into my ear over the wire: "Okay, pal. What do you want?"

"And who are you?" I asked.

"Now look, pal. We're trying to take a little chow, see? Why don't you play games with somebody else? The phone book is full of numbers."

"I'm laughing," I said. "You're a card, Mac. I think you're priceless. But why can't we get together on the joke? Are you coming down with Cora and surprise me?"

"This is Emerson 6-6217."

"What a coincidence! That's the number I want."

"Then who do you want?"

"Let's go slow. I understand a guy named Chick Graham lives at that number."

"That's right. Speaking."

"Oh," I said. "I'm *speaking* to Chick Graham."

"That's right. And what's on your mind, pal?"

"Nothing at all. If I'm talking to myself there's no use pursuing it."

"He's drunk," the voice said, turning from the phone. "Hey, Buster! Is this one of your deals?"

"Cross my heart and hope to die," Buster's voice called.

I hung up. So Buster was there. Buster was my business partner. I'd been with him in the office all day. He hadn't said a word about driving down the Peninsula after work. Unless something was up, he'd given me a ride. I figured he might have run into some joker we knew in the Army. Or maybe it was Cora's cousin from Los Angeles, Herb Cotter. I'd never met him to know his voice.

Fine; it was a rib. Well, I had the butter and the pork chops. Let them enjoy it awhile.

I walked over to Broadway and ate dinner at the Campus Creamery. Then I noticed there was a pretty good show on at the Sequoia, so I took it in. I left after the first feature. After all, I'd squeezed my side of the joke far enough.

As I stood outside the theater waiting for a taxi to come along, I noticed a man sitting across the street on the courthouse steps, a dog beside him. The dog was a big brown Doberman. I remembered that when I'd come out of the station after phoning, the man had been looking at the schedule of northbound trains. He was a tall man in a leather zipper jacket, vaguely familiar, and I'd said hello. When I'd come out of the Campus Creamery, the man and the dog had been half a block down the street, the man looking in a store window.

A taxi came along and I went home. I live three miles out of town, and it cost me a dollar and a half.

When I walked in the front door, Cora looked up at me sharply. The card table was set up in the living room. She was seated at it with

Buster and Ethelene, Buster's wife. The fourth chair was vacant, a hand of cards face down on the table before it, a highball glass beside the cards.

"I'm sorry," I said. "I was hungry and I guess I got sore."

Buster looked blankly from me to the door leading into the hall. He had a round innocent face, which now showed something akin to honest perplexity. "Did you go out the back door?" he asked me. "Say, where'd you get the hat and coat?"

"Stole eggs and bought it."

"And even a package in your hand," Ethelene said. "Chick, it's enough to scare somebody."

"Spring it," I said. "I'm waiting."

"Wait a minute," Cora said, indicating the hall door. "He's in *there*."

"Tell him to come out," I said. "I can't wait."

"And where," she asked me, "did *you* come from?"

"From heaven, I've been told. Though from what—"

I didn't finish, for a man came in from the hall. The other three looked from me to him. The man didn't notice me. He sat in the empty chair, picked up his hand of cards, studied it while taking a sip of his highball.

"Let's see," he said. "Who dealt this mess?"

Something prickled at the back of my neck. I had the uncomfortable feeling that I was dreaming. This was the stuff of nightmares. I had a crazy notion about mirrors. Because this guy who'd walked in from the hall was wearing my suit, my hair, my face, and even my ears. I ought to know that face. And a man generally figures without thinking about it that what he has above the neck is for better or worse a unique model.

The other three looked from me to him and back again. And then the man with my face saw me standing in the entrance hall, and his eyes widened and he gawped at me the way I was gawping at him.

"For crying out loud!" he said slowly.

I said, "And who the hell are you?"

"Chick," Cora said to him, "is he your brother or something?"

"I don't like this," Ethelene said to him. "It's no kind of a joke to play on anybody. It gives me the creeps."

The man put down his cards and felt of his face, as if to make sure he still had it. He stood up slowly. "What's the deal, pal?"

This was no rib. That guy with my face wasn't joking. Cora and Ethelene were dead white except for lip rouge. Buster's round face was working nervously.

"What do you want here?" the guy asked me. "I don't think I like this."

This guy was taking my place! He was sitting there in my chair wearing my clothes and my face and my ears. He was taking over. Well, that's just what *he* thought. I was plenty sore all of a sudden. This was no rib. He was trying to get away with it.

"Start talking, brother," I said. "And start talking fast!" I began crossing to the table.

"Jiggs!" the man said.

I stopped dead, and the hair seemed to rise on the back of my neck. My bull terrier had been lying before the fireplace. As my voice rose and I started for the guy, my dog had come up, growling at me.

"Jiggs!" I yelled at the dog. "Lie down!"

My dog showed his teeth at me, growling throatily. "Be careful, mister," Cora said to me. "Leave that dog alone."

"Just don't make any sudden moves, pal," the man with my face advised.

Buster jerked a thumb at me. "Say, who *is* this guy?"

"That's what I'd like to know," the man with my face said.

Cora said, "He must be the one who was phoning."

"I don't like this," Ethelene said. "I don't like it at all."

"Who is *this* guy?" I yelled. "What's going on here? What's wrong with my dog? For crying out loud!"

"What's the pitch, pal?" the man with my face asked. "Do you want something, or just what is it?"

"He just walked in," Cora said.

"We were just sitting here," Ethelene said. "We thought it was you. You'd gone to the bathroom, and I figured you'd slipped on your hat and coat and gone around the house and in the front door. Say, it was sort of creepy."

"Except your hat and coat are still on the sofa, Chick," Buster said to him. "That's what got me, the hat and coat."

"All right, pipe down!" the man with my face said irritably. And to me: "Now, pal. If you want something let's have it. And if you don't, why, goodbye."

I called him a name and started for him.

"Jiggs!" he said, just in time.

My dog stopped inches from me, growling, fangs eager and the hair erect over the shoulders and near the tail.

"You better get back and stay back, pal," the man said. "I'll let him take you, next time."

I moved back.

"Come here, Jiggs," he said. The dog went to him. "Lie down."

The dog obeyed. There was a plate of salt herring and cheese on the card table. The man tossed Jiggs a hunk of cheese. The dog caught it and gulped it down.

I'd spent a lot of time training that dog. It wouldn't obey anybody but me and Cora, nor take food from anyone else.

"This has got me whipped," Buster said to the man. "Except I was with you at the office today and drove you down here after work— When he came in that door, I could have swore it was you."

"I still don't get the pitch, pal," the man said to me. "What are you trying to get away with here, anyhow?"

"Cora," I said to my wife, "I don't know what's going on, but you know me. You know who I am. You know that guy's not *me*. His voice isn't the same. I never called anybody *pal* in my born life."

Cora looked around the table with astonishment. "Well, I never! Chick," she said to the man with my face, "he's trying to palm himself off as *you!*"

"I think we'd better call the cops," Ethelene said. "I think the guy's drunk, whoever he is. He might be dangerous."

"Buster," I said, "*you* know me, for God's sake! We went through a war together. We're in business together. I was with you today at the office."

"I'm not buying any," Buster said. "Chick, I think we'd better call the cops."

"I don't think he's *right*," Cora said.

"All right, pal," the man with my face said. "Get out of here. Goodbye, pal."

"Look, here's the pork chops," I said desperately, clutching at anything. "The pork chops and the butter, Cora. You told me to bring them home." It was unreal and insane that I should be trying to convince my wife that I was her husband. "We got up at six this morning, remember? You got breakfast while I shaved. Buckwheat cakes with an egg on top—"

"Oh, my God!" Cora cried. "Chick, can't you get rid of this guy? I can't stand much more of this!"

"Take it easy, Cobra," he said gently. That name, *Cobra*, was a secret name that I called her at intimate moments. Nobody but she and I knew that name.

"All right, pal," he said to me. "Out. Or I'll put the dog on you."

"Please go, mister," Cora said. "The dog's dangerous."

"Like hell I will!" I yelled. "I'll stay here and see this thing—"

"Gofer!" the man with my face snapped.

It was the word I'd trained Jiggs to obey if I spoke it. The dog raced for me and leaped for my throat. I flung up my arms and something that felt like a heavy electric shock went through my right wrist, shaking it, tearing it, numbing it. I heard Cora and Ethelene scream.

"Break away, Jiggs!"

The dog released my wrist and stood eagerly awaiting the command to attack again.

"Now get out of here," the man with my face said.

"I wouldn't argue," Buster said. "You'd better go, mister."

I didn't argue. I got out of there.

2

I walked down to the corner and looked at my wrist under the street light. My arm ached to the shoulder and there was a catch in my neck. Thanks to the overcoat sleeve the skin wasn't broken, but there were deep blue dents. I couldn't close my hand or open it; it was frozen in a claw. I still had the pork chops in my other hand, and I wondered dimly how I'd got the door open to get out.

I went over to Woodside Road and had walked almost to Valota, about a mile, when a police car drew alongside.

"Going someplace?" the cop asked. He was a red-faced, pleasant sort of cop.

"You're the answer to a prayer. I was hoofing in to get the police."

"What's up?"

"I just got kicked out of my own house."

"Yeah? What house is that?"

"My name's Graham. Charles Graham. I live over here off the Alameda."

"Get in," he said.

I was boiling mad. And a bit afraid. That joker who was trying to step into my place must be, I figured, unbalanced. Any normal man would know it simply couldn't be done. I had a madman in my house, in my shoes, in my face and my ears.

The dog? Well, something was behind that, too. I'd find out.

The police car pulled up before my place and we went to the front door and the cop rang the bell. It was a little thing, but it pointed up the fantastic situation—me standing with a cop at my elbow, waiting for somebody to answer my own door.

Buster opened the door. "Well, I see you got him, officer."

"This the character?"

"Well, I hope to hell there's no *more* of them," Buster said.

The cop shoved me ahead of him through the door. Cora and Ethelene and the man with my face were at the card table. The cop took a good look at me and at the man with my face.

"Well," he said, "I'll be damned! Twins?"

"I know just what you mean," the man with my face said. "And how do you think I felt, him walking in here and trying to take over? I've never seen the character before in my life. Just walking in and trying to take over."

"I don't think he's quite right," Cora said, and shivered.

Ethelene shuddered. "The whole thing gives me the creeps."

"We called the police just to be on the safe side," Buster said. "He was talking wild, and we didn't know."

"You done the right thing," the cop said.

"Lucky we had the dog," the man with my face said. "He tried to jump me."

The cop turned to me. "Okay, Mac. What have you got to say for yourself?"

"This is my house. That's my wife, right there. There's her brother, Buster Cox. I'm in business with Buster in the city. Cox and Graham, the Cogram System—public accountants. That's Buster's wife, Ethelene. And this joker over there who looks like me—I don't know who the hell he is but I'm going to find out."

"That's the way he talked before," Buster said.

Cora shrugged uncomfortably. "I don't think he's *right*."

"Cora," I yelled, "for God's sake!"

The cop squeezed my arm. "Pipe down, you." And to the others: "You could fool me, but I guess *you* know."

"Well, *I* certainly ought to know," Cora said. "I'm Chick's wife. If you really look at them, officer, you'll see a world of difference."

A creepy chill seemed to freeze a knot in my stomach. Maybe I'd been slow on the uptake, but a thing like that takes a while to soak in. You think you're going to wake up, or something. You think it will straighten itself out. *Well, I certainly ought to know*, Cora had said. *I'm Chick's wife. If you really look at them, officer, you'll see a world of difference.*

She did know. She knew who I was. She knew who I was, and she knew who the other man with my face was. She knew. Buster knew. Ethelene knew. They were part of it. They all knew. They were all against me.

"Well, I guess you can see it better than me, lady," the cop said.

"Hell, *I* ought to know Chick Graham," Buster declared in that frank and open manner of his. "I went through a war with Chick."

"Well, okay," the cop said. "Want to make a charge or what?"

"I don't want to get the poor devil in a jam," the man with my face said. "I think he ought to be under a doctor's care. Just so he doesn't bother us is all I care about."

"I don't think he's right," Cora said. "Maybe he escaped from a mental institution."

"I'll tell you," the cop said. "We'll hold him en route to L. A. and look into things."

"I think that's a good idea," Buster agreed. "He might just be a nut. And again, he might be dangerous."

"I can prove who I am," I said.

As I fumbled under my coat with my left hand, the cop grabbed my wrist. He patted my pockets, then let me take the billfold out. I still couldn't grasp with my right hand. I put the billfold on the table, opened it, and took out the things that proved who I was: driver's license, business card, Air Reserve Association card, and my old Army AGO card, the best identification ever devised, which was why I still carried it. It held my picture, signature, and prints of my index fingers, sealed in plastic.

"So there's where it is," the man with my face said. "I lost my billfold today in the city."

"Oh, you did!" I said sweetly. "And I guess you lost your fingerprints and signature right along with it, huh?"

"I can identify Mr. Graham's billfold," Buster said.

"If that isn't crust!" Ethelene said. "Lifting your billfold, Chick, and now claiming it."

The man with my face began picking up the billfold.

I grabbed his wrist. The dog growled and the man spoke to it.

"Take it easy here," the cop said. He smiled at the others. "You folks won't mind if we made sure of this. I know it's all right, but this guy talks like he means it."

"I like that," Cora said. "The police are believing him now."

"Well, it's a cinch this might be his billfold even if he's not your husband," the cop said.

"Relax, Cora," the man with my face said. "Of course I'm willing to prove it's my billfold, officer."

The cop got out a pencil and a notebook, opened the notebook on the table to a blank page, and covered the cards bearing my signature with a big red hand. "Write your name, Mac," he said to me.

I tried to grasp the pencil but my fingers wouldn't close. It felt as if rusty wires were pulling inside my wrist. This had to be a dream. A thing like this couldn't happen by planning. That dog could have bitten me on the left wrist. I pulled back my sleeve to show the blue teeth marks.

"They put the dog on me. I can't close my hand."

"He can't close his hand," Buster said.

"Well, maybe he can't," the cop said, turning to the man with my face. "Here, you write *your* name. One's as good as the other."

The man with my face wrote my signature on the notebook, not carefully but with the easy swing of long practice. The cop compared the signature with the cards.

"I just wanted to make sure," he said apologetically, and took my arm. "You better come with me."

"Wait a minute!" My voice was high and I knew that didn't help, but I couldn't control it. I had the horrible feeling that maybe I was crazy, maybe I *wasn't* Charles Graham, maybe I'd had a dream and was out of my head and really was somebody else. I grabbed the notebook. "It looks like my signature but it's a forgery! He could have practiced it! It's been done before! But one thing he can't copy is the fingerprints on those cards!"

"Never mind the fingerprints, Mac," the cop said. He swung me toward the door. "You come along with me and don't get gay."

"Maybe it would help, officer," the man with my face said. "I think he really believes it. It may help if we convince him.... Cora, we've got a stamp pad, haven't we? For that dating stamp?"

"Is all this necessary?" Ethelene said. "Anybody can tell, Chick, that he's not you."

"You don't have to prove it no more to me, Mr. Graham," the cop said. "And I got to report in. I'm late now."

"But it may help the poor devil, officer," the man with my face said.

"It will only take a couple of seconds. My wife's got the stamp pad now. I think the poor devil's got a fixation. Sometimes if you destroy one part of it, the whole thing collapses."

The cop turned me back to the table. "Well, if it will help him. He sure has got it bad."

Ethelene shook her head sadly. "Poor thing."

"Maybe it's only temporary," Buster said encouragingly.

The cop examined the driver's license and the AGO card, then he rolled the right thumb and two index fingers of the man with my face on the pad and transferred the prints to the notebook. The man with my face wiped away the ink with a handkerchief, calm as could be, while the red-faced cop compared the prints.

"I don't need a glass to tell these are the same," the cop said.

"Like hell!" I yelled.

He shoved his red face forward. "Yes, like hell. I've had some training in this work. I won't be a prowl cop all my life."

"Then take my prints," I advised, "and sign up for another correspondence course. How to be a detective in ten easy lessons."

"Okay, wise guy," the cop said. He put my prints on the notebook leaf. "Now, if you're not blind, take a gander for yourself."

I'm no fingerprint expert, but I could see the difference at a glance. The prints on my identification card had a pattern like a bull's-eye target. The prints from my fingers were characterized by loops like a series of mountain peaks.

The man with my face smiled with pity and understanding. He took my billfold from the table, put the cards into it, and tucked it into his pocket. If he was I, then who, in the name of God, *was* I?

"That's not the door," the cop said, as we went into the entrance hall and I pulled open the closet door.

"I know it isn't," I said.

On the other side of the door was a mirror. I looked into it wondering what I'd see.

I saw the same old face. Including the ears.

And, too, I saw something else. I saw Cora and Buster and Ethelene. Not in the mirror, but looking out of my own eyes at myself. I saw them as they really were. As they'd been all the time. I saw what they were doing, and why.

"Come along, Mac," the cop said.

I went out with him. And as we went down the walk toward the prowl car, I saw the end of the trail for me. The walk was a corridor.

The prowl car was the gas chamber.

It was so neat, so smart, so complete. They had planned it for years. And not until right now had I seen any part of it.

3

I was a brand-new shavetail assigned to a newly activated ground crew squadron when I first met Buster. I was walking down the road, feeling very important with my brass bars, when a chubby Pfc with a round face came out of the service club, stopped in his tracks, and saluted with his finger to his nose.

"Soldier," I said, "let's have a military salute."

Then he slapped me on the back and burst out laughing. I told him to stand at attention, and he shoved me in the chest.

"You, and you," I said to a couple of GIs, "take this drunk to his quarters."

As the GIs grabbed him, the Pfc began struggling. "Now wait a minute, Bert! Joke's a joke, but I might get in trouble!"

"Lieutenant to you, soldier," I said.

"Okay, Bert, if you've got the master race complex. I was only kidding. I didn't even know you was in the Army, and here I bump into you wearing brass. Hell, Bert, I was just saying hello. But if you don't want to be human, okay, Lieutenant Rand!" He gave me a salute. "And you can go straight to hell, you stuck-up bastard!" He obviously had mistaken me, ears and all, for somebody else. We went to a beer joint off the post and ironed the thing out.

The following Sunday I was in the orderly room signing passes when a rush of whistling and wolf-calling broke out. And then a girl came in. And what a girl! She was dressed in yellow, with a big picture hat, and her hair was the exact same shade as her dress. She wasn't merely pretty, she was a dream. She was the sort of thing most men don't get any closer to than the seat in a movie theater.

"I'm looking for Lieutenant Graham," she said.

"That's me," I said, conscious of my ears.

She gave me the big smile. The big happy smile that melts brass into putty. "Could I see you a moment, lieutenant?"

"You sure could."

Her car was outside, a Packard roadster, with the top down. As she got in, flashing a length of nylon, the whistles came again.

"I just wanted to thank you, lieutenant, for what you did for my brother. I'm Cora Cox. Buster is my brother—the Pfc."

"That's not at all necessary. Though I'm glad you called around."

"But he might have gotten into serious trouble with that silly mistake. Buster is awfully grateful. And so am I. We were wondering if you could have dinner with us tonight?"

And so I got to know Cora. She and the girl Buster was engaged to, Ethelene Crancall, had an apartment in town.

Of course, there'd been a girl before Cora. I was engaged to Mary at the time. Cora didn't mean anything to me. Not at first.

Buster wanted to be in my squadron. I arranged his transfer, and he wangled the mail clerk job. And I never did connect that up—the coincidence of his becoming mail clerk and the fact that Mary stopped writing. Not all at once. They were too smart for that. But instead of every day it was twice a week. Then once a week. Then once in a while. And then not anymore.

I wasn't exactly going with Cora. She was Buster's sister. The apartment was an awfully nice place compared with the officers' quarters. The four of us went to shows together, we had evenings together, we had dinners together. And all the while this gorgeous Cora was being very nice to me. As Mary's letters dwindled to silence, Cora was being gorgeous and charming. I'm human.

Latrine rumor had it that we were soon to be alerted for overseas. And I thought I'd go see Mary on my leave. I ought to find out, one way or another.

And then I got the card from Mary. The post-office card says USE THIS CARD TO NOTIFY YOUR CORRESPONDENTS OR PUBLISHER OF CHANGE OF ADDRESS. It advised me that Mary was moving from Fresno. The part that says, NEW ADDRESS, looked like it had been run over by a convoy of tractors.

"Gee, that's a shame, Chick," Buster said. "I noticed it at the APO. I reamed the guy out there—but what the hell? I'll tell you what, Chick. Why don't you send a special delivery airmail? It'll get forwarded, and she'll write right back. There's still time. Give me a pass and I won't even go to the APO. I'll buzz into town and put it in the post office."

Buster was so helpful. He'd do anything to see that my mail went right. Right where he wanted it. He was my best friend. That round face of his was more honest than the sun. It was like a baby's face, open and trusting. He was the sort of guy strangers ask to hold the stakes of a bet.

I got no answer from my special delivery airmail. I spent the leave with Cora and Buster and Ethelene. We went to Yellowstone in the Packard.

I was in England three years. Cora was writing. Sending pictures. Calling me pet names. When Buster and I got back, we married Ethelene and Cora in a double ceremony.

Inside of a short time, I realized that marrying Cora had been a mistake. Not that I kept comparing her with Mary. I'd made my choice. I was of age. And it wasn't merely that I found out a girl who knocks your eye out spends money on it. I couldn't see tossing thirty dollars away in a nightclub when we were starting up in business and scraping bottom. Nor was it that she had a habit of petty pilfering—ash trays, salt shakers, and so on—and that I came to learn some of it was not so petty. The thing that made the marriage a mistake was her attitude. She didn't love me. She tolerated me.

Then why should she have married me? Why—a gorgeous creature who could have had her choice of many men? I hadn't guessed. Who in a thousand years would suspect? There'd been little things, but they hadn't pointed to a pattern. Even today, the last day, when the years of preparation came to a focus, I hadn't seen anything particularly out of the way. It was something you could only see when you looked back on it, afterwards.

Yes, Cora had been on edge this morning, but what of it? And at the station, when the 7:12 pulled in to bear me away, she kissed me goodbye. A real kiss, not the peck of a wife as her husband catches the 7:12. A real kiss, a goodbye kiss. But what of it?

And when I got to our little two-room office in the city, Buster and Ethelene were obviously relieved to see me. But what of that?

When I went out to lunch there were extras on the street. $2,000,000 L. A. BOND THEFT! It was just another newspaper story.

The name of the man who'd done the job, Albert Rand, meant nothing to me. It had been years since Buster had mistaken me for somebody else. He and Ethelene and Cora had never since that time mentioned the guy I looked like. The picture of the guy, in the newspapers, didn't look too much like me or anybody else; it was a wire photo, taken from a poor snapshot, and it could have been anybody.

When I got back to the office after lunch, Buster and Ethelene were in the back room looking at the papers. Buster cooked up reasons, during the afternoon, for visiting all our accounts. That, of course, was to establish an alibi.

And after work the three of us had gone to Murphy's bar, for a drink. When I'd finished my rye, Buster held out his hand and said, "Well, Chick, good luck." Then Ethelene shook hands. A bit silly and formal, but nothing to catch hold of.

I got the butter and the pork chops, and caught the 5:29. And I didn't know that Charles Graham had become another guy. I didn't know it when I phoned Cora from the station. I didn't know it when I walked into my house and found another man in my place. I didn't know it when the dog was put on me. I didn't know it when I went back with the cop. I didn't know it until Cora said, *If you really look at them, officer, you'll see a world of difference.*

But now as I walked along the path with the cop toward the prowl car, I knew what Cora had seen in me. She'd seen her share of two million dollars, which is worth going to a lot of trouble to arrange.

As I rode beside the cop along Woodside Road, I kept flexing my right hand, the way a person will tongue a quick tooth.

The cop shook his head slowly. "Now, you ought to know better than try a deal like that, Mac. Maybe you got the idea if he was away and his wife was there—say, she's a dish. But when *he* was there—you ought to of knowed better." He shrugged. "I guess you need a doctor, all right."

I burst out laughing. I slapped my good hand on my knee and howled. The cop's red face turned briefly. "Okay, pipe down."

"You know," I chuckled, "I had Graham guessing, at that. Remember when I pulled out his billfold? Notice his face? For a minute I'll bet he was worried about proving who the hell *he* was! Me with his billfold. My picture on the AGO card. I'll bet he had a bad minute or so."

"Pipe down, Mac. You'll have plenty of time to laugh."

"Well, okay, officer. Maybe I went too far. But it was too good to pass up."

"Too good? I don't get it?"

"I found his billfold on the S. P. tonight. The 5:29. Right there on the floor between the seats. I picked it up and there was eighty-three bucks in it. Finders keepers."

"Yeah? You're supposed to turn in what you find."

"I did better than that. I took it back to the guy personally."

"You what?"

"What do you suppose I was doing out there?"

"That's why they called me, to find out."

"How the hell do you suppose *I* feel?" I said hotly. "Him putting his damned dog onto me. When all I was trying to do was give him back his billfold."

"It didn't sound like that to me, Mac."

"Okay, I had my little joke. Is that against the law? He had no business putting his damned dog on me."

"A lot of trouble, Mac, begins with a little joke."

"Look at it from my side, officer. I found this billfold on the S. P. In it was an Army AGO card. The picture on it, you'd think it was me. There was an address on another card, here in Redwood City. So I figured, hell, I'll just trot out and give the guy his eighty-three bucks and take a look at him. I was curious to see if the guy looked as much like me as the picture. Gives you a funny feeling, somebody looks like you. Funny we never ran into each other before, both living here."

"By the way," the cop said, "just who the hell are you, anyhow?"

I got a card from my vest pocket. A salesman had given it to me. It identified James Pease, Peninsula representative for Efficiency Business Machines, Inc. "You've seen me around."

He took the card. "Yeah. Both of you, I guess, thinking it was the same guy. Jefferson Street, huh?"

"Look at it my way," I said. "I was bighearted. I was taking the guy's billfold back when all I had to do was put it in my pocket. I spent a buck and a half of my own money on a taxi. Bighearted John. That's me. And he put his damned dog on me."

"Well, you got gay, Mac."

"Maybe you'd have done the same. When I got to the house, I saw the two girls and this baby-faced guy they called Buster sitting there playing cards. I didn't even know Graham was home. I thought maybe he was out looking for his billfold. So I figured, well, if I looked so much like him, why not pull a little rib? Why not pretend to be him for a few minutes?"

"That kind of a rib gets you in trouble, Mac."

"Okay, but it was all in fun. I didn't have to spend a buck and a half of my own dough taking the billfold back, did I? I wished I hadn't, now, that bastard!"

"Well, look at it from his angle," the cop said.

"He was the one who got tough. Not me. I walked in, and the two girls and Buster did a double-take. You see, Graham wasn't there. He'd just stepped into the john. And me walking in the front door with my hat and coat on, they thought they were seeing things. So I was just kidding them along. Just kidding. And Graham walks in from the hall and starts getting tough. Him getting tough when I was bringing back his billfold!"

"Maybe you give him a turn at that," the cop said. "Maybe he thought he was seeing things."

"Sure, that's okay, but he had no business putting the dog on me. A man hadn't ought to do that. If I hadn't got my arm up, the dog would have ripped my throat open."

"No," the cop admitted. "He shouldn't of put the dog on you, Mac."

"And then calling the police," I said. "That did burn me. Hell, I was going to call the cops myself. That's what I told you when you picked me up, wasn't it? I said I wanted a cop."

"Officer," the cop corrected. "Yeah, you said that, all right."

"But *him* calling the cops, when all I was trying to do was take his billfold back!"

"How did he know that? You sure didn't act like it when we went back there."

"Why should I, for hell sake?" I said. "He was giving me a bad time. He'd put his dog on me. He was trying to say I was crazy and needed a doctor. Well, okay, I figured to give him a bad time, too. I figured to let him fry awhile. You notice his face when I insisted on having my fingerprints taken? You know, I had him guessing. For a while he thought maybe *he* needed a doctor. I had him guessing right up to the last minute. Say, were you in the Army?" It was a safe guess, the way the cop had been calling me Mac.

He nodded. "MPs."

"Air Force," I said. "I was in England."

Nothing like a pair of veterans when they start fighting the war over again. He'd been in London, then Paris and Frankfurt. I was getting next to him. He figured he knew me. But those three miles were going fast, too. He drove through Five Points and along El Camino Real, and we were still fighting the war.

"Say, I live on Jefferson," I said, trying to be casual. "Why don't you drop over some afternoon and we'll crack a bottle? Maybe we both knew some of the same guys overseas."

"Well, I really ought to take you in, Pease," he said uncertainly.

"What's the charge? Those people at the house didn't make a charge.

Are you going to pinch me for taking his billfold back? I wish I'd kept it, now. Serve that guy right, putting the dog on me."

"Well, I don't know, Mac."

"Okay, lock me up," I said. "But stop at the house long enough for me to give these pork chops to my wife. The kids will be getting pretty hungry."

"Your kids haven't et yet? That's a hell of a note, Mac, you off getting in a jam and your kids waiting for supper."

I held my breath. He turned into Jefferson.

"Don't rub it in," I said. "I feel enough like a damned fool. And listen, my wife doesn't have to know, does she? If you've got to take me in, she doesn't have to know, does she? You know how a wife is. I don't want her to know. And the kids. Daddy in jail."

"You should of thought of that, Mac."

"I was only taking his billfold back. My God, will this be in the papers? I might lose my job."

"Well, there's really no charge, Mac," the cop said. "I was only taking you in for investigation. Graham didn't want to press it. But now if you find any more billfolds, turn them over to the police. That's our job."

"I guess I've been a damned fool, all right," I admitted humbly.

Luckily, the address on Jefferson was a new house with an illuminated number, easy to spot from the car. "This is the place. Right here on the left."

The cop pulled to the curb, and told me to stick around tonight in case he wanted to ask me some questions later. I said sure, and how about dropping around any time to fight the war? He grinned and waved goodbye. But he was a good cop. He stayed at the curb, watching.

A light showed at the front window. I went up the path and turned at the door. The cop was still waiting. I tried the knob. The door was unlocked. I opened the door, waved at the cop, and went in. I heard the prowl car shift through the gears going away.

I blew out a chestful of air. That had been close. Thank goodness that cop had been in the Army!

"Well?" a man said.

I was in a living room with a beamed ceiling. The man was sitting in an easy chair, a bottle of beer on an end table at his elbow, looking at me over the top of a newspaper. His shoes were off and he had his feet on a coffee table.

I looked about the room, my mouth dropping open. "I'll be go-to-hell," I said.

"Can I help you?"

"This isn't the place."

"What place do you want?"

"I'm awfully sorry, busting in like this. I just got a new house yesterday. I thought this was my house."

"Yeah?" he said, as if maybe he took it in and maybe he didn't.

"Isn't this the six-hundred block?"

"No, it isn't," he said, neither friendly nor otherwise.

I grinned. "Well, say, hello!"

He studied me, carefully getting his feet off the coffee table and onto the floor. A hand casually took hold of the beer bottle.

"Aren't you Jim Pease—Efficiency Business Machines?"

"That's right."

"I'm Chick Graham—Cox and Graham, the Cogram System—Mission Street. Remember, you were trying to sell me a posting machine the other day."

He took his hand from the bottle. "Oh, yeah. Hello, Graham. You just walking in that way, for a minute—"

"And I didn't know what-the-hell," I said. "I just walked in my own house and here you were. Then I saw it wasn't my house."

"Say, that's good, can't find your own house."

"We just moved in. And I get turned around in this town," I said. "From the outside the place is a dead ringer. But we don't have beamed ceilings."

"This is a hell of a town to get turned around in," he admitted. "And all these GI jobs look alike anyhow. They all come out of the same mold. Your car gone? I heard a car."

"I caught a ride from the station."

"Six-hundred block? You've got quite a walk. Wait'll I put my shoes on and I'll give you a lift."

"Thanks, Pease, but maybe I need the exercise. I had a couple of drinks in town. I guess that's how I made the mistake. And I'd better be okay when my wife sees me. She's going to be sore, anyhow." I displayed the pork chops. "I haven't even brought home the meat for supper. I'd better not show up tight."

"Suit yourself, Graham. About that machine. I still think you'll make enough to pay it off in six months."

"I'm sold on it, Pease. But Buster isn't. Work on him."

"Oh, I've just started on you guys. You'll see me again."

I went out and walked away, fast. Before that cop began wondering why, if I'd taken a taxi three miles out of town to deliver a billfold, I hadn't asked it to wait.

4

I walked into town. Parked at the taxi stand of the S. P. station was a police car. I didn't know if it was waiting for me, but there was no point in finding out. I went over to the Greyhound station. A highway patrol car was parked there. I walked on past.

"Hello, Mr. Graham!"

I must have jumped. I was passing a service station and the attendant was being friendly. He was a stubby character who'd been at the station a month or so. A chow dog was at his heels. I don't like chows and I'd been wondering about changing stations just because of that dog underfoot.

"Hi, Curly," I said, and went on. I remembered the tall guy in the leather jacket, with the Doberman.

If the cops were watching the bus and railroad stations, if they were looking for me, I'd ought to get off the public street. But I had no experience in this sort of business. What the hell does a guy do?

I stopped at Ed's Diner on El Camino Real for a cup of coffee and some thinking. There was a bunch of high school kids in the joint and the radio was howling. I was one of a crowd, and the chaos fit my mood.

I was on the second cup of coffee and fourth cigarette, my mind chasing its tail around a circle, when the music cut off and an announcer said, "We interrupt this broadcast to give you a special news flash. Albert Rand, the bank messenger who murdered a guard and disappeared with two million dollars in Government bonds this morning in Los Angeles, is known to be in Redwood City. Residents of the Peninsula are cautioned to be on the alert and to report any suspicious characters. This man is a desperate criminal and he will stop at nothing.

"Rand was apprehended less than an hour ago in a brazen attempt to impersonate Charles Graham, San Francisco businessman who lives near Redwood City, in Graham's own home. Arrested by the police on Graham's complaint, Rand escaped by impersonating James

Pease, Peninsula representative of a business machine company. He is now at large.

"State Police are cooperating with local law enforcement officers, the sheriff of San Mateo County, and the FBI, in a dragnet to apprehend this man. Cars are being stopped on all highways, transportation terminals watched, and a cordon of police is combing the Redwood City area. An arrest is expected momentarily.

"As announced previously over this station, there is a reward of ten thousand dollars offered for information leading to the arrest and conviction of Albert Rand. He is twenty-seven years old, five feet nine inches tall, though slender and appearing taller. Medium complexion. Gray eyes. Sandy brown hair. Rather prominent ears ..."

The counterman had an elbow on the bar in front of me, chin in hand, watching me. His jaws moved slowly on a toothpick.

"... Dresses neatly. When last seen was wearing a brown snap-brim hat, gray tweed topcoat, medium brown worsted suit, brown oxfords with tan socks, white shirt, tie with crimson and brown diagonal stripes ..."

The counterman took the toothpick out of his mouth and put his other elbow on the bar, watching me.

"... He is pleasant and presentable, talks easily, and is a very smooth character without appearing to be so. Any man answering this description should be reported immediately to the police or to this station. You are cautioned not to accept any identification whatsoever from a man answering this description. Albert Rand is obviously equipped with forged credentials under several aliases..."

The counterman was chewing his toothpick again. He seemed to be looking at my ears.

"... This man is a killer. Stay on the alert. Your phone call may be worth ten thousand dollars to you. Take no chances. Keep tuned to this station for further developments."

The music blared again.

"Say," the counterman said, "that almost fits you."

"What do you mean, almost?" I said. "It's me, right down to the necktie. You've got me, Mac. I surrender, dear. I am yours, body and soul."

"Well, it sort of does," he said.

"Sure it does. I'm Albert Rand. I'm a killer and smooth article. But I can prove I'm four other guys."

He grinned. "Sure, and I'm Joe Stalin."

"Why don't you call the cops? It might be worth ten thousand bucks to you."

"Yeah," he said. "I've seen you around town. All I'll get out of you is ten cents."

"Twenty cents. Two cups of coffee."

"Ten cents. I'm the sucker who sells the five-cent cup of coffee."

"Say," I said, nodding toward a high-school kid wearing a tweed topcoat. "That guy pretty well fits what the radio said."

"Sure. So do you. So do I if I want to put my coat and hat on. Why don't the three of us turn ourselves in and get thirty thousand bucks? Ten thousand apiece. I could use it."

"That's an idea," I said.

"You know what? If this guy Rand walked in here with a sign on his chest, you know what would happen? I'd try to call the cops and my phone wouldn't work. If I ran out the door and there was six cops standing on the sidewalk, my sign would fall down and hit me on the head before I opened my trap. That's how lucky I am."

I gave him a dime. He pretended to bite it to see if it was lead. He rang it up and I went out.

I walked out and stopped dead, staring at a policeman.

I was taken by surprise; my mind hadn't been on cops. Maybe it takes a little while to get used to being a fugitive. It's like being on the front lines. You know there are Germans over there. You know they're trying to kill you. You know you're supposed to kill them. But it takes a little while before you act without stopping to figure it out. Which is why casualties are high among green troops, no matter how well-trained.

I wasn't used to dodging. I walked out of the diner with my mind blank and there was a cop getting out of a car at the curb. Instead of walking on, I stopped and gawped at him. He looked at me.

But I was learning. An hour ago I couldn't have done it. Now I glared at the cop. I shoved my jaw forward belligerently. "Hey, cop!" I said. "Cop, come here!"

A cop doesn't like to be called a cop. He likes to be called an officer. He doesn't like to be ordered around. This cop scowled at me.

"I said, come here, cop! Snap into it!"

"Wait a minute, Bud," he growled. "Just who the hell are you talking to?"

"Don't stand there picking your nose, cop. You've got a job to do."

"Yeah? Who says so?"

"I'm telling you." I jerked my thumb over my shoulder. "That joker in there just charged me a dime for a cup of coffee. I've been gypped."

"Look, Bud, I've got plenty enough on my mind without you—"

"Yes, and you look, cop! I'm a citizen and a taxpayer. I'm paying your wages to uphold law and order. And I've been reamed out of a nickel."

"So what? What's a nickel worth these days?"

"That's a fine attitude, cop. A fine attitude, I must say. It's not how much, it's the principle."

"Bud, do you want to make a complaint?"

"What do you think I'm doing now if it's not a complaint? Now, look right there on the front of the place. It says, *Coffee, 5 cents*. A public sign. So I got myself a cup of coffee and had it warmed up a couple of times, and he charged me a dime."

"If you had it warmed up a couple of times, that makes it two cups of coffee."

"The hell it does," I said. "It's not two cups of coffee if it's only warmed up. I learned that a long time ago. If you only leave a spoonful in the bottom, it's the same cup of coffee. He only warmed it up a couple of times and charged me a dime."

"What the hell!" the cop said. "Go on, Bud, beat it. I've got things on my mind."

"Aren't you going to do anything about it? I'm a citizen and a taxpayer, and I demand—"

"Bud," the cop said grimly, "I told you to move along. I'm a patient man but I got my limits." His voice rose. "You get your pants the hell out of here or maybe I'll make something out of this!"

I moved along, mumbling.

"Gypped him out of a nickel," the cop growled, going into Ed's Diner.

As the door closed on him I moved along fast. Not too fast, but as fast as possible without appearing to hurry. Chances were the cop would say something to the counterman about the joker who made a gripe about paying a dime for having his coffee warmed up, these guys who always find something to bitch about. The counterman would say, what guy; nobody made any bitch to me. The cop would be irritable, and he'd say, no, well all he wanted me to do is pinch you, that's all. The counterman would say, I don't get it; what guy do you mean? The cop would say, that guy who just went out of here; he was griping about paying a dime for having his coffee warmed up a couple of times. The counterman would say you mean that guy in the tweed coat and snap-brim hat? The cop would say, yeah, the guy with the ears. The counterman would say, he thought coffee was ten cents anyhow; you mean some other guy. The cop would say, for Christ's sake I know who I mean; he had on a brown suit and a loud tie with red and brown stripes on it. The counterman would say, nobody bitched to me; you mean the guy who sort of fits what the radio said about that joker from L. A. who got away with the big haul? And about that time the cop would say, my God, he does at that. And the cop would leave his own five-cent cup of coffee unfinished and pop out of that door in a hurry.

That might not happen. But the chances were that something like it would.

On the corner of Broadway and El Camino, half a block from the diner, a car pulled in and a man hopped out and crossed toward the corner drugstore. He was wearing a T-shirt and moccasins, obviously a guy who'd popped down to the drugstore for a minute and was going to pop right back. He'd left his car lights on, the radio running, and the motor turning over.

Desperate as I was, I felt a curious surprise that I was doing this thing, as I stepped before him and with my hand in my coat pocket shoved a finger into his middle. It was a soft middle; no man with his waistline should go around in a T-shirt. Nobody in his right mind would go around in a T-shirt anyhow, the temperature being what it was.

"Oops!" he said, moving away. "I'm sorry."

I followed him aside, ramming the finger harder. "I'm Albert Rand. Know what that means?"

His eyes went round and his mouth sagged a little. He knew what that meant.

"I'm taking your car for a getaway. One squawk out of you and you're a dead pigeon."

His mouth sagged a little more. He tried to say something but it didn't come out.

As I went to his car I saw Curly, the service-station attendant, hurrying across the street, the chow at his heels. He waved at me. "Mr. Graham!"

I slipped into the car and gunned away. I was shifting into second when the guy in the T-shirt found his voice. And it was something to find. He had a voice like a grand opera singer, the kind of voice they hang a microphone forty feet away from at a radio broadcast, to save the tubes from shattering.

The cop was just breaking out the door of Ed's Diner, breaking out fast with a quick look both ways along the street, when the voice opened up. The cop hit the pavement at a run toward the yelling guy in the T-shirt.

I kept the car in second. The stoplight on the corner was red, three lanes of cars were piled up waiting, and a car was parked at the curb. An hour ago that would have stopped me. Now I gunned the car and broke over the middle lane to the left of the highway, then cut to the right around the waiting cars, tires shrieking, across the front of the three rows of waiting headlights.

A law-abiding citizen in one of the cars gave me a long and angry blast of the horn. Nothing a law-abiding citizen hates worse than to see somebody else flout traffic rules, doing something he secretly wishes he had the nerve to do.

After the short half-block I made another squealing right turn into the alley opposite the Greyhound station, gunned along the back of the stores and slid to a stop where the alley opened up into the parking area. I cut the ignition, lights, and radio, and, on foot, crossed through the block to Broadway.

To my right at the corner of Broadway and El Camino, the guy with the T-shirt was still yelling. Now he had two policemen to yell to. A siren began to wail. Another siren took it up.

I crossed the street and went to the corner, hurrying along with other citizens eager to see what it was all about. I joined the group at the corner who were watching the yelling guy across the street.

Traffic crowded for the curb and stopped. Signal lights were red in both directions. Sirens howled down Broadway. Sirens howled down El Camino,

"What's up?" somebody asked me.

"I just got here."

"That L. A. killer," somebody said. "He just made his getaway in a car."

"Who, the guy who got away with those bonds?"

"Yeah, the guy from L. A. Rand is his name. Albert Rand. He pulled that big bank job in L. A."

"What the hell's he doing up here, I'd like to know."

"That's what I say. Why don't those L. A. jokers stay down there where they belong?"

"We don't want 'em up here."

"He won't last long. He'll find out we don't go for that stuff up here."

I crossed the street toward the grounds of the Sequoia High School. The guy with the T-shirt was still in full voice. I couldn't have picked a better man to establish the fact that Albert Rand was making his getaway in a car.

And I was on foot. I had whatever time it would take the police to find the car parked fifty yards away from the guy with the T-shirt. And then what?

I half wished, right then, that I *was* Albert Rand. Or somebody like him. Somebody with a little background and experience in this fugitive business. I was green as grass.

Looking back as I went through the gates of the high school grounds, I saw a man following. It was Curly, the chow dog at his heels. That big surly chow, silent and alert. I never did like chows.

"Bert," Curly snapped. "Bert. Where the hell are you going? For God's sake, let me help you."

I stopped, partly from surprise, partly because of that chow. I have a healthy respect for chows. Or for any well-trained dog. And the way I'd seen that dog follow at heel, it was trained well.

"You're hot, Bert," Curly said. "You're hotter than a pistol. Why didn't you let me know, when you passed by the station a few minutes ago?"

I said nothing.

He said, "You didn't know, huh? Well, neither did I. I thought you was Graham. You remember I called, hello Mr. Graham. I didn't know until I heard it on the radio. Bert, you're hotter than a pistol."

"You're telling me," I said.

"When I heard it on the radio I closed up the station and started out looking for you. I seen you take that guy's car, then pop up on Broadway a minute later. That was fast thinking, Bert. You always were quick upstairs."

"Quit beating your gums, Curly," I said. As long as he thought I was Rand, it was okay by me. "I'm in a spot."

"Sure, Bert. My car's at the station. If we can get to it."

"We'd better do it quick while nobody knows the score."

I stripped off my topcoat, suit coat, and vest, took off my necktie and hat. I made a bundle and wrapped it in a newspaper lying among the shrubbery.

Curly and I emerged from the high school grounds, he in white uniform and I with shirt collar open and breathing deeply, acting like an adopted native son who believes in Climate Best by Government Test if it kills him.

With all the frammis going on, nobody paid any attention to us. Albert Rand was still firmly fixed in mind as a man in a car. At the station, we got into a '38 Plymouth parked by the grease rack. I crouched under the dash. The chow took what was evidently its customary position, hind legs on the cushion and front paws atop the dash, its body covering me. For just once I liked chows. I practically loved chows.

Curly backed out and drove into the street. The car bucked and the gears clashed. He evidently was plenty nervous, with a right to be.

Presently he said, "Bert, for Christ's sake make yourself small. They're stopping traffic ahead."

5

I tried to make myself small. The Plymouth stopped. A voice said, "Sorry to stop you, but we're checking all—"

The chow growled. The voice didn't finish.

"Easy, Boy," Curly said.

"He looked like he'd take a hunk out of me."

"Boy's all right, officer. But I wouldn't put my face in the car window like you done. Not with any dog."

"I didn't see the bastard," the cop said. "I don't like chows. I don't trust a chow."

"They're a one-man dog," Curly said. "What you stopping me for? Lights haywire?"

"We're looking for a guy from L. A."

"What's he doing up here?"

"That's what the hell I'd like to know. He'll find out. Those L. A. jokers can't pull that stuff up here."

"What did he do?"

"That guy who got away with a couple of million bucks in L. A. this morning."

"Yeah, I seen about that in the paper. What do you want out of me? I'm not from L. A."

"Get going. And that damned chow with you."

The Plymouth drove on, turned a corner. "Lucky we got Boy along, Bert," Curly said. "That cop kept his distance. He never even got his face close, after one growl. Yes, sir, there's nothing like a chow to command respect. I see what Bill Meadows meant, about having a good dog. Bill Meadows sure does train a dog."

At the name Bill Meadows, I remembered the man with the Doberman, the tall man with the leather zipper jacket. I knew where I'd got acquainted with him. Bill Meadows was the man who'd sold my dog Jiggs to Cora and me, when Jiggs was a pup.

Bill Meadows had trained this chow of Curly's. Curly thought I was Albert Rand. I was learning a little. At least the cast. Though I didn't know where the characters fit in.

"Bill's a good man," I said.

"One of the best," he agreed. "I like Bill. He's good company. He likes his liquor, but who doesn't? Bill's all right. I didn't like the dogs at first. Boy and Edgar. I was afraid of 'em. But it's like you said, Bert. You get attached to a dog. It's company. And you can depend on a dog. I had a drunk come in the station the other day and he started giving me a bad time. But not for long. Boy just sniffed at his pants and growled a little, and that drunk got real quiet. Nobody gives you a bad time with a dog around. Not even a drunk. Yep, Bert, I'm sure glad you got Bill Meadows to give me and Dolly the dogs. Like you said, Bert, you don't have no trouble with nosy neighbors, with a good dog. Dolly's attached to Edgar. That dog just follows her around day and night. Dolly will be sure glad to see you, Bert. I'll bet you've been lonely while we've been up here."

"I sure have been," I said. The car was driving a twisting road. Crouched under the dash, I had no idea where we were going.

"She was saying just yesterday, she said to me, 'Curly, I sure do miss Bert.' You know how a woman is, Bert."

"Yeah."

"And I'll bet you'll see a change in the baby. A baby that age. Even a couple of months you'll see a change. I'll bet you can't wait to see the baby."

"I've been lonely," I said.

"But why didn't you let us know, Bert? Me and Dolly, we're okay. You know that, Bert. You know we're all right. You know you can depend on us. So why didn't you let us know?"

I didn't say anything.

"Ain't I done my part, Bert? I went along with you, didn't I? I didn't even know what was cooking, but I went along. Not that I'm blaming you, Bert, in a way. What I mean—two million bucks. That's just too big to spread around beforehand. I mean, you wouldn't want that to get out. It's just too big. But you knew I was here. Me and Dolly. Waiting. Why didn't you come to me tonight? Why'd you just walk on past the station?"

"I didn't know I was hot yet," I said.

"Too bad it didn't work, Bert. It was a hell of a sweet play, as I see it. Of course, the minute I seen this Graham guy, after you sent me and Dolly up here, I put two and two together. Say, you're dead ringers, you pair. You figured to just walk in and take over, as I see it. Too bad it didn't work. What happened?"

I didn't know how much Curly knew of the original plan. "What the hell does it matter?" I said irritably.

"Sure, Bert. I know how you feel. You're sore as hell. There was a sweet hideout—walk right into another guy's shoes. Oh, that's it," he said. "Sure, Bert, that's it. That's why you had me and Dolly come up here. So if it didn't work, you'd have a place to stay."

"That's it, Curly," I said.

"I'm glad you really trust us like that, Bert. For a while I didn't know. After all, Dolly's my sister. Her having the baby and all, and you sparking around with that cashier's daughter. You can see how it was with me, Bert. I was just trying to see the right thing done by Dolly."

"Sure, Curly," I said. "I understand."

"I'm glad you do, Bert. It wasn't that I was trying to put the hooks on you. It didn't matter to me if I knew something about you the bank might like to get hold of. I'm not that kind of a guy, Bert. I didn't want the money for myself, Bert. It's like I told you. It was just for Dolly and the kid. After all, Bert, the kid's as much yours as it is hers."

"Sure, Curly," I said.

"I'm glad you see it my way, Bert. And you can count on me and Dolly. As long as you're going to do the right thing by Dolly, you can depend on us. You know that, Bert."

Presently he said, "Well, here we are." The car made a sharp turn and stopped.

I got out and stretched while taking a good look around. We were at a small house in the hills. Spotted about at infrequent intervals were lights of other houses.

The rear door opened. A girl stood in the doorway, a rather pretty girl with red hair. A chow was at her heels.

"Curly?" she asked.

"It's me. And guess who else?"

The girl came out slowly, peering into the darkness. She paused, seeing me. Her breath came tremblingly, then she flung herself on me, kissing me, clinging to me.

"Oh, Bert, *Bert!* I've been wild! Are you all right, Bert? The papers, and then I heard on the radio— Are you all right, Bert?"

"Sure he's all right," Curly said.

The girl clung to me, both laughing and crying. I didn't know exactly what technique Albert Rand used in making love. This impersonation business could go only so far.

"Are you hungry, Bert?" the girl said. "Oh, it's so good to see you. Have you had anything to eat? I'll bet you're dying to see the baby."

"We better get inside," Curly said.

"Good heavens, yes," the girl said. "Bert, they're looking for you."

We went into the kitchen, the chows following. One of the chows kept at Curly's heels and one followed the girl. Curly indicated a chair and got two bottles of beer from the refrigerator. The girl brought a baby from the bedroom.

"Hasn't she grown, Bert?"

"She sure has," I said.

The baby looked like any baby to me. I thought maybe I'd ought to chuck it under the chin or something, but I didn't know Albert Rand's habits in that regard.

The girl took the baby back into the bedroom, returned and began working at the stove. "Bert," she said, "you didn't do it really, did you, what the papers and the radio say?"

Curly winked at me. "I don't know what you've got to crab about, Dolly. Two million bucks."

"But it's dishonest," she said. "You wouldn't do anything dishonest, would you, Bert?"

"The Government won't never notice two million bucks," Curly said. "Billions is what they spend. Billions. This is a drop in the bucket. They won't never miss it."

"I guess if you put it that way," the girl said. She crossed over from the stove and sat on my lap. "I know you wouldn't do anything really bad, would you, Bert?"

"Look, leave him alone awhile," Curly said. "He's been through a rough deal."

"Well, so have I," she said. "Oh, Bert, it's so good to see you. Of course I knew you'd come up here, just like you said you would. But I've been so lonely for you. Haven't you missed me?"

"I certainly have," I said.

"Oh, leave him alone, Dolly," Curly said. "He's hungry."

She got off my lap. "Bert, you're different. What's happened to you?"

"What's happened to him? He's got all the cops in the state on his tail, that's what's happened to him," Curly said. "You'd be different, too."

"I've had a hard day," I said. "I'll be all right in the morning."

"Sure, you'll be okay, Bert," Curly said. "You always light right side up. I see why you sent us up here, now."

"I thought you would," I said.

"So if anything went snafu on your deal, you'd have a place to stay. It's too bad you couldn't just walk in and take over as Graham. That would have been a sweet deal."

"Maybe I'll get another chance," I said.

Curly raised a wise eyebrow. "Oh. This is just the prelim, eh!"

"This way," I said, "the cops will investigate Graham. They'll make sure he's what he says he is. When they're satisfied, I can walk in and take over."

"Say, that's cute, Bert. That's pretty cute. You always did have a head on you." He took a pull at his beer. "Two million bucks. Say, that's a haul. You done all right, Bert. Where is it?"

"You don't think I'm carrying it on me?" I said.

"Sure not, Bert. You're too smart for that. What I mean, I think two of us ought to know. What if you hadn't got away, down there in town a while ago? Anything might happen, Bert. More than just you ought to know."

"Those bonds are safe enough," I said.

"Sure, Bert. But what about Dolly?"

"I can talk for myself," Dolly said. "Leave him alone. He's hungry."

"Sure, you can talk for yourself," Curly said. "And look what you got for it. A baby."

"Well, Bert's going to marry me…. Aren't you, Bert?"

"Of course," I said.

"It must have been terrible, Bert," she said. "You're not yourself at all tonight."

"Oh, pipe down, sis," Curly said. "I'm trying to talk business."

"Why don't you both eat something?" she said. "I've got scrambled eggs and—"

Curly broke in with an oath. He sprang to the window and jerked down the blind. "Are we smart!"

"There's hardly anybody lives out here," Dolly said.

"Which makes it worse," he growled. "The farther out in the sticks you go, the more the neighbors know you. How long you going to be here, Bert?"

"I guess I hadn't ought to stay long," I said.

"You're not going to leave us," Dolly said. "You said you wouldn't, Bert. You said when you came up here we'd be together from then on."

We sat at the table. I wasn't hungry. I made the motions of eating. Curly wolfed his food, and spoke through it.

"You're good here for a day or two, Bert," he said. "But like I say, anything can happen. We ought to know where those bonds are."

"Why don't you leave him alone?" Dolly said.

"Bert, it's not that I don't know you're okay. I know you're okay. I always have. But I got to look out for Dolly. She won't watch out for herself. And there's the kid to think about. Anything happened to you, Bert, I ought to know where those bonds are."

"I'll think about it," I said. I put cream in my coffee, stirred it, and took a sip. "Good coffee."

"You've had a rough time, all right," Curly said. "Cream in your coffee."

"Good God," I said, "that's right."

"You poor dear," Dolly said. She emptied the coffee in the sink and refilled the cup. She put three spoons of sugar in and stirred it for me. "That's how you like it, isn't it, honey?"

I took a sip and tried not to gag. If there's one thing I can't stand, it's sugar in coffee.

"That's better," I said. How long this could go on, I didn't know. And with those two chows in the room, I didn't feel any too happy about the prospects of being found out.

"Where's the stuff, Bert?" Curly asked.

"Leave him alone," Dolly said. "For tonight, anyhow."

"You go in to bed," Curly told her. "Go on, beat it. We've got to settle this now. He'll be in pretty quick. Go on now. Beat it."

The girl obediently went to the bedroom. "Bert," she called through the door.

"Yes?"

"Don't be too long."

Curly laughed. "She's got it bad. You can't do anything wrong where she's concerned. A woman's not practical, Bert. She don't care. She'll believe anything you tell her. But you got to be practical, Bert. That's what I always say. Where's the stuff?"

"Can't we let it go for tonight?" I asked.

"Bert, it won't be no different in the morning than tonight. It ain't that I don't trust you. Sure I trust you. But, Bert, this is big time. This is two million bucks. And I got Dolly to think of, and the kid. Share and share alike, Bert."

"Okay," I said. "The bonds are in a briefcase. I put the briefcase in a locker at the S. P. depot in San Francisco."

"Locker?"

"Sure, where you put a dime in and then lock it and take the key."

"Where's the key, Bert?"

"You don't think I've got that on me, do you?"

"Sure not, Bert. Where is it, is all I want to know."

"I think we both ought to get it, when we do."

"Sure, Bert. But where is it?"

I said, "I put it in an envelope and mailed it to Frank M. Jeffers. General Delivery, San Francisco."

Curly grinned. "Swell, Bert. You better lay low here a spell. I'll go in and pick it up tomorrow."

"You'd better not miss a day's work. It wouldn't look right."

"I'm not on until two in the afternoon. Hell, you know that, Bert. I wrote you."

"I mean, as long as you're back by two," I said.

"Sure," he said. "Well, I better be hitting the hay. And you'll want to see Dolly." He stretched and went into a bedroom at the rear. The chow followed him. I was alone in the kitchen.

The other door opened. "Bert," the girl said.

"I think I'll walk around a spell," I said.

She slipped out and clung to my arm. The chow followed her. "No, Bert. No you can't. You don't know how it is, out here in the country. The neighbors know everything. Somebody will see you. You've got to stay inside. Come on, Bert."

She drew me into the bedroom and closed the door.

Her arms came around me. "Bert, I've been so lonely."

I felt like a fool, and worse. I stood woodenly while she kissed me.

"Bert, what's the matter?"

"Nothing's the matter."

"Don't you love me anymore, Bert?"

"Sure I do."

"Sure you do what?"

"I do. What more do you want?"

Her body stiffened. "Bert, what's wrong?"

"Nothing's wrong."

"Tell me like you used to."

"I feel silly."

"You didn't used to feel silly."

"A lot has happened today."

"Oh, my God!" she breathed.

I stood stiffly.

"I knew it," she said. "I knew it the minute I first put my arms around you. In the dark here, where I can't see you, I can tell. *You're not Bert Rand!* You're not him. You're somebody else. You're not—"

I took hold of her, then. With one arm around her waist I put my other hand over her mouth. She struggled. I heard a growl from the chow in the darkness. I moved with her to the crib.

"Listen," I said, "one squawk out of you and your baby will get it. You understand that? Just one squawk." I released her, pushed her away, and fumbled for the baby.

"What are you doing here?" she asked. "What are you doing? Who are you? You're not Bert."

"All I want is to get out of here," I said. "I'm taking the baby with me. You'll get it back in the morning if you do the right thing."

"What do you want me to do?"

"Just keep still. Say nothing. Don't tell Curly. Don't do anything that would hurt your baby."

"You won't hurt her. You wouldn't do that?"

"It's up to you," I said. "Is there an outside door?"

"Yes. Just a second." She moved through the room and a square of dim light showed from outside as she swung the door.

I went out. "Go to bed," I told her. "Say nothing. Do nothing. And you'll get your baby in the morning."

I went around the house to the car. I was almost upon it when a figure arose from the running board. It was the figure of a tall man with a leather zipper jacket. It was Bill Meadows. Beside him was the Doberman.

6

"Oh," he said. "So that's it?"

"Sure," I said.

"I was pretty sore," he said. "Here I call around and through the window I seen you in there with them. My God, Bert, what if I hadn't seen you?"

"Well, you did."

"Look, Bert, it's more than just your neck. You've got to think about the rest of us. You're supposed to be home with Cora, acting natural. Hell, the cops will drop in any minute of the day or night for a while. Me, I got sore, seeing you here. I thought you just had to take another crack at Dolly. But it's the kid. Yeah, I can understand that. The kid."

"Sure," I said.

"Okay, I'll be right back," he said. He slipped to the house, and I heard him say a word. The word was *Gumdrop*. He said the word sharply, and then from within the house came the ravening cry of dogs gone mad. The Doberman beside me began panting. It quivered in every muscle. There was the scream of a woman, and the scream of a man. And over all the savage fury of fighting dogs.

I stood rooted. It seemed as if my heart stopped beating. And then a bitter nausea hit me. I thought I'd go down. I knew that if I'd had any idea what was in Meadows' mind I'd have killed him before he'd got that word out.

He came gliding back but I couldn't look at him. "Come on, Bert," he said. He led the way across the hill through the live oak and acacia.

I was sick. I had to stop.

As I wiped the sour puke from my mouth Bill Meadows said, "Bert, I can see you're not a dog lover. There's nothing like a good dog, trained right. Just a word, Bert, is all you need with a good dog. The right word—"

"Goddamn you, shut up!" I yelled. "Shut up!"

A black Ford was parked by the road over the hill. We got in. The dog leaped into the back seat.

"Don't get hostile at me, Bert," Bill Meadows said as he drove along. "It was your idea. Christ, what's the difference, a dog or some other way? You had to get rid of them. They didn't fit. You shouldn't of ever got mixed up with that Dolly to begin with. Sure, it's your affair, but there's only one way it had to end. Don't get sore at me. What's the difference?" He glanced at the baby in my arms. "What you going to do with the brat?"

"Hell, I don't know."

"Leave it on a doorstep, Bert. Or let me. I know the people up here. I know a couple out in South Palo Alto—Mayfield—they've been trying to adopt a kid for a hell of a while. Kids are hard to get. I'll just leave it on the doorstep tonight."

"You're sure you will?"

"Now, damn it, Bert, you know me better than that. That chow idea might of been mine, but you told me you had to get rid of Curly and Dolly. Don't blame that on me."

"Sure, Bill," I said. "But it kind of got me for a minute."

"I know how it is. I didn't feel too good myself. But you got to do what you got to do. They would of tipped the play, sure as hell. You know Curly. You ought to. You've been paying him off every month. Paying him off just because he knew you back in the Army. What the hell would the payoff of been on a deal like this when he smelled two million bucks? We got to do what we got to do."

"Why don't you shut up?" I said.

"Sure, Bert. I know how you feel. I feel the same way. I'm sorry as hell, and I hardly knew them."

He drove to Woodside Road, turned left, and at the intersection of the Alameda pulled off the road and stopped. "I'll let you off here, Bert, in case the cops are over at Graham's house—your house. Good night, Bert. And don't worry about the kid. It will be in good hands."

I began walking along the Alameda, and when his car was gone I walked back and headed across the hills. The bundle containing my outer clothes—vest and coats—was still in Curly's car. I would need those coats. And I didn't want to leave that sort of identification on the scene.

I reached the place about an hour later. There was no sound from within the house. Not even a growl from the chows as I approached. I thought of them lying in a bloated stupor, and the insane idea came to go into the house with a club and kill them. I decided the idea was insane, and compromised by taking my clothes from the car. The coats were welcome in the night.

The keys were not in the car, but in the glove compartment I found a pair of Polaroid driving glasses. They weren't much as a disguise, but they were better than nothing.

I walked into the hills to a spot I knew, near the cross, where there were some camp stoves and tables under live oaks. It was isolated, as good a place to spend the night as any. I had an idea to sleep on one of the picnic tables, but I was just getting settled when I heard the whine of a car climbing the winding road. I went into the brush while the car slowly drove past, a police car with a spotlight sweeping back and forth. I stayed in the brush, dozing, smoking cigarettes, and walking about occasionally to warm up. It was a miserable night.

And now I had a purpose more than merely the personal one of trying to get out of this mess. I kept thinking of Dolly. A rather dumb girl, but trusting. And I thought of the baby, being raised by strangers because its mother was too trusting and its father was no good.

Something was going to be done about it. No matter how long it took. No matter how many years.

By morning I was beginning to itch, and I knew what I looked like. Daylight showed that the brush I was hiding in was the most prevalent shrub of California, poison oak, beautiful stuff with glossy leaves in groups of three. Some people can wallow in the stuff and I've seen it eaten. Some people get a few pink blotches a couple or three days after exposure. But on others it works as fast as sunburn, and these people turn pink and swell up. These people were my people; their ways my ways. When I looked at my hands in the daylight I knew exactly what my face looked like. I'd been all through it before. I'd been hauled off to the hospital from bivouac, in the Army, and again on maneuvers. I didn't need any mirror to know I didn't look like Charles Graham. My eyes were mere slits in a plump mass of bright pink. The sun glasses were almost coals to Newcastle; I put them on anyhow.

My watch had stopped. I wound it, setting it by guess. As soon as I figured it was late enough to be seen on the road, I began walking into town. The first turn of the road brought me to a shack with clothes on the line. No dog barked as I went by, and one item on the line was an old gray blanket. I went around the hill, cut over it behind the house and filched the blanket. Strange, the guilty and breathless thrill of stealing that worn blanket, a desperate character and killer such as I.

I took the blanket into some brush, making sure it wasn't poison oak, stripped to my underwear, folded the blanket lengthwise and wound it around me, then put on my clothes. I was grateful enough for the warmth, but my pants were tight enough to remind me of breakfast. I wasn't able to button the vest but the topcoat covered that.

I was now, I hoped, pleasantly plump, my body to some degree fitting my swollen face and hands. I kept on toward town.

Within a few minutes I began to sweat; I cursed that blanket. As the sweat broke out, the poison oak itched like fury. I slowed to a casual stroll, clenching my hands in my pockets to keep from scratching.

A jalopy came along and picked me up. I told the driver my car had broken down. He asked what model, and I said a '46. He said, "They don't make them like they used to, before the war." I said they didn't. He said, "What do you think about that big bond job in L. A.?" I said I wished I had a chance to cop two million bucks. He said, "Me, too, brother." I asked if they'd caught the guy yet, and he said, "Not the last I heard. I'd like a crack at that ten thousand reward." I said I would, too.

He let me off at El Camino Real and I went into Ed's Diner for breakfast. I had a dollar and eighty-four cents in my pocket. The rest of my money had been in that billfold. And despite what I'd told the red-faced cop, it hadn't been much. Cora had kept me too close to the line for that.

I ordered hot cakes and eggs and coffee, sixty-five cents. I had had the idea to test out my face with the counterman, but a different guy was on duty this morning. The mirror on the wall above the pie shelf showed the plump face of a man who either was on the verge of apoplexy or who had spent a couple of days on the beach at Santa Cruz worshiping the sun not wisely but too well.

I looked human but very little like Charles Bruce Graham, Esq. My watch, I saw from the wall clock, was only twenty minutes off. It was a quarter to seven.

When I was finished eating, it was a couple of minutes after seven. I decided to take the 7:12 to the city that morning. As usual.

I walked over to the S. P. station, bought a ticket and a morning paper, and leaned against a post to read about the big manhunt. There was a cop moving among the commuters waiting for the 7:12, and two local detectives I knew by sight were standing against the station wall taking everything in over their papers. I kept my paper low so my pink face was fully visible. The sun glasses got a glance from the detectives, but this not being L. A., they had no suspicion I was a movie star in street dress.

My tan Nash drew up, Cora driving, the man with my face beside her and the dog, Jiggs, in the rear. The two detectives perked up. One of them took a step toward the car, then changed his mind as the other touched his sleeve.

The man with my face got out of the car. Cora said, "Wait a minute, Chick. I've got the grocery list somewhere."

"Why can't you pick up the groceries? I hate to carry stuff in my arms."

"It's no bother to you, Chick, and I'd have to make a special trip to town," she said. "It's right here somewhere."

"I'll get a paper, dear," he said. He got the paper and went back to my car, leaning an elbow on the open window as he scanned the headlines. I wondered if the coin he'd put in the slot of the newspaper rack was a slug.

"There's a better picture of him in the paper this morning," he said. "He sure looks like me, all right."

"You know how those newspaper pictures are."

"Yes; but we saw him, dear. He does sort of look like me."

"At a casual glance. But he wouldn't fool anybody very long. The nerve of the guy, trying to walk in and take your place."

"He had plenty of that, all right," he agreed.

Cora shivered. "Thank goodness we had the dog. Except for Jiggs, I think he had the idea of maybe killing us and taking your place."

"Yeah, that's what the paper says. I think it was Buster and Ethelene who threw him off. They just happened to be there for dinner, thank God. He could have got rid of you and me, all right. Just stepped into my shoes and said you were away on a visit or something. But with four of us there, he couldn't get away with it."

"Chick, darling, be careful. Don't take any chances. He might try it again."

"He'd know he'd never get away with it, now. Anyhow, maybe they've got him."

"That dumb cop!" Cora said. "He had him, and let him talk his way out! Is that what we've got police protection for? What do we get for the taxes we pay?"

The train was pulling in. The man with my face kissed my wife. "Bye, bye, dear. Remember, keep Jiggs with you all the time. Don't take any chances."

He began hurrying for the train.

"Chick, the grocery list!"

"I hoped you'd forgotten it," he said, running back.

I got on the car behind him and followed him into the smoking car. He took the fifth seat on the right-hand side, my seat. I took the seat behind him.

I began reading the paper, to find out the details. But I didn't care about details. I knew all I wanted to know. Too, the car was warm and for the first time since the thing began I relaxed. I was limp. It was still something hard to believe, particularly watching the back of the man's head. No two humans could have ears like that.

I felt I was seeing things. And I felt I had to talk to somebody I knew before I'd got mixed up in all this—Mary. It was Mary I had to see. Mary, Mary, if I could only do it all over again. If I could see you like things used to be, instead of running back to you hurt after I'd messed up my life and got in a jam. But who else? In all this world, who else? I needed help. And more than that, I needed a friend. Somebody I could bank on. Somebody I could stake my life on.

Part of the plan, I saw as I looked back, had been to isolate me. To keep me from making friends, to wean me from old friends. Cora could be deadly to people she didn't like and it boiled down to the fact that she didn't like anybody except Buster and Ethelene. I'd lost one of our accounts, back when we didn't have any to spare, by inviting the man and his wife down to dinner. A neighbor who'd tried to be neighborly soon wouldn't speak to us. We had an abnormal social life. If we saw anybody in the evening, it was Buster and Ethelene. They either drove down to see us or we went to the city to see them.

When my old CO, Major Jody, phoned me at the office one day and said he was passing through, I had to meet him at a bar. I knew Cora wouldn't have him to dinner. So I had a drink with Jody and told him I'd like to have him down, but that my wife was under the weather.

"I'm tied up tonight anyhow," he said. "You married Cora?"

"Yes." Then I looked at him. "Why do you say it that way?"

He shrugged. "There was another girl. Mary Davis. She wrote to me."

"Mary wrote to you?"

"She knew I was the CO. She just wrote to ask how you were. If your health was good and so on. She used to write every once in a while. Just wanting to know if you were okay."

It was a couple of minutes before I said anything. They were bad minutes. "Why didn't you tell me?"

"None of my business. If you didn't want to write to her, it was your own affair. But I sort of wondered. There was something about her letters that sort of hit me. She seemed such a nice kid. Such a hell of a nice kid. Never complained, never explained, just wrote to see how you were. Such a nice kid."

"She was," I said. "They don't come any better."

"So I always thought, well, if I got out this way I'd look her up and say hello, anyhow. That's what I'm doing tonight. I'm having dinner with her."

"With Mary? You mean she's living in San Francisco?"

He gave me an odd look. "Didn't you know?" What he meant was, hadn't I cared enough to remember. "Have you got her address?"

"It's in the phone book. Under her brother's name. Should I tell her I ran into you?"

"No. No, I guess you'd better not." That was water under the bridge.

Next morning at the office I asked Buster, "What happened to Mary's letters?"

"Letters? Did you leave some letters around here?"

"You know what I'm talking about. You were the mail clerk. You stopped those letters. My letters and Mary's letters."

"Chick," Buster said in that honest way, "maybe I was a rat to do that. But Cora is my sister. She loved you, Chick. You're the only guy in the world she ever wanted. I'd do it again, for her." That round honest face. That sincere manner. Such high motives.

I'd had a couple of bad hours after that, thinking of what might have been. But it was done. Water under the bridge.

I'd run into Walt, Mary's brother, a few months later, on the street. We shook hands and told each other what a small world it was and how well we looked.

He said, "Living here?"

"On the Peninsula. Commuting."

He looked at the package in my hand, then tried not to appear to have noticed it.

"Yeah, I'm married," I said.

"Well, you're looking swell, Chick," he said. "Let's get together sometime."

"Sure," I said, "we'll have to do that."

And of course we never had and we'd both known we never would.

And, as I rode up to the city on the 7:12, sitting behind the man with my face, I saw how neatly it all fitted in. Cora hadn't wanted me to have friends, except Buster and Ethelene. She didn't want anybody too close to me, anybody who might get to know me too well and make it difficult for the man with my face to move into my place.

But maybe that was just as well. If I'd made friends, they might have gone the way of Curly and Dolly. It was dangerous for anyone to get too close to this.

7

"Hello, Graham."

I glanced up quickly, then shifted my eyes as I saw I was not being addressed. A man had paused at the seat ahead and was speaking to the man with my face. It was James Pease, the business machine salesman, whose identity I had used last night to get away from the red-faced cop.

The man with my face continued reading his paper.

"Graham," Pease said. "Mr. Graham."

The man with my face glanced up. He smiled. "Oh, hello, there. I'm awfully sorry. I was reading the paper."

He was, I knew, on the spot. He didn't know Pease from a turnip. One thing Buster and Cora couldn't have briefed him on would be his acquaintances on the commuter train.

Pease sat down beside him. "It sure is a funny deal, isn't it? Him trying to take your place."

"It's got me whipped."

"What do you think about my machine?"

"Your machine?"

"It will save you money, Graham. It will pay for itself in six months."

"I'll have to think it over," the man with my face said.

"I'll bring one around this afternoon. Once you give it a try, I know you'll never let it go."

"Sure," the man with my face said. "We'll try it out."

"Well, thanks, Graham." Pease moved down the aisle and took a seat behind us. I figured he must have thought he'd done some nice business. When he'd talked with me and Buster, Buster had been dead set against his machine.

The train pulled into the station at Third and Townsend. The man with my face strode outside, glanced at the sky, took a deep breath of morning air and strode up the street, as I might have done. He would walk to the office, say hello to Ethelene and Buster, and go with Buster to pick up Thursday's accounts.

I wondered if he knew anything about accounting. It wouldn't matter. Buster had cooked up the idea for the business while we were overseas. The idea was to keep the books of small businesses which were too big for the owner to do in his spare time and too small to afford a full-time accountant. The selling angle was that we'd save a business more in taxes than our service cost. We'd pick up all the records of a particular account once a week, bring them back the next day entered on the books, and take care of all statements and reports.

Buster had had big ideas of a hundred wage slaves toiling for us eventually. That's the reason we took the accounts to our office instead of working at the places of business. When we were hiring men, Buster had said, we didn't want them chiseling in on our clients. The clients would never see anybody but Buster and me.

Which made it perfect for Rand, stepping into my shoes. He didn't necessarily have to know a ledger from a mail-order catalogue. He would, this morning, take the books back to the Wednesday accounts and pick up the records of the Thursday accounts. Buster would be with him to answer all questions.

I went to a phone booth at the station and then wondered whom to call. Mary, of course. Mary, Mary, if we could do it all over again. I could bank on Mary. Her brother Walt and I had been great pals before I went away.

But could I come back crying, after what I'd done to them?

Who else?

It's a tough job, mulling over people you know, when you need help in a big way. I had to have money. I had to have a place to stay. I had to have cooperation in getting out of this thing.

Well, let's see. Despite the isolationist tactics of my erstwhile pals, I did know a few people. A guy has to, over the course of years. Okay, but *who?* I knew the conductor on the S. P., the newspaper boy, Murphy of Murphy's Bar, Larry of Larry's Grill. I knew guys to say hello to. I knew our accounts. I could ask a number of guys how the wife was. But who could I borrow money from? Who could I ask to put himself out for me?

Amazing, how alone a man is, outside a small circle. And my circle was certainly small.

Then I thought of Floyd Moon. Sure, there was the guy. I'd known him pretty well in the Army, and we'd had lunch together a few times since. Floyd had always felt indebted to me, embarrassingly so, because I'd fixed things so that he hadn't had to pay for a jeep he'd lost. Every time I saw him he brought up the matter and said how he certainly wished he could do something for me. Well, he could.

I called his number in Oakland. "Floyd? Chick Graham."

"Hello, Chick. Say, is that you I've been reading about in the papers? This guy from L. A. tried to take your place?"

"That's right. He did take my place."

"He what? Are you serious, Chick?"

"It's no joke. Remember Buster, the mail clerk?"

"Sure. You're in business with him."

"Let me tell you a yarn." I sketched the essential details. "What do you think of that?"

"It's an outrage, Chick. He can't get away with it."

"I'm afraid he has, Floyd."

"What are you doing about it?"

"Right now I've got a whole hide and my freedom. I've got to have a place to stay. Where I can think things out and decide what to do."

"Why don't you go to the police, Chick? Tell them the story just like you did to me."

"They wanted the police to take me in. That was part of the plan. I'm not going to play their game."

"It's kind of a problem, Chick."

"I need help," I said.

"Well, now, Chick, I wish I could do something. But if the police can't, what could I do?" He spoke very rapidly. "I don't know what you're mixed up in, but I've got a wife to think about. I don't want to get involved in something. You know how I feel about you, Chick. I wish there was something I could do. But a thing like this, Chick. I mean, murder and all. If it wasn't that I've got a wife to think about, Chick—"

"Could you let me have a little money?" I asked. "You'll get it back when I straighten things out."

"Well." He hesitated. "Why, sure, Chick. I'm a little pinched right now but I'd be glad to loan you a dollar. You're always good for a dollar with me, Chick. You know that. And never mind paying it back."

"That's swell of you, Floyd," I said, and hung up.

I next called Dud Egbert. Dud ran the Egbert Radio Repairs, one of our accounts. But Dud was a little more than a business acquaintance.

He listened to my yarn and said, "Wait a minute, Chick—customer." I waited several minutes. "Hello, Chick—still there?"

"Big as life."

"Chick, where are you? I'll come down and pick you up. Stay right there now. I'll pick you up in fifteen minutes. Where are you, Chick? Where are you phoning from?"

His voice was tight; he was breathing hard. I hung up. I knew that while I'd waited he'd gone to another phone and called the cops. Let's see, could they trace a dial call?

I opened the booth door, and standing before it, smiling confidently, was James Pease, business machine salesman.

"What the hell happened to your face, Graham?" he asked.

"I'm through with the phone," I said, turning away.

"I'm talking to you, Graham," he said, and indicated a cop strolling through the station. "Or should I talk to him?"

"My name is Berry, mister. Arnold Berry."

He chuckled. "Don't let's beat around the bush, Graham. You need some help, as I see it. And I'm a friend in need."

"Sorry, mister," I said. "Why do you think my name is Graham?"

"The ears, Graham. I was sitting in the back of the smoking car and I saw those ears. Two men with the same kind of ears, ahead of me. From the back, they were dead ringers. Maybe you ate some strawberries or something. They do that to some people. And you've got on sunglasses. But from the back, you and the other guy were the same. Let's sit down, and talk it over."

We sat on a bench. The cop wandered about the waiting room aimlessly.

"I done some thinking," Pease said. "You know, last night this joker Rand got away from the cops by pretending he was me. I saw him. I talked with him. But it's like I told the cops when they were asking me about him. I told them, maybe it wasn't Rand. Maybe it was Graham. Because, you see, the guy who walked into my house knew about that posting machine. A thing like that, how would Rand know about it? A little thing, like that? Of course the cops didn't pay any attention to me. They don't like to be told their own business. But still it was something to think about. And then coming up on the 7:12, I saw two guys with the same kind of ears. Dead ringers from the back.

"Well, I wanted to make sure. So I went up to this guy Graham, the one who'd come to the station with his wife and all—everybody watched that, you know, after what had happened. And I said his name. When I said his name, *you* looked up. I said his name again. And it wasn't until the third time that it soaked in and he looked up. Well, Graham, I knew right then that he wasn't you."

"You've got an interesting story, friend," I said. "I don't believe I understand."

"So he looked up and he didn't know just what to say. He didn't know if he was supposed to know me well or not. So I started talking about the machine. That didn't register, either. Then I said I'd leave one at the office and he said that was okay. Graham, you know very well that's not okay. Your partner wouldn't let me leave a machine when I called. The guy I was talking to was just feeling his way. I could have tripped him up worse if I'd wanted to, but I had plenty to satisfy me and I didn't want him to get wise. And when I look at you I can see behind what those strawberries done or whatever it was. If that other guy wasn't Albert Rand, then you are, buddy. And which will you have?"

"You're very clever," I said. "Are you also good at anagrams?"

"Meaning, what's it to me?"

"Something like that."

"Well, Graham, it looks to me like you could use a friend."

"I certainly could," I admitted.

"Let's go somewhere and talk it over."

We went out to a taxi. Pease gave an address on Twenty-sixth Avenue. He relaxed in the seat, smiling, the picture of a contented man.

"This is my big day," he murmured. "The day I've been looking for."

"I'd like to see you get that reward," I said. "But I don't think it will be easy."

"Reward?" He chuckled. "Peanuts. Peanuts, my friend. Peanuts."

"All right," I said, "it's your big day."

"I wonder how many guys there are like me? Here I am, a wife, a couple of kids, a pretty good job, paying on a house. I'm Joe Doakes, the average American. I'm the backbone of the country. I'm out mowing my lawn on Sunday morning. I'm taking my wife and family to the movies Friday night. My credit's good. I've served on a jury. I'm the salt of the earth and I'm as unhappy as hell. And the more I see of Joe Doakes, the average American, the more I wonder how bad he's made a mess out of his life like I have. Are you happy, Graham?"

"That's a question," I said.

"Oh, I don't mean now. Again, maybe I do. You're at least out of the rut."

"You're telling me."

"I mean, before this happened. Did you have what you wanted out of life?"

I shrugged. "Who does?"

"There's a question. Who does? If you ever get to know a guy real well, you find out something's eating on him. Kids, yes. Young bucks with the dew in their eyes, yes. But take Joe Doakes when he's married and has a couple of kids and realizes he's not going to knock the world off its pins. When he sees that he stacks up along with other Joes and can count on just about so much out of this life. And then, brother, you find an unhappy man."

"What's eating on you?" I said.

"Well, I married young. I was just a kid. She was pretty. I had normal impulses. We got married, and what the hell, Bill! We didn't even know each other, really. When the honey wore off, she wasn't my type and I wasn't her type. But the baby was coming, so we made the best of it. And that's the way it's been ever since. Just making the best of it. Joe Doakes, caught in the rut."

"I've heard of divorce," I said.

"So have I. But you know how a woman is about kids. She pulls out all the stops about ruining their lives. Hell, they're my kids, too. And her father is my boss, so she's got me there. We go around with a bunch of people, and what would they think? We've got a standing in the community. It all adds up."

"What do you want?" I asked.

"Well, there's another woman."

I glanced at him. He shrugged. "Sure, I'm just Joe Doakes. It's common as mud. I married the wrong girl."

"I know what you mean," I said, thinking of Cora. I'd made the best of it.

"It's been going on for about six years now," he said. "She's married to another guy. My best friend, the son of a bitch. I went deer hunting with him last fall. I got him in the sights of my rifle. With a little more guts I would have pulled the trigger—a hunting accident. But, you see, it wouldn't settle anything. I'm still working for my wife's old man. I've still got my own kids to think about. I'm still Joe Doakes, caught in the rut."

"It's a problem," I said.

"And don't think I haven't been figuring on it. Another thing, this other girl is used to more than I could give her. Her husband's in the chips. Not big time, but twenty thousand a year. If she gives up him for me, I'm not going to let her say she made a bad bargain. So I've been waiting. Waiting for the time. Waiting for something to turn up. And you're it."

"I'm glad you can see it," I said. "I can't."

He indicated the driver and said, "I'll tell you later."

Pease told the driver to stop on a corner. "I don't want to stop in front of her house," he explained as the taxi drove away.

We walked along the street. "It's a problem, Graham. I've tried every damned thing I know. I've put in plenty of thought. I figured, once, what if my wife and her husband got together? But it didn't take."

"Why don't you forget her?" I said.

"Don't think we haven't tried that either. It's not just an affair. It's been going on for six years. We've tried to break up. Once we agreed not to see each other for six months. And we didn't. But the day after, we were together. I didn't tell her where I'd be. I didn't know where she'd be. We just found each other. And, Graham, you're what I've been looking for. You're the answer. Yep, this is my big day."

"Where do I fit?"

"You're worth two million bucks."

"Me? Wait a minute."

"Oh, yes you are. This is something that hit me all of a sudden. It's the idea of a lifetime. With two million bucks, what the hell do I care about the neighbors and my friends and the house and the job? I can give my kids the best money can buy. I can go away with the woman I want, and what the hell, Bill! Money makes all the difference in this world. And you're money. This is the place."

We went up the walk and he rang the bell, pushing the button three shorts and a long. Footsteps came hurrying, the door opened, and a woman said, "Oh, Jim, I was just—" She saw me and stopped.

"A friend of mine," Pease said, taking my arm and going in.

"Jim, can your friend wait outside a minute? There's something I've got to tell you."

"Don't mind him. Go ahead."

"But, Jim, it's about—us."

"He knows about us. Go ahead."

The woman looked uncertainly at me. She was a dumpy ex-blonde with a lot of gold in her teeth. I figured it must be true love.

"But, Jim, you promised not to—"

"It's all right. This guy is going to fix everything for us."

"Jim, I think Bob knows. I think he found out about last Saturday. The way he's been acting, I'm afraid. You know how he is when he gets mad. I'm afraid. We hadn't ought to see each other for a while."

"Lil," Pease said, "we're going to see each other all the time from now on. This is Charles Graham."

"How do you do, Mr. Graham. You're a friend of Jim's?"

"In a way," I said.

"Charles Graham," Pease said. "Don't you read the papers, Lil? About that guy Rand who got away with two million bucks and tried to take Graham's place?"

"Oh," she said. "Well, this certainly is a surprise, meeting you, Mr. Graham. You had quite a time last night."

"He did," Pease said. "Rand took his place. Rand stepped into his shoes."

The woman frowned. "How in the world could he do that?"

"It's quite a long story," I said.

"But your wife. And the papers said some friends of yours were there—"

"They're all in it," I said. "They've planned it a long time."

"How horrible! What can you do, Mr. Graham?"

"That's where we come in," Pease said. "Lil, we know. We know that Rand switched places with Graham, here. We know he's the guy who walked off with two million bucks. We know, and we're the only ones who know. The cops don't know. Nobody knows but us. Graham, all you've got to do is sit tight until that strawberry rash goes away. Sit tight until you're yourself again. Then walk back into your old spot."

"And what about Rand?" I said.

"I'll take care of him. I'll take care of him proper."

"Jim," the woman said, "I don't like the way you talk."

"Lil, this is two million bucks. Two million bucks, velvet. What couldn't we do with two million bucks, you and me? For that kind of dough I'll do what has to be done. I've been waiting for this. This is my lucky day."

8

"But where will he stay?" the woman asked. "He can't stay here."

"The room," he said. "Our room. Where else? They never ask questions there. You can take him grub, take care of his laundry. The room's safe. Nobody asks questions. He'll be all right there."

"I don't like it," she said. "Jim, something might happen."

"What?" he asked. "Rand thinks he's safe. He don't think anybody knows. I can handle him when the time comes."

It was a little amazing to me, hearing him talk like that. He was a little man, one of the little men of the world; he was Joe Doakes, who'd made a mess of his life and let it remain a mess through sheer inertia. But the smell of money to him was like the scent of blood to a tiger. He was a man transformed by pursuit of the Holy Grail.

"Is the car here?" he asked.

"Yes."

We went to the garage. The woman drove.

"Jim," she said, "what if something happens? This fellow Rand. If he's done that, he's a desperate man."

"But he's playing a part. He's putting on an act. I've got an in. I'm selling him and Buster Cox a posting machine. I've got a reason to pester him. I can take my time. I can wait my chance. Sure he's a desperate man. But all cats are gray in the dark, and one man's head is like another's, if you give it to him from behind. Don't worry, Lil. I'll take care of this."

"Why do you think I can walk back into my place?" I asked him.

"What the hell, Bill! You mean your wife and partner? They ain't going to squawk if they see they've lost out. What can they do, admit they let a ringer move in? That's your problem, what you do with them."

"But it's been too carefully planned for that. They've thought of that. At least they've thought of everything else."

"They didn't think of Jim Pease," he said.

"I wouldn't try anything crude," I said. "It won't pay. It will be your neck. They're playing for keeps."

"So am I."

"Well, I'm just telling you."

"Look, Graham, all I had to do was call that cop in the S. P. station. That's all. And I would have picked up a nice little hunk of money. I could use that dough. Now, don't you tell me what to do. I know you're Graham. But it's something neither of us can prove. Do you want to play along for the big dough or do you want me to cash in quick for peanuts? I'm trying to help you. But I'll cash in now if you got to have it that way."

"I've had my say," I said.

"I'll let you off here at the corner, Jim," the woman said. "You can take a street car to the office."

"Office?" Pease laughed. "What the hell do I care about the office from now on?"

"Sure," I said. "To hell with the office. Why act smart? It's only two million bucks. It's not worth it, to play it safe a few days."

"Well, okay," he said. He got out of the car on the corner. "Look here, Graham. Let me handle this. This is my play. You just lay low in that room and don't eat any more strawberries. I'll see you later."

The woman drove on. Presently she said in a small voice, "He'll get into trouble. I don't want him mixed up in this. He'll get hurt. Why did you get him into this? Why don't you leave him alone?"

"It's his idea, not mine."

"Why didn't you stay away from him? How do I know you're Graham? You don't look like the picture in the paper. How do I know you're not Rand? How do I know you're either one?"

I said nothing. She drove into Golden Gate Park.

"I don't want two million dollars," she said. "Not if we get it that way. And Jim will get hurt. He's not very smart. He's always getting these big ideas. They never work out. He always backs out at the last minute. There's a dozen times we've had it all arranged, all fixed, all ready—and it always falls through. Something always comes up. And this time he might get hurt. He told you about me and him?"

I nodded. "Yes."

"It's never going to work out. It never can. It just gets worse and worse, and there's no way out. You get started and there's no way to quit. Bob's a good man. Jim's wife is a good woman. We can't hurt them. There's nothing we can do. And now Bob is getting wise. I think he knows about Saturday."

She pulled alongside the road in the park. "Why don't you leave us alone? We've got enough trouble without you. I'm not going to see him hurt. He might get killed. Why don't you leave us alone?"

I got out. "You're right," I said. "Good luck."

"Goodbye," she said. "Now leave Jim alone, please."

She drove away with her own troubles, leaving me with mine. I didn't know if it was good or bad, my getting away from Jim Pease and whatever ideas he had cooking. I was just where I was before he came along.

I walked into town. My feet were hurting. I wasn't used to walking and the poison oak had spread. The blanket was a strait jacket, smothering me. I went into a bar and got rid of the infernal thing in the washroom.

What to do? It was impossible, on the face of things, for Rand to step into my place. But he'd done it. And with such confidence that he'd turned me over to the police. He wasn't, then, afraid of investigation. He wasn't afraid of anything I might say. He wasn't afraid of my proving who I was. He was supremely and insolently contemptuous of my threat to him.

I was he. I was Rand. I was a killer who had gotten away with two million dollars' worth of bonds. I was a fugitive.

But there is more to identification than the shape of a man's ears and the testimony of people who know him. Or is there? For the average man, what more is there? Rand could write my name as well as I could. What else was there? Fingerprints? He'd taken care of that. Aside from that, a man is who he is because he has established a place in society. He has a wife and friends. There are clerks in stores. There are neighbors. He just fits in his groove. And Rand was in my groove.

I wondered about Jim Pease's idea. To wait until my face was normal, then to get rid of Rand and step back into the groove. It was an idea, but meanwhile there was the question of food and shelter.

After eating lunch, I had thirteen cents to my name. My feet hurt. I was worn out. I had to do something.

I went into a drugstore and phoned Mary's number. As I listened to the phone ringing on the other end, I wondered what I could ever say to her. How could I ask her help?

The problem became academic. Her phone didn't answer. She would, of course, be at work somewhere. By five-fifteen that afternoon, my pride was gone. I'd walked the streets. All day long walking with a calculated stride, a pink-faced businessman about his business. No loitering where I might be picked up. Not even a spare dime to take the weight off my feet for a glass of beer; I needed my money to phone. I wasn't going to walk in on Mary and face her down. I'd give her a chance to refuse, and that's easier over the phone. Walking all day long, not limping in order not to draw attention, while blisters rose on my feet and then broke, sticking my socks to my shoes.

Five-fifteen. She should be home. I dialed her number and she answered. "Hello." That voice, so warm and sweet. Mary, Mary, how I've missed you!

"Hello, Mary."

"Oh," she said.

"This is Chick. Chick Graham." I knew she'd recognized my voice by the way she'd said, "Oh," but I had to say something.

There was a silence. I wondered if she'd hang up. She had a right to. "Hello, Chick," she said.

"It's been a long time, Mary."

"Yes, it has. Walt said he ran into you, a while ago."

"Yeah. At Fourth and Mission."

"That's what he said. Fourth and Mission."

I took a deep breath. "Mary, I'd like to see you."

There was another silence. Not longer than a couple of weeks with double time for Sundays and holidays. "I'm pretty busy these days, Chick. Working and keeping house for Walt."

"Couldn't you spare me a few minutes?"

"Walt said you were married."

"Yes, I'm married."

"We'll probably see each other around, Chick."

It was the brushoff. She'd been hurt by me, and anyhow she was no toots to hop out with a married man when he had a spare hour.

"Mary, do you remember Jody? Major Jody, my CO at the squadron?"

There was another silence. "Yes."

"I saw him the time he was through here. He said he was having dinner with you that night. I didn't know, before then."

"Know what, Chick?"

"I didn't know, before then, that you'd kept writing me. Mary, I didn't get a letter from you for months before I went overseas. And no letter from you overseas."

"I don't believe I understand."

"That's one reason I want to see you. I want to explain. Your letters were stopped. My letters to you were destroyed."

"This is a little … surprising. The Army wouldn't—"

"Mary, it wasn't the Army. It was a guy I thought was my best friend. He wanted me to marry his sister. He stopped your letters. He stopped my letters. He was the mail clerk."

There was another of those silences. "I'm—glad to know it was that way."

"When can I see you?"

"But, Chick, if it—I mean, after all, it happened. And it's too late now to do anything about it."

"I just wanted to explain. If it hadn't happened, I might still have been the heel you think I am. But I like to think if we'd gotten each other's letters, things might have been different."

"I'm glad you called anyway, Chick. I want to believe you. But that was a long time ago, and don't you think it's just as well to let it lie? We've made our adjustments, and—goodbye, Chick."

"Goodbye, Mary."

It was over. She was right. Let it lie.

"Chick!"

"Yes."

"Is that all you wanted to tell me?"

"Yes, that's all."

"Has something happened?"

"Why do you ask?"

"If you saw Major Jody and he told you—that was some time ago. Why did you wait until today to call me?"

"It was water under the bridge."

"Why isn't it still?"

"I didn't know of it until last night."

"Then something has happened."

"Yes."

"Are you in trouble?"

"Up to my neck and ears."

"Where should I meet you, Chick?"

"Can I call around?"

"Of course. This evening?"

"I'll be right over."

"Okay, Chick. Goodbye."

She had an understanding heart. I heard her end of the line click shut and then I said, "You're sweet," into the dead phone, and hung up.

9

The apartment was on Turk Street. I pushed the button alongside the card saying *Davis*, and the speaking tube above the bell said, "Chick?" I said it was. The electric door lock began clicking and I went in. It was an old house with brown wallpaper and a musty smell.

"Second floor, Chick," Mary's voice called from above.

I went to the stairs and looked up. She was leaning over the railing with her hair falling forward, and I knew then that beauty isn't something that comes from the skin or the features or the bones. Beauty comes from within. Beauty shines from inside.

"Oh," she said. "I'm sorry. I was expecting—"

"It's me. I guess I look a sight."

"Chick!" She came running downstairs, then paused on the third step from the bottom. "Chick, what in the world? What happened? Walt didn't tell me—" She caught herself, her hand flying to her mouth. "I'm sorry, Chick."

"Just poison oak," I said. "I'm not sensitive about it. It's sensitive about me." And I thought, wouldn't it have been so simple, if *that* was the reason she hadn't got letters from me, because something had happened to my face.

She held out her hand. "Well—hello."

We went upstairs. Walt's jaw dropped at sight of me. I said poison oak, and he said, "California is a lovely place."

Mary asked, "What can you do for it?"

"Not a great deal. Calamine lotion helps."

"You look all in, Chick. Take off your coat and sit down."

I began unbuttoning the topcoat. Then I said, "First I'd like to tell you something. Maybe I won't be welcome."

"Don't be silly. Sit down, anyway."

It was good to get the weight off my feet. I told them the whole story of what had happened to me. It took about an hour and it wasn't easy. They would think me an awful cluck. It is hard to admit being duped; that's why confidence men get by.

"That's—why, it's awful!" Mary declared when I'd finished. "They can't get away with that."

"Well," I said, "they have."

"I don't get it," Walt said.

"What part?"

"The whole thing. You claim they've been working on this deal since before you went overseas. That's a hell of a long time."

"Sure it is. But the stakes were high."

"I can see that. And this guy who looks like you—Albert Rand—he had to get in the right spot to pull the job. There was a lot to be arranged. Everything had to be exactly right. For it was a terrific job. But look at it reasonably, Chick. The whole deal is pretty hard to swallow. It's too involved. It's fantastic. You're sitting here now. We know you. Anybody in the world would believe that yarn, it's me and Mary. But I don't know. It's fantastic. Things like that just don't happen."

Mary declared, "That's a fine attitude, Walt."

"Well, it's how *I* feel," Walt said. "This is serious business, Chick. The police want you for murder, and you're putting it into our laps by coming here. The least you could do is come clean."

"Come clean? I've told you everything." If Walt didn't believe my story, who *would*? "I can't help it if it's fantastic. It's just how it is. I can't change it."

"Then what does it make of you?"

"In what way?"

"Chick, Cora's a crook. Buster's a crook. Ethelene's a crook. And you've known them for years. You married Cora. You went in business with Buster."

"Walt, for heaven's sake!" Mary said.

"All right, let's face it," Walt cried. "If I know anything about it, a crook is a crook. He can't help it. He may be planning for the big stuff, but he'll still turn a dishonest dollar on the side. Chick, you've been very close to three crooks for a long time. Are you claiming you're dumb—or were you in on it?"

"You can't ask him that," Mary said.

"I'm finding out the score," Walt said. "How about it, Chick?"

"I knew things weren't right," I had to admit. "Overseas, Buster lived pretty high for a corporal. He claimed he got money from home. After I got back and was married to Cora, I saw that she certainly wouldn't send money to anybody. She lived up to the last dime I made. There was just one answer. We'd been bothered by a thief in the squadron. The last man anybody would suspect was Buster. That innocent baby face."

"So you knew he was a crook. And you stayed in business with him."

"I put it up to him and he admitted it. Walt, you don't know Buster. To look at him and talk to him, he's just so damned honest. He said it wore on him overseas. He just had to get out at night and forget. You'd know how it was if you were there."

"I know how it was," Walt said. "I went to the Pacific. But we were all in the same boat. I didn't steal from the other guys."

"When I put it up to him, Buster said he only took it from guys who could spare it," I said. "He told me he'd paid them back, with interest, since getting home."

"You swallowed that?"

"He was Cora's brother," I said. "I was trying to believe. From here, yes, it looks like I was a chump. Maybe I was. At the time it seemed reasonable. You can't believe anything bad of Buster when you talk to him. He's convincing as hell."

"What about your wife?"

"I knew she took little things—ash trays and salt shakers and napkins. But after the fur coat deal she promised she wouldn't do it anymore. I was trying to get along and make the best of things."

"Fur coat?"

"She came home one day with a fur coat. When I made a fuss she admitted she'd copped it at a cocktail bar. She said if I couldn't give her what she wanted she'd get it in her own way. Well, I started to pack up. I was going to pull out. Then she was very sorry. She begged me not to go. We mailed the coat back. I thought it was just one of those things. She promised never to take anything again. How could I know that she just couldn't afford for me to pull out? I couldn't guess a thing like this. Nobody could guess it ahead in a million years."

"Of course, Walt," Mary said. "You're looking backwards."

"It's time somebody did," Walt said. "Chick, you claim this deal has been cooking for years. It has been carefully plotted. Yet Buster is supposed to have figured out the whole thing in a flash when he first bumped into you and mistook you for Rand. It was the next Sunday, you say, that Cora came around to see you at the orderly room. The deal was cooking then. And now, years later, it pans out. That's one hell of a long time to look ahead."

"It is," I said. "Except that it happened to me, I wouldn't believe it."

"Chick was overseas," Mary said.

Walt frowned. "So what?"

"Walt, you're going on the assumption that this bond robbery yesterday was what they planned from the beginning. It doesn't have to be that way at all. Chances are it wasn't. From their viewpoint, it was a golden opportunity—here was Chick, who looked exactly like Albert Rand. No doubt they cooked up a plan, and it fell through. We don't know if this bond robbery was the first plan, the second plan, or the tenth plan. It just happens to be the one where everything went exactly right, and paid off.

"Whatever they were working on originally must have fallen through when Chick went overseas. Rand was in the Army, too. The Army has a way of upsetting the best of plans. They had to wait until after the war. And there's no way of telling how many ideas didn't pan out since then. They were shooting at big stuff. Everything had to be right. And this time it paid off."

"Well, okay," Walt said.

"Rand was in the Army?" I asked.

They looked at me curiously. Walt said with a touch of sarcasm, "It seems to me that you'd be one guy who would at least read the newspapers about the case."

"I haven't had time to catch up. And this thing floored me."

"He was in Europe," Mary said.

"What do you know about Buster and Cora and Ethelene?" Walt asked. "What about their past life?"

"They never talked about that."

"Where were they born? Go to school and so on?"

"Walt, they just never talked about such things."

Walt's face had a look of suffering patience. "You were married to Cora. You went through a war with Buster."

I didn't feel so hot. Walt and I had been pretty close, back when I was going with his sister. He knew I was straight. But if he sat there with ironic disbelief in his voice and suspicion in his eyes, what chance did I have with strangers? Where would I get convincing the police, for instance?

"I took them at face value," I said. "Why shouldn't I? There is loyalty in friendship. You don't suspect it, you defend it. Part of friendship is overlooking faults. If things happened that I didn't like, I tried to make the best of it. If they turned off questions about the past, I didn't probe. You say yourself that their plan is fantastic. That's its strong point. I wouldn't suspect a thing like that. Not in a hundred years."

"Yeah. But what I'm getting at—"

"Now, quit it, you two," Mary broke in. "I know what's wrong, we're all hungry. Walt, we've still got some of that wine we had at Christmas. Get Chick a glass while I fix dinner."

They went into the kitchen. I unbuttoned my coat and relaxed, without energy enough right then to stand up and take it off. I'd been worn out on arrival and now I was washed up. The ordeal of telling everything, then trying to convince Walt, had drained me dry.

It was so good to be able to relax, to be off the streets.

Walt brought wine from the kitchen, a couple of fingers in the bottom of water tumblers. It was port, sweet and rich, and it seemed to flow into my aching joints. From the kitchen came the clink of dishes and the maddening smell of food. Walt studied me over his glass. The old easy friendship was gone. Well, why should he love me?

"Chick."

"Yes?"

"I see by the papers tonight where they've added another five thousand to the reward. That makes fifteen thousand." He put his glass carefully on the floor beside his chair. "That's a lot of money for lifting the phone."

I considered that. "I certainly can't stop you."

"And don't get smart about it, damn you. You know I won't. That's why you're here. You know you can count on us. Just who the hell do you think you are, putting this in our laps? Why do you come crying to us when you're in trouble?"

He kept his voice low, so Mary couldn't overhear from the kitchen. "Haven't you done enough to her already? She's not a girl to pick up with a new guy every week. She went overboard for you and you put her through hell. You didn't even have the guts to write her and break it off clean. You didn't care enough. You just stopped writing, and let her dangle. She was nothing to you. You were having a good time with Cora. What did you care about little Mary?"

"I told you that Buster stopped the letters."

"I know what you told me. I know what you told me just now. But it wasn't important enough to tell me when we bumped into each other on the street a while back."

"Walt, it was water under the bridge."

"That's just what I'm getting at. Water under the bridge. It's over and done with. When I saw you on the street you didn't even ask how Mary was. You didn't care, then. It was nothing to you. We never would have seen you again if you hadn't got in a box. Why come crying back to us now?"

"Okay, Walt," I said. "I deserve it."

"You're no baby. You knew Mary wasn't the sort to promise a man and then just drop him. You knew she'd wait. You knew that if anything happened, you'd hear about it."

"You can believe it or not, Walt. I had a bad time."

"I'll bet you did. That yarn about Buster and the mail is pretty damned thin. Even if it's true, you took it lying down. You didn't care enough to dig into things. You could have wired Mary at any time before you went overseas, and stayed right there at the telegraph office for an answer. That is, if you'd really cared."

"Walt, I know I've been a fool. You're not telling me anything."

"I am telling you something. I'm telling you to look at yourself. You were having an affair with Cora. You'd met this gorgeous dish. What did you care about Mary? Let her dangle. Let her heart break. What did you give a damn?

"She went through hell, Chick. If it wasn't for Major Jody, she wouldn't have known whether you were killed or missing or maybe bunged up in some hospital. She had faith in you. She knew you could explain. She knew it right up until I bumped into you on the street and found out you were married to somebody else. That's how she is. And you didn't care enough to find out what was wrong with the mail. You didn't give a good goddamn. So now you get in a box and here you are, in our laps. Just where do we fit in, in this mess? You'd had plenty of time to make friends. You've shown pretty definitely what we mean to you. Why pick on us now? Why get us involved in a mess? Why come whining back to Mary?"

"You're right, Walt. Thanks for the wine."

I got up, then reached out to steady myself, and made it into a gesture of understanding as I gripped his shoulder. My feet must have been in pretty sad shape. They had swelled while I'd been sitting down. They wouldn't hold me up.

"Tell Mary I went to the drugstore for some calamine lotion for my poison oak."

"The hell I will!" He knocked my hand from his shoulder, and I grasped the back of a chair for support. "I'll tell her the truth. I kicked you out. And good riddance."

I felt silly and embarrassed. It was two steps to the door and I didn't want to show weakness. I kept hold of the chair for one step. The doorknob was then within reach. On the landing there was the railing to cling to.

Outside the front door, I leaned against the wall a while, getting my feet used to the weight. Then I sat on the steps and loosened the shoelaces. My shoes now were tight by about two sizes. I got up and walked along the street, taking it easy, getting used to it. My hip joints seemed filled with emery dust, the way they'd been back at basic training after a twenty-four-hour stretch of guard duty.

I had been the independent guy. The master of my fate. I'd run away from home at thirteen, and been on my own ever since. I made my own way and didn't ask anything of anybody. That was me. Yep, I'd been pretty snobbish about that. I couldn't spare compassion for the ones who ended up bad. If a guy had the stuff, he'd get along. Luck and be damned, I'd said. A guy gets in and hits the ball, he'll get along. A man starts bellyaching about tough luck, I'd said, when he's thrown away his chances.

Yes, I'd been pretty smug about it. Me, the independent guy. Come right down to it, I hadn't really missed much, in not having close friends. Cora had been smart in restricting my social life, but it hadn't hurt. The only thing that had griped me was that we saw too much of Buster and Ethelene. I didn't want people as friends, I wanted novelty and entertainment. I was the independent guy.

And now Fate had kicked me in the teeth. I knew what luck meant. Except for meeting Buster, none of this would have happened. I would have been married to Mary, now. We might have had a child. That was luck. Just luck, running into Buster. I knew what luck meant.

And I knew what independence meant. It's cold out there. Cold and dark.

10

A hand fell on my shoulder.

I turned slowly, alert. Walt's face was hard.

"Where do you think you're going?" he asked.

"What the hell is it to you?"

"You haven't got any place to go, or you wouldn't have come back to us. You wouldn't have faced Mary if there was one single other place to go."

I shrugged his hand from my shoulder. "I don't want anything out of you."

"Got money?"

"Sure."

"Let's see it."

"Go to hell, will you?"

"And don't get tough with me, Chick, or I'll let you have it. If I had any guts at all I'd let you have it. If I was anything but a soft-hearted fool, I'd collect fifteen thousand bucks. I could use it. Come on. Supper's ready."

"I wish I could, Walt. But there's just a hell of a lot to do. Thanks a million, and I'll take a rain check. I've had supper, anyhow."

"You lie like hell."

"I wasn't intending to stay, Walt. I just wanted to get it off my chest. I had to talk to somebody. Now I've got an idea, from talking to you. I think I'm going to straighten this thing out in a hurry."

"Look," he said, "I'm trying to help you. I blew up and now I'm sorry. If you don't shut up I'll pop you in the kisser. Come on. Supper's ready."

I went back with him.

In the bathroom I got out of my clothes. The poison oak had spread; there were red blotches all over me, my ankles were swollen and the stuff was showing on my feet. The feet themselves were in pretty sad shape. I gave myself an alcohol rub with the idea of getting rid of as much of the volatile oil as possible. I didn't take a bath, which would have completed the spreading action, but washed my face and hands four times, lathering well, washed my feet and put some sulfa salve from the medicine chest on the broken blisters.

Walt brought some calamine lotion from the drugstore, and I patted it on the pink areas. When I came out, wearing Walt's bathrobe and house slippers, the lotion was drying to a whitish crust and I looked like something out of this world. One good thing, my wrist, where the dog had bit it, seemed okay.

I felt a lot better with a full stomach. We sat around afterwards, talking the thing out. Walt tried to be cooperative but he obviously wasn't happy about my presence.

"Chick," Mary said, "there's one point that bothers the dickens out of me. Did you ever give your fingerprints to them? To Buster or Cora?"

"Fingerprints? Why should I?"

"Last night the billfold you carried had Rand's fingerprints on your driver's license and Army identity card."

"Cora substituted fake cards," Walt said.

"Certainly. That's obvious. What I'm getting at, don't they take your fingerprints in the Army?"

"At the induction station," I said.

"The fingerprint business has me baffled," Mary said. "Now, we've got to give Rand credit for being smart. This whole thing is almost inhumanly clever, and all of them have gone to no end of pains. Rand is no fool. He knew it didn't matter how much his face was like yours. If it came to a showdown your identity could be established by the War Department's fingerprint file. You can't argue against fingerprints. So he had to get around that, somehow."

I said, "You mean he's switched the fingerprint cards in the War Department file, somehow?"

"He had to do something about it."

"You two are going off the deep end," Walt said. "It's stretching things too far. Granted that a guy in the right place in the Army could have switched fingerprint cards. It would be easy enough for Rand to lift them out of the file and put a card in bearing his own prints. Or he could know some GI in the right spot. But it's just too much to suppose he just happened to be in the right spot or have the right connections, *and* that Buster just happened to bump into Chick, *and* that Chick and Rand happened to look alike. That won't hold water. The Army had plenty of snafus, but you didn't shove the Army around."

"I don't know the answer," Mary said. "I'm just pointing out what would have had to be done."

"Aside from that, I can't see through it," Walt said. "Now look: Buster and Cora worked on Chick and got him into position. All Rand had to do was to pull that job in L. A. and step into Chick's shoes. Why do fingerprints enter? The average man never has occasion to prove his identity by fingerprints. All they had to do, Chick, was bump you off and let Rand step into your place. Cora could have poisoned you. Your body could be at the bottom of the bay or in a pit of lime—"

"Walt!" Mary cried.

"Yeah," I said, "let's not go into detail."

"Let's face it. It wasn't because Rand was squeamish. He killed the bank guard. In getting ready for the job, he sent this girl Dolly and her brother to Redwood City. They were there in case they'd be needed. When they weren't, Bill Meadows gave the word to the chows. That was a girl Rand had had an affair with. She'd had a baby by him. He must have felt something for her. So your life wouldn't matter to him, Chick. So why aren't you dead? That's what I don't get about this business.

"They needed you here yesterday to establish an alibi. Buster took you around to see all the accounts, on one pretext or another. That established you as yourself and as being here at the time of the bank robbery. But the minute Rand walked into your house in Redwood City, your job was done. For the two of you to be seen together was a dangerous thing. Why weren't you killed? Why did they take the risk of turning you over to the police? I don't get it. What if the cops had taken you in and questioned you? What if there'd been just a little slip, and the cops had dug into the case? Why was Rand a big enough fool to let you live?"

"It beats the hell out of me," I admitted.

"Now, let's take one thing at a time," Mary said. "First of all, the fingerprints—"

"Oh, to hell with fingerprints," Walt said.

"Walt, that's the beginning," Mary said. "Let's just suppose all this hadn't happened. Let's suppose Rand had never heard of Chick. Suppose he hadn't known he and Chick looked alike. All right, Rand steals two millions in Government bonds and disappears. Chick is here in San Francisco with a perfect alibi—but he looks exactly like the man who stole the bonds; his picture is on the front page of every newspaper. Supposing that, Chick would have nothing to worry about, as an innocent man. *But*—his resemblance to Rand would cause him to be picked up by the police and investigated. He would have to prove, beyond the shadow of a doubt, who he was, and that he wasn't the wanted man.

"How would he do it? Simply by fingerprints. That would be the final proof. You see, Rand had a job in the bank where he was entrusted with transporting two million dollars. A man's fingerprints are taken by the bank if he has that kind of a job. So Rand couldn't just murder Chick and move into his place. He knew he'd have to prove he was Charles Graham. By fingerprints. And in the same way he'd have to prove that Chick was the wanted man.

"That's why I asked you, Chick," Mary said, "if you'd ever given a standard fingerprint card to Buster or Cora."

Walt said, "That fingerprint stuff is complicated as hell. I can see how it might be done. I've read in detective books how they make a rubber mold of a man's fingerprints."

"They wouldn't need any rubber mold," I said. "I remember now. It was soon after the war ended, while Buster and I were sweating out the trip home. We had this idea of going into the accounting business, and Cora sent us an application for bond and a public accountant license. And she enclosed two fingerprint cards for each of us."

"And that," Mary said, "is how your fingerprints are on file at the bank where Rand worked as messenger."

"He might have made the switch there," Walt admitted. "Chick, did you send the applications and fingerprint cards back to Cora?"

"Buster took care of the actual mailing," I said. "Good old Buster. My pal."

"The whole deal on that was phony," Walt said. "I'm a public accountant and I'm bonded. Nobody ever asked for my fingerprints. On top of that, you couldn't get a PA license while you were still in the Army. The whole deal was just to get your fingerprints on a standard card."

"Rand probably took out the PA license and the bond in your name," Mary said. "He would want everything in order. And he used your fingerprint cards to establish himself at the bank and possibly somewhere else."

"That would take some doing," I said. "I've never worked in a bank, but they wouldn't let a guy fool around with stuff like that, certainly."

"That would be easy enough," Mary said. "If you two had been around during the war, you'd know how easy. Every place you worked during the war required your fingerprints. There's a standard card, and if you wanted to put your prints on one card and then slip another in its place, it could be done a dozen ways. I remember when I went to work at Richmond shipyards as a welder. I'd brought along my birth certificate and some papers showing I wasn't a spy. I filled out a lot of papers. They took my fingerprints. They gave me a badge and identity card.

"I gathered up my papers, they gathered up theirs. It was the first time for me; I didn't know, and I took the fingerprint card along with my birth certificate and other stuff. I'd been on the job several hours when an office man came and told me they'd misplaced the fingerprint card and would I come to the office to make another.

"That happened to me by mistake. If I'd arrived with a fingerprint card in my purse bearing the prints of somebody else, there certainly would have been a chance to substitute it for my own. What I'm saying is that Rand pawned off your prints at the bank. It was part of the plan. He had to do it. If that hadn't worked, he would have had to use the other card he'd got from you at some other place."

"Okay, okay," Walt said. "This whole thing is getting me dizzy. I still don't see how he got around the fingerprints in the Army. But we'll let it drop for now. What gets me is that dog. Chick, your own dog jumped you. The dog you raised from a pup. That's what gets me."

"Bill Meadows," I said. "He can train a dog. He had those chows trained. He'd given those chows the word, and they were tailing Curly and Dolly. Just waiting. Waiting for the word. When he went up to the house last night, all he said was one word. Just a word, and the chows went to work."

Mary shuddered. "Chick, let's not talk about that. Thank goodness, you did save the baby."

"But he couldn't train your own dog to bite you," Walt said. "Hell, you'd trained that dog yourself. You'd raised that dog from a pup."

"There's only one answer," I said. "That wasn't my dog."

"Hell, don't you know your own pooch?"

"I was upset. I wasn't expecting another dog. And Jiggs had a pedigree as long as your arm. We bought him as a pup from Bill Meadows. There was a litter of four or five pups."

Walt nodded. "I guess that's possible. A pedigreed dog fits a pattern. That's what they prize in a dog. If his tail's wrong or his ears or the color of his eyes, he's not a good dog. Bill Meadows trained another dog of that litter. That was the dog that jumped you."

"It's the only way it fits, Walt."

Mary asked, "Where does Bill Meadows fit in?"

"I don't know. Of course he's in it, but I don't know the connection. He was at the station yesterday afternoon while I was waiting for Cora. Him and his big Doberman. He was waiting across the street with his dog when I came out of the show. And he was outside the house when I brought Dolly's baby out. I'm telling you, it gave me a start, running into him there. That Doberman is big as a horse. But I don't—"

"My God!" Walt cried, leaping up.

"What is it?" Mary asked.

"Doberman!" Walt cried. "I'm asleep! Why didn't it sink in? Isn't a Doberman one of those big brown dogs with slick hair, and they clip their ears to a point?"

"Of course," I said. "So what?"

"Chick, I went across the street to the drugstore for your calamine lotion. And when I came back a dog like that was sniffing at the front door."

In the silence, as we looked at one another, I had the chilling realization that it wasn't just my own fool neck anymore. I'd dragged Walt and Mary into the mess.

Mary asked quietly, "Are you sure it was a Doberman?"

"I'm no dog expert," Walt said. "But it was one of those German kinds. Not the police dog, but the brown one with the sharp ears and slick hair."

"That's a Doberman," I said. "The question is—is it Bill Meadows' dog?"

"I ought to have my head fixed," Walt said. "I went across to the drugstore and this big brown mutt was sniffing at the door when I came back. I didn't think a thing about it until you started talking about Bill Meadows and his Doberman."

"They could have given the dog your scent with one of your shirts or something, from home," Mary said. "But surely a dog couldn't track you all over San Francisco."

"My pal Buster," I said. "He knows how I felt about you. He could guess easily enough that I didn't have anybody else to go to. I'm sorry about this. Walt, you were right. I never should have got you two mixed up in it."

"Oh, shut up," Walt growled. "We're in it now." He went into the bedroom.

"Let's not get all excited," Mary said, "until we're sure. It might just be a stray dog sniffing at a door."

Walt came out of the bedroom with a .45 automatic. "Here's something the Army don't know I brought home." He shoved a clip of ammunition in the handle, threw a shell in the chamber, and put on the safety catch. "Okay, let them try something."

"You look wonderful, Walt," Mary said. "You look like Horatio Alger on the bridge. But we don't even know if that's Bill Meadows' dog or not. If it is, the gun's no good. What do you intend to do, have a gun battle with the police?"

"Well, okay," Walt growled. "What are we going to do, just sit here and wonder?"

I slipped into the bedroom, pulled the door shut behind me to cut out the light, and carefully eased aside the curtain of the front window. The street was deserted. There was a Ford parked at the far curb, down the block. It looked like Bill Meadows' Ford, but there are a lot of Fords in the world.

I went into the living room. Walt and Mary looked at me questioningly.

"Damned if I know," I said. "But I didn't see the dog."

"It could be on the porch," Walt said.

The buzzer sounded.

Walt asked, "Who's at the door?"

I shrugged. "Don't know. He must have been under the porch when I looked out."

The buzzer sounded again, a long buzz, insistent.

"There was no police car in front," I said.

"Who is it, please?" Mary said into the speaking tube.

"Western Union," a voice came back. "Telegram for Miss Mary Davis."

Walt took her wrist as Mary reached for the button to unlock the front door. "That's the oldest gag in the world," he said.

"Put the wire in the mailbox," Mary said into the speaking tube.

"There's an answer requested, miss."

"Put it in the mailbox. I'll answer it later."

"Okay, miss."

We ran through the bedroom to the front window. Below, a tall figure in a leather jacket appeared from the porch. At his heels was a Doberman.

"That the guy?" Walt asked.

"That's Bill Meadows," I said.

"And that's the dog I saw sniffing at the door. If we'd let Bill Meadows in with that brute—A gun's not much good against a dog."

Bill Meadows stood uncertainly before the house. There was an unlighted cigarette dangling from his mouth. He said something to the dog, just a low word, then crossed the street and went into the drugstore on the corner. The dog remained on the sidewalk before the house.

"He's going to phone the police," Mary said.

"He had plenty of chance to before now. What's he been doing?" Walt said.

"It doesn't do any good to guess," Mary said. "He's tried to get in now. That didn't work and he'll try something else. We can't just sit and wait for it."

"I'll slip out the back door," I said. "I'll phone you tomorrow and we can—" I didn't finish. The dog had cocked its head, then suddenly run along the sidewalk and disappeared around the corner of the house. Presently it appeared and took up guard again at the front.

"That's a smart dog," Walt said. "It's watching the back door. We had some smart ones in the Army. Some of them were practically human."

Across the street a man was walking along smoking a cigarette. As he passed the lighted front of the drugstore I noticed the smoke from his mouth wafting ahead of him.

"Walt," I said, "let me have a pair of your shoes and your overcoat, quick! … Mary, have you got some strong disinfectant in the apartment?"

"Yes—in the bathroom. What are you going to do?" I left Walt pawing in the closet and followed Mary into the bathroom. She got a bottle of Lysol from the cupboard below the basin. I dumped the whole bottle into the basin, filled the basin with water, took off the house slippers and put each foot in turn, sock and all, into the mixture. I went into the living room, unmindful of the smelly tracks I was leaving on the floor, to find Walt with a brand-new pair of shoes.

"Old ones, Walt," I said. "The oldest ones you've got. Something with your smell soaked right through them."

"I get you, Chick."

I put my suit on in the bedroom, then got Walt to lace the shoes on me. He'd unearthed an old pair of Quartermaster low-cuts that really were beat up. I slipped into his gabardine overcoat. It was big in the shoulders, but not too bad a fit.

"Mary, you watch the window," I said. "If Bill Meadows comes out of the drugstore before I get out, give a whistle. If it's after I'm outside, let me handle it. Walt, you handle the back door. Make some noise getting it open and shut."

"I've got it," Walt said. "You'd better take the gun, Chick."

"If it doesn't work, a gun won't help much. I've never shot one of the things."

"Chick," Mary said, "where will you go?"

"I don't know yet. You and Walt stay together here. Don't let anybody in. I'll contact you tomorrow. Where do you work?"

"Bay Title Insurance. We both work there. Do you need money?"

"Well …"

She got ten dollars from her purse. "I can have more tomorrow." Something must have showed on my face. "Chick, don't be silly. It's only a loan."

"Thanks.… Ready, Walt?"

"Let's go."

We went downstairs. I stopped at the front door while Walt walked along the hall to the rear door. He paused, hand on the knob. I gave him the highball. He opened the door and slammed it shut.

I heard the dog's toenails scratching the sidewalk. I slipped out the front door, leaving it open. I took the front steps at a leap and raced downwind past the front of the house. Then I fought myself to a walk, and realized my feet were hurting.

Behind, I heard the dog running back along the side of the house, having found nobody at the back door. There came the sounds of Walt slamming the front door. The dog's toenails scratched on the pavement and clawed the wooden steps of the porch. Then there was silence.

For some silly reason I was afraid to turn around. I knew the dog wouldn't recognize me by sight; a dog goes on smell. But it was hard glancing over my shoulder, and hard not to. When I did look back, the dog was at the front of the house, watching the doorway.

I was glad to have Walt's shoes. They were two sizes larger than mine and, right then, they fit comfortably.

I was near the corner when Bill Meadows came out of the drugstore across the street. He looked at his dog, then walked up the street toward the parked Ford. He paid no attention to me.

11

I found a place to stay on Howard Street. Beds, thirty-five cents. Rooms, fifty cents. I went all-out and got a room. Nothing too good for a man living on borrowed money. Too, I needed the privacy and the use of the 25-watt bulb hanging from the drop cord. It was about time to take a look at the newspapers.

I'd bought the afternoon papers, the *News* and the *Call*, and the predated *Chronicle* and *Examiner*. I put them on the bed with the overcoat and went to the community bathroom down the smelly hall to wash some of the lively odor off my feet and out of the socks. When I got back to the room I found I'd had a visitor.

Walt's overcoat was gone. There was a sign on the door, NOT RESPONSIBLE FOR ARTICLES LOST THROUGH FIRE OR THEFT. LEAVE YOUR VALUABLES WITH THE CLERK. I wondered if the clerk made tenants regret ignoring that sign.

My visitor had left the newspapers, at any rate. And what does a man want with an overcoat in sunny California?

I locked the door, undressed, and, after examining the sheets suspiciously, got into bed. The *Chronicle* carried a review of the whole case.

Albert Rand had got away with the bonds neatly and simply. As bank messenger, he was carrying two million dollars in Government bonds in a briefcase locked to his wrist by a steel chain. He was accompanied by an armed guard, but the greatest safety factor was that nobody, presumably, knew what was in the briefcase. Rand himself was not supposed to know. Rand had made hundreds of trips as messenger. Generally he carried papers of importance but of no possible negotiable value.

However, it had been revealed that Rand did know what he was carrying. Under grilling by police, the cashier of the bank, H. R. Alexander, had admitted that he had told Rand the previous night what he would be carrying, and had warned him to be careful. Rand had the cashier's confidence because of the fact that Rand was engaged to the cashier's daughter.

This, then, explained the uncomfortable position Rand had been in with Dolly and her blackmailing brother. Getting close to the cashier, through the daughter, was essential to Rand's scheme.

I found a feature story in the *Examiner* on the girl who'd been engaged to Rand. From her picture, Alicia Alexander seemed a nice enough kid. She had gone to Palm Springs, the story said, for rest and seclusion. In other words, to get away from it all.

With Rand cuddling up to the cashier's daughter, the way would be cleared of several obstacles. Making the switch of the fingerprint cards would have been possible. Rand had got his job through the cashier's recommendation. Which meant that nobody would be standing over him with a club while he filled out the necessary papers. It was possible.

I went back to the *Chronicle* story. It seemed that in carrying the briefcase of bonds, neither Rand nor the accompanying guard was in uniform. Rand had been trained to keep his coat sleeve over the chain fastened from his wrist to the handle of the briefcase. To the casual observer, two men were walking down the street, one with a briefcase. Which was part of the protection.

The trip was three and a half blocks each way. One block along Broadway, a block to Spring, a block and a half along Spring, and return. The bonds were carried on the return trip.

The guard suddenly became faint. Rand helped him into a bar and onto a stool at the counter. Rand suggested calling a doctor, but the guard said it was just one of his spells. (Investigation revealed that he had a bad heart and didn't want the bank to find it out.) Rand ordered a shot of whiskey for a bracer and said he'd pop in the drugstore next door and get something. The guard made a vague objection, but he was very ill.

Albert Rand walked out. And away.

It was that simple.

As Rand walked out, the guard tossed off the shot of whiskey and, momentarily braced, began following. He collapsed on the floor. The bartender, thinking the man was drunk, dragged him into a rear booth and got him awake enough to drink some black coffee. The bartender did not know, of course, that the man was a bank guard or that Rand was a bank messenger.

The guard passed out again. A half hour or so passed. Rand didn't return from the drugstore. The bartender asked a cop to take care of the drunk. The cop called the wagon and the guard was taken to the station. There, his identity was established by the contents of his pockets. Technically the guard was a policeman, a brother-cop. So the police at the station did the natural thing in trying to shield him. They didn't notify the bank. They didn't want the guard to lose his job. That was a bit of luck Rand hadn't counted on. Whether he needed it or not was an academic point.

The cops called in a doctor to sober up the guard. The doctor didn't suspect, until the bank put out an alarm, that the man had been poisoned. The guard died that afternoon of heart failure induced by poison. It was assumed that Rand had given him poisoned candy. The guard was known to have been very fond of candy.

Albert Rand walked out of the bar with the bonds at about a

quarter to nine in the morning. It was past eleven o'clock, more than two hours later, when the alarm went out for him. Rand had, at or about the time he walked out with the bonds, phoned the cashier that there would be a delay while the other bank checked serial numbers. His intended father-in-law hadn't checked on that. This phone call helped stall suspicion when Rand didn't show up.

Rand had next appeared, according to the *Chronicle*, at the home of Charles Graham at Redwood City. He bore a remarkable resemblance to Graham, and evidently planned on murdering Graham and taking his place. I skipped the account of Graham, feeling I knew that part. The story said Graham owed his life to the fact that he had had company for the evening, and to his dog. Rand obviously had plotted the thing carefully. Had he been able to murder Graham and Graham's wife, he could either have taken a trip under Graham's name and disappeared, or he could have, at his leisure, murdered Graham's business partner and slid into the new identity.

Whatever his plan, he had been thwarted, had been captured by the police, and had escaped by impersonating yet another man, James Pease, salesman. And Rand was now at large, a dangerous and desperate criminal of resource.

Such was the affair which for headline purposes was already known as the "Switch Case."

On an inside page of the *Call*, I saw pictures of Curly and Dolly. MAN, SISTER, KILLED BY PETS, the head said. Their two dogs, of which they were very fond, according to neighbors, had turned on them in the night. The dogs had been destroyed and their brains tested for evidence of rabies. The child of the unmarried mother had been found unharmed in bed.

Bill Meadows, then, had taken the baby back. Which was a smart move. It would have been very odd if the baby had been found on some doorstep. The attack of the dogs might not have seemed so accidental.

Police, according to the *News*, were digging into Rand's past but finding precious little pay dirt. He had served in the Air Force in the European Theater during the war, being discharged with the rank of captain. In Los Angeles he had lived a model life, had been an active church member, and had not associated with any but respectable people.

Curious, I thought, Rand being a captain of the Air Force in the ETO, just as I had been. There were millions over there in the Air

Force, but still somebody might have mentioned that I looked like a Captain Rand of such-and-such-a group. On the other hand, inasmuch as both of us were Air Force captains, we could have been mistaken for each other. But, still—

I looked back over the part I'd skipped. The part about myself, Charles Graham. The type seemed to leap out of the page.

Graham was a technical sergeant in headquarters at Ft. Douglas.

I jumped out of bed and ran down the narrow hall in my underwear. Then I remembered my previous visitor and ran back. I threw on my clothes and ran down the hall again; I put a nickel in the pay phone on the wall of the eight-by-eight lobby and dialed Mary's number. There was nobody behind the desk, but the door behind it opened a crack. What did I care? Let him listen. Let the whole world listen!

When Mary answered the phone I decided to tease it along. It was too good to give right out cold.

"Everything okay there?" I asked.

"Nothing has happened. Bill Meadows is still out front. He's in that parked Ford across the street and the dog is at the front of the house."

"The police didn't come?"

"Not yet."

"I hope he catches pneumonia."

"I can't understand why he hasn't called the police. They turned you in once. Why don't they now?"

"Did I get you out of bed?"

"I was just going to pile in when the phone rang. You should see this, Chick. Walt's having more fun than he's had since he was in the Pacific. Now I know why men go to war. They love it. Walt has fixed a pile of pots and pans at the door in case somebody tries to get in during the night. And he took his gun to bed with him. He wouldn't have missed this for a million dollars."

"I don't want to keep you up, but—"

"Oh, I wanted you to call, Chick."

"And I wanted to call."

"I wanted to know you were okay. And Walt and I have thought of a couple of other things. They can't get away with this."

"You're telling me."

"Chick, there's the driver's license with your thumbprint. The one in your billfold was a phony, but you can get a duplicate of the original from the Department of Motor Vehicles in Sacramento. It only costs fifty cents or something. And that will prove—"

"I'm afraid that's out."

"Why?"

"My lovely wife Cora. The day we bought the car I came down with something. I thought it was the flu. Now I wonder if it was something in the coffee. Anyhow, I was home in bed and she brought me the application and the little card you fill out and put your thumbprint on."

"But, Chick, they won't let you do that. They won't even let you whisper while you're filling out the test, let alone bring the papers home. And the man at the desk makes out the card and puts your thumbprint on."

"Cora admitted it was irregular. But she said she'd pulled some frammis on the guy to get it. When she wanted to be nice she could charm a bird out of a tree. No man could withstand that great big smile."

"Then you've been carrying Rand's driver's license all along?"

"I'm afraid so."

"Didn't you ever notice the print on it?"

"Who does?"

"Well, that's out," she said. "It still was a good idea. But there's your teeth."

"Teeth? What about them?"

"Your dentist will have a chart of your teeth. If we can get a start, something to begin throwing suspicion on Rand. That's all we need, Chick. And don't tell me your dentist disappeared to the South Seas with a blonde."

"Mary, I don't live right. I've got a perfect set of teeth."

"Oh, now, Chick."

"I've only got one filling in my head, and that was put in by an Army dentist at the Mount Street Dispensary in London. I broke a tooth on one of those rolls they served at the Grosvenor House mess. Proving I should have bought my dinner honestly instead of borrowing a mess card when I was in on leave. Though the dentist did say there was a cavity anyhow. The point is, finding that Army dentist would be a miracle. And I'm sure the records wouldn't still exist."

"Chick, if you have good teeth it's just as good as having a mouthful of gold. It stands to reason that Rand's teeth won't have just one filling identical to yours. Your dentist can prove who you are."

"But I haven't got any dentist. My teeth are okay."

"Haven't you even had them cleaned?"

"I know—see your dentist twice a year. Just try to, around here. I've been going to make an appointment to have my teeth cleaned, but I haven't gotten around to it. Anyhow, I brush them well three times a day and they don't need it very badly."

"Gee, Chick," she said, a bit wanly. "Walt and I figured we'd made progress."

I figured she'd dangled long enough. "Mary, the reason I called is that we've got Rand."

"Got him? You mean the police—"

"I mean us. We've got him where we want him."

"Chick, what do you mean? Don't make me wait!"

"Rand is trying to ride my service record in the Army! I was overseas in the Air Force. He was a tech sergeant at Ft. Douglas. There's his slip-up! According to the papers, it was the other way around. He has given out the story that as Charles Graham he was at Ft. Douglas during the war."

"How does that help us, Chick?"

"Mary, the Army had millions of men. It knew all about how to tell one from another and keep track of every single one. The War Department files will show which is which."

"How hard is to get access to them?"

"I don't know, but we'll do it. We've got him!"

"Chick. this is so—oh. I just wish you were here so I could—" She didn't finish that, but I hoped I knew what she meant. "I just *knew* there was a way, Chick. He can't get away with a thing like that. He just can't. Oh, I want to go running out in the streets and yell, or something."

"Let's yell together," I said.

We did, trying to outshout one another on the phone. "Hey, you, pipe down," the clerk said through the crack of the door behind the desk.

Mary and I laughed together. It was so good to be laughing together again. Back in the old days we'd done a lot of that. Maybe the old days would come again.

"Chick," she said.

"Yes?"

There was a little pause. Then she said, "Good night, Chick."

"Good night, Mary."

I went back to bed. I didn't know whether I was happier about finding Rand's mistake or about the way she'd said, "Good night, Chick."

12

I slept like a baby. I wasn't even annoyed when somebody hammered at my door at a quarter to eleven next morning and said if I didn't clear out of there in fifteen minutes I'd have to pay for another day.

I washed up in the community bathroom, taking all my clothes with me, and went out whistling. I whistled for almost half a block. And then I saw a newspaper rack with the bear edition of the *News*.

The streamer said, "SWITCH" DISCOVERED YEARS OLD! The subhead said, RAND SERVED IN ARMY UNDER ASSUMED NAME, FBI CHECK REVEALS; ROSE TO CAPTAIN UNDER ASSUMED NAME; HAD PLOTTED IDENTITY SWITCH FOR YEARS.

I decided to skip breakfast. Just a cup of coffee, please.

As I sipped the coffee I went over the story. It seemed there were two Charles Bruce Grahams in the Army. One at Ft. Douglas and one overseas with the Eighth Air Force. The FBI, checking War Department files, had discovered that Albert Rand had served in the Air Force under the name of Graham.

On getting the job with the Los Angeles bank, Rand had presented a photostat of his certificate of service. Microscopic examination of the photostat had revealed that the original certificate of service had been altered, and not too well. The name had been changed from Charles Graham to Albert Rand, both where the name was typed and at the signature.

A nice touch, I had to admit. Not only a phony certificate of service (being an enlisted man, he would have received a discharge, rather than a certificate of service)—not only a phony, but a phony that had been carefully altered in a clumsy manner. A very nice touch.

I decided to have another cup of coffee. Yes, please; black.

So Rand had used my name in the Army. My name fit his fingerprints. The newspaper story said that the information given the Army by both men—next of kin, place and date of birth, mother's maiden name, and so on—was identical. The signatures were identical. So was the physical appearance of both men, and measurements down to the shoe size.

The sole proof, then, of which man was which, boiled down to the positive identifications of Cora, Buster, and Ethelene.

They had made for Rand a perfect alibi. I was the alibi. And I was out where it was very cold.

Could I have another cup of coffee, please? Yes, black. The blacker the better. As black as it comes.

Well, anyhow, I had my health.

Then I noticed the picture of James Pease in the paper. VICTIM OF ATTACK, the head said. It seemed that James Pease had been mysteriously assaulted in Golden Gate Park the previous evening. He had gone to the park for exercise, and while walking along a path a figure had leaped on him from behind. He did not see his assailant, nor could he give any reason for the attack. Police were working on the theory that it was attempted vengeance on the part of Albert Rand, the murderer and bond thief, retaliation for information Pease had given the police.

Well, there was one thing about this deal, it made me understand the newspapers. I wondered if I'd ever believe anything I read from now on.

Pease, of course, had been caught up with by Lil's husband. He'd been worked over, and of course he didn't want to admit the reason. Albert Rand was a nice goat.

I wondered how many cases the police would solve if they caught me. I'd probably be accused of everything from stealing the atomic bomb to the raping of young girls.

The prospect wasn't very funny.

My face, I'd noticed in the wavy mirror while in the community bathroom, was really coming in bloom. I felt dopey, but not too bad. If I'd had a nice bed and a good excuse, I might have admitted I felt like hell. But I hadn't, and I didn't. My feet were still sore but the crisis seemed over in that department. Walt's shoes were a trifle loose this morning.

I felt my whiskers, and remembered seeing an electric razor in Walt's bathroom. I didn't want to try scraping that inflamed hide with a blade. Ordinarily, I wouldn't have shaved at all until my face was getting back to normal. But I didn't want to get picked up as a bum.

I finished the coffee and went to the phone in the back of the café.

I phoned the Bay Title Insurance Company.

"Just get up?" Mary said brightly when I was through to her. Bright and brave. "How did you sleep?"

"You saw the papers?"

"Chick, he can't get away with it. He just can't."

"He's sure making a stab at it."

"Walt and I have been talking it over. We've got another idea. Why don't you meet me for lunch and we'll talk it over?"

"I'm not really hungry."

"Have you had any breakfast? Or did you see the papers before?"

"What's your idea?"

"I won't tell you a single word until I see some food disappearing into that red face. Not a word. Can you meet me here?"

"They might be watching you. You'd better meet me. And make sure you're not followed."

"All right. I'm not used to dodging, yet. I can't remember."

"It takes a little time. Was Bill Meadows still there this morning?"

"Yes; and he looked rocky from sleeping in the car. His dog was at the door when we went out."

"I hope that mutt starves to death. And Bill Meadows, too. If the dog gets hungry enough he might eat Bill. Did he follow you?"

"I didn't see him. I think he stayed outside the apartment."

"Did anybody else follow you?"

"Chick, how do I know? I couldn't tell if I was being trailed by a regiment of spies."

"I'm thinking of Buster. Did you notice a tubby little guy with a round innocent face? A baby face, just so honest and sweet you want to reach out and pat him on the head."

"Well, I really didn't—yes, I do remember, Chick. Come to think of it. A wide innocent grin? Getting a little bald, hair cut short—just like a baby's face?"

"That's Buster."

"There was a fellow like that waiting on the corner this morning. He got in the streetcar with us."

"Then you'll be followed when you go out to lunch."

"Chick, there's a drugstore on the corner of Fifth and Market. I'll be there at twelve-thirty. At the soda counter. You come in and take a stool and if everything's all right I'll say hello. If I don't, just go out. How's that?"

"Mata Hari couldn't do it better. And, say, could Walt meet us there with his electric razor? I don't want to get picked up for a bum."

"Sure thing. I'll be seeing you. 'Bye."

I felt better, just talking to Mary. And she had said she had an idea. I had a hunch it might be a good one. We'd used up, it seemed to me, just about all the possible bad ones.

I had an hour and I decided to get rid of what dynamite was in my pockets. If somebody had copped my suit coat, instead of Walt's overcoat, I would have been a cooked goose.

I went into the washroom of a bar, hooked the door, and emptied the stuff out of my pockets. My key case had my name stamped in gold. I dropped the case in the overhead tank of the old-fashioned toilet, but kept the keys. There seemed no immediate use of the keys to my house and car and the office, but throwing them away would be a defeatist attitude. I'd been carrying seven letters in my breast pocket, the sort of stuff a man totes around without any good reason. Two of the envelopes were of the window variety, a transparent opening showing the name and address inside.

I took the letters out, tore off my name, and on the back wrote in a disguised hand, *Mr. C. Bramwell Greene, 781 Santa Clara Street, San Carlos, California*. I folded the letters so this would show at the windows, and put the envelopes back into my breast pocket. I also kept my checkbook.

I had entered the washroom a nameless fugitive. I emerged as C. Bramwell Greene, a couple of letters with good return addresses and the initials C. B. G. on the back of my wristwatch to prove it.

At twelve-thirty I arrived at the drugstore at Fifth and Market. Mary wasn't there. I had a cup of coffee at the counter. My appetite was back with a vengeance. I sipped the coffee and watched the clock above the mirror. I also watched the mirror.

I made the coffee last twenty minutes, and got another cup. I was getting the quivering shakes from all that coffee on an empty stomach. Or maybe it was because Mary wasn't there.

What had happened?

It was three minutes to one when, in the mirror, I saw Walt come in. He didn't walk in, he sauntered in. He browsed awhile at the magazine rack, picked up a newspaper and came to the counter alongside me. He gave the clerk a quarter and said, "Paper."

As the clerk turned to the register, Walt muttered, "Bill Meadows is outside."

The clerk gave Walt twenty cents change. Walt asked him "Where's the Egypt?"

"Where's Egypt? Why, it's to hell and gone over there in Asia or Africa or somewhere. Why?"

"I mean the Egypt Café."

"Egypt Café? Beats the hell out of me. We serve lunch here."

"I was going to meet somebody there. I think it's on Third, just off Market."

"There's a phone book over at the booth. You could look it up."

"Thanks. I think that's where it is. On Third, just off Market."

Walt went out.

"Say," the clerk said, indicating the leather case of an electric razor by my coffee cup, "did that joker leave this here?"

"No," I said, "it's mine." I put the case in my pocket.

"I didn't see it there before he come in."

"The hand is quicker than the eye."

The clerk gave me a look of distrust but didn't pursue the matter. I waited until ten after one and then went out the side door.

I don't remember what I was thinking about right then. Probably it was very profound stuff. But the point is that I was thinking. I was soul-searching, and not keeping my head up.

It was by the merest chance that I saw at the edge of my vision a brown snout protrude from the Market Street side of the building. A brown snout sniffing the air. Then a pair of eyes looking, and two needle-pointed ears alert. Then, above, an unlighted cigarette followed by Bill Meadows' face.

Bill Meadows looked at me for a long moment. His eyes went to the dog, which had moved into full view and stood quivering with eagerness. His eyes came up to me again. Then his unlighted cigarette bobbled as his lips moved to say a word. Just a quiet word. A single word I couldn't hear.

And the Doberman came for me.

The dog had about thirty yards to go. I moved as fast as I could, with the horrible feeling of slowness that comes in a dream. The corner stoplight had just changed to green and the traffic was beginning to move. I took two steps to the curb, jerked open the door of a green Chevrolet and slipped into the front seat. The dog hit the door, slamming it shut.

"Say—" the woman driving the car began.

Then she saw the great white fangs at the window and she bucked the car ahead.

"My God! My God!" she muttered, terrified. She was so rattled she made an illegal left-hand turn, cutting across the line of traffic.

I looked back to see the dog standing quietly beside Bill Meadows on the corner. Bill, tall and impassive, watched me until the green Chevrolet melted into the traffic.

My puffed face and sun glasses no longer were a disguise. Now they knew what to look for.

The woman driver took me on one of the wildest rides I ever hope to have, for three blocks. "It's okay, now," I said. "I'll get out here. The dog didn't chase the car."

I didn't want a traffic cop stopping her and asking questions.

She pulled in at the curb. "I think the cops ought to do something about that." She was a small woman, not quite enough nose or mouth or chin or hair. "I was never so scared in my life. That big brute jumping at the window. He might be taking after somebody else. The cops ought to do something about that."

"I'll report it," I said. "I was just standing there minding my own business."

As she drove away she smiled and waved. We had shared an adventure. I waved and smiled. It was a big thing in her small life. It was a big thing in my small life, too.

The Egypt was upstairs on Third Street, off Market.

It had booths around the sides, and over them on the walls a homemade mural showing the Nile winding, contrary to all natural laws, up- and down-hill among palms and pyramids. Mary was in the end booth.

She smiled all over, her face coming alight, and I wondered why the camera couldn't catch that in a picture. I sat down opposite her and we squeezed each other's hands. We were sharing an adventure, too.

"Chick, it's so good to see you," she said. "I've been on pins and needles."

"Oh, I got the message. My rapierlike brain at once deciphered Walt's clever code."

"Buster followed me from the office. I know what you mean by that round baby face, all innocence."

"You got rid of him all right?"

"Yes. First I went back to the office and told Walt to stay there until I phoned him. Then I did everything I could to shake Buster, but when I got to the drugstore where I was to meet you, he was still tagging me. A taxi came along and I grabbed it. The last I saw of Buster he was trying to find a cab. I didn't want to go back there so I phoned Walt I'd be here. Did you have any trouble?"

"I got here okay. What's this idea of yours?"

"We won't talk about that until you get some food. I'll bet you haven't had a thing all day except coffee."

The food was far superior to the murals. A swarthy little man with a great mustache brought us barbecued lamb on skewers, some boiled whole wheat with a sauce mixed in it, what looked like cups of clabbered milk, and a dessert composed of many layers of flaky pastry with melted honey over it. Mary said it was Syrian food, but that the place was run by Armenians.

"Armenians? I wonder if the waiter knows Saroyan?"

"All Armenians are very proud of Saroyan."

So when the waiter brought us tiny cups of thick coffee I asked him, "Do you know Saroyan?"

"Oh, yes, yes. Very good friend." And then he asked, "*Which* Saroyan?"

"Which Saroyan? You mean there's more than one Saroyan?"

"Oh, yes. Name is like Smith in America."

Mary claimed this brightened her day.

"I have eaten like a good little boy," I said to her. "And now for the big idea."

"It may lead to something, Chick. But—I don't know. You might get into trouble."

"Now there's something to worry about, for a man with no troubles."

"At least you're free now. And with the poison oak—"

"They know me," I said. "Bill Meadows followed Walt to the drugstore. The dog found me out."

"Chick, what happened?"

"I got away. But the poison oak is no good any more for a disguise. They know what they're looking for."

"Then I guess my idea is better than staying here," she said. "At least, you'll be away from them."

"I'm for anything that means doing something. I'm tired of this infernal chase. All I've done is run away. I haven't accomplished a single thing to improve my position."

"I've got a good hunch you have, Chick. I think you've done exactly the right thing."

"You're being kind. That is sweet, but it doesn't help."

"I'm serious, Chick. Walt and I were discussing it. Why is it that Bill Meadows and Buster are trying to do the work of the police? They knew you were at the apartment last night. Why weren't the police notified? Why haven't they told the police you are in contact with me and Walt?"

"Maybe they're after the reward. You can't pick up fifteen thousand bucks every day."

"Fiddlesticks."

"All right. But they did turn me over to the police once."

"Chick, to get that reward they don't have to capture you personally. The reward is for information leading to the capture of Albert Rand, dead or alive. If it was the reward, Bill Meadows could have had it last night by lifting a phone."

"Then what is it?"

"Chick, they're scared. They're desperate. They're trying to catch you by themselves. You've put them on the spot. I don't know the reason but I do know they're terribly afraid."

"I don't get it."

"It's perfectly plain," she said, "that Rand is in a bad position with you free. He was aiming one way. We've got to admit that his plan for stepping into your shoes was perfect."

"He thought of everything," I admitted.

"But, Chick, he was looking only one way. He closed every possibility for you to prove that you are *you*. He never intended you to be free to prove you're not *Rand*."

"Isn't that juggling words?"

"Not at all. You might not be able to prove you're Charles Graham. But if you prove you're *not* Albert Rand, it amounts to the same thing. Don't you see?"

I let that sink in. "Maybe you've got something there. It still doesn't explain why they turned me over to that cop two days ago and were afraid to last night."

"Perhaps they're afraid of something you know now that you didn't know then."

"But what can I do that the police and the FBI can't?"

"Chick, you have the enormous advantage of knowing the whole thing."

"Sure, but nobody would believe it."

"And you can be yourself. You can be Charles Graham. That, perhaps, is why Rand is scared right now. You can prove you're not he."

"Simple as that."

"Now let me finish. When I saw you yesterday it was for the first time in years. Your face was red and swollen. You were wearing dark glasses. You looked so little like your normal self that you got on the train in Redwood City that morning with the police at the station watching for you. But when I saw you, I knew you."

"You were prepared. You knew I was coming. I'd phoned ahead. You knew my voice."

"True enough. But James Pease also recognized you on the train."

"He saw both me and Rand from behind."

"Chick, if a girl's been close to a man—what I mean, let's suppose Rand had come to see me, pretending to be you. Let's say I had no idea he wasn't you. Do you think he could fool me very long? And what about Dolly? You know what happened there. You put cream in your coffee. You didn't say the right things. You made a number of little mistakes of habit. Dolly thought you were Rand. She excused little things because she thought you'd been under a terrible strain and were upset. But she finally knew that you weren't Rand. One more thing—why did you get away from that policeman the other night, before you knew just what you were up against?"

"I did know, pretty well."

"Yes, it was obvious—why? Simply because Cora and Buster and Ethelene pretended not to know you. Particularly Cora. She accepted him against you. So you knew she was against you. She *had* to know which man was which."

"Yes," I admitted, "that's what did it. But where is this getting us?"

"Chick, don't you see? Rand was engaged to a girl in Los Angeles. That girl will know you are not Albert Rand. She is no good in proving who you are, but it's just as good for our purposes to prove who you are *not*."

"Remind me sometime to put you in for the Bronze Star," I said. "It was right there under my nose but it took you to see it. The cashier's daughter—Alicia Alexander. There's our starting point. And their weak point."

"She will *know*, Chick. She will know in a minute that you're not the man she was engaged to marry."

"What about the fingerprints?"

"I don't care about all that foolishness. Once there's a shadow of doubt cast on Rand's impersonation of you, it's doomed. Anything that was possible for him to do, is possible for the police to unravel. If you can establish that you are not Rand, his whole play will fall through."

"Mary," I said, "you've got something. Let's celebrate with a small bottle of wine."

13

We drank a toast to Alicia Alexander. To her good health, long life, and high IQ.

"I hope," I said, "that she has loved Rand not wisely but too well. I hope she knows him as no nice girl should."

"Chick, what a way to talk," Mary said. "But I do, too."

"Well, I'm off to the races. I've got something to do. And that's a great relief. I'm tired of being shoved around."

"Now, don't get overconfident, Chick," she warned. "Be careful. It will be difficult making contact with her. But once you've seen her, and she knows you're not Rand, I think you'd better go to the police."

"Police? That's suicide."

"Chick, we've been through that. That's what we've just been talking about. Rand is deathly afraid the police will get you. Otherwise he would have had you apprehended last night. And give the police some credit. This sort of thing is why we have a police force. It's their business, not yours. They know how to do things. The very best brains of the country are on this case. With the Alexander girl throwing doubt on your identity as Rand, the police will have a starting point.

"You and Walt and I have figured the entire thing out in its essentials. Not because we're particularly smart but because we had a starting point. We started with the premise that you were not Rand. Give the police the same starting point and they'll figure it out the same way. More than that, they'll prove it. They've got the organization for doing it, and we haven't."

"You're right, as usual," I admitted. Alicia Alexander was the pin. Pull out the pin and Rand's false structure would collapse. "The paper said Alicia had gone to Palm Springs. I've always wanted to see Palm Springs."

"Well, if I'm not smart," Mary declared. "Walt and I talked this over and of course I knew you'd need money. But I didn't draw any. Now

I've got to go back to the office and go through the business of shaking Buster and getting together again."

"That's no calamity," I said. "Alicia Alexander will keep an hour or so. I'm ready to go through a little frammis any time to see you again."

"This wine is going to your head," she told me.

Mary and I went out arm in arm. It was good to see the end. Alicia Alexander was money in the bank. She would be burning with humiliation; she'd cooperate gladly once she knew I wasn't Rand. She'd do anything to nail the guy who had made love to her for the sole purpose of getting next to her father in order to rob the bank. She was my pigeon.

We went down the narrow stairs to the street, laughing at the fun of being alive. It was a bright day. The sun was bright and life was bright.

"Extry!" a newsboy was yelling on the street. "Extry! Read all about it! Rand's girl dead! Extry! Read all about it! Cashier's daughter found dead! Extry! Read all about it!"

We read all about it, standing together beside a storefront. Alicia Alexander had, the previous afternoon, started for Palm Springs. She had phoned her father that evening that she had arrived. The next morning, which was today, her car had been found awash in the surf of a cove near Santa Cruz, some five hundred miles north of Palm Springs. The car had gone over the cliff during the night at high tide. The girl was drowned. Bruises on her head indicated she had been stunned by the accident. A check of her phone call to her father proved that it had come from Santa Cruz, not Palm Springs.

"They saw it, too," Mary said. "They got her. Chick, what can we do now?"

"Oh, hell," I said.

"Chick, there will be another way. We'll think of something. There has to be some way."

Suddenly I quit feeling sorry for myself. I grabbed her arm. "Mary, you're in the same spot she was. You know the same thing she did. I want you to go back to the office. Stay with Walt. Have Walt carry that gun. Don't take any chances. Promise me, Mary."

"Of course, Chick. I'll be careful. But I'm thinking about you."

"Quit thinking about me. You've never got anything but trouble from doing that. Be smart."

"But, Chick, what are we going to do?"

"We aren't going to do anything. This is my baby. I won't have you hurt by it. You take care of yourself. Stick with Walt. We're up against killers."

"When will I see you again, Chick?"

"I'll phone you," I said.

"You will let us help you. Promise me."

"Sure," I said. "Of course."

"Be seeing you."

She walked away and I knew I wouldn't see her again. Not until I was out of this. If I ever got out of this. I'd been a fool going to her in the first place. A weak fool. Now she was in danger. She was in the same danger Alicia Alexander had been. The same threat hung over her. It was my fault. I had to do something. Something. Something.

What?

I spent some time over a beer, seeing if there was something in the newspaper to take hold of. The police had discovered that Albert Rand had chartered a plane the morning of the crime. He had walked out of the bar in Los Angeles with the bonds, climbed into his car parked at the corner, driven to the airport and taken off in the waiting plane.

His method of escape had not been discovered until his car had been located at the airport. The pilot, it seemed, had kept mum because he was not licensed to carry passengers for hire. The car, according to a quote from a Los Angeles captain of detectives, had provided an important clue that could not be revealed at this time.

The whole thing, I felt, was shouting in a barrel. Just what good did it do to know exactly *how* Rand had reached Redwood City? But that was the police—dig, dig, dig; nothing too small to overlook. The only thing they seemed to have overlooked was the one thing that counted. To my mind the "important clue" provided by Rand's car was either the usual frammis the police used in trying to scare a fugitive, or something given by an obliging detective to a reporter friend who just has to have some angle to hang a story on.

I finished my beer and went back to the washroom with the idea of shaving. There wasn't any wall plug for the electric razor. I walked to a dime store and bought a double socket and a screw-in plug. On the way back to the bar I picked up the *Call*. I was getting to be a fiend for newspapers. I went into the washroom, took out the bulb, put in the double socket, screwed the light in one side and plugged the razor in the other, and shaved. Then I went out to the counter, got another glass of beer, and read the *Call*.

The beer on top of the wine made me feel lousy. Or maybe it was the poison oak. Or maybe I would have felt lousy anyhow. I had a perfect right to feel lousy. I felt defiant about it. At any rate I didn't want that second beer. But I had to keep off the streets, and there was no place to go except bars or movies. I had enough plot on my hands without borrowing from the movies.

The *Call* carried a byline piece about Rand's war record (that is, mine). This was familiar enough to me, except for a curious paragraph:

> Rand, while serving under the name of Graham in England with the Eighth Air Force, made a practice of slipping back to the United States for brief visits with his girlfriend, Alicia Alexander, in Los Angeles. While the War Department professes no knowledge of this, the same thing was done by other members of the Air Force during the war. It was not too difficult for an Air Force officer with the right connections to get on a military plane as an unofficial member of the crew. A five-day leave was ample time to make the round trip and have a day with the girlfriend. Rand's appearances in Los Angeles were very hush-hush, and he added to the mysterious glamor by hinting he was on some top-secret deal so super-important that he couldn't even receive mail. Thus his girlfriend never did discover there was no such person as Captain Albert Rand in the Army.

And to bolster up this odd sidelight on Albert Rand (or myself), there was a story datelined El Paso about a former crew chief named Theron Carter who claimed that on two occasions he had let the man he knew as Captain Charles Graham take his place on a flight to the ZI while Carter had a good time in London.

Anybody in the Air Force knew that such things occasionally did happen. Though personally I hadn't been so lucky. I had a horrible moment wondering if the crew chief had traded places with still *another* guy who looked like me and had the same name. But obviously Theron Carter was either mistaken, or he was a crank seeking a little notoriety.

Rand, stationed at Ft. Douglas, had had ample opportunity to pop up occasionally in Los Angeles in a captain's uniform and an ETO ribbon, to soften up his girl and lay the groundwork for the big job.

Then I remembered Major Jody, my old CO at the squadron. If the exact dates of Rand's appearances in Los Angeles could be determined, I might be able to prove through Jody that on those dates I was on duty in England. Human memory is faulty, the daily records of our squadron were burned before we flew home—but still it was something to work on, and better than sitting in bars drinking beer I didn't want. All we had to prove was one single date when Rand was in Los Angeles and I was in England. He might have popped up in L. A. the day of some big mission—some specific date that could be ascertained, and at which time Jody could swear I was sitting in the same office with him.

Jody had corresponded with Mary and had dropped by to see her once. She might have his address. I hadn't intended contacting her again, but this was important and it wouldn't involve her.

I phoned the Bay Title Insurance Company and asked for Miss Davis, please. Walt came to the phone. "Chick, I'm glad you called," he said in a breathless way. "Mary wants to see you."

"Put her on."

"She's not here. She went to meet you."

"She what? Walt, what happened? How did she know where to go?"

"Well, she—you know it takes some time to shake Buster. She said she'd slip him and then phone me where she was, so when you called you could meet her right away."

"Damn it, Walt! I told her not to go out alone! They killed the Alexander girl. Mary's in the same position. Why did you let her go out? She could have waited for me to phone. If she had anything to say she could have said it over the phone—"

"And that's enough out of you!" he cried. "Don't you talk to me like that! I didn't ask for any part of this. This is your mess, not ours. You got her mixed up in this. Now she wants to see you, and you get on your bicycle and get there in a hurry!"

"All right. What's cooking?"

"I don't know. Don't sit there beating your gums! She wants to see you!"

"Okay, okay. Where is she?"

"It's a place on Bush Street. Just a minute." After a small wait he gave me the address. "It's close to Van Ness. The door's unlocked. Just walk in. She says it's a place you can stay. Now get going. Hurry!"

"Okay. I'm off."

"Chick!"

"Yes?"

"For God's sake, don't say anything to anybody!"

"Do you think I'm crazy?"

"I'm just telling you. Keep this under your hat!"

I took a taxi. It went out Market to Van Ness, along Van Ness to Bush, and made a left turn. The house of the address was an old frame building, high and narrow, painted gray.

"Keep on going," I said to the driver. "Don't stop. Keep on."

"Okay," he said. "Where to?"

I directed him, right, left, uphill and down, until I was sure nobody was following. Then I had him stop at a little grocery store tucked into a half basement. I told him to wait. I went into the grocery and dialed the Bay Title Insurance Company. I asked for Mr. Davis, please.

When Walt's voice answered, I said, "All right, let's have it."

Walt stuttered a bit.

"Come on, let's have it!" I yelled.

"Good God, do you want something to happen to her? Haven't you been there? Didn't you go?"

"They've got her," I said.

His voice came flatly, barely audible. "Yes."

"Why the hell didn't you tell me?"

"How did you find out?"

"It added up. The way you talked. Warning me not to say anything to anybody. The fact you didn't know why she wanted to see me. But never mind that. Let's have it. What happened?"

"Chick, don't blame me. They've got her. I had to do it. I'll tell you how it was. A few minutes after she got back from seeing you at lunch she got a phone call from you—"

"I didn't call her."

"She thought it was you. She said you'd trapped Buster and got a confession out of him. She went to meet you, to take the confession down in shorthand."

"Yes, that would bring her," I admitted.

"Chick, for God's sake! We've got to do something! They might right now be—"

"Shut up and tell me what happened. How did you get that address on Bush?"

"A little while after she'd gone, a messenger delivered a package to me here. It had in it one of her gloves, a lock of her hair, and the lipstick with her initials on the case I gave her for her birthday. I'd just opened the package when there was a phone call. A voice told me Mary had just one hour to live unless I did exactly what I was told. Chick, the hour's almost up!"

"Keep hold of yourself. She's bait for me. She's no good to them dead."

"And neither was the Alexander girl! Don't pull that on me! They've got her! Why didn't you go to that place on Bush?"

"Don't be a damned fool, Walt. When they had us both, it would have been you next. Let's quit this crazy fighting and get down to cases. What's the rest of it?"

"That's everything, Chick. The voice on the phone told me to contact you and tell you to go to that address on Bush. I told the guy I couldn't contact you, that I'd have to wait until you phoned me. He said if you weren't there in an hour, Mary would be dead. He said the same thing would happen to her that happened to Alicia Alexander, and that if I notified the police— Chick, I was wild! By God, what time is it now? What are we going to do?"

"Walt, give me a half hour more. Give me until three o'clock. Will you do that? If you don't hear from me by three, call the police. Tell them everything. Every single thing. It will be my neck, but that can't be helped. We've got to think of Mary. But give me just a half hour, Walt. Give me until three o'clock. The police may be too late, and I've got a chance."

I hung up before he had a chance to argue. If he didn't call the police, which he might do, I had a half hour.

14

I walked out of the grocery and got into the taxi. The driver looked around. "Where to now?"

I flipped a mental coin. Mary wouldn't be at that address on Bush. That was just a spot for me to walk into. I fancied Bill Meadows might be there with his Doberman. That left Buster's apartment or the office. Assuming that she—but, yes, she *had* to be all right.

"Cox and Graham, The Cogram System," I told the driver. "It's on Mission. I'll show you where."

There was traffic. Every stoplight was against us. I felt like jumping out and running. I kept putting my watch to my ear.

It was twelve minutes to three when the taxi pulled up below the office. I told the driver to wait.

"Just a minute, Bud," he said, jerking a thumb at the meter. "You look okay, see, but we're sort of building up an account here. And every place there's a front door, there's a door in the back."

I pulled out whatever money was in my pocket, slapped it in his hand, and went inside. I ran up the flight of wooden stairs and along the hall to that familiar door of our office. I put my ear against the lower panel, not showing the outline of my head against the moss glass above. There was no sound from inside.

I got out my key, rammed it into the tumbler lock, twisted it and the knob, and barged in.

Ethelene was at the antique desk in the little reception room. She whirled, eyes wide. Her mouth began going wide and I got a hand over it just in time. She struggled, clawing at me, trying to bite my hand, trying to get my instep with her heels, trying to knee me. It was no time for chivalry. I hit her in the middle with all I had. It took the wind and fight out of her. She doubled onto the floor, grimacing, clutching at her middle.

I slid up to the door of the back office and then went through fast. The back office was empty, except for Mary. She was tied to my old chair with heavy cotton twine, a gag in her mouth and a blindfold over her eyes.

"Mary, it's me." I cut her right arm free with the big office shears. She got a handful of my hair and almost scalped me before I got the blindfold off. Then she let go my hair and made a gurgling sound. I cut the rest of the twine while she got rid of the gag.

When we went into the front office, Ethelene was still sitting on the floor feeling of her middle. She opened her mouth. "Kidnaping is no joke," I said. She closed her mouth and drew in a shaky breath. I picked up the desk phone and dialed the Bay Title Insurance Company. When Walt answered I told him everything was under control.

"Yes," Mary said over the line, to convince him, "I'm all right, Walt." Then we got out of there.

"Golden Gate Park," I told the cab driver. He was just shifting into high gear when Mary broke, clinging to me and sobbing.

Near the corner of Franklin and Fell, I told the driver to stop. He seemed to think I had a hard time making up my mind. I told him that was all; goodbye. He shrugged, and drove away, and I remembered I'd given him all my money. No, not all. There was a dime down in a corner of my pocket. I got two nickels for it in a drugstore and phoned Walt. I told him where we were, and to meet us in a hurry.

"I don't think anybody is watching you," I said. "They're probably still waiting for me on Bush Street. But don't take chances."

"Okay, Chick. I'm sorry that I—"

"Forget it."

"I was such a silly fool," Mary said to me as we waited. "I walked right into it. I ought to have my head fixed. But I didn't suspect. When you phoned and said you'd got Buster and he had confessed—"

"I didn't phone you."

"Your voice did."

"You mean Rand's? His voice is entirely different from mine."

"That's just what you think. Nobody knows what his own voice sounds like. Were you at the fair when the telephone company had that trick phone that repeated back what you said into it? People were startled to hear their own voices. They couldn't believe they sounded like that. Maybe Rand has practiced your voice, just as he has your signature. Or maybe it's something to do with looking so much like you—the shape of the mouth and so on. Anyhow, he didn't say much, and it was over the phone. And I wasn't suspecting. We should have a code. After this, when you call me, mention poison oak. Then I'll know it's you."

"Sure," I agreed. I wouldn't be calling her anymore. That was certain.

"The voice I thought was yours told me to go to a place on Bush Street," Mary went on. "When I got there, *he* was there. Chick, it was horrible! That face. Your face. Just like you. It was like a nightmare."

"I know just what you mean. Was Rand there alone?"

"No. Buster and Bill Meadows were on deck, and that big dog. Bill Meadows told me the dog would tear me to pieces if I made a sound. He took me to your office on Mission and tied me to the chair. It seemed days before somebody cut my arm loose. From the voice I thought it was Rand. Did I almost scalp you? Why is Walt coming here to meet us?"

"I've got an idea."

When Walt arrived in a taxi, I told the driver to wait. Walt and

Mary hugged one another. I could see he was close to tears. That big bohunk thought a lot of his sister. Well, so did I.

He turned to me. "Chick, I feel like such a heel. But when I thought—"

"Forget it. You were under the gun. Will you and Mary do something for me?"

"What," Mary asked, "are you two talking about?"

"Walt got a little sore at me for putting you in danger," I said.

Walt gave me a thankful glance. "What do you want us to do?"

"Can you get off from work?"

"We'll take off," Mary said. "What can we do?"

"I think we can trip Rand up. I'd like both of you to go to L. A. and line things up. Find out who Rand's dentist is. Talk with Alicia Alexander's father. Rand must have left some strings dangling down there. See what you can turn up."

"I think that's a good idea," Walt admitted. "He lived there for years. A man has to leave a track."

"Write to me here, General Delivery—C. Bramwell Greene."

"C. Bramwell Greene, General Delivery," Mary said. "I'll write it down. Oh, my purse! It was there by that bookkeeping, machine when Bill Meadows tied me up."

"We won't go back for it," I said. "I think you'd better take a plane. Have you got enough for the taxi and plane fare?"

Walt looked in his billfold. "I've got enough to get us there. But not much more."

"I'll have money for you tomorrow. I'll send it to General Delivery. You'll have it in the morning. I know where there's lots of money."

"Chick," Mary said dubiously, "you're talking so strangely—"

"They've tipped their hand and they're wide open," I broke in, talking fast. "I can prove I was overseas when Rand was making his mysterious trips to L. A. Mary, have you got Major Jody's address?"

"Yes. In the apartment. In a little green address book in the desk drawer. Maybe I'd better get it for you."

"No; I want you to get to L. A. right away. Find out the dates Rand showed up there. His girl's father ought to be some help in that. I can get the address book. They won't be expecting me back at the apartment. I'll go in the rear door anyway."

"Okay," Walt said. "Here are the keys."

I hurried them into the waiting taxi and waved goodbye.

And then I didn't feel so hot. They would be safe in Los Angeles; it would be a nice trip. But I was back where I'd started. Alone and broke. No, not exactly broke. I had five cents.

I walked toward Mary's apartment on Turk Street. At least I'd have a place to stay. A base of operations. And it was high time I did some operating.

Coming to Turk, I walked past the corner, looking down the street to where the old-fashioned apartment house stood in the middle of the block. I couldn't see anything suspicious. Still, I didn't take a chance on the front door. Walt had given me three keys. The only one that fit the rear door wouldn't turn the bolt. I tried the knob; the door was unlocked. I went upstairs.

At the door of the apartment, I could hear a radio inside. The doorstop, near the rim latch, had been sprung. There were marks where it had been pried loose for a knife blade to slip in and push back the striker of the latch. I sighted through the crack left by the tool. The latch was now back; the door was unlocked. I went in.

The floor was ankle-deep in papers and books and sofa cushions. Drawers were scattered around. The radio had, of course, drowned the noise of the search.

I snapped the rim lock shut, for whatever good it would do, and began pawing through the mess, tossing things into a corner. I didn't find the address book. Nor had I expected to.

The radio was giving the news: "The death of Alicia Alexander, whose body was found this morning in a car which had plunged into the sea from a cliff near Santa Cruz, has been revealed as murder. Her killer has been named, in a joint statement by police and FBI, as the girl's fiancé, Albert Rand, Los Angeles bank messenger who murdered a guard and absconded with two million dollars in Government bonds Wednesday morning.

"The statement reconstructs the crime as follows: Late Thursday afternoon Miss Alexander left her home in Los Angeles, saying she was going to Palm Springs, where her father maintains a weekend residence. It has been discovered that she received a phone call from San Francisco shortly before she left. The call unquestionably was from Rand, who lured her to her death by protesting his innocence and asking her aid to help clear his name.

"Instead of going to Palm Springs, the girl drove north to Santa Cruz. She phoned her father from a service station there, telling him she had arrived safely at Palm Springs. The girl was next found dead this morning after her car had plunged off a cliff into the sea.

"The murder was carefully planned to appear as an accident. An examination of the girl's body brought the first suspicion of foul play. Her head was too severely bruised for the contusions all to have been sustained in the plunge over the cliff. Upon examination, her car was found to be in low gear with the hand throttle partly out. Her killer had knocked her unconscious, started the car in low gear toward the edge of the cliff, and leaped out.

"A man's shaving kit was found inside the car, containing toilet articles and a heavy flashlight, all of which bore Rand's fingerprints. Strands of the girl's hair were caught under the on-off button of the flashlight, and police are subjecting it to further examination in the belief it was the murder weapon.

"Rand lured the girl to a rendezvous, obviously with the plan of using her help to make his escape from the vicinity. When she realized his true motive she refused to become an accomplice. He knocked her unconscious, drove to the cliff, set the hand throttle and leaped out.

"We wish to warn the listeners of this station again of the desperate character of this man. If you see a suspicious character in your vicinity, notify the police immediately ..."

I snapped off the radio. More fingerprints. It would be simple enough, of course, to have put my shaving kit and my flashlight into the girl's car. Which of the three men, I wondered—Rand, Buster, or Bill Meadows—had actually murdered her? Not Rand. With that face he couldn't risk a trip to Santa Cruz. And last night Bill Meadows had been watching the apartment. Bill had stayed all night in his Ford across the street while the dog kept guard. Which left Buster. My pal Buster. My best friend. Chubby, open-faced Buster, the guy strangers wanted to pat on the head.

Unless, that is, there were others involved. But if there were others, why hadn't they put a man on the back door last night when they knew I was in Mary's apartment? I had escaped because they hadn't. If there were others, people I didn't know, surely they would have tailed Mary and Walt, rather than leaving the job to Buster and Bill Meadows. So those three were the only men involved. Rand had to play my part. He had to catch the 5:29 to meet Cora at the station. He had to be me, Charles Graham, right down to the last gesture and habit.

What about Cora and Ethelene? Cora would have to be Mrs. Charles Graham, playing that part to the hilt. She couldn't be scouting around

Santa Cruz in the night. Ethelene? Why not? But, no, Ethelene couldn't have gotten away with it. Because she was a girl. A pretty girl. If Alicia Alexander was met at Santa Cruz by a pretty girl as liaison for Rand, she'd have no part of *that*.

It had to be my pal Buster. He could do it. That round open face. That childlike innocence. Yes, Alicia Alexandar would trust him. She'd believe him. She'd go with him to where he said Rand was hiding out, unjustly accused and a victim of circumstances. She'd trust Buster all the way down the line. People did. She would put her life in his hands. And he'd taken it.

I went over this in my mind calmly. As I saw it, there was something to be done and it was my job. The FBI and all the police in California were barking up the wrong tree. I was the guy who knew the answers. It was on my head. It was my job and I had to do what had to be done.

There was nothing noble about how I felt. It was just something that had been tossed at me and I had to catch it. Murder is a plague. It, like the black death, is spread by rats. There is no end to it until you exterminate the rats.

That was my job, to get rid of the rats. If I couldn't do it legally, I'd do it any way I could. I wished I had accepted Walt's gun. Well, I could get a gun.

For the first time I understood why men ran amok. Put enough pressure on any man, and you've got a savage.

15

I straightened up the apartment, in much the same way a man will clean out his desk while mulling over a business problem. Then I investigated the refrigerator and the kitchen cupboard. I fried eggs and bacon, opened a can of corn, made coffee.

After eating, I washed the dishes, then listened to the radio awhile, killing time. At six o'clock I dialed the office. I listened to the phone ring on the other end of the wire for long enough to know it wouldn't be answered, then hung up.

Rand had caught the 5:29. Buster and Ethelene were at their apartment having dinner. I had my key to the office.

It was getting dark when I reached the office building on Mission. On the right wall were the names of the tenants. Cox and Graham,

The Cogram System, 2nd Floor. I read the directory, including the sign at the bottom, OFFICES FOR RENT, while taking a look at the street. Then I went in, up the stairs, and let myself into the office.

In the front room, Ethelene's antique desk had been cleared off neatly. The typewriter on the little table beside the desk had been covered. I went through the desk, paper by paper, replacing everything exactly as it had been in the drawer before starting on another drawer. There was nothing there; it would have been sheer luck if there had been.

In the back room, the day's accounts were on the table beside the posting machine, three ledgers side by side, the week's papers in envelopes atop them, all ready to take back in the morning. Despite a busy day otherwise, Buster and Rand had got out the day's work. That, of course, was essential. They couldn't afford anything funny in the business. They didn't want anybody to say, "Things were different, before Wednesday."

I picked up the ledgers and the envelopes. These, our Friday accounts, were Walker Jewelry, Johnny's Garage, and Nutter & Post Hardware.

It would be highly inconvenient to Cox and Graham, the Cogram System, if they couldn't produce those ledgers. Yes, indeed. Rand and Buster would be between the sword and the wall. They could stall the accounts off awhile, but there would have to be a showdown. Or they could claim the place had been burglarized. Whatever they did would mean investigation. And investigation was the one thing they were trying to avoid. The motive for stealing three ledgers was going to be very hard to explain. In fact there was no way to explain it. There was no reason for it. I wondered if they'd try to burn the building down to conceal the loss—but that again would mean investigation.

Yes, they would be on the griddle.

As I let myself out, the ledgers under my arm, the door across the hallway opened and a big man came out. He was heavy, with a solid face and prominent black eyebrows. On Wednesday that office had been vacant; it was just my luck that it had been rented and I'd bumped into a witness. Or would it, from the viewpoint of Rand and Buster, matter? There would still be an investigation.

"Evening," the man with the eyebrows said.

"Good evening," I said.

He locked his door and I locked mine. We went to the stairs together.

"Little homework?" he said, indicating the ledgers.

"That's what a man gets, working for himself," I said.

"I just moved in," he said. "Getting things straightened around." And as we went downstairs: "What's the Cogram System?"

"Accounting."

He held the front door open for me. "Maybe we can do business. What do you charge?"

"It would depend on the work," I said.

"My car's here. I'll give you a lift and we'll talk it over."

"Thanks. My car's just around the corner. I'll see you in the morning and we'll go over it."

He took my arm. There was no way of telling whether he just didn't know his strength or whether he just didn't want me to move.

"If you've got a minute, I have a problem. I'm in bad with the income tax people. I'd like to go over it with you."

"I'd have to see your books," I said. "I'd have to go into them. What time in the morning, sir?"

"My name's Rivers," he said. "Bob Rivers. Investments."

I took his right hand. His left still held my arm. "Glad to know you, Mr. Rivers. If you'll excuse me, I'll see you in the morning. Just drop across the hall. Any time—I'll be there. We'll go over it."

He pumped my hand. "I'm very happy to know you," he said. "I know we can do business together. And maybe I can help you. I think neighbors should work together. Do you have any investments?"

As he spoke, a car's headlights swung from the traffic to the curb. The big man was speaking to me, but watching the car.

A face showed at the car window, a face that looked even worse than mine. One eye was swelled almost shut and the nose had a blue hump on it. The lips were puffed and one cheek didn't match the other. The face belonged to James Pease, the business machine salesman.

"Graham," Pease said, "I've been looking all over for you. Why the devil didn't you stay in the room? What have you been doing? Don't you know your friends? Don't you want me to help you?"

"Get in, Graham," the big man said, and I found myself in the car. I couldn't exactly claim I had been pushed inside, but certainly I hadn't been held back. Bob Rivers climbed in and slammed the door. Pease drove on.

"What held you up?" the man with the eyebrows asked Pease.

"There was a joker double-parked," Pease said. "I couldn't get the car out."

"Always a good alibi."

"I came as fast as I could, Bob. I couldn't help it if he was double-parked."

"What's the score?" I asked.

"We're trying to help you, Graham," Pease said. "Don't you want any help? What got into you, anyhow? I got a room for you. I fixed it with Lil to keep you in grub and anything you needed while your face cleared up. Why didn't you let me help you? Why did you have to leave?"

"I've been pretty busy," I said.

"Well, sure, Graham. I understand that. You had a lot to do. You've been busier than a one-armed paper hanger. But you could have used the room. You told me yourself you didn't have anywhere to go and that you were flat broke. How have you been getting along? You could of let us help you. You don't want to try to do everything alone, do you? You can count on your friends, Graham. You know that. We only tried to give you a helping hand."

"Pease," I said, "why don't you be smart and stay out of this?"

"Why be selfish, Graham?" Bob Rivers said. He put a big hand on my shoulder, palsy-walsy. "Let's get along, why don't we? Why try to hog it all for yourself? There's plenty for everybody. Why be greedy?"

"If you just crave to be unhappy, you two guys," I said, "you're sure on the right track. If I were you, I'd—"

I suddenly found myself on my knees between the seats. I'd reached for a cigarette and the big man had grabbed my wrist and wrenched it. His other hand went over me, feeling for weapons.

"I'm sorry, Graham," he said, helping me onto the seat again. "I just thought maybe you didn't realize who your friends were."

"What did he try to do?" Pease asked from the front.

"I wanted a cigarette," I said. "Is it quite okay by you?"

"It was sort of a sudden move," Bob Rivers said apologetically. He squeezed my shoulder. "No offense, Graham. I'm sorry. We only want to be friends."

"You'll be friends if you have to kill me to prove it," I said.

"You don't want to mind Bob," Pease said. "He's impulsive. He acts before he thinks."

"Is that what happened to you?"

"I got the wrong idea of Jim," the big man said.

"Oh, you're Lil's husband?"

"What was I to think?" he said defensively. "Some dirty sneak tipped me off that Jim and my wife were playing around together. How was I to know? And last night when I followed them out to the park, it looked bad. You've got to admit it looked bad. I lost my head."

"There's no hard feelings, Bob," Pease said. "I'd of done the same thing, if I thought somebody was playing around with my wife."

"Yeah—but I might have listened to you," Rivers said. "You tried to explain. I wouldn't listen."

"Then you know it was all right, now?" I said.

"Sure. Jim and Lil were buying me a smoking jacket for my birthday. That's why they were together Saturday. Lil wanted a man along to pick it out. And then last night they went to the park to talk about you. I jumped Jim before he had a chance to explain. Hell, Jim, I'm sorry about it."

"I've told you a hundred times it's all right," Pease said.

"I'll bet it's a load off your mind," I said. "There's nothing worse than worrying about your wife."

"I was just a damned fool," Rivers said. "I should know better than that. All the while I've been married to Lil. And Jim's my best friend. I don't know what got into me, thinking a thing like that. The guy I should of beat up is the dirty rat who told me Jim and Lil was playing around. Don't worry, he's got his coming."

"Bob," Pease said, "for God's sake, let it lay. We don't want any fuss right now."

"Sure, I know. First we get this job over with. But still he's got it coming. You just wait and see."

"It was my fault," Pease said. "I didn't want to try to swing this deal alone, from the first. I took you over to Bob's house yesterday morning, didn't I, Graham?"

"That's right," I said.

"I wanted to catch you before you went to work, Bob. I knew you had a head on your shoulders. I wanted some brains in on this. But Lil got afraid. She didn't want you in on it. So I let her talk me out of it."

"You shouldn't ought to listen to a woman, Jim," Rivers said. "You knew damned well I'd want to be cut in on a deal this big. Two million bucks!"

"Sure, Bob. But you know how a woman is. So I fixed up Graham with a room to stay in, and asked Lil to keep him in grub and whatever else he needed. Well, I went around to the room yesterday evening and he was gone, so I went to find out from Lil what happened, and you jumped me."

"Well, that's over now," Rivers said. He patted me on the shoulder. "We found you, Graham. We had a damned good hunch you'd be coming back to your office. We want to help you. Who's the girl?"

"What girl?"

"Come on, Graham. Let's try to get together. That's the only way we can ever help each other out. A little before three o'clock you came to the office and come out with a girl. Pretty good looker. You got in a taxi with her and drove off. We lost the taxi in the traffic."

"You do the driving after this if you want to, Bob," Pease said. "We didn't get started until the taxi was a block and a half ahead. And, hell, all taxis look alike. All Yellows."

"Who was the girl?" the big man asked me.

"A girl I knew before the war. She was trying to help me and they snatched her." I sketched briefly what had happened, without identifying Mary and Walt or telling where they'd gone.

"And what did you come back tonight for?"

"For what I could find. Rand can't keep this up forever without dropping something. And I had an idea about these ledgers. If he and Buster can't produce the books for these three accounts, they'll be in hot water."

"Just causing them trouble, huh? I see how you feel."

"It's more than that," I said. "If the police ever start investigating Rand, something's going to crack. However well Cora and Buster knew me, they didn't know everything. However well they coach Rand, they'll miss something. There are too many little things happen in a man's life, for another man to take over—if the police ever start digging. I just want to give them a start. I'm going to keep him in trouble until they find something."

"Pretty cute," Rivers said.

"I told you he had a head," Pease said.

Pease drove through the park and into the garage of the house I had been to the previous morning. We went upstairs. Rivers' wife was in the living room. Her eyes showed fear.

"Why don't you keep out of this?" she said. "Why don't you turn him over to the police and take the reward? You keep on and something's going to happen. I know it."

"Shut up," her husband said. He crossed to the front window and pulled the blind. "If a man listened to a woman he'd never do anything."

"Yes, and there wouldn't be any wars and there wouldn't be any trouble," she said. "That would be just too bad, wouldn't it?"

"Lil, for God's sake. I'm trying to make a stake. I can make enough on this so we'll have the world by the tail."

"Why?" she cried. "Why? You're doing all right. You've got a business. You're making good money. We've got some put away and we've got everything we need. What for?"

"Oh, for Christ's sake," he said. "Look, will you leave me alone? Do you mind? Now, will you get out of here and let me be?"

"I'm just trying to help you, Bob. You and Jim. I don't want you to get in trouble."

"Just scram. That will help us a lot."

Lil put her hands to her face and was crying when she went out.

"There's a woman for you," Rivers said. "The very idea of picking up a couple of million bucks breaks her little heart."

"Well, I can see her point," Pease said. "She don't want anything to happen to you, Bob. You ought to be glad she's that way, instead of the other."

"Sure. I am. But it gets in your hair." He turned to me. "Well, where is it?"

"What?"

"The bonds? What do you think we're after?" His heavy face had formed a knowing smile.

I said, "You're talking to the wrong guy."

"Oh, no." He shook his head slowly. "I'm talking to you—Albert Rand."

And as if that wasn't enough, I caught a quick motion from Pease behind me. As I tried to turn, Rivers grabbed my shoulders. Then something conked me from behind.

16

It was cold. Cold and damp. Very cold. I was shaking with the cold. I opened my eyes. I was lying on the floor of a room about six feet wide and eight feet long. A single light burned in the ceiling. Pipes, white with frost, were along the walls. A compressor throbbed, beating at my aching head. Meat was hanging from hooks on the ceiling; there were bins along the end wall. Pease and Rivers were sitting on a deep-freeze unit, watching me. Smoke coiled slowly around the light from their cigarettes.

They were wearing overcoats and gloves. Pease had a towel over his head and tucked under the lapels of his overcoat. Rivers wore a hunting cap with ear flaps.

I wasn't smoking, but from my breath you might have supposed I was.

"Ten degrees cooler inside," Rivers said. "How do you like our show, Rand?"

"I always wondered about that," Pease said. "Ten degrees cooler than *what?*"

"Don't get up, Rand," Rivers said. "Stay there. It's cooler on the floor."

"You've got the wrong guy," I said. I stuttered it a bit; my teeth were chattering.

"Well, think it over, Rand," Pease said. "We're in no hurry, are we, Bob?"

"I got all the time in the world," the big man said.

Pease looked around. "You know, this is pretty nice, Bob. I wish I had a walk-in like this."

"It comes in handy," Rivers said. "During the war I had all the meat I wanted."

"Run you much?"

"Not too bad. It's just so damned handy. You don't have to run down to the store every time you want a chop."

"I think I'll have one like this, no matter what it runs."

"You can have anything you want from now on."

"That's me, Bob. What I want, I get. Why worry about the price? What the hell, Bill!"

"The beauty of this," Rivers said, "it's clean. It's velvet. The old guy with the whiskers doesn't get his nick in. Figure that way, it's not two million. It's more like ten million—twenty million. It's tax-free dough. Hard money. A dollar's a dollar."

"We've still got to get rid of the bonds," Pease pointed out. "We can't do that dollar for dollar."

"So what if we only get fifty percent? That's still a half million apiece."

"I hope I'm not interrupting you millionaires," I said. "But I'm getting cold. Let's settle this thing. What makes you think I'm Rand?"

"Well, friend," Pease said, "why should we think otherwise?"

"You knew better, yesterday morning."

"A lot has happened since then."

"For instance?"

Pease looked at the big man. "Should I argue with this joker?"

"Call his bluff," Rivers advised. "Let's get this over with."

"Yesterday morning, Rand," Pease said to me, "I jumped at conclusions because I thought you'd known too much to be Rand when you dropped in on me the night before and talked about the posting machine. I was just too smart for my own good."

"But you talked with Rand on the train. And he didn't know as much as he should have, about that machine."

"I talked with *Graham* on the train," Pease corrected. "Sure, he acted a little funny. Why shouldn't he, after what had happened to him?"

"And when did you decide I was Rand?"

"Me and Jim put our heads together," Rivers said. "It don't add up any other way."

"And it adds up the right way more and more," Pease said. "Yesterday morning I didn't know all the trouble you'd gone to, to establish yourself as Graham. And me, I'd jumped to conclusions because you knew about me trying to sell you a posting machine!"

"Okay, but how *did* I know that if I was Rand?"

Pease grinned. "What the hell, Bill! The way you know the rest of it—from Buster's wife."

"Ethelene? You're nuts."

"Okay, I'm nuts. But you walked into your office this afternoon when Ethelene was there, and you walked out again with this other dame. And nobody called any cops. So Ethelene is on your side. That pink face and those glasses wouldn't fool her—and what were you doing there, anyhow? Unless Ethelene was in with you, she would have called the cops. And if you were Graham and she was with you, Rand wouldn't be taking your place there. It only adds up one way, Rand."

"I told you what happened," I said. "They snatched Mary and I—"

"I know what you told me," Pease agreed. "You're a smooth article. You talked your way out of Graham's house in the first place, when your deal didn't work. You talked yourself away from the cop. You talked yourself away from me twice. But you're not going to talk yourself out of this."

"All we want to hear out of you," Rivers said, "is where the bonds are."

"And never mind the song and dance," Pease advised. "If you were Graham, you would have gone to the cops. That's what any guy in his fix would have done. Instead, you ate some strawberries to puff your face—"

"It was poison oak," I said.

"Okay, it was poison oak. What's the difference? You changed your face for a week or two when your first try fell through. And we knew damned well you'd make another try. That's why we got the office across the hall, for when you did. You're not dumb, Rand. Maybe you figured it this way from the first. It's pretty cute. You wait until the cops have made damned sure that Graham is really Graham. And then you bop him some dark night and step into his place."

"That is cute," Rivers agreed. "And meanwhile you're doing your homework. Taking the books home at night so when you step into Graham's place you'll know all about his business."

"What about Buster?" I said. "What about Cora? What about Bill Meadows?"

"What about them?" Pease said. "Maybe more than Ethelene is in this with you. Maybe they all are. That don't change anything. You're setting Graham up for the kill. Who's in it with you, I don't even give a damn. You're the guy with the hairy ears."

"Yeah," Rivers said. "You're the guy who can put his hands on those bonds."

"We're going to have them, Rand," Pease said. "If you want to lay there and get pneumonia, that's your business. We've got all the time in the world."

"You can't take it with you," Rivers said. "Jim, see if that coffee's perked. It's chilly in here."

Pease opened the heavy door and went out. He came back in with a pot of coffee and two cups. The warm smell of the stuff was like a breath of heaven. I saw the woman's face at the door as he pulled it shut. Pease poured the coffee and the men cradled the hot cups in their gloved hands as they sipped.

"Give me some of that," I said. "I'll tell you where the bonds are."

"Now you're talking," Rivers said.

Pease got another cup. "We'll call this," he said, pouring, "the million-dollar cup of coffee."

"Cheap at the price," I said. I gulped it down. It warmed me inside, but I shook worse. "Do we have to stay in here?"

Then I tried to grab a leg of lamb hanging from a hook. It was hard as rock and would have made a club. But my fingers were stiff and they slipped along the cold surface instead of tearing the string loose from the hook. Pease hit me with the coffee pot and then Rivers began slugging me. When I went down he kicked me until Pease said, "For Christ sake, Bob, don't kill him. Not yet."

Pease pulled the big man away. They sat on the deep-freeze. "Thanks, Jim," Rivers said. "I've got to watch my temper. I don't know what gets into me when I get sore."

"You shouldn't of done that, Rand," Pease said to me.

"It was a poor idea," I agreed.

"Well, like I said, we got all the time in the world."

"I'm sorry, Rand," the big man said. "I didn't mean to mess you up. I've got nothing against you. But you shouldn't of done that."

"The bonds," I said, "are in a locker at the S. P. station. Third and Townsend."

"Locker?" Pease asked.

"One of those where you put a dime in and take away the key."

Rivers got off the deep-freeze and began going through my pockets.

"I searched his pockets," Pease said.

"It won't hurt to look again."

"I'll show you where the key is," I said.

"You'll tell us," Pease said.

"You'd never find it. I'll have to show you."

"Like hell. We're not going to walk into anything. You'll tell us."

"All right. The key is in the office. The Cox and Graham office. Have you been in there?"

"No."

"There's a front room and a back room. In the back room there's a table with a posting machine on it. Under the right front leg of the table there's a crack in the floor. The key is in that crack."

"Pretty cute," Rivers said.

"Okay," I said, "you've got what you want. Let me out of here."

"We haven't got it yet," Pease said. "And, friend, it had better be there. What's the number of that locker?"

"Five sixty-three."

"Five sixty-three. You stick with him, Bob, while I find out."

"Maybe I'd better go with you," Rivers said.

The two men regarded each other. Neither wanted the other to go for that key.

"How the hell are we going to work this?" Pease said. "We can't leave him here alone, and I don't want him along. I'll tell you, Bob, Lil can go with me. We'll phone you if the key's there."

"Sure," the big man said, relieved. "You and Lil go." He lifted me to my feet. "No use you catching your death of cold while we're waiting."

He took me into the living room. I relaxed on the sofa, drinking in the warmth. My body shook all over, tearing at my ribs where he'd been kicking. From the garage below we heard the car back out and whine away. Rivers got a bottle from a sideboard and poured me a shot of whiskey. It helped.

"This is a hell of a messy business," he said.

I said, "What a man won't do for money!"

"Funny, isn't it?" he said. "Look at me and Jim. Honest, steady—not perfect but as good as the next man. Something like this comes up, and where the hell are you?"

"You'll get the reward, anyhow," I said.

He frowned. "What?"

"You'd better take a shot of that whiskey. You'll need it."

"I don't drink; that's for guests. What do you mean?"

"Jim Pease has got the key," I said.

"Him and Lil," he said. "She went with him."

"He's got the key," I said. "He searched me. I had it in this vest pocket. Do you think I'd leave it in the office, you dumb fool?"

He grabbed the front of my coat and raised me up, his other hand poised in a fist.

"Go ahead," I said. "Beat my brains out. That won't get you the bonds."

"What are you telling me?" he said. "Damn you, let's have it."

"They've gone off together," I said. "You big oaf, can't you see it? He's been two-timing you for six years. Have you seen the room?"

"What room?"

"The room they took me to yesterday. How do you think he found a room for me so easily? A place where nobody would ask questions? It's *their* room. Do you want to go with me? Should I show you the room, with her stuff in it, with her black silk nightgown in the closet? Do you want me to take you there? Go ahead, sock me. That's all that's left for you. He's got the key. He suggested that she go along and leave you holding the bag. Do you remember going deer hunting with him? Did you ever glance around to see him with his sights on you? He would have done away with you years ago if he'd had the guts. Sock me, if it'll make you feel better. You've got me. You can take the reward. But he's got the bonds and your wife."

The fist came open. He grabbed me by the shoulders, squeezing, shaking me. "I'll bust you in two." He hurried me to the cold room, shoved me, and slammed the door behind me.

I counted fifty and then tried the door handle. I couldn't move it; it had been fastened from the outside.

I flipped off the switch of the compressor. Not that the room would warm up in the time I had. I tried the door handle again, and gave it up.

Then I saw the meat saw and cleaver hanging on a nail in the wall. It was a heavy butcher's cleaver and I went to work on the door. It would keep me warm, anyhow.

I hacked through a layer of flooring boards composing the inner surface of the door and found a four-inch layer of rock wool. I pulled this out and hacked at the next layer of wood. When I had a hole through this I reached through and felt for the latch. Rivers had padlocked it. There was nothing to do but cut my way out, hoping the neighbors wouldn't call the cops and that I had time.

I was crawling through the hole in the door when the phone rang. I went to the front room and picked it up.

"Bob?" Pease's voice said.

"Yes, Jim."

"The key ain't here."

"Try Jell-O with its six delicious flavors."

"Say, who is this?"

I hung up and got out of there.

17

Saturday morning. And I was stiff. Every time I moved, a hook caught my rib on the left side. I didn't try to move too much. I stayed in bed until ten-thirty, got up and made coffee, drank a cup and decided I wasn't mortally wounded.

I'd stayed in Mary's apartment. I washed, dressed, and after taking a look out the front window went across to the drugstore and spent my lone nickel for a paper. Back in the apartment I fixed breakfast—using the last egg—and looked over the news.

The Switch Case had been demoted to the bottom of page one; the story was a rehash of what had already been said. On page three I found an account of a brawl in an office building on Mission Street. Police had arrested James Pease, Robert Rivers, and Rivers' wife Lillian, on a charge of disturbing the peace. It seems there had been what the paper called a "love triangle." Pease had been hospitalized. His wife said she'd stick by him. Pease admitted that the attack on him in the park the previous evening had been by Rivers. Mrs. Rivers had declared she loved her husband dearly and didn't know why he did it. Rivers had made no comment. And there was no mention of either me or my shadow.

Money. I'd promised to send money to Mary and Walt. Well, why not? I still had my voice. I could still write my name. I took out my checkbook, made out eight checks to C. Bramwell Greene for $73.45 each, and signed them Charles Graham. It would be a pleasure. A downright pleasure.

Albert Rand was sitting on two million dollars' worth of bonds. But he couldn't cash them. Not right away. Every newspaper in the land had carried their serial numbers. Those bonds were hot. Rand would have a plan for disposing of them. Of course he would. But it would take time. He'd have to let them cool off. And, meanwhile, it would be such a pleasure to make him finance me.

He was going to find out that Cora came high. And that money didn't grow on bushes. In stepping into my shoes he had taken over my bank account. That account now held, according to my check stubs, exactly $58.16. On Tuesday $54.10 of that was due for the monthly payment of my house. Leaving him a total of $2.06 to his name until the company accounts paid up at the end of the month. Cora was always right up to the penny; she'd probably have that $2.06 earmarked.

Yes, Rand was going to be horribly embarrassed to find his account overdrawn several hundred dollars. He couldn't claim forgery—that would indicate two people could write the name of Charles Graham equally well, and, in fact, the signature on those rubber checks could be proved genuine if it came to a showdown, while his own imitation might not stand up. On top of that, three sets of books were missing, and I hardly believed Rivers or Pease would bother returning them.

It could just be, I thought, that these two things might start people wondering. At least they'd think it was mighty funny, this guy Charles Graham doing things like that. He never used to. And somebody might pop up with the idea—he's not acting the same, I wonder if he *is* the same? Could be.

I dialed the Lock Drug, one of our Tuesday accounts. That is, if I could still consider myself a member of Cox and Graham, the Cogram System.

"Lock Drug. Mr. Lock speaking."

"Hello, Ned. This is Chick Graham. How are you?"

"Say, Chick, I've been reading about *you*."

"Don't believe all you see in the papers."

"Isn't it the damnedest thing you ever heard of?"

"You're telling me."

"They haven't got the guy yet?"

"I wish they would. I don't like it, him around. Why I called, Ned, there's a man here in the office and I'm giving him a check. I bank up in Redwood and I wondered if you'd cash it as a big favor? He's up from San Carlos and he's got shopping to do."

"I might, Chick, if it's any good."

"Pure rubber. I don't want to run you short, but I'd appreciate it. It's for $73.45."

"That's all right. I'm going over to the bank anyhow."

"Thanks a million, Ned. His name is Greene. C. Bramwell Greene. He'll be right over." I lowered my voice, as if Greene were in the room. "He's got identification, but you'll know the guy—reddest face you ever saw in your life."

Lock chuckled. "Okay, Chick."

I made seven more phone calls of similar nature, then walked to the Lock Drug and cashed the check, endorsing it with a stylized backhand. Lock didn't give me a second glance. It was a cinch.

"Got a match, Chick?"

I don't know how long it takes to learn how to be careful walking out a door. Before me on the street was a tall man wearing a leather zipper jacket. An unlighted cigarette was between his lips. It was Bill Meadows. One hand idly fondled the pointed ears of a big Doberman Pinscher which watched me alertly.

I got out a book of paper matches. Bill Meadows made no motion to take it. The unlighted cigarette bobbled as he spoke.

"You are Chick Graham? I wouldn't want to be fooled a second time."

"Make a guess."

"I'm surprised at you, Chick, trying to cash a check. That's not up to par. You've been pretty quick in the head, up until now. That was

cute, playing Rand the other night with Curly and Dolly. And you
even took me in. But this check business, I'm amazed at you, Chick."

"We all make a slip now and then," I said.

He glanced down at the Doberman. "Chick, I want you to meet
Tige. Tige is quite a dog. You know I can train dogs, Chick. I trained
those chows, and chows are tough to train. Tige, now, he's really a
dog. I like Tige. He's almost human. What I do, Chick, I tell him two
words. I already told him one, so he's ready. When I say the other
word, he'll tear your throat out. It's just a common word. He's listening
for it now. He'll be listening for it a month from now, waiting for that
other word. I could put it in a sentence like this while I'm talking to
you. If he hears that word he'll kill you. And he's already got the
other word, so he'll kill you if you try to make a break. If you even
move fast he might jump you. And, once he jumps you nothing in the
world will get him off until you're dead, except another word that
just Tige and me know."

"I could have guessed that," I said.

The cigarette gave a little flip toward his Ford parked at a fire
plug. "Give you a lift?"

"No argument," I said.

As we crossed to the Ford a motor cop pulled up, leaned his bike on
the stand, got out his little book, moving with that exaggerated
nonchalance of motor cops at such times.

"This your car?"

"Could be," the tall man admitted.

The motor cop poked his head through the window to look at the
certificate on the steering column.

"Easy," Bill Meadows said.

The cop froze in an awkward position, looking sidewise at the big
dog. "Hey, now," he said cautiously. "Wait a minute here."

"He's all right, officer," Bill Meadows said. "But you shouldn't ought
to go poking your head in my car that way without telling me first.
He knows it's his car."

The cop carefully withdrew his head. "Look," he said plaintively,
"you're parked at a fire plug."

"It was only for a minute. I seen my friend here walking by. I
stopped to give him a lift. It hasn't been a minute."

"Yeah, but I got my job to do like anybody else. I let you get by with
it, and there's somebody else. What if there was a fire?"

"You're right, officer. We're just getting in to leave."

"Well, okay." The cop got on his bike, watching the dog. He glanced back at it as he gunned away.

Bill Meadows grinned. "Nothing like a good dog to command respect." We got in. The Doberman sprang into the back seat. I could feel its watchful eyes on the back of my neck. The tall man made a right turn, drove to Tenth and turned left into the 101. "I never have no trouble with cops, with Tige along. Or with anybody else. Nobody ever gets tough with me."

"You've got a way with dogs," I said. "We bought that pup from you—Jiggs. There were two males in that litter. The dog that jumped me at the house was the other male."

"Could be, Chick. You don't mind if I call you Chick? I've heard so much about you."

"Let's not be formal, Bill. You trained Jiggs' brother for Rand. Maybe you took the dog down to L. A. occasionally so Rand and the dog would know each other."

"Could be. Say, what did you do to your face?"

"Poison oak."

"Say, that's pretty smart. I like that. You're a pretty smooth article, Chick. But I'm surprised at you, trying to cash a check. That wasn't up to par. You might have known we would notify everybody to give the office a ring if somebody tried to cash a check. So Lock phoned us to check and Buster told him, sure, we'd just called, and go ahead and cash it. And I went down to meet you. We had that figured out but we never expected you to try it. We didn't think you'd be that dumb. You slipped up that time."

"You've established the point," I said testily. "Drop it."

He shook his head slowly. "But that poison oak deal, that's a honey. I'll remember that. You hardly look human. When I tagged Walt to that drugstore yesterday I took a look at the guy sitting at the counter, but I didn't tumble until it was too late."

"Not much too late," I said, remembering the dog's fangs against the window as I slipped into the green Chevrolet. "If you didn't tumble, why did you stay there? Why didn't you keep following Walt when he left the drugstore?"

"Could be it was that little leather case he left beside your coffee cup."

"I didn't need a shave *that* bad."

"I didn't tumble, but you can't fool old Tige." Bill reached back to pat the dog. "When he got your scent it didn't matter to me what your face looked like. Or whether you had any. You sure made a fast dive into that Chevvy."

"If your dog's so smart," I said, "why didn't it know I wasn't Rand Wednesday night when I walked out of Curly's house with the baby?"

"Tige knew who you was, all right, but he didn't know the score. He hadn't been put on your trail yet. I hadn't given him the word. You almost got me in bad that night, Chick. Why, if I'd left that baby on a doorstep there would have been hell popping. Say, how did you get out of that apartment night before last?"

"What apartment?"

"You was there all right, Chick. With Mary Davis and her brother. Can't fool old Tige. He was on watch all night, and I slept in the car. Next morning Buster was on deck to identify the Davis girl—you used to carry her picture in the Army. The big guy with her had to be her brother Walt. Buster tailed them, and I hung around the front door until somebody else came out and then I went in before the door closed. I worked the apartment latch with my pocket knife and the place was empty. How did you get out? The dog was on watch every minute. Over the roof?"

"Sure," I said. "There's a skylight."

He reached back to pat the dog. "Figured it that way. You couldn't of got past Tige any other way. No, sir. There's a dog. Oh, by the way, Chick, what did you do with those three ledgers?"

"What ledgers?"

"Rand is sore about that. You trying to make trouble for him."

"He's got a right to be," I said. "He never made any trouble for me, did he?"

Bill grinned. "There's a smart lad, Chick. You're up against some smooth characters in this deal."

"You hate yourself."

He chuckled softly. "I wasn't including myself in on that one. I don't claim to be smooth. I'm just a country boy trying to get along as best I can with what few brains I've got. But the rest of them—they're a crew, Chick. That wife of yours is nobody's fool. Buster will do until a brighter boy comes along. Ethelene has got plenty upstairs. But, now, you take Rand, it's a privilege to work with a guy like that. He's one smooth article."

"He might be too smooth for your own good."

"I can take care of myself."

"Curly thought that, too."

"Could be I'm protected."

"I'd make sure of that."

"Maybe I'm no whiz on the deep strategy stuff, Chick. But if you put a piece of bread five hundred yards away I'll tell you with the naked eye which side has got the butter on it. Oh, yes."

"You might be sorry."

"Don't try to plant cruel suspicion in my little mind, Chick. Say, do you wear a shoe that big, a guy your size?"

"They're Walt's."

He reached back again to pat the dog. "So that's why Tige didn't pick up your scent outside the drugstore. I wondered about that. Good old Tige. You can always depend on a dog."

"What happened to my dog—Jiggs?"

"Your dog? Well, Chick, it was a shame, a fine dog like that. But we could hardly afford to have two of them looking alike and answering to the same name. It was a shame, Chick, but we just couldn't afford it."

I called him a name.

He said, "He didn't suffer. I got a soft spot for dogs. A little cyanide gas in a box; they don't suffer."

I called him another name.

He shook his head slowly. "After all that's hit you, what you get sore about is your dog. Not a word about that pretty bitch of a wife and her brother, building you up for the kill. You get sore about a dog."

"Jiggs is the only one out of the lot *worth* getting sore about. Two million bucks didn't mean a thing to Jiggs. You couldn't buy him with a stack of T-bone steaks as big as a house."

"Yeah, I know what you mean. I feel that way about a dog myself. There's nothing like a good dog, Chick." We were coming down the grade into South City. Bill parked at a bar fronting the highway. "Excuse me while I make a phone call. Be right back."

He went inside, leaving me in the car with the Doberman. Out of confidence or sheer impudence, he even left the ignition key in the lock. I didn't try to slide over into the driver's seat. I didn't so much as lay a finger on the door handle. I had a healthy respect for that big dog. My respect matched Bill's confidence.

In about ten minutes the tall man came out with liquor on his breath mixed with clove. He drove through the underpass with the stream of traffic and onto the freeway. Ahead to the left was the airport from which Walt and Mary had taken off yesterday afternoon. They were out of it, anyhow.

Bill Meadows spoke musingly. "I know how you feel about a dog. I hated to do it to Jiggs, but Rand was standing over me. I'm that way myself about a dog. Dogs are my business. With a good dog what you've got is safer than in a bank vault. Train him right and nobody will poison him. He'll starve to death before he'll take a mouthful of food from anybody else. A dog can't be bluffed. They ain't afraid of a weapon. You can depend on a dog. People, now—well, it takes all kinds to make a world. The hard ones get along so good because us soft chumps are such easy pickings."

"Us soft chumps? You're including yourself?"

He shrugged. "I'm doing my share for peanuts."

"Why?"

"Oh, it's interesting work. And like Rand says, I'm not really contributing anything. I just do what I'm told."

"There's fifteen thousand reward. That's not peanuts."

He grinned, shaking his head. "We're all in this, Chick. You know that. As the saying goes, we'll hang together or hang separately."

"One thing I can't figure, Bill. Wednesday night Rand called the cops. He insisted that the cop take me in. But from then on none of you have wanted the police to get me. I can't figure that."

"Well, you'll have a little time to figure on that one," Bill Meadows said. "What are you worried about answers for? Who are you going to tell them to?" And he lapsed into silence.

18

At Palo Alto he turned left off the Bayshore. His place was on the flat near the bay, about two acres, surrounded by a high hedge of Catalina cherry grown with poison oak, and planted too thickly with walnuts and acacias. The house was of the novelty rustic period, painted yellow, with a low-pitched, tar-and-gravel roof. The kennels made a horseshoe out behind.

The dogs set up a clamor as we drove in. Bill had me wait outside the kennels, the Doberman at my heels, while he put feed in the pens. He had bull terriers, great Danes, chows and cockers. Beautiful dogs, except that I never could see anything beautiful about a chow. Or, right then, a Doberman.

When he'd tended the dogs we went inside the house. It was a shabby place, the overstuffed set in the front room lumpy, the rug threadbare, a fan of red crepe paper stuck in a fireplace whose smoked front showed it had been made wrong.

"Just a living," he said, noticing my look around. "That's why I'm in on this deal. I'm not getting any younger. I got to look ahead. Take the weight off your feet."

He went into the kitchen and came back with glasses. He poured drinks from a bottle he got from behind some books on the shelves built alongside the fireplace. "You'll be all right anywhere in the house, but don't try to go outside without telling me. And don't try to feed that dog. Here's how."

"Mud in your eye." The liquor was vile. "Why do you keep chows?"

"Chows? People buy chows. I'm in business."

"That's one dog I've got no use for. A chow would just as soon jump you as look at you."

"A lot of people like a dog that's not a pushover for anybody who pats him on the head."

"I'd hate to stumble and fall in that chow pen when they're hungry."

Bill Meadows paused in the act of pouring himself a slug. "Would you?" he asked softly. He began pouring one for me. "Say when."

I let him pour a stiff one. I needed it.

The dogs out back began barking. Bill peered out the shade of a front window, then moved very fast. He hid the bottle behind the books and ran into the kitchen with the glasses. He came back chewing a clove Life Saver, and tossed one to me.

"It's the wife. Not that I hit the bottle. I can take it or leave it alone. But I like a little celebration now and then, and I've been under a strain."

His wife came in. She was a square-faced woman with a wide mouth and large teeth and a mop of frizzled copper hair that looked like the frayed end of a telephone cable.

She looked at me steadily. "This ain't him, is it?"

"It's him."

"He don't look too much like Rand."

"He's got poison oak. He does otherwise."

"Maybe. He's got the same ears. Thank goodness this mess is over. Maybe now I can use the car once in a while. Me hoofing around town after groceries, walking from the bus. Had lunch?"

"I ain't hungry."

"Let me smell your breath." She did. "I thought so. You've been drinking."

"I had one small shot on the way down," he said. "Ain't that right, Chick?"

"That's right," I said.

"You better eat something," she said to him. "I would of had some lunch ready, but how did I know when you'd be back? I was over next door visiting. Over to the Webbs. That baby's getting cuter every day, the little rascal. I'll fix it and you better eat it." And to me: "I don't care, but if he drinks he don't eat. And thin as a rail. There ain't any vitamins in liquor."

We had lunch, then whiled away the afternoon playing sluff. It was getting dusk when a car drove in. A young couple wanted a cocker pup. Bill went out to the kennels with them.

"Guess I'd better fix supper," the woman said.

I followed her to the kitchen, the Doberman at my heels. "What's your end of this?"

"Look around you," she said. "We're not getting anywhere. I want to get Bill out of the dog business. He'll never make anything at it. I don't know how many times he's turned down a good sale because he didn't like the looks of the people. If he don't think the people will give the dog a good home, he won't sell them one. He's too soft-hearted about dogs. Somebody who likes dogs and will give them a good home, Bill will practically give them one. That's no way to do business. I tell him, let me handle the business part and we'd get along okay. He's just too soft-hearted about dogs. I want to get him out of it. What I want, with a little capital we got a chance to buy into a highway spot—dinners and drinks. It's a gold mine. A person's got to look ahead. We're not getting any younger."

"You're sure of getting this capital?"

Her large teeth flashed. "Oh, yes."

"Curly thought he had a cinch, too."

"We'll get ours, don't worry. Rand won't get funny with us."

"And something for your old age, maybe."

She looked at me narrowly. "I didn't say that."

"You don't have to. You're taking a cut because of what you know. Getting it won't make you forget. Something for your old age. If you have one."

Her square face hardened. "We're protected. Why don't you go in the front room and let me fix supper?"

About a half hour after we'd eaten, the dogs out back set up a clamor as a car drove in. The Doberman watching me was unnatural. It had never made a sound.

Buster and Ethelene came in. Ethelene's hand touched her stomach, where I'd hit her, at sight of me. Buster gave me a searching glance and then averted his eyes. He sat on the lumpy couch, his moon face showing some embarrassment.

"What in the world happened to you, Chick?" Ethelene asked. "What happened to your face?"

"Poison oak."

"You look like you've been boiled."

"How did you get away from that cop the other night?" Buster asked. "You sure gummed up the works. He never quite explained that."

I said, "He was my brother."

"Okay, okay."

"Leave him alone, Buster," Ethelene said. "You know how he feels. Leave him alone."

"Sure, I know how he feels. How the hell do you think *I* feel?" he cried. "We knock ourselves out on this deal. We eat it and sleep it. Hell, I can't hardly remember back far enough when we weren't working on this deal. And this dumb cluck talks himself away from the cop and gums it up. I know how *he* feels!"

"If this dog wasn't sitting on my feet," I said, "I'd give you a rough idea of how I feel."

"Take it easy, boys," Bill Meadows said. He turned to his wife. "How about it, Bess? This is an occasion."

"All right. But I'll fix them. And nurse yours along because you'll only get three all evening."

"I'll watch to see I get full measure." Bill went out with his wife and Buster followed along, pouting with innocent fury at the outrage I had perpetrated by spoiling his plan temporarily. Ethelene remained with me and the Doberman in the front room. She couldn't meet my eye.

"Why feel bad?" I said. "You gave me my chance and I didn't take it."

A number of times Ethelene had been a bit cozy with me at the office while Buster was out. I hadn't followed through.

"I didn't give you your chance," she said dully. "I was just lonely, and sorry for you. I wish things could have been different, Chick. I ought to be glad what happens to you, the way you socked me in the belly yesterday afternoon. But maybe I had it coming."

"I often wondered why you and Buster stuck together. Going to leave him now it's over?"

She shrugged. "It's not over. The thing has only started. It will be years before they quit this case. They'll have you but they won't have the bonds. They'll keep on working."

"I think you'll earn that money," I said.

"We'll earn it, all right."

"None of you trusts the others. You've each proved what you'll do for money. Each one is scheming to cross the others."

"Let's not go into that."

"Okay. If you don't want to think about it tonight, there will be plenty of other nights."

"Once you're in it there's no out," she said. "You can't stop or go back. Sometimes I wish I was—well, what I'm supposed to be. Just the wife of a guy trying to get ahead in a small business. This is like a nightmare. And it comes every night. It's like having your life on number twelve and the little ball spinning. All those other numbers, and you've got everything on number twelve. Then the ball hits number twelve. But that's not the end. It's got to spin again. The ball will always be spinning around the wheel, with your life at stake."

"Thank God I'm honest," I said. "How are you going to get rid of the bonds?"

"Let's not talk about it, Chick. It's foolproof. Everything is foolproof. One foolproof thing leading to another. On and on. Always a hundred percent foolproof. It has to be. If you're only ninety-nine percent foolproof, that's all, brother."

"I'm glad to see you're happy," I said.

"Chick, you dope. You poor sweet dope. You're a square guy. Why does it have to happen to you?"

The others came in, and Bill's wife served drinks. They talked together about the small things people know in common, leaving me out of the conversation. The Doberman, sleek and deadly, lay at my feet with one clipped ear cocked. I had the yen to kick him in the ribs. It was the sort of impulse you get to jump off a high building. You never do it, but the idea comes.

The dogs out back began barking. Cora came in, followed by the man with my face.

"Hello, pal," Rand said to me. "You've been giving us a bad time."

"That's a shame," I said.

Cora hadn't looked at me. "We went to a show," she said, "and slipped out during a heavy love scene. No, I'll keep it on," she told Bill's wife as the woman offered to take her coat. "I'm cold through. I don't think I'll ever warm up until the heat's off."

"That's good," Buster said, and laughed.

"Shut up," Rand snapped. "You didn't come straight here, did you?"

"Nobody followed us," Buster said. "I came down El Camino and then drove around San Mateo and cut over to Bayshore."

"Okay. We've got to play it safe. The cops have got to keep busy. The heat won't be off until they get him." He indicated me. "What's wrong with him? What happened to his face?"

"Poison oak," Bill Meadows said.

Rand asked me, "How long will it take before you begin to look human?"

"I've got my pockets full of the leaves," I said. "I rub them on my face every day."

"See he's taken care of," Rand said to Bill Meadows. "We've got to clear that up."

"Why?" I asked.

"You'll answer, pal," Rand said, "when somebody talks to you."

It was a bit strange, seeing my face hard like that, tough talk coming from my lips. It just goes to show there's nothing in physiognomy.

I said, "You'd better treat me nice. Maybe I'll kill myself before my face clears up. Then where will you be? Or what if I go out to that chow kennel and stick my hands inside and rag those chows? Then where's your fingerprints?"

"Chick!" Cora cried, looking at me directly the first time.

"He won't do it," Rand said. Bill's wife brought in drinks for Rand and Cora. Rand gulped his highball, handed back the glass. "Straight for me the next time, Bess. He won't do it, because a man always hopes."

"You don't know what I'll do!" I yelled. "You've done this to me, and by God, I'll get back at you!"

"Listen to him, would you. Somebody must have been feeding him raw meat."

Buster said, "It's our own damned fault. We had him. I still think we made a mistake Wednesday night. He walked in, the deal was set. We had him. We should have let the dog finish him."

Rand turned on him with withering contempt. "And that's all out of you, you dumb fool. Don't you get it *yet?* People don't let a dog kill a man for no reason except that he walks into their house. You're still acting, for Christ's sake! You've got to believe it. You've got to live it. Never a doubt in the back of your mind. *I* am Charles Graham. *He* is Albert Rand. Get that now and nail it down. Act like a normal human with that belief. The plan was perfect, except he talked himself away from that dumb copper. If the cop had taken him in …"

Rand shrugged, and took a glass of whiskey Bill's wife had brought in. He threw it off and began pacing up and down. "Okay, we've got him again. We've got him for keeps. All we've got to do is sit on him until we're ready again."

"We've got him," Buster said. "So why not close the deal tonight?"

"That's what I need," Rand said. "That's all I need. Some more good advice out of you guys."

"Well, why not?" Bill Meadows asked.

"Good," Rand said. "You're asking. That's something. You're not just going ahead, like you did Wednesday night. You guys have got to see that a plan isn't cast-iron. If a thing works, okay. But if one part of it don't work, then you can't go on with the rest. Bill, you damned near got our neck in the wringer. If you'd left that damned baby on the doorstep of a house— And what the hell do you suppose I had Curly and Dolly up here for? I could have got rid of them down there. I got them up here in case anything went wrong. Something did go wrong and you still put the chows on them, just like everything had gone off. Now let's get together here."

"What's that got to do with closing the deal tonight?" Buster said. "As long as he's loose, we don't know what the cops are digging into. We don't know how close they're getting. Once they've got him, they'll quit looking. They'll quit digging for Albert Rand. We're sitting on a powder keg and I don't like it."

"Do you think I like it?" Rand snarled. "We've got to be sure, this time. One more dumb play and it's our necks."

"What's the difference what his face looks like?" Buster said. "Anybody can get poison oak. They'll identify his body by the fingerprints, and the heat's off us. And the quicker the sooner."

Rand raised his hands in an imploring gesture of suffering despair. "Listen to the man. He wants to go to the San Quentin gas chamber. I've got to argue with him. I've got to plead. I've got to beg him not to go to the gas chamber!"

"You don't have to treat me like that," Buster said.

"Then act like you've got good sense. We've got to work together. Let's not have any more fool impulses. Bill almost got us in the soup yesterday, putting the dog on him at the drugstore."

"I was surprised, him with his red face," Bill explained. "I didn't stop to think."

"It's time somebody stopped to think," Rand stated. "We're all going to do some solid thinking. This time it's got to go through without a hitch."

Buster said, "But as long as he's alive, we won't know—"

"I know, I know, I *know!*" Rand cried. "Don't you think I know we're walking on eggs? But it's not as simple as it was Wednesday night. Now he's had time to think it out. Now he knows what's what. Now he's had time to tell his story to people. You dumb fool! If the police found his body tonight, what would happen? How long would it take Mary Davis and her brother to run to the cops and spill the whole thing?"

"Okay," Buster said. "And what can they prove?"

"What can they prove? What have we been sitting on pins for since he got away Wednesday night? You just let the cops start looking in the right direction, and you'll find out what they can prove! We've got to close the deal this time and button it up without any *doubt*. We've got to nail it shut and bend over the nails on it." He turned to me. "Okay, pal, where are those books you took last night?"

"What books?"

"Where is the Davis girl and her brother?"

"Don't you have the address?"

"Like that, huh?"

"Something like that."

"Buster, you take the girls to the house. It looks like this monkey has got to be worked on."

Cora's face showed horror. Ethelene took her arm and began moving to the door.

"How long will it take?" Buster asked.

"I don't care how long it takes. We'll get it out of him if it takes all night."

"I'm the dumb one," Buster said acidly. "How smart is that? You're supposed to be at a movie tonight. What if the cops drop around to have a chat, and you're not there all night?"

"All right, all right," Rand snapped. And to me: "Look, pal, don't think you're not going to do what we want you to. You'll either do it nice, or you'll do it the hard way. Think it over.... Bill, tomorrow's Sunday. Me and Cora will go to the beach for the day. We'll circle around and drop by here about ten, and go to work on him."

"Okay, Bert," Bill Meadows said.

Rand stiffened. *"What did you call me?"* He shoved his face close to Bill Meadows'. "You dumb fool! One slip like that when the heat's on can queer the whole deal!" He controlled himself with an effort. "Let's get out of here before I go nuts. Buster, you and Ethelene drive down to Mountain View, then cut across to El Camino and come up to the place and drop in. We were out earlier, so you took a drive down the Peninsula and stopped by on the way back.... You can handle him okay, Bill?"

Bill Meadows nodded at the Doberman. "Me and my helper."

Cora said, "I'd like a word with Chick."

"Well?" Rand asked.

"I don't mean you."

"Oh, with *Chick*. What do you want to say to him?"

"That's my business."

Rand grabbed her arm. "And it's mine too, baby."

Her chin came up. "Take your hands off me. I married the guy. I lived with him. And I'm going to say goodbye."

19

Rand smiled thinly. It was fascinating, watching the play of emotions in that face identical to mine. It was seeing myself as others saw me. And somewhat disconcerting, those ears from the back. Just as well a mirror gives a man a limited view of himself.

"Okay, baby. Kiss him goodbye. But make it snappy."

They all went out. Cora looked at me with tenderness, her eyes filled with tears.

"You're looking bad," I said. "You must be under a strain."

"Chick, I ... don't know what to say."

"It was nice knowing you, Mrs. Graham."

"It might have been different. If we had it to do over again ..."

"We can try it in the next world, the right way."

"Chick, you're the swellest guy I ever knew. And I had to do it to you. Don't think I like it. It's something that when you start you can't stop."

"I don't think your new husband will wear too well."

"Him?" Her lip curled. "He'd better not touch me. I'll pull out when things settle down."

"Does two million dollars ever settle down?"

Fear showed in her beautiful eyes. Fear had ridden the faces and the voices of everyone in the room. It seemed to me that, curiously enough, I had been more at ease than anybody else.

"Cora, you're going to earn that money."

"I guess so. I guess you're right, Chick."

Rand poked his head in the door. I'll never get used to seeing my face appear like that. "Let's go. Let's go. Kiss him goodbye." He ducked out.

"I guess I won't see you again," Cora said.

"Good luck, kid. You'll need a lot of it."

"Oh, Chick, I don't—" Her voice broke and she began crying into her hands. I stepped over the big dog and put my arm over her shoulder. She came against me, crying on my lapel, her body shaking.

Maybe I should have slugged her, but right then I couldn't feel too bitter about Cora. She was weak. She was helpless when it came to something she wanted. I remembered that fur coat. She'd done her best to be a good wife. And if her best wasn't too good, it was nothing to get sore about. Considering her position, she had done very well. And despite herself, she'd fallen in love with me. That made it tough on her. The last thing she'd wanted was to go soft about me.

I patted her shoulder and let her bawl her flinty little heart out.

Bill and his wife came in when the cars had gone. The woman went to bed. Bill Meadows waited a few minutes, then tiptoed into the kitchen and came back with glasses. He got the bottle from behind the books, poured us equal drinks, and then with a quick twist of the wrist sweetened his. I wondered if he would get tight enough to open up. But there wasn't much left in the bottle.

"Who is this Rand guy?" I asked.

"He's you."

"Then who am I?"

He grinned. "Don't you know?"

"Save it."

"You mean his connection with Cora and Buster and Ethelene? They met on a traveling breakfast food deal. You know how it works. Hit a town, put on a demonstration in a local store, get out samples, and so on. They worked out a few small side grifts and grew into bigger things."

"Then they must have been in trouble, one time or another."

"You still underestimate Rand." Bill poured himself another drink, emptying the bottle. "When he does a job, it's done. They say genius is the capacity for taking infinite pains. That's Bert Rand. No trouble's too much for him, on a job. Nothing's too small for him to pass up."

"You seem to know a lot about him, Bill."

"Me and the wife was in charge of the breakfast food crew. That was before I went into the dog business. I hadn't seen any of them for years when Rand got connected with me just after the war ended. He needed an outside man. You've no idea how much work goes into a deal like this."

"I still don't see how they figured the whole thing out so quick from the first."

Bill tilted the bottle for the last drop, and regarded it mournfully. "I've heard that if you keep a bottle around you can get a drop a day for thirty days. I ought to try that." He put the bottle behind the red crepe paper in the fireplace and with a wink drew out a full one. He began working on it.

"They didn't figure it all out at once," he said. "It grew. When Buster bumped into you, he'd got caught up with by the Army and Rand was off somewhere hiding from the draft. Buster knew the situation had possibilities, so Cora invited you to dinner. They didn't know just what they were going to do with it, at first.

"It was a month or so before Rand showed up, just passing through. He saw right off the bat that it could be a big thing. A hell of a big thing. The only trouble was, you'd established your identity by getting into the Army. Rand saw there had to be two guys with the same face and the same name in the Army, to overcome that. It made a patriot out of him. He enlisted under your name.

"He had a quick deal cooked up. But the Army shoved him around. The way the Army does. You know. And it pushed you around, too. You went overseas and the deal fell through. I don't know just what that one was. Rand never said much about it because a man don't talk of the ones that get away.

"With you overseas and the deal snafu, Rand really showed the stuff he was made out of. Yes, sir, that lad has got the stuff. The ordinary guy in his fix, would have said to hell with it and gone AWOL. But by that time Rand had figured up a bigger deal. He just kept on working."

"Sterling character," I admitted.

"He'd met this Alexander girl, whose father was cashier of a bank. So he softened her up. When he'd get some time off he'd show up in L. A. in officer's uniform and overseas ribbon, under his own name—if his name is Rand. Hush-hush stuff. Quick secret trips from overseas. That military secret stuff went over big during the war. She couldn't write him; he wasn't allowed to get mail. He went over with a bang with her, and after the war he stepped into the job at the bank. And about that time he contacted me. It was really simple. All good things are simple. Then he just had to sit tight and wait for the right time. I don't know how many times we were all set to go, and something wasn't just right. With Rand, it's got to be right. And on this deal we could afford to wait. We could wait ten years for this one. It's the chance of a lifetime."

"Cora claimed to have a cousin in Los Angeles—Herb Cotter," I said. "That was Rand?"

"Yeah. It was a cover, if she or Buster had to make a trip to L. A."

"Where did Curly and his sister come in?"

"Curly and Dolly? I thought you talked to them. Curly knew Rand in the Army, and bumped into him in L. A., under another name and working at a bank. Curly made a good thing out of it. Rand paid him a little each month, and got it back through Curly's sister. He got his money's worth."

Bill yawned, and I deftly poured him another drink. He grinned. "You're trying to get me tight. But it's okay by me. I've been under a strain and it's going to be a mess, working on you in the morning. I like to lay in bed on a Sunday. I don't like to have to get up for a job like that."

"How does Rand know you won't cross him?"

"Now quit that," Bill reproved gently. "We're all in this together. If one of us gets nailed we'll all go through. Don't try to sow cruel suspicion in my mind, Chick. None of us could walk out of this now if we wanted to."

"What if something happened to you?"

He shook his head. "Nothing's going to happen to me, with my dogs around. Old Tige there is the best life insurance a man ever did have."

"I still don't see why you didn't put the cops on me when you knew I was in Mary's apartment."

"Still worrying about that?" Bill poured another drink. He forgot to offer me one. "I'll tell you, Chick. We had it fixed Wednesday night. You walked into your house and found Rand there. You got sore and he put the dog on you. Then he called the cops. The cop brought you back, and Rand established the fact that he was Graham and you were somebody else, which was important to fix with the cop. The cop even had your fingerprints in his notebook.

"The next part of the deal was for the cop to take you to the station. In about three minutes they would have known you were Albert Rand, the bank robber from L. A. But you see, Chick, they didn't need you alive to tell that. They could get that off the ends of your fingers. And we didn't want you shooting off your face and putting wrong ideas into the cops' heads. We didn't want you to go to jail. We didn't want you to stand trial.

"The clean, quick way was to establish the fact that you were *not* Charles Graham. The cop done that out at the house. Once that was established, the quicker we got rid of you the better. So I was waiting at the police station that night, Chick. Me and Tige. When the cop brought you in, I would just happen to be passing by. And something would happen to Tige. A sad accident, Chick. A dog like that. A kid's dog. The kindest dog in the world. But suddenly he'd go mad. What a shame! He'd jump you and I wouldn't be able to do a thing with him. I even had a gun along, to shoot my dog when it went mad. Missing a couple of times and getting you, of course, just to make sure. A dog like that. A kid's dog, going mad. Just one of those things. But after all, the victim was a bank robber and a killer anyhow. Maybe the cops would think that dog was pretty smart, after all."

"By the skin of my teeth," I said, remembering how I'd talked that red-faced cop out of taking me in.

"You've had luck," Bill admitted. He put a slight emphasis on the *had*. "So have I, in a way. You see, if it had gone off, I would of lost Tige. And I hate to sacrifice a good dog."

"A simple matter of values," I said.

"And this time it's got to be the same way," he said. "Rand will cook up something. He's a bright boy. Something quick and clean. Want to tell me where Mary Davis and her brother are at?"

"You won't get that out of me."

"Yes, we will, Chick. I hope you don't do it the hard way. You're not a bad guy. Why don't you be smart?"

"Why have you got to go after them? They can't possibly prove anything."

"But they can sing a song, Chick. They can get up on their hind legs and howl. Sure, the evidence is all against their yarn. They can't prove a thing. But you see, Chick, the cops are dumb. They wouldn't be coppers unless they were plenty dumb. They're so dumb they never know when to quit. If Mary and Walt Davis pop up with that wild story the cops might not believe it, but they're just dumb enough to go to work on it anyhow. And they might catch hold of some little thing. We can't let that happen. We're sewing it up tight."

"How do you know they've gone anywhere?"

"They telephoned the company and said they'd be gone a few days. We checked on that."

"You dumb fool!" I cried. "You keep telling me how smart Rand is. Do you think he's dumb enough to give you a split? When the time comes, he'll fix you just like he did Curly and Dolly. Or like he got Buster to fix the Alexander girl!"

"He'll wish he hadn't," Bill growled. Then he cocked an eye at me. "How did you know Buster done that job?"

"Who else? You were watching Mary's apartment that night and Rand couldn't have risked it. He had to be home playing me."

"You're a pretty smart lad, Chick. Too smart to force us to get messy in the morning."

"Why didn't you just make the girl's death look like an accident? What was the idea of my shaving kit and flashlight in the car?"

"I keep telling you, Chick—Rand is a smart customer. It's awful hard to get away with murder. Try to make it like an accident and some dumb cop is sure to pick up some little thing you've overlooked. The bright thing is to make it murder to begin with—murder that looks like somebody *tried* to make look like an accident. Plant the things for the cops to find. That shaving kit and flashlight, Chick— that clinched it for the cops. They've got it pinned on you. Rand's a smooth article. What say we hit the hay?"

"I could use some sack time," I admitted. I figured I had the details pretty well. "I'm pretty tired."

"And I'm pretty tight," Bill said grinning. "But don't get the idea you've been pumping me, Chick. I just filled in a few harmless details. The condemned man's last wish and so on. And I like to talk to people. Sure you won't change your mind? It will be messy in the morning."

20

There were two bedrooms in the house, connected by a hallway. The door of the bathroom opened off the hallway and directly across from it was the kitchen door. I had the rear bedroom. The windows were open and it was just a step to the ground. With the Doberman at my heels, I didn't make that step.

I went to the bathroom to wash up, and in the doorway remembered that Bill's wife had left a towel over the foot of my bed. I turned in the doorway, and that dog moved like a streak of light to follow me back. I paused again in the hallway outside the bedroom door, to test the dog out. It waited, pointed ears alert. I slipped quickly inside the bedroom and tried to shut the door before the dog got in. I was almost knocked off my pins as the dog hit the door and my legs at the same time. I took the towel from the bed and played the game again, at the bedroom door and the bathroom door. The dog had learned that trick in a hurry.

I wondered how far I could go with the brute. It had never growled or barked. I had an idea the first sound I would hear out of it would be the last thing I'd hear.

I waited in the bedroom an hour, sitting on the edge of the bed. It was hard to keep still. I was out of cigarettes. The dog lay at my feet, sleeping with an ear cocked. When I stood up, it was up instantly. I turned the knob of the bedroom door carefully, then jerked the door open and slipped through into the hallway. The dog hit my legs and we went through together. I switched on the hall light and listened. From the front bedroom came snores as Bill and his wife slept the sleep of the just.

I turned the knob of the bathroom door slowly. The dog's eyes were on my hand. My other hand was against the doorjamb, and I hoped the animal didn't know what that meant. I shoved the door open quickly and lunged forward until my chest struck the jamb. The dog, dashing in, half upset my balance. Then I gave all I had to the hand against the jamb, shoving myself backwards and pulling on that doorknob. The dog's toenails clawed at the tile floor as it tried to reverse. The shutting door struck the brute's hindquarters, throwing the Doberman off balance. Then I was in the hall and the dog was in the bathroom.

If I hadn't heard a sound out of that Doberman I heard it now. It wasn't a pretty sound. Immediately, too, all the dogs in the kennels out back began yelping. The Doberman fought at the door, beating against it, clawing at it, snapping, giving throat to a ravening snarl of rage and frustration.

I ran into the kitchen for some weapon. "Tige!" Bill Meadows yelled. "Tige!" And then he yelled "Feather!" and I wondered if that was his word for breaking the dog from an attack. Whatever the code, the dog kept at that door.

Bill's wife screamed, "The dog's killing him! I never did trust that dog! He's killing him!"

I grabbed a skillet off the kitchen stove. It was heavy and black, an old-fashioned cast-iron fry pan. I reached the hall door again just as Bill, running from his bedroom dressed in cheap, blue cotton pajamas, grabbed the bathroom doorknob. He didn't look around. He didn't know I wasn't inside with that mad dog. As a matter of fact, he didn't know anything, for I swung that skillet with all I had. He went down in a heap, his skinny bare legs twisted grotesquely beneath him.

The lower panel of the bathroom door was cracking under the dog's attacks. Everything was bedlam, the dogs outside yelping like mad. Bill's wife screaming from the bedroom, "Bill! Call him off! He'll kill him! I never did trust that dog!"

She appeared in the doorway of the front bedroom, saw her husband crumpled on the floor and me standing over him with a skillet, and her screams broke off with a gasp, the back of her left hand flying to her mouth. She was wearing a pink rayon housecoat and her frizzed copper hair looked like a fright wig.

"Quiet that dog!" I yelled. "Call him off!"

"Tige!" she called, moving to the bathroom door. Then she grabbed the knob, screaming, "Get him!" and I had to hit her.

She had the door shoved partly open to let the dog out at me, and it was just luck that the brute was lunging against the door from the other side and knocked it shut as the woman crumpled atop her husband. I ran to the kitchen and jerked out drawers. Silverware, kitchen knives, ash trays, string, bottle openers. No weapon that would stand up to a mad dog.

The panel of the bathroom door gave, and the slavering snarl of the Doberman was suddenly louder. As I ran that way, the head and the great impatient fangs were through the panel. The dog was working its body through, impeded somewhat by the two figures piled before the door.

I slammed the door leading from the kitchen into the hall, then raced through the kitchen and utility room behind it to the rear door just as the dog appeared around the house, having gone through a bedroom window. There was a storm door on the utility room, the bottom half of plywood and the top of screen, over which could be fitted a sash in bad weather. The sash wasn't in place now. The dog leaped for the screen and fell back. It leaped again, and once more. The screen was bulging inward, pulling loose at the bottom and one side.

I retreated to the kitchen and closed that door. It was a flimsy affair; the lower panel had been broken out sometime before, no doubt by a dog, and tacked back in place with a couple of shingle nails. The breakfast nook was built in; there was no table to put against the door. Chairs wouldn't do. I crossed to the refrigerator and was dragging it across the linoleum when the Doberman began hitting the flimsy panel of the kitchen door. The refrigerator stuck. My feet slid on the slick linoleum. The electric cord, plugged into the wall, was holding the refrigerator.

I tore the cord loose. And then I saw I didn't have time to drag the refrigerator to the door before the flimsy panel gave way. I ran into the hall, leaped the bodies on the floor, and went into the rear bedroom. I grabbed the covers from the bed.

The panel of the kitchen door shattered and the dog's toenails clicked across the room, along the hall, through the bedroom door, and then quit clicking as the brute left the floor in a lunge for my throat.

I was braced with the bedclothes hanging in front of me, my hands gripping their top edge at my chest. I still had the skillet in my right hand. I waited until the dog was in the air, its fangs rising for my neck, and then I flung the bedcovers overhead at arm's length and threw them forward. My only hope was to cover the dog, muffle it, ensnare it, fall on it.

I must have gone a little crazy for a while. I don't know how long it was before I realized the dogs outside were quiet. Bill's wife was leaning against the doorjamb, one hand feeling gingerly of her head, watching me impassively. The only sound was the dull thud of the skillet as I beat at the tangle of bedclothes.

I realized the dog beneath hadn't moved, or made a sound, for some little time.

I got up, crossed by the woman into the hall, and turned Bill Meadows over. He had a pulse, very faint, but there.

"He's dead," she said dully. "Dead and gone. Bill's dead, and what did we get out of it? All we wanted was something to get ahead on. We weren't getting any younger. Just enough to buy into a place where we wouldn't have to worry. That's all we wanted. And now he's gone and what have we got? Bill wasn't a bad man. He liked to squirrel away bottles and then he wouldn't eat. But Bill never looked at another woman. He loved dogs. You can bank on a man that loves dogs. And now he's gone."

"Just a man trying to get along and store up a little for his old age," I admitted. I didn't tell her he was alive. I grabbed her shoulder. "And I'll kill you, too. You've got it coming."

"I don't care," she said dully. "Bill's dead. I don't care what happens to me."

I grabbed the front of her housecoat and ripped the flimsy garment down the front. That woke her up. She gasped, cowering, her eyes coming alive with terror.

I leered at her. "You don't care what happens. That's fine!"

"For God's sake! Bill's there! He's lying there dead!"

"It depends on how you treat me, what will happen to you."

"What do you want?"

"Where's Jiggs—my dog?"

Her eyes shifted. "We—did away with him."

"I guess we'll have to make you sorry." I grabbed the frizzled hair. "Like hell you did away with him. Bill's a pushover for dogs. You both said you were protected. Jiggs is your ace in the hole."

"Rand isn't that big a fool. He made sure. He was here when Bill gassed the dog."

"Okay, lady. You asked for it."

"Please! No! Bill's lying there dead. Yes—the dog's here. In a pen behind the feed room. The gas was ether instead of cyanide. We can't leave Bill just lying here like that."

I carried Bill into the front bedroom and put him on the bed. He had a terrific lump rising on his head. The pulse was still there, very faint.

The woman went into a closet and came out wearing a blue bathrobe. We went out to the kennels and through the feed room. In back, in one of the private pens generally used for bitches with new litters, I saw Jiggs. My dog began leaping against the mesh, whining. I let him out and he jumped all over me. I boxed with him a little until he settled down. And until I did.

"Where are the papers?"

"What papers?"

"The papers on this dog and his brother."

Her eyes shifted. "In the bank. Safety deposit vault."

I grabbed the front of her bathrobe. "I thought we were through with that?"

"I'm telling you the truth!"

"The hell you are. Bill believed in dogs. He told me a dog was better protection than any bank vault. Where are those papers? Or should I go in and set fire to Bill's bed?"

"In the house," she said.

We went in. She got a manila envelope from among a pile of old magazines in the broom closet of the utility room. In the envelope were pedigrees of Jiggs and his brother, paw prints of both dogs, photographs, detailed descriptions. Something for their old age.

"Bill's alive," I said.

The woman ran in to him. I went into the front room and pulled the phone cord out by the roots. Then I went out to the garage. The key was in the Ford.

I drove to the Redwood City Post Office, addressed the manila envelope to the police department, and dropped it in the slot. The police would have to pay a few cents postage due, but they probably wouldn't mind. It would come out of the taxpayers' money anyhow.

I drove out Main and took Woodside Road from Five Points. I turned off Woodside Road at the Alameda de las Pulgas. Then I turned into my street and pulled up before my house.

Buster's car was in the driveway. I went up the path with Jiggs at my heels, and walked in the front door. This was where I'd come in. The scene was almost exactly the way it had been that other night. Wednesday night. Cora and Buster and Ethelene were at the card table. The fourth chair was empty, a hand of cards face down before it, a highball glass beside the hand. And the dog before the fireplace.

They looked at me sharply as I came in, but didn't move, didn't say anything. Jiggs bristled at the other dog; this was his house. I spoke to him. Cora spoke to the other dog. I went to the empty chair, picked up the hand of cards, took a sip from the glass, and said, "Your play."

Cora and Buster and Ethelene looked past me to the hall door at my back.

"I thought you might try it," Rand's voice said behind me. "Bill's wife phoned from a neighbor's house."

I glanced around. Rand had come from the hall door. His coat was off, tie loosened. He was the picture of a man at ease in his own home over a game of cards with friends, except for the gun in his hand. It was the Luger I'd brought back from overseas.

"Who is this guy?" I said.

"It's the other way about," Rand said.

"He sort of looks like me," I said. "But look at him closely and you'd never be fooled a minute. Would you, Cora?" I took another sip of the highball and studied my cards. "Not a bad hand. I hold the aces."

The hard end of the Luger pressed against the back of my head.

"Not here," Cora said. "For God's sake, not here."

"Get up," Rand said.

"Cora," I said, "tell him to put that thing away before he hurts himself with it."

"I know how to use it, pal," Rand said. "And don't think I won't. I said get up."

"You'd better tell the guy, Cora," I said, "that he'll lose a hand if he shoots that gun. The ammunition I brought home is for machine pistols. Plenty of soldiers in Europe got hurt using machine pistol ammunition in Lugers. Some of them got killed. The cartridge fits, but the Luger isn't built for it. It flies to pieces."

"Oh, no, you don't," Rand said.

"It's what he told me, Bert," Cora said.

"He ought to know the game's up," I said. "If he couldn't kill me earlier tonight, he can't now."

"You're forcing it, pal," Rand said.

"You're damned right I am. That's why I'm here. You sit down and I'll tell you where *you* come off. Sit down!"

"Okay, pal," he said. "Let's hear your song."

He took a seat on the couch behind me.

I spoke to the other three. "He's washed up. But you've got a chance. My escape Wednesday night blew a hole a mile wide in his plans. His scheme depended on a nice, quick, clean finish. He got me into the hands of the police. The red-faced cop was taking me in. Bill Meadows was waiting at the police station with his dog. I would have been killed as I stepped out of the police car. On the tips of my fingers was proof I was Albert Rand. It was all cut and dried. But I got away."

"How did you know that?" Buster asked nervously. "How did you know about Bill waiting at the police station with his dog?"

"I know all about it," I said. "I can blow it wide open. If you're smart you'll ride along with me."

21

"He's bluffing," Rand said.

I spoke to the other three. "It was a good plan, but it blew up. I shot it full of holes by escaping."

"What holes, pal?" Rand asked.

"One hole was Alicia Alexander. If I got to her, she would know I wasn't Rand. That would show that the man taking my place *was* Rand. Why should he be afraid of what she'd say? Because there were other holes. Rand had courted her during the war by appearing in L. A. with a story of hush-hush trips from Europe. Once suspicion was aroused, just as soon as the police began wondering which of us really was Rand, they'd start checking the dates of those trips. Buster, you remember our CO at the squadron, Major Jody. He and I had desks back-to-back in the same office overseas. He's a colonel now in the Pentagon."

I didn't think Jody would mind being promoted, or being shoved back into the Army, or even the Pentagon, considering. "Did you know he kept a diary, Buster? He can prove that on certain dates I was on duty while Rand was in Los Angeles."

I was getting them. They were coming around. I kept on: "And I'll tell you what I did last night. I typed the whole thing up. The whole story. And this morning I mailed it out. One copy to Colonel Jody in the Pentagon. One copy to the FBI. One copy to the police. They'll have it Monday. You couldn't afford to go to the police when Bill Meadows found I was in Mary's apartment. You couldn't afford for me to talk. All right, I've talked. I've put it in writing. Monday, the heat will be on. Rand is washed up. He's finished. But you three have got a chance to pull out. You'd better drop him and save your own necks."

Yes, it was getting them. I'd shaken them to their shoelaces. I was making a gamble, and it stood a fair chance of paying off.

"You're bluffing, pal," the man behind me said.

"Let's add two dogs to it," I said to the others. "Two dogs named Jiggs, right here in this room, who are practically dead ringers. And there's no use trying to shoot one of them and get rid of it. Because I've mailed the pedigrees and photographs and paw prints of both dogs to the police. That was Bill Meadows' ace in the hole. That was something for his old age."

Rand swore. "I should of took care of him."

"You would have, when he wasn't needed any longer," I said, turning toward him. "You don't intend to split those bonds with anybody. But now you're washed up, Rand. You know an impersonation can't hold up if it is once suspected. They can't even run a race horse for another if there's a breath of suspicion. Once the law gets a hint that you are Albert Rand, it never will let go. Especially since the police never can get the bonds out of me.

"You know that. That's why you got rid of Alicia Alexander. What would her unsupported word be against the evidence of fingerprints and identification by Cora and Buster and Ethelene? It wouldn't hold up a minute in court. But it would start suspicion. It would give the law an idea. All the law needs is that one idea. Once the law starts thinking that way, you're cooked and you know it."

I turned to the others. "You three still have a chance. You can claim you were honestly fooled by the impersonation. You can hang it onto Rand and Bill Meadows. Bill furnished the dog. Cora, you can say you took Jiggs to Bill's kennels Wednesday to have the dog wormed, and didn't know you got a different dog back. Buster, you and Ethelene can say that when I left you Wednesday afternoon, Rand came in a few minutes later and you thought he was I. You can say you drove him down here, that he was established in your minds as I, when I walked in. With him here, you naturally thought I was the impostor. You were victims of an impersonation.

"This is your chance and you'd better take it quick. There have been murders and you're accomplices. You're as guilty as he is. You'll never spend that two million anyhow. That's gone up the spout. The police will know Monday morning that there were two dogs. They'll know there is something funny about the whole deal. Once they start from the premise that Rand took my place, they can figure out the rest of it just as I did. They'll find out about those switched fingerprints. They'll know why Alicia Alexander was murdered. They'll prove I couldn't have been in Los Angeles during the war while Rand was seeing her. All the law needs is suspicion, and now it's got it. You'd better get out from under."

There was fear in the three faces at the table. And desperate hope. There was no struggle of loyalty. Avarice was all that had held them together.

Cora put a hand on my hand. "Chick, do you think that we—I mean, if you and I started over?"

"You're lovely," I said, and that was the truth. "There's never been a girl made quite so beautiful."

"You know how I feel about you, Chick. I tried not to fall. I tried my best not to fall. But I love you, Chick."

I squeezed her hand. "We all make mistakes. We can forget all this and start over."

"It's a cinch, Chick," Buster said. "That rat fooled us for a while, but we saw through him. Sure, that's the angle. That's our story. He pulled the wool over our eyes for a while. But now we know."

"That's the angle," Ethelene agreed. "If we hang together we can pull out of this. I never did like it anyhow.... Chick, are you with us? Will you ride with us against him? All the way down the line?"

"If we stick together," Buster said. "We're out of this."

"You can forget, can't you, Chick?" Cora said. "We can be so happy together."

"Don't be fools!" Rand cried. "He's pulling a fast one! Do you think for a minute that guy's going to stand by you after what you did to him? Don't be fools!"

"Chick's a square guy," Ethelene said. "He's not like you. If he says he'll stand by us, he will. How about it, Chick?"

"He couldn't save you if he wanted to!" Rand yelled. "Once the cops start in, they can connect the four of us up! And if the cops can't get it any other way, they'll get it from me. You try to cross me up, I'll squeal. I'll spill my guts."

"Spill what?" Cora asked. "Sure, we knew you before the war, Bert. That's how we got acquainted with Chick. Buster mistook him for you. But we never saw you since, until you showed up here and tried to take his place."

"Yeah," Buster said. "We never saw you since before the war, until Wednesday night."

"That will hold up, won't it?" Rand sneered. "If you knew both of us, the cops will wonder why you didn't tumble the night we were both here together!"

"I was upset," Cora said. She was beautiful. She could make that sound convincing.

"Sure, that's it," Buster said. There was life in his round face again and he saw an out. That magnificent innocence glowed. "We knew Bert Rand before the war. But we heard he'd got killed. So there were two guys here Wednesday night who looked alike, but we didn't know who the other one was. Hell, with the dog and the fingerprints and all, who can blame us for being taken in?

"But then Cora began noticing little things that made her suspicious. At the office, I began to see that the guy didn't know what he should about the business. And then the newspapers came out with the story that Rand had served overseas with the Air Force but that Chick was at Ft. Douglas. That did it. We knew. Hell, I knew Chick was over there in England. I went through a war with good old Chick. So we got together to see what we could do. We figured to play it smart and not let Rand find out we knew he'd taken Chick's place. We figured to get close to him and get the goods on him. Yeah, that's it! That's our out!"

"I don't see anything wrong with it," Ethelene said.

Cora squeezed my hand lovingly. "Chick, it's going to be so wonderful, back with you again."

"Bert, this is a hell of a note," Buster said to Rand. "But you see how it is. You're cooked anyhow. There's no use all of us getting it. I wish it wasn't this way, Bert. But you see how it is."

"I see how it is," Rand said tightly. "I always did know *you* for what you are. All three of you. Don't think you ever fooled me a minute. You were with me for what you got out of it."

"Don't be nasty, Bert," Cora said. "There's no use crying over spilled milk."

"For God's sweet sake," Ethelene said, "let's hang together on this."

"We'll go over it again," Cora said. "Let's get it right and get it cold and hang to it."

"No, by God!" Rand yelled. He leaped from the couch. His face was white except for a small pink spot on each cheekbone. "We're in this together, and we'll make it or go down together!"

"Bert, why don't you keep quiet while we discuss this?" Cora said.

"We can still pull out of this, you fools!" he yelled. "We've got too much in this to toss it away. We can still bring it off. *I'm still Charles Graham!* Get that! Get it and don't forget it. I am Charles Graham. This guy is Rand. He came back here tonight and I shot him. As I've got a perfect right to. To hell with the dog business. All we know about is one dog. We'll fix Bill Meadows so he'll never talk. And his wife.

"That's it," he said tightly. His eyes were alight with a bright fire. "That's it. It was Rand and Bill Meadows. They worked together on the deal. They cooked up the ringer for Jiggs. It was part of the plan for them to take my place. Rand tried it Wednesday and it didn't work. He came back tonight to try it again and I shot him. That's it. All we've got to do is sit tight and hang together. It's all we can do. You fools, we're not licked yet!"

And he brought the Luger up, directly at my chest.

I spoke the word my dog had been waiting to hear.

"*Gofer!*"

With a snarl Jiggs was at him. The gun swerved to the dog. There was a terrific explosion. Then the two dogs were at each other. I ran out to the garage for the mattock, hit the end of the handle on the floor, dislodged the head, and came back in with the handle.

Ethelene and Cora were shrieking as the dogs fought back and forth across the living room. With the two dogs together, I knew which one was Jiggs. I laid the mattock handle on the other dog, where it would count. Then I said, "Break away, Jiggs," and turned to Rand.

He was sitting on the couch holding his right wrist and staring stupidly at what was left of the hand.

"I warned you about that ammunition," I said.

"Don't rub it in," he muttered. "Leave me alone."

"Here, let me put a tourniquet on that," somebody said, "until the ambulance gets here." A red-faced guy was beside me. He was not in uniform, and I watched him expertly stop the bleeding before I recognized him as the cop I'd had dealings with Wednesday night.

"So I'm the goat," the cop said. "I get a reprimand. The boys rib me. Okay, who got Rand? And on my day off, too. Say, Rand, let's see that Army identification card of yours."

"I'm not Rand," Rand said. "Talk to him."

"I'm talking to you, Rand."

"What Army identification card?"

"Okay. I didn't figure you'd still have that. Funny how that came to me this morning at breakfast. Little thing, but I remembered it. I was in the Army myself. MP's."

"What about the card?" I asked.

"I'll tell you, Graham. Rand claimed he was you and that he'd been a tech sergeant in the war. Well, that identification card with his fingerprints on it was an *officer's AGO card*."

"You clumsy fool," Buster said.

"No; it was smart for a quick deal," the cop said. "It nailed identification in my mind. That's what it was for. Nobody knew anything about war records at that time. There was no reason why Graham's supposed war record should even be checked, if the thing had gone off on schedule. And Rand didn't know the cop he called would be an ex-GI from the MP's. If I'd taken Graham in Wednesday night—well, Bill Meadows was waiting at the station with his Doberman. I've just had a little talk with Bill Meadows, and he figured he'd better squeal and try to save his own neck. So if the deal had worked Wednesday night, Graham would be dead, his identity established by fingerprints as Rand, and nobody would have paid any more attention to the guy who was supposed to be Charles Graham. Yes, it was a nice deal all around. Pretty neat.

"It only hit me this morning, on my day off," the cop went on. "I slept in and I had a late breakfast. And I kept turning the case over in my mind. I was under the gun, the way the boys was ribbing me. And I remembered that AGO card. Funny how a little thing like that will pop up in your mind over a cup of coffee. An ex-GI with an officer's card. Where did he get it? Why would he have it? Well, if the card was phony, I figured, let's turn the thing upside down. Let's figure everything backwards. Let's say the guy who claimed he was Graham Wednesday night really *was*."

"A starting point," I said.

"Sure. And once I started looking at it that way, it fit. It explained the Alexander girl's death. Sure. She could tell the two guys apart and no fooling. Well, then, why couldn't Graham's wife and her brother and the brother's wife? Sure, they could—but what if they were in with Rand? Crazy, you know, me turning it upside down. Just feeling around with it over a cup of coffee. Wait a minute, I figured—what about the dog?

"Then I remembered Bill Meadows there at the station when I reported in. I remembered the guy and his sister who'd been killed by a couple of chows they'd bought from Bill Meadows. Did Bill Meadows fit in? He raised dogs. He could have furnished a ringer. Sure, the whole thing's crazy, but I'm just sitting there with a cup of coffee and a cigarette, letting it snowball. It didn't make sense, but what about that phony AGO card? How about the Alexander girl?

My day off, what have I got to lose? If it does pay off, who's the goat? And then I thought I remembered something Buster had said Wednesday night. I wasn't sure. But if he'd said that, it had to be that way."

Buster was white-faced, waiting.

The cop grinned reflectively. "So I start at the other end. What can I find out about Buster and Ethelene Cox and Cora Graham? Well, I didn't find anything out. And that was funny. Nobody really knew anything about those three. So I got off a wire to the War Department asking about Buster's war service, to see if he'd been in any trouble in the Army."

"You've got nothing on me," Buster said. "I was mistaken just like you were."

"Let me tell you a few things about Buster," Rand said.

"You shut up," the cop told Rand. "I figured this out for myself and I don't want no confessions until I'm through talking. The boys will be here pretty soon and give you all plenty of chance to sing.... Well, so it's my day off and I'm playing around. Busman's holiday. And tonight I'm sitting in a picture show behind Cora and the guy who might be Rand. You wouldn't exactly say I'd been tailing them. I was just keeping my eyes open and tagging them around. So what happens? They slip out in the middle of the show. Right in the best part. And it's a good picture, too. Why did they come to the show if they didn't want to sit through it? That's an old dodge to shake a tail—go into a movie and slip out in the middle of a big scene. It was interesting, and I was having fun anyhow. So I wondered where they had to go to that maybe they didn't want to be followed, or if they wanted to see enough of the show to be able to say they'd been there when they were somewhere else. I was playing around. I followed them.

"I lost their car when it crossed Bayshore and I had to wait on the light. So I drove over to Bill Meadows' place, just for the hell of it. And there was the tan Nash. And Buster's car, it looked like. Well, well, well. Things were making sense."

The cop nodded at his own astuteness. "So then I drove back to Redwood to see if I'd got anything from the War Department. I had. Buster hadn't been in any trouble in the Army, *but he was in the same squadron as Graham—or Rand, as the case may be—overseas.*

"That hit me right between the eyes. That was what I'd been trying to remember from Wednesday night."

THE MAN WITH MY FACE

Listen, I had to admit it hit me, also. There, under my nose, had been the way to blow the case open at any time. I guess my mind isn't trained in police work.

"You see?" the cop said. "If the guy who was overseas in the same squadron with Buster was *Rand*, then Buster should have been right on my doorstep telling us all about Rand. But he hadn't let out a peep. And when the two of you who looked so much alike were here Wednesday night, Buster would have known that one was Graham and one was Rand, even if he didn't know which was which. *Buster was the one man who knew you both very well.* Then why hadn't he opened his head that night? Why hadn't he said he knew a guy overseas who was a dead ringer for his business partner? Even if he hadn't seen the papers to know about the big L. A. bond job, he could have put the finger on Rand right there and then. And why hadn't he? Why—unless Buster was in on the deal and Rand had taken Graham's place? That did it.

"Once I figured that out, I put it down in black and white. Just in case. Then I drove back to Bill Meadows' place. I found Bill nursing a bottle and a big lump on his head. His wife really spilled it, Graham. She'd given you that envelope about the two dogs. Where is it?"

"I mailed it to the police on my way here," I said.

"Good boy, Mac. Bill's wife told me about your face. Have you tried calamine lotion?"

"Yes."

"So I come here and was just pulling up when the shooting and yelling began. I come in the back way and seen I wasn't needed, so I called the station while you took care of the dogs. I guess that buttons it up, except for the important thing."

"What's that?"

"The reward, Graham. Hell, that's fifteen thousand bucks! I'm doing this on my day off, on my own time. We ought to settle it between us before the others get here. That's a lot of jack, and you watch, somebody's going to try to horn in."

"I don't want that kind of money," I said.

The cop grinned. "That's because you haven't felt it. How about fifty-fifty? If we hang together, we can cop that reward."

22

I guess it was Wednesday night, four days later and a week after the thing had started, when Mary and Walt walked in. I'd been answering so many questions I hadn't kept track of time too well. But by this time everybody seemed to be pretty well briefed, even the FBI, and I was sitting in my living room with a bottle of beer in my hand and Jiggs at my feet, feeling pretty lonely, when in walked Mary and Walt.

"Speak of the devil!" I cried. "I've been phoning your apartment and the Bay Title Insurance Company every time I got a free minute. Where have you been?"

"Where have we been?" Walt yelled. "Don't you remember?"

"I've been in Los Angeles, waiting on tables," Mary said.

"Waiting on tables? What for?"

"And I've been diving for pearls," Walt said, holding up his hands. They were red.

"Washing dishes? What for?"

"To keep body and soul together and a roof over our heads, is what for!" he cried.

"Oh," I said.

"You were going to send us money," Mary said. "Remember?"

"Gosh—honest, I forgot all about that. There's been so much going on. I just forgot all about that."

"That is what we figured," Mary said stiffly. "Of course we knew you were okay, from the newspapers. You were all right—and what did you care about us? You simply forgot all about us. We didn't matter, if you were okay."

"It isn't that way at all," I said. "You don't know what I've been through the last few days, answering questions."

"Never mind," Walt said. "We understand. The only reason we're here, I want my overcoat."

"Overcoat?"

"Yes, overcoat. You borrowed an overcoat from me. And a pair of shoes."

"And you borrowed ten dollars from me," Mary said. "We thought at least you'd send us that."

"Sure, I'll give you back the money. Can't you understand I just forgot? And, Walt, I lost your overcoat. Somebody copped it."

"Somebody impersonated it right off your back," Walt said. "And me in L. A. without an overcoat!"

And then he broke suddenly, or maybe it was Mary who broke first. I guess my face was funny enough, the look on it, not to mention it was coming into the mottled period and was daubed with calamine lotion.

The two of them burst out laughing and howled until they were weak. Walt sat down, yelling, and I thought Mary might fall so I held her pretty tight, purely for safety's sake.

"Chick," Walt said when he could talk, "I promise to dive gladly for pearls every time you didn't murder a flock of people and get away with two million bucks."

Were you at the trial? Then you know how I felt about Cora and Ethelene. Of course, Buster and Rand and Bill Meadows got the treatment, and they're sweating it out right now as I write this, sweating out that long wait in death row and marking the days on the wall. We expected Bill's wife to get the works, and nobody was surprised when she drew forty years. After all, she didn't have the looks.

But it went without saying that no jury would deal harshly with Ethelene. Justice is justice, but we have to face the facts of life. With ten men on the jury, it was a cinch. She was a cute dish, those long legs crossed on the stand, daubing her eyes daintily and giving soulful looks at the jury.

And of course a beauty like Cora was a cinch for nothing more than a tap on the wrist. If you were one of the lucky ones who got a seat, and saw Cora on the stand, you know what I mean. She was gorgeous. She could charm a bird out of a tree.

So if you were there you know how I felt when both Ethelene and Cora got life.

And incidentally, the mysterious clue the police in L. A. claimed they'd found in the car Rand left at the airport in making his getaway with the bonds really was important. It put the hooks into that fingerprint business. Rand had carefully wiped off the steering wheel, the dash, the knobs and the door handle, and, with an unconscious gesture of habit, he'd made sure the parking brake was on before he got out. Leaving a perfect set of prints that weren't mine.

And so you might say it is all over for me. My marriage to Cora was annulled because it was contracted through fraud. Mary said yes to the important question, the bank got its bonds, the bonding company got off the hook, the red-faced cop got a promotion, I got my identity—and so you might suppose that was that, and that I forgot it and lived happily ever afterwards.

But I believe Mary knows it can never be quite all over. Not for me. There's something dangling. You don't walk through a thing like that without a scar.

In the morning when I go into the bathroom to shave, I come up to the mirror the way a man goes off a high diving board. It's never casual. I'm never quite certain of the face I see. Crazy; but it's there. And when I come home at night with a sack of groceries under one arm and the paper in my pocket, there's a moment then, as I walk in. There's always that moment, as I walk in the door. And I think Mary understands, because she's always there, right there with a smile and a kiss. Then I pat Jiggs on the head, and I'm okay.

THE END

THE GRINNING GISMO
GISMO
- - - - - - -
Samuel W. Taylor

1

The letter was in the morning mail. It was one of a dozen or so, neatly stacked and with the envelopes slit to save my precious time, which were on my desk when I arrived at the office. The desk was of walnut, approximately the size of a billiard table. It held the stack of letters, a picture of Caroline in a leather frame, two telephones and an intercom. Beside the desk was a Dictaphone. The office itself would have made a respectable dance hall, at least for a nightclub. To get to it, to invade my precious privacy, a visitor had to pass through an anteroom guarded by my secretary, and another anteroom guarded by my confidential secretary. The whole setup was as phony as a three-dollar-bill.

I sat at the throne and reached for the mail. Then I shoved the letters aside, unlocked a drawer of my desk and took out the fly-tying equipment. Tomorrow I'd be in the mountains, and for two weeks it would be mosquitoes and campfire smoke and the thrill of hooking a big one on light tackle. Then I'd come back ready for another year of make-believe. Or, if not ready, resigned.

I was making a royal coachman when I got the high sign from my secretary on the intercom. I cleared away the fly-tying equipment, locked the drawer, grabbed a letter from the pile, and was the picture of a busy executive when my father came in.

"Good morning, Henry," Father said, as if we hadn't had breakfast together. This was part of the make-believe, that business and social life existed in separate airtight worlds, even among the family.

"Good morning, sir." I didn't call him *Father* here at the plant, nor *sir* at home.

"Let's see, your vacation begins tomorrow, doesn't it?"

"Yes, sir." At home, I'd talked of nothing else for the past month.

"Got the decks cleared, everything ready, instructions for carrying on while you're away?"

He said it deadpan, perfectly serious. As if I didn't know that every decision I made, every letter I dictated, was screened, weighed and edited. Henry Chatworth Oates III must not make a mistake. Not even at the price of his self-respect.

"I'll be busy today," I said soberly. "But I'll have things ready before I leave."

"Good. Well, I won't waste your time, Henry." Then, as if it just happened to catch his eye, he picked up the leather frame containing the picture of Caroline. "Lovely girl." He gave me the wink, the heavily playful one of the boss to the hireling, which he could do here at the office but not at home. "Faint heart never won fair lady, Henry!" With a chuckle he replaced the leather frame on the desk and went out.

I picked up the leather frame. Caroline was nice enough, but neither of us felt that way about one another. She was willing to do it dutifully for family reasons, but I didn't want marriage that way. So I was being obstinate, unreasonable, foolish, dogmatic, and several other things.

I pressed the hidden catch of the frame and Caroline's picture swung out. Then I was looking at Trudy. Trudy had loved me without knowing or caring who I was. That's how I wanted it. And we might have been married now, except—well, we can't all be Edward VIIIs.

I snapped the frame shut, covering Trudy with Caroline. It was a long, long time ago. Water under the bridge.

I shoved aside the letter I'd pretended to be reading for Father's benefit, and began getting out the fly-tying equipment. Then I did a double-take on that letter.

The letter was from Jim. Aside from the scrawled signature, I knew the smudged type and the high *E*'s of his old folding Corona. Jim was Trudy's brother. He'd been my best friend before I proved myself a heel to his sister.

The letter was something of a shock because Jim Daniels had been dead for three months.

The letter was dated July 14th, two days ago. The envelope showed it had been airmailed from San Francisco on that date. Yet Jim had died the night of April 7th. It said,

Dear Hank,
Surprised?
It's a long story and one I don't want to put in a letter. Sufficient that I'm caught in a hinge and you're the only guy who can help me out.
This is what I want you to do: Come to San Francisco and get close to Clara. But don't let Clara know who you are. This will be easy because Clara is still working for that dentist, Leo Cranston. Make an appointment with Cranston to have

your teeth cleaned, strike up an acquaintance with Clara, and follow through. But don't follow through too far—for she's still my wife, remember. I'll contact you there.

Do this for me, Hank. I don't have to tell you it's important.

It was signed, "Jim," and a P.S. said, "Burn this letter."

The letter unquestionably had been written on Jim's typewriter. I knew that smudged type with the high *E* as I did my own face. Jim had toted the folding Corona overseas in his barracks bag, and I'd borrowed it hundreds of times to write letters to Trudy. His signature was on the letter, his initials under the P.S.

I fished among the junk of the fly-tying drawer for Trudy's letter. The last one. I'd burned all the others because I couldn't face the fact of what they made me. And then after a gap of years this last one had come, in April.

Dear Hank,

The enclosed clipping will be a shock to you. I wish I could do something to soften the blow.

Though Jim is now gone, there is still something we can do for him. We know that Jim wasn't the sort of person to take his own life. I know you will want to help clear this stain from his memory.

Please come to San Francisco immediately. I have good reason for believing Jim did not suicide.

As ever,

Trudy

The clipping was headed, almost casually, ANOTHER SUICIDE FROM GATE BRIDGE. The story said that the car of James Daniels, 29, real estate man, had been found abandoned on Golden Gate Bridge with a suicide note in it. A pedestrian, L. M. Arnold of Sausalito, had reported the abandoned car to the toll gate at 3:10 A.M. A wrecker had immediately removed the car to avoid the danger of collision in the heavy fog. No reason for the suicide had been given by the note, except that it was "the only way out of this mess." A search was being conducted for the body.

At the time, I had felt that Trudy was simply upset, distraught, unwilling to face the cold fact of her brother's suicide. So far as Jim not being the type to take his own life, who can say that of any man?

Hell, rich men suicide; so do beautiful girls who apparently have everything, even movie actresses who are the envy of the entire world. The decision as well as the cause is subjective; nobody knows what eats inside another person.

For example, yours truly, Henry Chatworth Oates III. Born with the golden spoon, raised in luxury, given the advantages of travel, education, social position, being groomed to take over the business when my father stepped aside. And where, you might ask, could you find a happier man? Go down on skid row and pick out just any drunken bum. He might be a derelict and a has-been, but at least he's living his own life.

So I'd written Trudy of the shock and the sorrow. I'd said I was sure the police would uncover any evidence of foul play, but that I was willing to stand the cost of an investigation by a private detective agency. After all, what could I do personally? Father would like it, me getting involved in some mess. He would like it, me rushing off to San Francisco to see Trudy again. Oh, yes.

But now, with the two letters before me, I knew Trudy hadn't been merely upset and unwilling to face the situation. With good reason she had suspected something was phony about that suicide. Jim's letter proved it. He wasn't dead at all. And now he was asking for help.

I crumpled both letters, together with the clipping, put them in an ash tray and touched a match to them. I watched the flame with a certain hard satisfaction. It was a feeling I hadn't had for a long time; not since the War, when, just as Father was pulling strings to get me a nice safe berth in the Pentagon with brass on my shoulders, I'd slipped down and enlisted as a private. Father had never completely trusted me after that.

It was fortunate that the letter had arrived this morning, the day before vacation. Father wouldn't question my whereabouts for two weeks. Nick Van Cott would cover up for me with the other members of the fishing party. Nick worked at the plant; he knew which side of the bread held the butter. Father would be retiring in a few years, leaving me at the head; Nick would cover up for me.

The phone call came just before noon. "There is a party on the line who insists on speaking to you, Mr. Oates," my confidential secretary said over the intercom.

"Who is he?"

"He refuses to give his name, but he says to tell you it's about Jim."

"Put him on."

I lifted a phone and a voice said, "Hank, did you get a letter from Jim Daniels this morning?"

It was a muffled voice. I had the idea it was coming through a handkerchief over the mouthpiece of the phone. Too, there was something fuzzy and indistinct about the words, as if the speaker couldn't talk very well even without the handkerchief. It was a man's voice.

I said, "Who is this?"

"Just call me Smith." He pronounced the name as a child might— *Smiff*. "Did you get the letter?"

"I don't know what you're talking about."

"I think you do. The letter should have hit your desk this morning. If it didn't, you'll get it in the next mail. A letter from Jim Daniels, asking you to go to San Francisco."

"Just what do you want?" I asked.

"This is just a little free advice, Hank. Don't go."

"Free advice isn't worth much."

"It can save your life," the voice said.

"Aren't you being a little melodramatic?"

"That's right. It couldn't happen to you, could it? Not to Henry Chatworth Oates III. Nothing happens to you that isn't laid out in a neat little plan beforehand. But you'll find out, Henry Chatworth Oates III. There are plans and plans. This one isn't the kind you're used to. This one is made by other people. For their profit, not yours."

"I don't think you can frighten me, Mr. Smith," I said.

"I'm not trying to scare you, Hank. I'm just telling you. If you go to San Francisco, you will be murdered."

"Why?"

"Money, Hank. It makes the world go around."

"Nobody could profit from my death."

"They could profit by Jim's death, which is the same thing. Look, Hank, I'm trying to save your life. You don't want to get mixed up in this. There's nothing you can do for Jim Daniels by sticking your neck out. All you'll do is end up dead. Be smart, Hank."

So Jim evidently had faked suicide to avoid murder. He needed my help. Just why I was the one, or what I could do, I didn't know. But somebody was very determined I shouldn't give that help.

"Just why are you so generous with the advice?" I asked.

"Same reason, Hank—money. I'm not as dumb as they think I am.

Hank, would you like a scandal involving your mother?"

"Now, wait a minute!"

"Keep your shirt on, Hank. This isn't blackmail; just advice. Don't go to San Francisco. You'll live longer and your mother will be a lot happier."

"What has Mother to do with this?"

"There's an old family skeleton in the closet, Hank. You wouldn't want it dangled in the newspapers for everybody to see, would you?"

The line clicked dead. I hung up wondering if Smith had filled his mouth full of mush to help disguise his voice. Then I wondered if it was somebody I knew—or why bother to disguise it? He had, I felt, gone too far. As to a family skeleton, that was simply too preposterous for serious consideration. Which meant that the threat to my life could also be discounted.

However, the phone call wasn't just the work of a crank. The person knew about Jim's letter. For some reason the person who had phoned didn't want me to go to San Francisco to help Jim. Which meant that there was actually something I *could* do by going. Which, in turn, erased any lingering doubts I might have had about going.

I played make-believe at the office during the remainder of the day, and that night packed up for a trip to San Francisco. How long a trip, I didn't know.

The alarm went off at four-thirty next morning. I shaved, put on my fishing clothes. When I went downstairs I found Mother in the kitchen, sleepy-eyed, with breakfast fixed for me. She wouldn't ask the cook to fix breakfast for me that early, but she'd do it herself. And, mothers being what they are, she had to get up to say goodbye. I wondered again about the threat of scandal, and dismissed it. It was beyond belief.

She waited until I was having a cigarette with the second cup of coffee, then she said quietly, "Where are you going, Henry?"

I might have known I couldn't fool her.

She said, "I didn't mean to pry, but I was checking your luggage to make sure you had everything, and ..." She waited for me to finish it.

So I told her about the letter from Jim.

"Of course you have to go," she said.

"Yes."

"Your father would never understand."

"No."

"Do you still love Trudy?"

I met her eye. You couldn't lie to Mother. "We can't all be Edward VIIIs."

She seemed about to say something, then she didn't. She put a hand on my shoulder and squeezed it. "I've been hoping your father …"

"Nothing can change Father's mind."

"Nothing ever has," she admitted.

I considered a moment, then told her about the phone call. Fear came behind her eyes, and I wondered about that skeleton. Then she said, "Henry, do be careful," and I decided the fear was just a normal mother's concern for her only chick. "Well, you'd better be going." She said it in the same casual way that she'd said, back during the War, "If you feel that way, of course you'll have to enlist."

It was for her sake that I hadn't rebelled against the make-believe. Because of her I hadn't left the old homestead. Of course she supported me when I wanted to marry Trudy. I could have done without the gold spoon. But it would have been a deep wound to Mother, having her only child cut adrift, disowned, disinherited. Yes, love is everything; but there is more than one kind of love.

I stopped at Nick Van Cott's to unload the fishing gear and change into a suit, then headed west. It was a clear morning, bright and with the promise of heat to come. I'd been on the road a couple of hours before I realized I was being followed by a green Chevy.

2

It was, of course, incredible. Why should anyone be following me? Maybe that's why I was slow on the uptake. Too, the highways are free to anyone, and a car behind you is no cause for alarm. It was only after my second stop that I began thinking back. When I had swung out of our bluestone driveway, the green Chevy had been parked in the street. I'd noticed it without thinking about it because it was the only car in sight that early in the morning. After stopping at Nick's to change clothes, I'd noticed a green Chevy parked down the street from his place.

I'd stopped to gas up, and stopped again an hour or so later at a roadside café for a cup of coffee; and when that same green Chevy was behind me as I drove on again, I began thinking back. If that

Chevy wasn't following me, it certainly was a remarkable coincidence that both its route and its stops were the same as mine. Either that or the roads were alive with green Chevys, all with dents in the right front fender.

I began trying to get a good look at the driver. In doing so, I proved beyond a doubt that it was tagging me. If I slowed down, it did; if I poured on the gas, it speeded up. I played this game carefully, for if I was being followed it would be an advantage not to tip off the car behind that I knew it. But instead of being on my tail waiting for a chance to pass, the Chevy always stayed its distance.

I intersected Highway 40, which I intended to follow to the Coast, at Terre Haute. Here, in the traffic, the Chevy couldn't stay too far behind without losing me. Watching my chance, I pulled suddenly into a lone parking space. There was no other parking space the length of the block, and the Chevy couldn't just stall traffic, it had to keep coming. So that I was apparently paying rapt attention to the business of locking my front door when it came past.

A man was driving, with a woman beside him. The man was in his sixties, and while it's hard to tell the size of a person in a car, he gave the impression of being small. At least he was lean. And from the looks of the yellow nylon shirt, green plaid sports jacket, and rayon scarf that took the place of a necktie, he either was from Hollywood or subscribed to *Esquire*. Probably Hollywood, I figured, since the Chevy had California license plates.

The woman beside him might have been good looking. It was impossible to tell, for the exterior was strictly a manufactured job from the carefully waved and hennaed hair to the cupid's-bow lips to the brilliant fingernails of the hand delicately holding a cigarette so the ash wouldn't fall in her lap. She was probably crowding thirty.

Neither of them looked at me as the Chevy went past. I figured I was seeing spooks. If I was being followed, it wouldn't be by a couple like that. Lay it up to coincidence.

I went into a drugstore for a pack of cigarettes. It took a minute or so to get waited on, and when I came out the Chevy was passing again, having gone around the block. Well, that could be coincidence, too—looking for a parking space. While I'd never had experience at being shadowed, from the mystery books I'd read overseas (Father didn't allow them in the house) a shadow either was a sinister character or a beautiful and mysterious glamour girl. This scrawny man and synthetic woman didn't fit at all.

I left Terre Haute on Highway 40. Within an hour the Chevy overtook me and went ahead. So it was coincidence, after all. I put it from my mind until, going through Effingham, I saw the man with the Hollywood clothes beside the highway just beyond town. As I approached, he raised his thumb and grinned hopefully, showing a set of gleaming plates. He was even smaller than I had supposed, a scrawny little man. I passed him by.

Then the game began. Within a few miles the Chevy overtook me again and went ahead. The woman now was driving, the little man not visible. On the outskirts of Vandalia he was there on the highway with his thumb out as I went by.

This little game kept on for the remainder of the day and all the next day, as I passed through Missouri and Kansas and into Colorado. Just about every time I passed through a town, the little man would be on the outskirts trying to thumb a ride. Now he was waving to me; my old pal.

The following day I picked him up at Steamboat Springs. He was going to an incredible amount of trouble to be picked up by me, and I was curious to know why.

"Much obliged, friend," he said, getting in. I said nothing, and he added, "I've been getting a lot of lifts, but short ones. Going far?"

"Frisco."

"I'm going to San Francisco myself." He emphasized the full name of the city slightly, politely correcting me. So he wasn't from Hollywood, despite the garb. He flashed his plates in a grin. "My name's Arnold, so people call me Hap." I said that my name was Hank Oates. He let that pass until we passed a billboard which showed a child's beaming face, a package of breakfast food, and the slogan, *Strong As Oaks with Oates' Oats.*

Hap Arnold looked from it to me. "Say, that kid—Your name is Oates?" So I admitted the picture of the kid was me at the age of two and that I was Henry Chatworth Oates III. Which he knew anyway.

We spent the morning in a pumping contest, both talking a lot and saying nothing. His plan, I could see, had been a good one. A person will tell more to a hitchhiker than he would to his closest friend, both to impress the guy and because he never expects to see him again. The only trouble with that plan was that I knew he had gone to a great deal of trouble to be picked up. Why, I didn't know. Hap Arnold could talk the hind leg off a mule without saying anything. He was cute, too, at leading questions. I tried to be as cute.

Anyhow, it was something to do on a monotonous drive.

The green Chevy, I noticed, was now keeping just in sight behind. We came through a canyon and into Salt Lake City about ten that night.

"Last town before we jump off for the desert," Hap Arnold said. "We better stay over and get an early start."

Since this was his suggestion, I weighed it. But there seemed nothing sinister in spending a night at Salt Lake City, so we checked into a hotel, taking adjoining rooms. We had dinner, then Hap suggested we stretch our legs. We walked a half dozen blocks—which is a long hike in Salt Lake—and Hap suggested we stop at a beer joint for a cool one. I didn't feel like beer, so I ordered ginger ale.

"No ginger ale," the waitress said.

"Then make it root beer."

"No soft drinks at this time of night."

"Why?"

"It's against the law."

So I ordered beer. "What kind of a law is that?" I asked Hap when she went for the beer.

"State liquor control," he said. "No drinking of hard liquor in public places. If you got a soft drink you might mix it with something from the hip."

We were sipping the beer when Hap Arnold suddenly cried, "Millie!" And guess who had walked in the door. The woman of the green Chevy, no less. Now things began making sense.

He brought her to our booth and introduced her as Millie Barron. For my benefit they told each other how they happened to be here. Millie had been on vacation. Hap's car had broken down while East on a business trip. Millie explained to me that Hap was a retired businessman. Hap told me that Millie was secretary to the president of a big corporation. Meanwhile we had another beer.

When Hap left us to go to the washroom, Millie confided, "Don't believe that stuff about his car breaking down. He hitchhikes all the time. Since retiring, he's been getting material for a book." And when Hap returned and Millie excused herself for a minute, Hap whispered, "She's not a secretary but she'd skin me alive if she knew I told you. Her old man left her five million—chain store money."

It was the buildup.

Millie returned and began giving me the business—the knee under the table, the knowing look, the baby talk. Aside from the fact that I was two jumps ahead of them in the game, I wouldn't have been excited. Her copper-red head was a mouse brown at the part. The cupid's-bow outline of the lipstick was a paint job over thin lips. The eyelashes were pasted on, as was the complexion. The idea of seeing what was under all this the morning after was not an exciting one. And I never went for baby talk.

Presently Hap yawned. "I got to hit the hay. Can't take it like you kids anymore."

I'd been expecting this.

"You don't have to go, Hank," Millie said. "Have one more beer with me. Me don't like to drink all alone."

"I'd better go," I said. "We want an early start in the morning to get across the desert."

"Well, I'll stay for another," Hap decided.

"I need the sleep," I said. Then I held out the teaser. "Why don't we get together tomorrow night, at Lovelock?"

So we left the joint. Millie wanted to drive us to the hotel, but after Hap had accepted the ride I said I wanted to stretch my legs.

I walked down Main Street feeling annoyed at myself. Why fool around with this pair whose design was so obvious? Besides, I'd had too many beers. I'm strictly a one-bottle man. One bottle of beer makes me relaxed and mellow. But I'd had four and I felt a bit green around the gills.

At the hotel, I got my car from the garage and drove to an all-night service station on State Street for a lube job. I took another walk while the car was being serviced, and stopped in a café for two cups of black coffee. I knew I was going to feel like hell in the morning. Four beers were at least two too many.

When the car was serviced, I drove to the hotel and told the clerk I was checking out. He said he would have to charge me for the night. I said that was okay, and paid him. I took the key, went up the elevator to the fourth floor, and let myself into the room. Millie Barron was sitting on the bed.

Millie had made herself comfortable. She was wearing stockings, panties, and brassiere. Her dress was over the foot of the bed. On the floor at her feet was a fifth of Scotch. It was nearly empty.

"You's been so long, darling," she said. "Me's been so lonely."

She held out her arms and stood up. It was a mistake, standing up after all that Scotch on top of the beer. Her eyes crossed and she slumped to the floor, out cold. I took my bag and got out of there.

An hour later I was passing over the salt flats, level and white in the moonlight. About now, I figured, Hap Arnold would be bursting into my room to reveal himself as the betrayed husband. And all he would find was Millie, sleeping it off. This seemed very funny.

Then suddenly it wasn't so funny. While Hap and Millie had obviously tried to clip me with a badger game, that wasn't the point. The point was that they had known I would be driving across country; they had been waiting in that green Chevy when I left the house on the trip. And that was something I hadn't known myself until I got Jim's letter. They had known beforehand that it would be sent.

Was the attempted badger game, then, not merely for money, but to put me into a position where I would have to obey orders on threat of scandal? The phone call from "Smith" had threatened scandal.

I began swearing aloud. As usual, I'd been thinking only of myself. By avoiding a badger game, I'd missed a chance to help Jim; I'd let slip an opportunity to find out something about the people who were trying to stop me. I was doing great.

It was a couple of hours later, as I drifted along at seventy on the long straight road across the Nevada desert, that something suddenly popped up in my memory. I remembered the clipping about Jim's suicide. The abandoned car had been reported to the toll gate by a pedestrian. Just what had a pedestrian been doing, walking across Golden Gate Bridge at 3:10 A.M. of a foggy morning? The pedestrian's name had been Arnold.

A fine time to remember that. Yes, I was doing great.

3

I reached San Francisco early the next afternoon and I never felt worse in my life. After driving all night, I'd stopped at Reno with the idea of getting some sleep, but I was no more than drowsing off when something tried to blow my skull apart. I'd felt lousy anyhow, driving all night after four beers, my mouth brown, shoulders aching, eyes burning; and it was hot.

A shower cooled me off, the toothbrush took off a layer of the brown taste, and I'd felt pretty good—good and tired—as I hit the sack. And then all of a sudden—bang! there was a rat inside my skull, trying to eat its way out. I'd had headaches before, occasionally, but nothing like this. The pain was getting fiercer by the minute. So I got up, dressed, and after stopping in at a drugstore for a bromo, drove on, determined never to combine four beers with the desert heat again.

The headache was gone by the time I reached San Francisco. There was a cool breeze off the ocean; in fact, it was slightly chilly after the desert. I'd never been there before, yet in a curious way I had, through Jim. Jim was a good talker and he'd loved his home town. Many an evening overseas I'd taken a vicarious walk with Jim through the streets of the city.

I got a room at the Mark Hopkins, showered, shaved, brushed my teeth, and went to bed. Tomorrow, rested and full of pep, I'd make an appointment with the dentist Clara worked for, pour on the charm, get next to her, and wait for developments. Such were Jim's instructions.

I went to sleep thinking of Trudy.

The rat chewing inside my skull woke me. It was eating into my eyeballs, gnawing at my brain, leaping against the top of my skull. I got up, then sat down on the bed, holding my head to keep it from exploding. What had I eaten? I wondered if Hap or Millie had slipped something into my beer; though that wouldn't explain the headache returning after going away once. The trouble with being healthy is that you have no experience in knowing what's wrong with you.

I wondered about calling a doctor, and put the idea aside. Our family didn't go much for doctors. Perhaps part of the enormous success of the Oates' Oats Company was Father's firm conviction that the product made for health and strength, and to be sick was a slap at this belief. I've seen Father carrying on when hardly able to walk, violently protesting there was nothing whatsoever the matter with him. And while I didn't quite subscribe to his beliefs, I grew up in the environment; the idea of calling a doctor for a headache was a passing thought.

I rang room service and asked for some aspirin.

The aspirin stopped the gnawing, but now I wasn't sleepy. Tired, but not sleepy. It was still early afternoon, and Jim's letter had suggested urgency. I looked up the phone number of Leonard Cranston, D.D.S.

Clara's voice answered the phone: "Dr. Cranston's office." It was a low voice, with a full and throaty quality, and it took me back to a Nissen hut where a plastic phonograph record went around and around, bringing mist to Jim's eyes. Over the phone, the voice of his wife was exactly the same. "Dr. Cranston's office. Hello."

"Oh, hello," I said, returning to my room in the Mark. "I'd like my teeth cleaned."

She murmured something about a future appointment. I said, "Couldn't you make it this afternoon? I'm a stranger in town, and—well, I'm getting married tomorrow morning."

"Well, in that case, Mr.—er—"

"Brown. Robert Brown."

"In that case, Mr. Brown, we'll slip you in. Just cleaned? You don't need other work?"

"Just cleaned. I've never had a filling in my life."

"You're fortunate, Mr. Brown. Let's see, now. Could you make it by three o'clock? That's half an hour."

I said I could, and hung up.

I gave my teeth another brushing and, tired of driving, took a taxi to Cranston's office on Sutter. The taxi had hardly got under way when the fire in my brain came alive again. I'd left the aspirin in the room so I had the cabbie stop at a drugstore on the way.

By the time I got to Cranston's office, the agony had eased off. But after this third time I was beginning to get unpleasant thoughts about a tumor of the brain or something. I figured I'd better be seeing a doctor, Oates' Oats or no. A hell of a note if it was something serious popping up suddenly, just when I was supposed to be at my best for whatever Jim needed me to do.

Cranston's office was on the sixth floor. As I opened the door of the reception room, a muted buzzer sounded. There were a half dozen people patiently waiting, wearing that expression of brave terror typical of such places. Clara appeared from a hallway to the left, smiled professionally. "Mr. Brown?" I admitted it. She indicated a chair, murmured something about waiting a few minutes, and disappeared. I selected a movie magazine and sat down.

So that was Clara, in the flesh. I understood now how Jim could have been just a little bit crazy when it came to Clara. She had something that didn't come through in the pictures Jim had carried around in his wallet and pinned above his bunk in the Nissen hut. She wasn't beautiful. She was too solid to get anywhere in Hollywood. But she had something in the flesh. She would be a wow as a night club entertainer—say, doing a strip tease. Because everything she had called to a man—everything from the vibrant voice to the corn-colored hair to the full breasts to the living hips to the little hollows above her ankle bones. Whatever it's called, she had it. I imagined that women would hate Clara.

Then over the top of the magazine I saw her. She was standing at the door of the hallway, staring at me, her eyes round, the full lips slightly parted. And as I met those eyes, I knew she'd recognized me. A hell of a note; Jim had told me not to let her know.

She crossed to my chair. "Hank," she whispered huskily. "You *are* Hank Oates, aren't you?" I nodded; I could hardly deny it now. She reached impulsively for my hand, then became conscious of the other people watching. "The doctor will see you now, Mr. Oates."

I followed along a short hall to a tiny office containing a desk and three file cases. On the desk was a picture of Jim and myself at the nose of a B-17. I should have thought of that. Or Jim should have. Of course she would recognize me.

She stopped, turning. I'd expected her to go around the desk, and I crowded into her. But as I stepped away she followed me, her face upturned, the pressure of her body against mine.

"Hank, it's good to see you. I've known you so long, through Jim." And then she kissed me, with those full lips soft and open.

Yes, she had it.

I found myself in a chair, elaborately acting as if I wasn't fussed. She took the armchair behind the desk. "I told Jim I'd do that when I met you," she said, smiling. "And Jim said, 'Hell, you'd better!'"

"I wanted to meet you," I said. "But I thought maybe—" I finished with a shrug.

She leaned forward, taking my hand. The neck of her starched uniform bulged. While I didn't stare, it was quite obvious that she wore no brassiere. "I understand, Hank. What could you have done, personally? You're not a detective. There's the family name to consider, if you got involved in a mess. As you wrote Trudy, it was a matter for the police. I appreciated your offer to pay for a separate investigation by private detectives." She smiled wryly. "Poor Trudy. She was out of her head. She and Jim were so close—orphans, you know."

I didn't know exactly what to say. Jim's instructions were to make up to Clara without letting her know who I was. "It was a blow to all of us," I murmured.

"But now we know that Jim is alive!"

I don't know what my face showed. I said, "Alive?" and made it noncommittal.

"Hank, quit trying to act like a private eye. You saw it in the newspapers. Why else are you here? Why else did you make a dental appointment as Robert Brown?"

"All right," I said, wondering what had been in the newspapers. "But I've been traveling—I haven't seen the papers for a couple of days. Any new developments?"

She looked at me steadily. "How did you come out here?"

"Drove."

"Then Jim wrote you. Or phoned you. The piece was in this morning's paper, and it took you several days to drive here."

I was doing just fine. I said nothing.

"Oh, all right, keep it to yourself—you men!" she said, as if humoring a child. She leaned forward again. I wished she wouldn't do that; it was distracting. "If Jim didn't want me to know anything, then why did he phone me?"

"Phoned you?"

"You *haven't* seen the papers or you'd know that."

"Are you sure it was Jim? Over the phone—"

"Could anyone fool me about that? Like all married couples we had a little secret language. He's alive, Hank."

"Did he explain why he disappeared?"

"No; except that—"

She stopped speaking as the door behind her desk opened. A plump woman came out of the dental office. Clara made an appointment for her. The plump woman went along the hallway. Clara said to me in her professional voice, "The doctor will see you now."

I followed her into the dental office, where Leonard Cranston, D.D.S., was drying his hands. Clara performed introductions. Cranston and I exchanged the usual banalities of people who have known of each other through a mutual friend.

Cranston was a big man, getting bald at the temples, with a broad pink face. He looked like an ex-football player gone soft, which, as I knew, he was. Jim had said Cranston had been a fullback for Stanford or California—or maybe it was UCLA; anyhow, some Coast school— and had been known as Special Delivery Cranston from his ability to deliver a few yards in a pinch.

I got into the chair. Clara clipped the bib on me and went out. Cranston began an examination. I told him I just wanted a cleaning job. He murmured something and continued the examination. I resigned myself to it.

Presently Cranston's large pink face lost its professional smile. He began making little "hmm's" and "ah's" in the manner of one who is finding something unexpected and unpleasant. He withdrew the mirror and looked at me steadily. "You haven't been to a dentist in some time."

"Not since the war," I admitted, somewhat embarrassed at what the examination might have revealed. Good teeth and good health were hereditary in the Oates family; and Father was firm in the belief that teeth needed nothing but a thorough brushing three times a day and a bowl of Oates' Oats every morning. It was something of a family skeleton that Mother wore a partial plate. Father attributed this to the fact that she hadn't had Oates' Oats each morning until after her marriage.

"Too bad," Cranston said. "If you had caught it in time ..." He shrugged, and made a smile. "Well, we won't form a judgment until we see the X-rays. Maybe it's not as bad as it looks."

I had the feeling of a guy who goes in for a routine insurance examination and finds he has cancer. "What do you mean, Doc? What's wrong? I've never had any trouble with my teeth."

He put a film in my mouth and told me to bite down on the lip provided for the purpose. Clara came in as Cranston swung the pointed snout of the X-ray machine to my cheek. She looked at him questioningly and he murmured some Latin term. Her breath came in with a gasp, and she looked at me pityingly.

"Oh, Hank," she said. "I'm sorry."

"Let's not borrow trouble," Cranston said. He stepped aside and pressed the button. The machine clicked a few times and went off. He put another film in a different position. "We'll hope for the best."

"But Doctor," Clara said, "nothing can be done. You remember young Sutton—"

A glance cut her off. The machine clicked again.

When all my teeth had been X-rayed, Clara took the films into the little lab adjoining the office. "What is it, Doc?" I asked Cranston. He said that Latin name again. I said, "To hell with the medical terms. What does it mean?"

"Do you have headaches? Sudden and violent headaches?"

"No," I said, remembering my years of good health. "That is—"

"Good," he said, cutting me off. "Then it hasn't gone too far."

"Well, I did have a couple of headaches today. But I had too much beer last night, the desert was hot, I was tired from the drive."

"Here?" he said, tapping my temples. "Back here?" He tapped the base of my brain. "It feels like your head is trying to split wide open?"

"Yes, but it only started this morning in Reno. I never had it before."

"But the headaches *have* started?"

"It's too early to tell. With a couple of headaches you can't say it's chronic."

"Once they start they don't stop," he said. "Not until the cause is removed."

"What cause?"

"I'm afraid," he said gently, "that all your teeth will have to come out."

As my mouth sagged open he put the mirror in and began another examination. Butterflies fluttered in my stomach, and for some reason I thought about Jim. Now I understood. Not the reason that Jim had faked suicide and disappeared, but the fact that something just as unexpected as this could have come up, just as suddenly, causing him to do what he did.

Cranston took the mirror from my mouth, smiled professionally. "It might not be as bad as it looks. The X-rays will tell." He picked up an instrument, put the mirror in again, began probing. It felt as if he was sticking that instrument right up into my brain.

"I just couldn't figure it, when Jim suicided," he said, as if he was trying to get my mind off my teeth. "And now, when we know he didn't—I'm really thrown. I can see it was easy enough to fake. Drive onto the bridge, park, and walk away. Late at night in a heavy fog. People jump off the bridge every week or so; with the current, the bodies often aren't recovered. A neat trick—but why? That's what throws me. Jim was in good health, happily married to a wonderful girl like Clara. And he'd fallen into the chance of a lifetime. His uncle Jasper died and left him a piece of property. Jim was subdividing— stood to make a half million clear, after taxes. It beats me. Hurt?" he asked as I gasped.

There came the buzz of the reception door; Clara came out of the laboratory to answer it. Cranston probed again. I gripped the arms of the chair; sweat broke out. Cranston squirted water into my mouth; I spat it into the bowl. He shook his head.

"I'm sorry, Hank. I'm afraid it's too late."

Cranston went into the laboratory, returned with wet film clipped to a metal frame. He held the frame to the window, studying the film. I waited with the butterflies dancing madly. He turned, smiling.

"You're lucky," he said. "When you told me the headaches had started, I was afraid it was too late. But I think we can save most of them."

I had the sort of joy that comes to the condemned man who learns the sentence is commuted to life imprisonment.

4

Cranston held the film between my eyes and the overhead light, so I could see. "Look here. That's pus at the roots. Let's see—one, two, three—yes, and this molar. They'll have to be extracted. The quicker the better. Aside from the headaches, have you had any aches or pains lately?"

"No; except I'm stiff from driving."

"You will have, if we don't extract those four right away. Arthritis or heart disease—something will lay you low when your vitality is overcome. The headaches have already begun. And see here. Cavities. An almost microscopic break in the enamel from the outside. But inside—Well, see for yourself."

Cranston counted up eight cavities. I'd had a little experience with X-rays, having spent a month in the Army assigned to a chest examination unit while waiting on gunnery school. So I knew how to look at the film. Though any fool could have seen the difference between the good and the bad teeth as Cranston pointed it out.

"It's progressive, Hank," he said. "Like rotten apples in a barrel of good ones. You were lucky, dropping in today. Though eventually you would have gone to a doctor about the headaches, and he would have sent you to a dentist. But if you'd waited a couple of weeks or so … this is like a prairie fire in your mouth."

Clara came in. Cranston showed her the film. "We'll only need to extract these four. Inlays will save eight others. He'll need some treatments, but we caught it in time."

"That's wonderful!" Clara exclaimed. She squeezed my shoulders. "You don't know how lucky you are, coming to Leo Cranston. We had a man in here just last week. Another dentist had told him he'd lose all his teeth, but Leo saved them, all but six. He's wonderful."

"Advertising," Cranston said, "is unethical, Clara."

"Well, you are," Clara declared.

"Jim swore by you, Leo," I said. "I remember he had to have a filling in the Army, and he said the first thing he was going to do when he got home was come in and have you do it over right." I watched the two of them getting ready, and it dawned on me what was going to happen. "Hey, wait a minute. You can't do it today."

Clara gave me a sympathetic smile. "I know just how you feel, Hank. A fellow was in just the other day. Never any trouble with his teeth in his life. He'd had a few bad headaches but he didn't think much about it. His name was Sutton. He just came in to have his teeth cleaned—and found it was too late."

Cranston stepped into the laboratory and returned with a set of plates, upper and lower, grinning teeth horrible without a face to go with them. "He'll be in this afternoon for extraction and he'll walk out with these. If we'd caught him in time, just a few weeks earlier— if he'd gone to a doctor when the headaches first began ... I always believe in saving the natural teeth whenever possible. Plates aren't the same."

"But—damn it," I said. "This thing has bowled me over. I've got to get used to the idea."

Cranston's pink face froze. "Of course, Hank," he said politely, "if you wish to check first with another dentist—"

"It isn't that. It's just—hell, I'm knocked for a loop. Never in my life—"

"It's your decision, Hank. I can only advise you." He absently worked the plates up and down in a chewing motion. The buzzer sounded; Clara went out. "You've had no trouble. But the headaches have started. The insidious part of this condition is that a man doesn't know he's facing dental catastrophe until it's often too late." He put the plates on a tray, took a toothpick with cotton on the end, dipped it into a little bottle. "You won't even feel it." He rubbed my gums with the cotton, took up a hypodermic.

I shut my mouth tightly, feeling both a coward and a fool. Cranston shrugged and put down the hypo.

"Not right now," I said. "Give me a little time to get used to it."

"Those headaches have started," he said. "In a few days you'll be glad to have your teeth out. Anything for relief." He unclipped the bib. "Tell you what, Hank. Drop down to a bar and hoist a few. Then come back."

"Okay." I got out of the chair, probing with my tongue the sore places I hadn't known were sore before.

Cranston took my hand, gave it a reassuring squeeze. "I know just how you feel, Hank. Hoist a few drinks and get used to the idea. Check with another dentist if you wish. I'd rather you did, if there's any doubt in your mind. Or go to a doctor about the headaches. But whatever you do, get that condition straightened out immediately." He clapped me on the shoulder. "A few slugs under the belt and it won't seem so bad."

I opened the door to go out but a girl was in Clara's office, standing with her back to the doorway, blocking the exit. She glanced around, moved away from the door to let me pass, and continued talking with Clara.

The girl was Trudy. I hadn't seen her since Camp Shanks, in the autumn of 1943. She'd come to New York to marry me before I went overseas. We were to be married next day, and that night our outfit got the word and there was no way to tell her. We sailed for Europe at dawn while she was asleep, or perhaps while she lay awake thinking of her wedding day. And I'd often thought what might have been, had the orders come just one day later.

After I got back, my father put it up to me and I saw how impossible it all was. It's easy enough to say a man should give up everything for the girl he loves. But it's not so easy to throw away a lifetime of training and tradition. I didn't fancy starting out broke. More than that, I didn't fancy giving Jim the axe. Jim and I, overseas, had dreamed great schemes for going into business together. I knew how far we'd get, with Father not only refusing financial backing but out to teach me a lesson and bring me crawling back on hands and knees. He would have done it, too. So I hadn't seen Jim since the war, nor Trudy since Camp Shanks. And here she was.

She was so tiny. The top of her head didn't come to my shoulder. I realized what a kid she must have been, back then. But I wasn't as old either, back then. She had matured, and for the better. Her hair was auburn, with glints of fire, the skin delicate to go with that kind of hair; small pointed breasts, slender hips, nice legs. This girl I might have got into no end of trouble by making her my wife.

"… postmarked here," Trudy was saying to Clara. "So why did Jim write a letter? Certainly Jim knows that I—" She turned, realizing the person behind her hadn't moved past. She edged farther from the door. "It's as if he didn't trust me. But—" Her head snapped quickly around again, eyes wide with recognition.

"Hello, Trudy," I said.

Her lips had parted in surprise, her face softening in the way I remembered, back when it had all been possible. We began drawing together. Then her lips tightened and the moment was over. She stiffened and deliberately turned her back on me. It was a nice back. All of her was nice.

"Trudy," I said, "I know now Jim is alive. I'm here to do all I can. I want to help."

"Will you tell this person to go away," she said to Clara. "I don't know him and I'm not in the mood to be picked up."

"Trudy," Clara said reprovingly. "You must realize—"

"I don't want anything to do with this person," Trudy said. She added bitterly, "Jim's best friend!"

"Why don't you two quit acting like a couple of kids?" Cranston said from behind me. "We've all got to pitch in and help Jim."

"He's not interested in Jim," Trudy said sharply. "He proved that once."

Clara made a helpless gesture to me. I went along the hallway and through the reception room, Clara following. She gave a reassuring smile to the victims there, opened the door and came into the corridor with me. "Hank," she said. Then seeing the corridor wasn't empty, she lowered her voice. A man was waiting at the elevator. He was a man with a big nose, wearing a trench coat and chewing absently at a humpbacked cigar. Clara whispered, "Where is he, Hank?"

"Jim? I wish I—"

"Shh." She indicated the man at the elevator and came close. Closer than necessary. I felt the yielding pressure of hip and breast, and I stood frozen against her soft warmth. "Hank, you can tell *me*," she whispered throatily, pressing closer. "I've got to see him. You can arrange it."

Jim had written to get next to Clara. I wondered if he knew how easy it would be.

"Tell me where he is, Hank," she urged softly.

"I don't know that."

Her upturned face made a knowing, confident smile. I decided she was fully aware of what she did to men. And she was trying to do it to me.

"Just tell me this—is he all right?"

"I know nothing about it."

"Then why did Jim tell me over the phone that everything would be all right when you got here?"

"He told you that?" My voice rose with surprise. She laid a finger against my lips. The elevator door opened. The man with the trench coat got in; a voice from the elevator said no smoking, please; the door shut.

"Yes," Clara said. "That everything would be all right when you got here. Then when you called around, naturally I thought— Haven't you seen him? Really, Hank?"

I don't know what my face showed, but I was never any good at poker and I felt almost as smart as a trained chimp. Jim's letter, telling me to get close to Clara without letting her know who I was, had intimated that she was implicated in his disappearance. And yet Jim had, after writing me such directions, phoned to tell her I was coming. It was entirely possible that she wouldn't have recognized me, despite the photograph, unless she was expecting me.

Nothing added up. Maybe, I thought, conditions had changed from the time Jim wrote to me. Too many things were coming at once. Discovering that Jim was alive. Being trailed by Hap and Millie. Finding that my teeth were on the verge of explosion. Meeting Clara and Trudy and getting a high-voltage shock—though of a different kind—from each. At least, too many things for me.

"No, I haven't seen Jim," I said, answering her question.

"But you've been in contact with him. All along. That's why you didn't come out here when Jim wanted it to appear as suicide. That's why you're here now, when Jim is ready to come back to us. You've been helping Jim, all along."

I began mumbling a protest and her fingers touched my lips again. "No lies, Hank. Where are you staying, so we can keep in touch?" I gave her my room number at the Mark. She said, "I'll see you later; we're busy right now." She went into the reception room and I went to the elevator.

Outside, I found the world had turned dark since I'd entered Cranston's office. Now a high fog hid the sun and it was cold. I decided the exercise would do me good and began walking to the hotel. But it seemed impossible to walk fast enough to keep warm. Jim had told me July could be the coldest month of the year in San Francisco.

I hurried along with my hands in my pockets, wishing for the topcoat in my luggage while my tongue probed at the sore places in my mouth. Four teeth. A hell of a note. A full set of plates if I didn't get it attended to right away. Cranston's suggestion of hoisting a few for courage was no good. Alcohol didn't work on me that way. Strictly a one-highball man. A soft, pampered product of wealth. Couldn't even face the prospect of having a few teeth pulled. A fine specimen.

I was puffing from the climb, but still chilled, when I reached the
hotel on top of the hill. The warmth of the lobby felt good after the
raw wind outside. The clerk gave me my key and an envelope that
was in the box. My name was typed on the envelope, in that smudged
lettering with a high *E* key.

At a glance I knew it had been written on Jim's battered Corona.
While the high *E* was the most distinctive feature, there were a
dozen little things about that machine that added up to recognition,
just as you know somebody's handwriting without knowing why.
The note inside said:

> Couldn't you have worn dark glasses or something? Now Clara
> is hep to you. I hope you didn't spill your guts to her. Watch
> your step, Hank. This means everything to me.
>
> *Jim*

How did he know? I thought of the victims in the waiting room. Of
the man with the cigar waiting for the elevator. Of Trudy. Of Cranston.

I asked the clerk. "Who left this message for me?"

"I really couldn't say, sir. We were busy. I found the envelope on the
desk so I put it in your box."

I went up to my room with an old familiar feeling. It was that
feeling of tight expectancy that had come on those early mornings of
the air war, when I'd filed into the briefing room with the combat
crews and sat there waiting for the officer to pull the white sheet
from the big map and disclose the destination of the mission. It was
a feeling that things had been planned ahead for you and that there
was nothing you could do about it.

5

In the room, I walked up and down a while. Then I unpacked my
luggage. My suits, pressed by the desert heat, looked as if they'd
been slept in wet. I walked up and down some more. Why the hell
hadn't Jim told me how to make contact with him? Didn't he want to
see me?

I put on my topcoat, phoned for my car and went down. At the
desk, I told the clerk to have the valet take care of my suits. I went
out into the raw wind and waited, thankful for the topcoat, until my

car swung up before the entrance. The boy who brought it told me how to get to Golden Gate Bridge.

I followed California to Van Ness, made a right turn along it and watched for the sign. As the boy had said, I couldn't miss it. I followed the sign to the left, along a divided boulevard. The fog was getting thicker here, and by the time I reached the bridge approach I snapped on the headlights, not to see but to be seen.

I stopped for the toll gate, then drove slowly across the bridge, windshield wipers clicking back and forth. Suddenly, halfway across the bridge, I broke out of the fog into brilliant afternoon sunlight; and before I had reached the end of the span the topcoat was feeling too warm. A hell of a climate. I drove along the highway carved through the hills until I found a place to turn around, then headed back.

As I came onto the bridge from this side I saw the fog piled up like dirty whipped cream, shrouding the city from the sun overhead. The bridge span faded into the high bank of grayness. No wonder everybody worked in San Francisco but lived elsewhere, across the bay or down the peninsula. Driving into that bank of fog was like going into a refrigerator; within a hundred yards the climate had changed completely.

I realized that it would be easy enough for Jim, at night in a heavy fog, to park on the bridge and walk away, leaving a suicide note in his car. Or someone could have followed in another car to pick him up. It wasn't a matter of how, but why. I drove back to the hotel.

The door of my room was unlocked. I went in to find my suits, freshly pressed, lying on the bed, and the valet using the phone. The room smelled of the humpbacked cigar in the valet's mouth.

"No, I couldn't say," the valet was saying as I came in; then, quickly: "Here is Mr. Oates, now." He gave me the phone. "It's for you, sir."

I said hello, and Clara's throaty voice said, "How are you, Hank?" Somehow she could put more sex into a simple line like that than a strip tease. I said I was fine. "Getting settled?" she asked. I said I was. "Leo—Dr. Cranston—asked me to call. He's been expecting you back. Do you want him to wait?"

"Well, I don't know about this afternoon, Clara."

"He's careful, Hank. There'll be no pain."

"It isn't that. I—just can't get used to the idea. Let me sleep on it."

"If you wish, Hank. Any more headaches?"

"No."

"Has Jim contacted you?"

I said, "No," wondering how phony my voice sounded. I'm no good at a lie.

"My thought was, Hank, that you'd better get this teeth business out of the way while you can. You might be busy later."

"You're right, Clara. But today—" Suddenly something hit me. I yelled, "Hold the phone!" and ran out.

But the elevator had already gone down. I walked slowly back to the room, reflecting that I had indeed lived a sheltered life. It just hadn't dawned on me at the time that a hotel valet doesn't wear a trench coat and smoke a humpbacked cigar while on duty. That was the same man who had been in the corridor waiting for the elevator outside Cranston's office.

My things, I found, had been pawed through. Which was bad enough without the pawer leaving marks on my white shirts. Nothing seemed to be missing.

I was engrossed in examining the luggage when I heard the phone click. I went to it and said hello, but the line was dead. I put the phone on the cradle. There was no point in calling Clara back; I had to get used to this teeth situation, and another day wouldn't be the deciding factor. I dampened the corner of a hand towel and began working on the paw marks on my shirts.

Somebody knocked on the door. I opened it to find myself face to face with Trudy.

There was a bright spot on each cheekbone that wasn't rouge. I said hello. She said, "Well, aren't you going to ask me in?" I stepped aside and she swept past me, her back stiff. I offered her a chair. "This is not a social call," she said, and remained standing. "This is embarrassing, for both of us."

"Cigarette?"

She ignored the extended pack. "You know I don't smoke."

"I know you didn't. But people change."

"Don't they?" she said.

"Trudy, it wouldn't have worked out. Though I don't expect you to understand."

"Never mind the excuses. It was the luckiest thing that ever happened to me. When I think how close I came to marrying a spineless, comfort-worshipping mama's boy like you ... We can be thankful for some things."

"I'm glad you feel that way about it."

"How else would I feel? Oh!" She laughed. "You mean my broken heart? Pining for you? Sitting night after night with a light at the window? Never looking at another man? You hate yourself, don't you? What do you expect—that I'm here now to throw myself at your feet and beg for a pat on the head?"

"It's your inning," I admitted.

Suddenly her stiffness was gone. "Hank, let's not quarrel. The past is over and done with. I came to apologize."

"For what?"

"Hank, where is he? I've got to see Jim."

"I know nothing about Jim."

"But you're here because— Oh, Hank, you know what it means to me. Knowing he's alive and not knowing ..." She sat down and began worrying the finger of a glove. She was a lovely girl. A miniature watch-charm of a girl. I wanted to put her in my pocket or something.

I wondered what might have happened if I'd seen her, just once, after coming back from overseas. The memory of the flesh-and-blood Trudy had dimmed after two years in Europe. But if I'd seen her again, held her in my arms, the family dignity might not have seemed so important. Being disinherited might not have been so important. Nothing but being together might have been important. But that was water under the bridge.

"I realize that if Jim wanted me to know—but still it seems that of all people I might ..." She made a little shrug. "I know how men are. They never trust a girl. Or they don't want her mixed up in something. As if I couldn't take it! As if I wouldn't do anything in the world to help Jim! But I want him to know—and you to know—that if there's anything I can do ... Anything at all. That's why I'm here now."

She regarded the finger of her glove intently. "I've been such a fool. Now I understand. All along you were doing what was best for Jim. That's why you didn't come out here when he—disappeared. You knew that Jim wanted to hide. And now that he needs help, you're here. And I thought that you— Can you forgive me?"

I felt like an impostor. But there didn't seem to be a way of explaining without saying too much. Until I saw Jim and learned the situation, I had to keep mum.

The phone rang.

"What happened, Hank?" Clara asked.

"A man was searching my room."

"What! Who was he?"

"You remember the joker who was waiting at the elevator when you and I were talking in the corridor?"

"I'm afraid I don't." Her voice softened. "I was looking at you, Hank."

"Well, it was the same guy, anyhow."

"You turned him over to the police?"

"He got away. I didn't report it. I don't know what's going on yet; and he didn't take anything."

"Maybe it's best to say nothing. Who was the guy who answered your phone?"

"That's the joker I'm talking about. I thought he was the valet. When I walked in he handed me the phone; it didn't sink in for a while."

"Oh," she said, and I realized I had not made myself out either a mental giant or razor-sharp. "We're closing the office now, unless you want to come over. We'll wait for you."

"Let me sleep on it."

"Fraidy cat."

"I've got to get used to it." There was a polite tap on the door. I nodded at Trudy, who crossed to it.

"I know how you feel, Hank. You need a night out, to forget your troubles."

This was my cue to ask if she was free for the evening. "Hank!" Trudy cried. "It's a letter—from Jim!"

A silent coolness seemed to come from the other end of the phone, as if a refrigeration unit had been connected to the line.

"Oh," Clara said. "I didn't know you had company." She hung up.

I put the phone down and turned to Trudy, who was oblivious of any *faux pas*. "It's from Jim!" she cried, waving an envelope. "Only one typewriter in the world could have written that name on the envelope!"

I took it. "Who delivered it?"

"A bellhop. I tipped him. Open it, Hank!"

As I turned away to open it she crowded close, peering over my arm. "That's not polite."

"Polite and be damned. He's my brother."

"Trudy, Jim sent this to me. Until I see him and find out—"

"Oh, for heaven's sake!" She snatched the envelope and ripped it open, dodging as I tried to grab her. She darted into the bathroom and slammed the door. She locked it when I tried to follow.

"A fine thing, trying to follow me in here!"

"I'll spank your bottom!"

"Shut up, I'm reading Jim's letter."

After a few moments of waiting, I said, "Well, what does it say? If it's any of my business."

She came out, the letter in her hand. "I can't figure it out." She gave it to me. It said:

> Hank,
>   Target: Skyline; 2100 hours. Rev it slow and form on group signal. Follow formation to aiming point.
>
> Jim

I crumpled the letter into an ash tray, struck a match. "Wait," Trudy said. "Do you understand it?"

"Yes." I touched the match to the letter.

"Well, all right. Keep it to yourself."

"I intend to."

She doubled her fists. "There are times when I wish I was a man!"

"There are times when I'm glad you're not."

"Oh, go to hell." She whirled and went out, slamming the door.

I was left with the memory of the glimpse of her pretty knees as she whirled, and of what might have been. I felt very tired and I could still taste the stuff Cranston had painted my gums with. I brushed my teeth, then got into pajamas. I phoned the desk to ring me at seven, and climbed into bed.

The rat in my skull woke me. He was ravenous now. Rabid. I staggered blindly to my coat for the aspirin, swallowed a couple, gulped a glass of water. Then I sat on the bed, pressing down on my eyeballs until the pain began to die away, slowly.

What the hell kind of a coward was I? This sort of thing didn't cure itself. Whoever heard of an infected tooth getting well of itself? The four bad ones could be out by now. Whatever pain came after the hypo wore off wouldn't be as bad as the biting and gnawing in my brain. I crawled back into bed, dopey, exhausted from my jangled nerves.

I'd hardly closed my eyes when the phone rang. It wouldn't quit. I wobbled to it. "Yes?"

"Seven o'clock, sir. You left a call."

"You're crazy!"

"You didn't leave a call, sir?"

I looked at my watch. "Yeah, thanks."

I felt like hell. Sleeping in the daytime, too long for a nap, too short for a sleep. There was fur on my teeth and my eyeballs felt like somebody had stepped on them. After a shower and a tooth-brushing I felt better. I looked at my teeth in the mirror. White and even, apparently perfect; a beautiful front for decay and pus.

I got dressed, phoned for my car. I was going down the elevator when the infernal ache began pounding in my head. I felt as if it would fly off my shoulders. I left the elevator and made a beeline for the hotel drugstore. This time I got a large bottle of aspirin. I took three of them.

Outside, I knuckled my eyes while waiting for the car, as the aspirins and the rat fought a death battle. "Hank, are you sick?"

Trudy was beside me.

"What the hell are you doing here? Leave me alone."

"What is it, Hank? You look awful. You passed right by me in the lobby. Is it your eyes?"

"Just a headache. I took some aspirins."

"You ought to see a doctor. A headache is a warning signal that something else—"

"I know, I know. It's my teeth. Four of them have to come out."

"Why don't you have it done?"

"I will. Tomorrow."

"Leo Cranston is very good. There's no pain. I've lost two—wisdom teeth."

My car swung before the entrance. Trudy slipped under the wheel. "I'd better drive."

I got in. The rat seemed to be getting used to aspirin. I swallowed a couple more. Presently my head began to feel more normal. "Hey, wait a minute. Where are you going?"

"With you."

"The hell you say."

"While I didn't understand the note, I know that 2100 hours means nine o'clock tonight. I thought we could have dinner together and talk things over—about Jim."

"Okay, but you're not flying this mission with me."

She didn't answer that one.

She turned right into Market and followed it into the hills, where it became Portola Drive. We came out of the hills onto Junipero Serra Boulevard, and a mile or so further on pulled up at a drive-in. I said,

"Can't we do better than this?"

"There's a dining room connected, and the food is good. You don't have to impress me, Mr. Oates; I know you're rich."

We went into the dining room. Trudy excused herself. I supposed she'd made a trip to the little girls' room, until she rejoined me and said, "I was right, Hank. We are being followed."

6

The head waiter took us to a table, handed us menus and, his duty done, bowed away.

I said, "Are you sure?"

"Of course not!" Trudy said sharply. "Things like that just don't happen to Henry Chatworth Oates III."

"Let's forget personalities. I was followed across four states on the trip out here. Somebody is very anxious to keep an eye on me."

Her eyes went to the menu. "Sorry, Hank. Yes, I'm sure. In driving through town I just happened to hit three stop lights at the change; a car behind me ran through the red. It was still behind me on Portola Drive, so I made some crazy turns in the hills and it followed. And now it's parked at the drive-in."

"A green Chevy with a dent in the right front fender?"

"No, it's a brown car—an old jalopy. As you go out, it's the farthest car on the left."

"I'll take a look. Order me a T-bone, medium."

I went out and turned left around the semicircle of the drive-in, looking about in the manner of someone searching for the little boy's room. A red-headed car hop smiled and said, "Clear around to the left."

I thanked her and kept on. A brown Auburn was parked in the last space of the semicircle. At the wheel, trying to make himself fit behind a strawberry soda, was a big-nosed man wearing a trench coat. A humpbacked cigar, soggy and mangled from gnawing, was on the door tray. I stepped alongside.

"Small world."

He came out from behind the strawberry soda and gave me the eye. It was a small eye, but steady. "Henry Chatworth Oates III."

I was surprised; I'd expected him to claim he'd never set eye on me before. "You were searching my room."

"You say so."

"What's your aim in life?"

He took the humpbacked cigar from the door tray and looked at it with distaste. He flipped it away. "What I would really like is a four-bit cigar."

I laid a half dollar on the tray. "Buy yourself one."

He had a small mouth under the big nose. It became tiny as the lips tightened. "Pick it up," he said. "You can't buy me."

I picked it up. "That wasn't the idea."

He didn't say anything.

I said, "Why are you following me?"

"Who says I'm following anybody? Maybe you drive a Lincoln convertible and me a bucket of bolts, but I've got just as much right as you to stop at a drive-in for a strawberry soda."

There didn't seem much point in going into the matter. I turned away.

"Hank."

I turned back.

He said, "All cats are gray in the dark." Then he put his attention to the strawberry soda.

I went inside and rejoined Trudy. Our salad had arrived. I asked her, "Do you know the guy?"

"I've been trying to think. I know I've seen him some place before." She pressed her fingertips to her temples, shut her eyes. "If I saw him in a familiar place … Maybe it will come to me."

"Maybe it's important."

"I realize that, but it doesn't help. I'll keep thinking about it. And now tell me about Jim. Is he all right?"

"I know nothing about Jim except for a couple of letters. One was written a few days ago—the fourteenth—mailed from San Francisco. It said he needed help, and asked me to come out. You saw the other, about the rendezvous tonight."

"That's what it meant? That you're meeting him tonight?"

"Yes."

"Hank, I can't wait!"

"You won't be seeing him."

"Don't be silly! You just try to shake me!"

"Somebody's got to take care of our friend outside. I can't be followed."

"What can I do?"

"He's a man and you're a pretty girl, yet you ask that?"

She sighed. "Okay, damn it."

"I need some background on this. I know nothing at all. You wrote a note to me at the time he—when it appeared suicide. Why were you suspicious?"

"Hank, he had absolutely no reason. His health was good, he was happy, he stood to make a great deal of money—but more than anything, I just knew Jim wouldn't take his own life."

I considered this, and her. The small, innocent, little-girl appeal went over very well with big strong men. But I happened to know she had a brain.

"Don't you know, or don't you want to tell?" I said. She looked up from her salad, resentful. I said, "Whether he jumped off the bridge or faked it adds up to the same thing—he had to have good reason."

Our steaks came. Something had given me good appetite, perhaps fighting that rat. I waited for Trudy to say something. She looked across the table appealingly, but I met the look with the expectant expression of a man waiting for an answer.

"At the time Jim disappeared, I—" She hesitated, then finished with a rush: "—I suspected Clara of killing him for the insurance."

"His ten thousand GI?"

"No; he didn't keep that up. But a year ago he took out a policy for fifty thousand. That's a lot of money. Some people will do anything for money. I—was wrong to suspect Clara."

"That's a pretty heavy insurance load," I said.

"Jim took it out for business reasons. He went into partnership with Irving Kline. A real estate development. Jim and Kline each took out fifty thousand in insurance for mutual business protection."

"Who is Irving Kline?"

"A real estate man. He and Jim had been friends for a number of years, before they went into business together."

"They took out the insurance about a year ago?"

"Last July. Just a year ago. Jim and Kline were doing very well, too. They were subdividing and building on an estate Jim inherited from Uncle Jasper. That's what made me unable to believe he would commit suicide. I suspected Clara of killing him for the insurance. That's why I wrote you. Though I didn't want to put what I thought into a letter."

"But if he suicided, she wouldn't get the insurance."

Trudy shrugged, making an embarrassed smile. "Yes; I found that out later. The policy was void if he suicided within a year. But I didn't know that at the time. I was terribly upset."

"With most companies it's two years."

"One year in this case. I've seen the policy."

"Clara is the beneficiary?"

"Yes."

"That isn't good business practice."

"I wouldn't know about that. But she is."

"Assuming she could have collected, is she the kind who would do it?"

"No."

"You're not making sense."

"This is embarrassing, Hank. I thought so at the time. Now I'm sure she isn't."

"What made you think so?"

"Do we have to go into it?"

"I think we'd better."

"Well—Clara had an affair with her boss while Jim was overseas—Leo Cranston."

"Oh," I said. "Jim found it out and—"

"No." She cut me off sharply. "You don't understand Clara. I didn't. Jim and Clara got along fine after he returned. And now I know that Jim was the love of her life."

"Just how do you know that?"

"You should see their apartment. It's a little frightening, how Clara refused to accept things. It would give you the creeps. What I mean, we all thought Jim was dead. But she wouldn't accept it. She kept his clothes hanging in the closet. His pipes and house slippers by his chair. His hat on the radio. His tools just where he had left them, in the garage workshop—the magazine rack he'd been making still in the glue clamps. Clara never talked as if Jim were dead and gone. It was as if he might walk in any minute." She made a little shiver.

"You've made a baffling portrait of Clara. On the one hand a girl who wants a good time; on the other, a one-man woman gone neurotic over the loss of her husband."

"That's why I didn't like to go into this. Now we know Jim is alive. I misjudged Clara. To her, being true to a man and being in love with him are separate things."

I remembered a WAC I'd known overseas who fit that so well. Which, I decided, was another thing Father wouldn't understand.

"What was this real estate deal of Jim's?"

"I don't know much more than what I told you. He and Kline were subdividing and building on some property left by Uncle Jasper. Kline is making a lot of money for Jim."

"But the partnership is dissolved with Jim's suicide."

"We know Jim is alive."

"Legally—"

"No body was found. Jim is legally alive. Kline is keeping on with the business in Jim's name."

"Why is Clara working for Leo Cranston? She should be looking after Jim's business interests."

"She has no authority to, under the partnership agreement. And she needs the money she gets as wages."

"I thought you said Kline was making money for Jim."

"He is, but he won't give Clara any. He says it's impossible. I don't really understand it, Hank."

It seemed to me that there were wheels within wheels. I took down Kline's name and address. "Dessert?" Trudy said she had to watch her figure. I fancied some pie and ice cream, but passed it up. I was afraid overeating might wake up that rat. So I got the check, paid it, and we went out.

"Darling!" Trudy cried as we came around the front of the drive-in. She rushed to the brown Auburn and might have embraced the flabbergasted man within except that he edged to the other side of the seat. Trudy piled inside, behind the wheel. "Darling, where have you been keeping yourself?" She waved gaily at me. "You go on, Hank. Honey will take me home!"

I drove on. As I wheeled out of the drive-in, Trudy yelled, "Hank, I remember! His name is White!"

His name was White. Now that was a big help.

7

The dashboard clock showed one minute to nine. I was parked in a clump of acacia near a little lake which the map called Laguna de la Merced. I knew the trees were acacia because Jim had once, while on leave to London, taken me to Kew Gardens and pointed out a spindly specimen under glass. This spot was, according to the map, the beginning of Skyline Boulevard.

The fog was roiling thick, boiling like smoke as headlights groped past. Since leaving Trudy I'd done some dodging around; I was sure nobody had followed me. I'd been out of cigarettes for half an hour. I got a twisted stub from the ash tray, straightened it, got it going. Then I started my car, snapped on the lights and began creeping slowly along Skyline, waiting for whatever was to happen.

It was nine-fourteen by the dash clock when fuzzy headlights snapped on behind me. A car, blacked out, had been following my taillights. It swept around and went ahead; from the brief and fuzzy look at it I couldn't tell the make, or even the color. Then from ahead its twin taillights blinked on and off four times. After an interval they repeated the signal.

This was what I'd been watching for; and, briefly, in the fog, it seemed as if I was again at the waist of a B-17 as the bombers circled for altitude. After an hour or so of climbing in the fog over England they would break into the cold sunlight; in all directions could be seen the tiny four-engine bombers climbing out of the clouds like swarming bees as a thousand or more formed for the attack. And there were the old assembly planes, tired and war-weary bombers stripped of armament and painted outlandishly in stripes and dots, with big electric letters on their sides, spewing rockets so the thousand planes could form on them, group by group. Which used to be a military secret. And the assembly ship of our group shot four red rockets.

Was Jim in the car ahead that had given me the old group signal? If so, why couldn't he stop for just a few moments to shake hands and say hello? But mine not to reason why.

The lead car set a good pace, crowding the turns of the winding road. Presently it turned to the right, into a side road that switched back and forth downgrade. This road lasted but a few miles, ending in a T-intersection. As I turned left after the car ahead, my headlights picked up a reflector sign; I was on Highway 1.

From the right came the boom of breakers, a moist roar in the night faintly audible above the whir of the engine. Soon the road tilted upwards, winding among cut and fill as it sliced through a series of ragged ridges and canyons. We reached the crest and began the descent.

The stoplight of the car ahead glowed on and off intermittently as it braked for the curves; it was going too fast for a steep road slick with moisture. The stoplight blinked on and stayed on, swerved sharply in a hard left turn into a narrow side road. My tires squealed as I followed, and I imagined Jim grinning in the car ahead. He used to scare the daylights out of me in a jeep.

The side road followed a brush-grown ravine. I hadn't followed more than a hundred yards when the car ahead swung sharply off the road against a bank of overhanging brush, and stopped. The lights blacked off. I snapped off my lights, got out. The door of the car ahead slammed. From somewhere nearby, the boom of the surf came heavily through the fog. With lights out, I could see nothing at all. Footsteps scrunched toward me from the car ahead.

"Hank," a voice said.

"Jim!"

Then the figure melted into view. It wasn't Jim. This man was too short, too thin. In the night fog, the face was a blur between hat and upturned overcoat collar.

"I'll take you to him, Hank."

I had the impression of age, partly from the voice and partly from the jerky agility of the man's movements. I had the feeling, too, that I should know this person. But he didn't stop to get acquainted.

Snapping on a flashlight, he pointed it at the ground and led the way back along the side road to the highway. Headlights appeared out of nowhere. The flash snapped off and we stood motionless as a car whisked past and vanished around a curve.

"Better do without a light from here on," he muttered. "Keep close, Hank; it's dark as a pocket."

We crossed the highway, walking up the slope. On the left and far below came the boom of the surf. A stone guard rail alternated with sheer rock walls. I wondered how much it had cost the taxpayers to slice this highway through the mountains. In most places, roads were made where roads were possible; in California, roads were made where they were wanted, possible or no.

Another set of headlights appeared. I turned away from the glare until it had passed; I could see a little now and wanted to keep my eyes in shape. I continued along beside the little man, who set a steady pace up the grade. There seemed neither time nor distance in the fog. Cars swept by every few moments. I wondered where people had to go in fog like this. Though maybe they were used to it and didn't let it bother them. Once as I turned away from the glow of an approaching car I was facing a signboard. It contained a warning not to go down to the beach. There were ten white crosses representing those who had lost their lives here. Do you, the sign asked, want to be number eleven?

I asked, "Where are we?"

"Devil's Slide."

We walked through a cut in the rock mountain. Then the little man turned left onto a rough concrete driveway rising steeply. This brought us to a high mesh fence, the gate secured by chain and padlock. A sign was fastened to the gate, but the lettering was too weathered to read.

"We'll go around the fence," the little man said, pointing to the left. He was puffing from the walk. "It ends at the face of the road cut. Don't fall."

The fence paralleled the highway below. We edged along, clinging to the dank mesh, scrambling for footing on the slick slope. As a car swept by below and for the first time I got the perspective of height, I knew a fall would be highly unpleasant. The fence ended in a fan of barbed wire. I inched around this and followed the little man down a steep slope. A low building, set into the side of the mountain, melted out of the fog; I felt concrete again beneath my feet. The little man squatted on his heels, puffing.

"Out of shape," he gasped. "Cigarette?"

I took one. The little man struck a match, and as he brought his cupped hands to his face I got my first good look. He raised the face, grinning. "Surprised?" Then he flipped the match away.

It was Hap Arnold, my pal of the highway.

I said, "What the hell is this?"

"Jim sent us to follow you out here—me and Millie."

"Jim didn't send you on a badger game."

"Badger game?" he asked. Then he laughed. "Hell, Hank, Millie was just trying to be friendly. She's like that, when she's had a few drinks." He laughed again. "So that's why you scrammed out of Salt Lake?" He chuckled. "Me, I was asleep when she come hammering at my door in the middle of the night. Said she was waiting for you with a bottle, and must have passed out when you come in. When she woke up, you was gone. Don't get the wrong idea of Millie. She's a nice girl. Just friendly."

"I don't think I buy it."

He shrugged. "Figure it out for yourself, Hank. How would we know you'd be leaving for the Coast? Why would I be there with my thumb out, every time you passed through a town?"

"You tell me."

"Jim sent us. We knew when his letter to you would arrive."

"Why?"

"Protection, Hank. That's why we didn't tell you nothing. We was just to keep close to you."

"Protection from what?"

"Hank, Jim ain't playing for fun." He brought a bottle from his overcoat pocket. "Drink?"

"Not right now. What's he mixed up in?"

"He'd rather tell you that. You wouldn't believe me anyhow. Nobody would believe it, except an old friend. That's why he needs you." He unscrewed the cap and tilted the bottle. He lowered it with a deep sigh of satisfaction. "Good for what ails you on a night like this. Sure?"

"No, thanks. Where is Jim?"

He jerked a thumb at the mountain. "Up on top."

"Let's go."

"Jim will keep a couple minutes longer. Got to get my wind back."

I indicated the low building built into the mountain. "What's this place?"

"Radar station during the War. Good hideout."

"Why has he been hiding out?"

"He'll want to tell you about that." The little man stood up, rubbing stiff knees. "Not getting no earlier."

We went up concrete steps set into the side of the mountain. I crowded the bank, for there was no guard rail. Nothing could be seen off the low side except that the mountain pitched steeply away. The steps seemed endless, one after another rising upward into the grayness. Hap stopped twice on the way to get his breath and take a pull from the bottle. There was a tightness in my throat that wasn't entirely due to the climb. Jim was waiting on top. Soon I'd know everything.

We reached the top of the stairs. Hap Arnold struck off along the ragged crest of the mountain. The footing was rough—raw stone with scrub brush growing in the creases. Hap stopped on a bare shelf of rock; his breath wheezed noisily. He was too old and out of condition to have made that climb. He pointed into the fog.

"Jim's over there."

I moved that way, then stopped suddenly, loins tightening. The rock shelved off directly at my feet. Through the fog below, far below, came the boom of the surf. One more step would be too many. And the little man had pointed, saying, "Jim's over there." Hap had expected me to step off into oblivion.

At the moment I felt only the tight and frantic exasperation of a man who realizes that he's been a chump. Hap Arnold had almost taken me once, on a badger game, and now I'd let him take me for my life.

I turned, knowing what I would see. The little man's right arm was pointed stiffly at me. The legs were braced. His breath was wheezing. He had a gun in his hand.

"Keep walking," he muttered.

"Why?" I said. "What have I done to you?"

"It's your own fault, Hank. I told you not to come. I tried to stop you. It's your fault, not mine."

"You were the voice on the phone—Smith?"

"Yes, with my teeth out and my scarf over the phone. I tried to make you stay away. Then I tried to stop you with Millie in Salt Lake. I done my best, Hank. Don't blame me."

"What about the threat of scandal involving Mother?"

"It's too late, Hank. You're here, now. He's going to kill you, for Jim. He thinks I'm a fool. I can see through it. Where would that leave me? He gets the money and where am I? He proves Jim is alive and then he kills you for Jim, and what have I got?"

The little man was beside himself, speaking very rapidly, his breath heavy and labored.

"Who?" I asked. "Who is killing me for Jim?"

"Speck. But why should you care? You ain't going to tell nobody, Hank."

So someone called Speck was attempting to kill me at Jim's orders. Hap for some reason had tried to spike the plan but now was going through with it for personal reasons.

"Hank, there's no use talking. Step back. Step off."

"No."

"Then I've got to shoot you, Hank."

"You won't shoot me."

"Why won't I? By God, I will! I got to!"

"Not with the safety catch on," I said, and jumped for the gun.

I had a fraction of a second as Hap's eyes went to the gun. Then the weapon went off, practically in my face. I crashed into the little man, bore him over.

Arnold was spry and clever. He fell without resistance, then gave a sudden twist in mid-air and was on top. I crashed heavily. A knob of rock caught me in the short ribs. My breath and strength suddenly were gone.

The little man scrambled away. I pushed myself slowly to my knees, and it was like a dream where you have no strength or speed. My breathing apparatus was frozen; I was numbed and groggy. Arnold had dropped the gun when I hit him. Now he dived frantically for it, as if he expected me to be springing after him.

He snatched the weapon from the flat rock and whirled, springing backwards to avoid the expected charge. And he went backwards too far.

He started toppling off the lip of the cliff, balanced on one toe, tense and terribly intent. Then suddenly he began flailing his arms. The toe slipped on crumbling rock. He fell, catching himself by his forearms on the edge of the cliff. The gun went off as it struck the rock. He hung by his forearms on the rock shelf, frozen, afraid to move.

"For God's sake," he croaked tightly. "I'm going over."

I was sick and numb, still unable to get my breath. The fingers of Arnold's left hand were wedged in a crack of the rock. The right hand was useless; he'd numbed it striking the rock while holding the gun. The gun was lying under the useless hand. I crawled toward him.

"For God's sweet sake," he pleaded, "hurry."

I reached for the gun, just to make sure. The little man misinterpreted the move, released his hold in the crack and snatched at my wrist. His fingernails raked my hand as I jerked back. He clawed for another handhold and then slipped over the edge of the rock. His scream came on a descending note, like the whistle of a train that has gone past. It ended suddenly. Then nothing could be heard but the boom of the surf below.

I remained on hands and knees, wondering if my breath ever would come back. I felt futile and empty as well as sick. If I'd been able to talk, I could have reassured the little man. Arnold had misunderstood the gesture for the gun.

My breath came back in a gasp. I sank face down on the wet rock, just breathing.

Presently I realized I was chilled through. The legs of my pants were wet from wading through the brush. I sat up, put the gun in my overcoat pocket, got to my feet and began walking through the fog toward the landing of the concrete stairs somewhere ahead. There was a sinking feeling in my short ribs with each breath. I couldn't forget Hap Arnold's face as it disappeared from sight—that expression as the little man realized his time on this earth was over.

Jim. My best friend. He had engaged someone called Speck to kill me. The letter asking me to come to San Francisco was for the sole purpose of luring me to my death. Hap Arnold didn't want me killed. He'd tried to stop me with a phone call. Then he'd tried to frame me with Millie, to stop me that way. And finally he had tried to kill me himself. Why? Why would he try to save my life, and then try to take it? The only difference was that now I had come to San Francisco; for some reason that meant he had to kill me instead of save my life.

I remembered what Clara had told me. Jim had phoned her, saying everything would be all right when I arrived. Now I realized that meant his reappearance depended upon my death. Which would mean that he had disappeared in the first place because of me. But what could be the reason? I hadn't seen Jim since the war. That was a long time ago. How could I have made it necessary for Jim to vanish? How could my death solve his predicament?

I put my hands to my face, remembering the hot blast of the weapon. My left ear stung, but I could feel no wound, no warmth of oozing blood. I was somewhat surprised at what I'd done, leaping for that gun. It wasn't in character for Henry Chatworth Oates III. Or was it? Anyone will fight if cornered. Perhaps it had been the lip of the cliff behind me. There is something horrible about falling to death. Leaping at a gun is far the lesser of two evils.

Jim.

I began swearing thinly. I couldn't believe it. Not of Jim. Yet Arnold certainly had no reason to lie to me. The facts pointed all one way.

I wondered ... Trudy. I'd thrown Jim's sister over. Which had resulted in canceling the grand plans for Jim and me to assault the business world. Had Jim brooded over that? Had it festered over the years? Yet Jim wouldn't have done that. Not the Jim I knew. He wasn't the sort ...

Wait a minute, Hank, I told myself. Follow the facts. Quit thinking of what Jim *was*. People change. If he had been resentful because of my treatment of Trudy, because of lost business opportunity ...

But that didn't hold water. It didn't explain why Jim had disappeared in the first place. Nothing added up, except that I was alive now by sheer luck. It didn't matter that Hap was somehow double-crossing a man called Speck by killing me before Speck got a chance to; except for Jim, there would have been no attempt on my life. And now that Hap had failed, Speck would try to do the job.

Except that my left ear burned and my short ribs tore a little at each breath and that Hap Arnold's scream still echoed in my ears and that I was stumbling along the rocky ridge in the fog, I wouldn't have believed any part of it.

I reached the landing, went down and down the endless concrete steps. Something tight and hard and heavy was like a lead fist inside me. It wasn't just that someone was trying to kill me. I'd flown a tour of missions, I'd been shot at. What made all the difference was who was doing the trying.

Jim.

I reached the bottom of the stairs, passed the low military building, went around the fence, walked down the highway to the side road and followed it to the two cars parked against the brush. In Hap's car might be something to explain all this. I tried the right-hand door of the Chevvy. It was locked.

A footstep crunched directly behind me. Then as I whirled, the fog momentarily disappeared in a shower of stars.

8

A rock was digging into my ribs. I tried to move and couldn't. Something heavy was atop me. Everything was black; something was tied over my eyes. I was cold. I tried to move again, against the pressure. My wrists were behind my back, lashed together. My ankles were bound tightly.

"Awake, Hank?" a voice whispered into my ear.

"Get off me."

"Cigarette?" the whisper asked.

"Okay."

The cigarette came. It came against my neck; the hot end. I struggled to get away from it, but didn't get far. I was lying face down; someone was on my back, someone on my legs, someone ramming my head against the sharp pebbles of the hard surface on which I was lying.

The cigarette was taken away, and the whisper came, "We're not fooling, Hank."

"You've made your point," I admitted.

"Where's Jim?"

"I don't know."

The cigarette touched my neck again. "I don't know!" I yelled.

"You were to meet him," the whisper said.

"But I didn't."

"What happened?"

"I just didn't make connections."

"Where's Hap Arnold?"

"I don't know."

The cigarette touched my neck again. I decided there was no point in verbal sparring. Get this over with.

"He's dead. He tried to kill me at Devil's Slide, and fell over."

"Why would he try to kill you?" the whisper asked.

"Keep that thing away from my neck. I don't know why he tried to kill me, except that it was because of Speck."

There was a bit of silence. "Speck?" the whisper asked. "Who is Speck?"

"I don't know; probably somebody who wears glasses. He said Speck was going to kill me on Jim's orders, after Jim had come out of hiding. Hap said Speck was double-crossing him—double-crossing Hap—so he had to kill me. It doesn't make a great deal of sense, because twice Hap tried to save me."

"Hap tried to save you? How?"

"I got a letter from Jim, asking me to come West to help him. On the same day I got a phone call from somebody calling himself Smith, warning me not to come." I decided to say nothing about the threatened scandal involving Mother. "Hap admitted tonight that he made that call. He tried to frame me with a badger game in Salt Lake, to keep me from coming here. But since I got here, the only thing left for Hap was to kill me. Why, I don't know."

"Then you didn't see Jim?"

"No."

"You don't know who Speck is?"

"No; and I don't know who you are. What are you after?"

"I want to find Jim," the whisper said.

"So do I," I said grimly.

"Hap told you that Speck had orders from Jim to kill you?"

"That's right. He said Speck was to kill me for Jim."

"And you don't know why?"

"No. Don't you?"

"You don't know anything," the whisper said. "You're not worth bothering with." I felt something cold against my temple. "Here's your pocket knife, Hank, under the blindfold."

The weight eased off my back, then the weight of the other person— who had said nothing—eased off my legs. Footsteps hurried away. There came the slam of a car door, growl of a starter, whine of an engine; then the crunch of tires moving away, and presently nothing could be heard but the dull boom of the surf.

I don't know how long it took, scraping my head against the ground, before I decided that was no way to dislodge the pocket knife in the blindfold. I got to my knees, bent over, and shook my head until I was dizzy. The knife fell out and clattered away. Then it was a matter of feeling for it with my hands behind my back, inching along on the seat of my pants. This took a quarter of an hour or so. Once I found it, cutting my wrists free was relatively simple. I took off the blindfold, got my ankles free. I was on a road, and that was all that could be seen in the fog.

I began walking, and presently came to a T-intersection. A car was coming along in the fog. In the brief fuzzy glow of the headlights, I saw where I was—at the intersection of the side road where Hap and I had parked. I walked back along the side road to my car, got in and drove away from that place.

My head was aching again. I didn't know whether from the teeth or because of the lump behind my right ear. I swallowed some aspirin on general principles. I turned on the heater of my car and was feeling almost human by the time I got to the city.

I walked into the lobby of the hotel to find Clara and Cranston there.

"Hank, what happened?" Clara said, rushing to me. "It isn't true, is it? I know it isn't true. Oh, you poor dear, look at your suit! You didn't do it, did you?"

"Do what?"

"Jim phoned that—"

"This is a bit public," Cranston said. We went to a corner of the lobby and sat down. "Something happened," he said, eyeing my disheveled appearance.

"Jim phoned," Clara said. "He said you'd killed Hap Arnold at Devil's Slide. Is it true? You wouldn't kill a man, Hank."

I didn't know exactly what to say. Here was Jim's loving wife, neurotic, Trudy had told me, about the loss of her husband, keeping his pipes and slippers in place, everything just as it had been when Jim walked out, as if he might walk back in any moment. I could never convince Clara that Jim was trying to murder me; nor was there any need to try. She didn't have to know that part of it. Yet.

"You know Hap Arnold?" I said.

Cranston said, "A patient of mine. What happened, Hank?"

"He was supposed to meet me tonight and take me to Jim. I got a note from Jim—"

"Yes, Trudy told us," Clara said. "You didn't kill Hap, did you, Hank?"

"What did Jim tell you when he phoned?"

"Just that you'd killed Hap at Devil's Slide, instead of coming to meet him."

"Hap took me to Devil's Slide and tried to kill me," I said. "I don't know why. In the fight he fell off the cliff."

"Hap tried to double-cross Jim," Cranston said. "We know that your arrival here means a great deal to Jim. He told you, Clara, that everything would soon be all right when Hank arrived. And, Hank, Hap tried to put you out of the way."

If they wanted to think that, it was all right by me. I said, "The police will get to the bottom of it."

"Police?" Clara said. "Hank, can you prove that he tried to kill you?"

"I will explain exactly what happened."

"Where's the body, Hank?" Cranston asked.

"In the surf somewhere below the cliff."

"They'll probably never find it," Clara said. "People have drowned there in sight of those above, and the bodies have never been recovered. Nobody has to know."

"The authorities have to know," I pointed out. "He's a human being, and now he's dead. You can't just ignore that."

"The police might think you murdered him," Cranston said.

"Don't be silly. What reason would I have?"

"What reason did he have for trying to kill you?"

"He didn't say."

Cranston's big pink face formed a wry smile.

"I'm telling you the truth," I said, a bit sharply. "He didn't explain. He just pulled a gun and told me to walk off the cliff."

"Okay, Hank," Cranston said. "That's how it happened. But how will that sound to the cops? All they've got is your word for it. Look at it from their viewpoint. You walk in and announce that you've killed a man. They ask why. You say it was because he tried to kill you. They ask you why he tried to kill you. You tell them that you don't know. Then they find out that you're Henry Chatworth Oates III, a rich playboy—"

"I'm not a playboy."

"Any young man of prominent family is automatically a playboy if he gets into a mess. The newspapers will see to that. Public sentiment will be against you; people resent wealth."

I thought of what the headlines would do to Father. And to Mother.

"Henry Chatworth Oates III, rich playboy, walks into police headquarters and announces that he's killed a man," Cranston said. "He claims self-defense, but he hasn't the foggiest notion of why the man tried to kill him. He tells a wild yarn about some mysterious notes and a rendezvous. Where are the notes? *Why, they are burned.* Who were the notes from? *From a dead man.*"

"But you two know that Jim is alive. It was in the papers."

"It was in the papers that Clara reported a telephone call from her husband. That's not proof."

Clara said, "Isn't it much simpler just to say nothing about it?"

"You will be charged with murder," Cranston said. "No doubt you'll beat the rap. Your father will get the best lawyers in the country; money can do anything. But there will be months of chaos, tons of publicity, the big trial. You'll never live it down."

"Be sensible, Hank," Clara said. "This can ruin your entire life. It can crucify your parents."

"Sleep on it, Hank," Cranston advised. He looked at his watch, stood up. "And that's what I've got to do. Drop in in the morning and we'll get to work on those teeth. I wouldn't let it go on."

He went out. Clara said, "I could certainly use a drink."

We went into the bar. She ordered a double Scotch, and I repeated it. There are times when a man wants more than his quota. I was confused, upset, appalled. Policemen had always been, to me, protectors of the *status quo*, standing between me and the unwashed rabble who yearned to get a fist into the Oates moneybags. The prospect of being grilled, accused, cast behind bars—that was something that just didn't happen to my sort of people. I didn't even know the sort of people who got into messes in the papers. Such things happened, but to a class of unfortunates I couldn't even comprehend.

But now I saw it could happen to me. And I knew only too well that Cranston spoke the truth about publicity. When a member of a prominent family *did* get into a mess, it was headline news from coast to coast, week after week and month after month. I would never outlive it. Not to mention what it would do to my parents. And what good would it do anyway? Hap was just as dead one way as the other. Why should I blight my future and crucify my family because he had tried to kill me?

Clara watched me, perhaps reading my thoughts, as she finished the drink. "Don't do anything for a while, Hank. Think it over. Don't do anything you'll regret."

"I think I'd better let it ride for a while. Until I find out what's behind all this."

"Good. Well, now that I know you're safe, I'd better go home."

She didn't have a car, so I offered her a lift and drove her to a stucco duplex near Nineteenth Avenue. She invited me in for a nightcap and I figured, well, why not? She'd been closest to Jim, and I hadn't yet had a chance to talk with her fully.

Her living room was furnished cabana style, except for a big leather chair that clashed with the rustic motif. I knew about that leather chair very well, for Jim had built it into a symbol of all the things back home. Jim used to talk about being back in that leather chair with his feet on the footstool, pipes at one elbow and the radio at the other.

And that was the way the chair was now, footstool before it, Jim's slippers alongside. An end table at one arm of the chair held Jim's rack of pipes and a tobacco humidor. The humidor was of glass, beaded with moisture inside, the tobacco moist and ready for smoking. At the other arm of the chair was the radio, Jim's hat atop it. On the wall above the radio were pictures. Jim and Clara at the beach. Jim and myself before a Nissen hut. Just Jim.

Clara indicated the leather chair. "Sit down, Hank."

I took the cabana couch.

"Why don't you take the easy chair, Hank?" she asked.

"It's Jim's."

She made a hard laugh and rushed past me. She grabbed Jim's rack of pipes and threw them. The rack broke against the wall and the pipes skittered on the oak floor. She flung the tobacco humidor, spraying tobacco over a corner of the room. She snatched Jim's hat from the radio, crumpled it furiously, threw it on the floor and stomped on it. She tore the pictures from the wall and smashed them onto the floor, kicking at the frames and grinding the glass beneath her heels.

Then suddenly she began laughing. It was a high laugh that got higher and higher until it broke.

"Jim! That son of a bitch!" she yelled. "He tried to kill you!"

Then she flung herself into a chair and began bawling.

9

Nothing makes a man feel quite so helpless as watching a woman in tears. Presently I got up, went through the dining alcove off the living room, pushed a swinging door, found a light switch and began poking around in the kitchen. The liquor was in a cupboard above the refrigerator and there were glasses above the sink.

As I poured out whiskey I found my hand trembling. It was creeping up on me. As it had done on Clara. And I remembered the last mission of the tour. That last one that the combat crew sweated out. The one which meant going home—if we came back. And it was a milk run. No enemy fighters. No flak. No nothing. And then as we came back to set down safe, the landing gear went haywire.

The pilot circled the field while he and the co-pilot and the navigator tried to get the landing gear down. But it wouldn't come down and when the gas ran low they had to put her down on her belly. And as the bomber came in for the belly landing we knew it had been too easy. Old Lady Luck had just been holding back, with this up her sleeve. And when the plane screamed against the concrete, hell broke loose.

There was a tearing and a grinding and she did a ground loop and was afire, with the crew piling out and running for it before she blew up. But we all got out and everybody was casual as hell about it. Casual as hell, until a couple of hours later when we all began to shake. As I was shaking now, an hour or so after Hap Arnold had tried to kill me.

I sloshed another couple of fingers into the glasses, put in some water and took the drinks into the living room.

Clara turned up a tear-stained face, made a brief little smile of thanks, straightened up in the chair and took the drink. I sat on the couch across the room. We worked away at the whiskey. When we were to the bottom, my hands had quit shaking and she no longer was drawing long quivering breaths.

She made a little smile. "I'm sorry."

"It did you good."

"I'd better clean up this mess." She got a broom and dustpan, swept up the room and carried the debris out, came back in and picked up the glasses. "I'll make another."

I didn't object.

From the kitchen came the clink of glassware, the slam of the refrigerator door. Then silence. After a bit I began wondering if she'd fainted. I was on the verge of investigating, when she came in with the drinks and I understood the delay.

She had changed into a red housecoat. The zipper hadn't been closed to the neck, or anywhere near the neck, while it parted at the bottom to flash a length of white leg with each step. The housecoat was made of some slinky stuff that clung to every curve; there was no outward evidence that she wore anything beneath it.

She gave me the drink and sat beside me. "Hank, what do you think of me?"

"I'm confused," I admitted truthfully.

"Trudy thinks I'm slightly psycho. Jim's chair. Jim's slippers. Jim's hat on the radio. One must accept things. One must make adjustments." She gave a hard laugh. "I've known all along that Jim didn't suicide. I knew it was a fake."

"Then why act as if he were dead?"

"Did I? I've kept the place as if he might walk in any minute."

This made sense; it was a little startling seeing a new reason and a simple one.

"When he disappeared, he took a bag and his typewriter. They weren't found in his car on the bridge. What happened to them? A man doesn't pack up to jump off a bridge."

"You didn't tell the police about this," I said.

"Not even Trudy. I didn't want her to know."

"Wasn't that unkind to her?"

"I didn't want to let her know her brother. What he really was." She turned toward me on the couch, her face close. "Hank, Jim tried to have you killed tonight."

"You're upset," I said.

"Of course I am! And that's why! How would Jim know that you had killed Hap at Devil's Slide? How could he possibly know, except that if you were alive Hap *had* to be dead! Jim knew Hap was going to kill you tonight." She settled back on the couch, looking across at the opposite wall. "I've protected Jim Daniels long enough. Because he's my husband, I tried to excuse one murder. I could figure he was driven to it. A man can be tempted. Who was I to judge? And—yes, I had a selfish interest. But this is too much."

"Jim disappeared because of a murder?"

"Yes. But I'd rather you didn't know the details. You don't want to get involved. Keep out of this, Hank."

And I had been protecting Clara from the knowledge of what Jim was and what he was trying to do.

"I am involved," I said, and told her what had happened. "Have you any idea who Speck is?"

"Obviously a nickname for someone with glasses," she said. She looked at my neck where the cigarette had burned, went to the bathroom and returned with some salve for the blisters. "This whispering person, Hank—could you tell the voice if you heard it again?"

"Probably not. One whisper is like another, and that's why he was whispering. Either I know the guy or he expects me to soon, and the whisper was to disguise the voice. What I can't see is where I fit into this. If I knew that, I'd have the key to the whole thing. Hap tried to keep me from coming West with a warning telephone call. He tried to frame me with Millie for the same reason. Yet once I was here he felt he had to kill me. A man named Speck is supposed to kill me at Jim's orders. Somebody else hit me on the head and gave me the business with a lighted cigarette, to find out where Jim is. It beats me."

She smiled wryly. "You thought you knew Jim pretty well."

"That's it. I did. The Jim I knew was a swell guy."

"Yes, he used to be," she admitted reflectively. "He was everything you thought he was. Charming, solid, honest, good company—a swell guy. But he changed. It soured and began to fester. Outwardly he remained the same. But here at home the real Jim came out. It festered inside him."

"What did?"

"Jim missed his chance in life because of you."

"I—don't understand."

"You would if you'd face it. Jim threw Trudy at you. And it clicked. If your outfit had gone overseas one day later, his sister would have been married into the Oates millions."

"You're wrong there," I said sharply. "Neither Jim nor Trudy knew about my family at that time. To them I was just Hank Oates, a GI. I didn't tell Jim about my family until a year or so later."

Clara smiled. "You innocent child."

"How do you know so much? Jim hadn't even met you when I got acquainted with Trudy. He ran into you for the first time on his furlough home before going overseas, and you hooked him into one of those fast war marriages."

"You're not being kind, Hank."

"You're not being exactly nice about my friend! I don't know what happened since I saw Jim, but certainly I knew him then. And he just wasn't the kind of guy you're trying to make him out!"

"We need another drink," she said, and went out with the glasses.

When she came back, I fancied the zipper was lower than it had been. To hell with her. I knew Jim. What was she trying to do, anyhow?

She sat beside me, and the housecoat fell away on either side of a white leg. Nuts to you, babe.

She said, "I made a mistake."

"Okay. Let's drop the subject."

"My mistake was in not preparing you. I watched this grow over a period of years. And then I hit you with it in one jolt. No wonder you're dubious."

She twisted toward me, leaning forward a bit, and I tried not to look at that zipper. "Hank, I didn't mean that Jim cold-bloodedly arranged with his sister to hook you into marriage because of your money. Trudy never knew of your family until later. Until you and Jim were planning to go into business after the War would be over and you'd get home. I remember she told me when you wrote her about your family. She was flabbergasted—and a little afraid. I guess she had a hunch what would happen. And it did."

I looked into my glass. This wasn't a matter I liked to think about.

"As for Jim knowing your identity," she said, "go ahead and call me a liar, but *I* knew who you were when I first met Jim, and that was before you went overseas. How Jim found out, I wouldn't know. But he did know who you were. Now, wait a minute," she said as I began objecting. "I'm not intimating there was anything sinister about it. Jim would have liked you anyhow. Too, he was reasonably bright, or you wouldn't have liked him. You know he was ambitious. All right.

It didn't make him like you any *less* to know who you were and what you might do for him. When you and Trudy fell in love it didn't make him unhappy to think of being a brother-in-law to Henry Chatworth Oates III. That didn't make him a rat, did it?"

"No," I admitted. It was just human nature. "As a matter of fact, that's why I told Jim who I was. I wanted him to take a position with the company after the War. I might have offered it to him anyhow, but certainly a good part of the reason was because I expected him to be my brother-in-law."

"Exactly. The situation was understood on both sides. On that basis, plans grew. Instead of him taking a position with the company, you and he began planning to open a business of your own when you got back. Maybe you were just talking, but Jim was serious."

"I wasn't just talking. After I got back—well, you know."

"Exactly. The whole plan collapsed because you dropped Trudy. That was the end of the grand plans. Not because you and Jim wouldn't have been friendly enough if you'd run into one another. But he was no longer the prospective brother-in-law. Do you see my point?"

I admitted, shamefacedly, that I did.

"You'll never know, Hank, how much Jim counted on that. You don't know what success means to the average guy. You were the key to all Jim's dreams. You knocked that in the head. And he really loved his kid sister. You built her up for marriage, then dropped her cold."

"Let's not go into that."

"I'm just making a point. After what you did, can you expect Jim to love you?"

I took a deep breath. "I guess you're right."

"He was terribly hurt. A man doesn't make more than one or two intimate friends in a lifetime. You were his best friend, and you did that. And Jim began to sour on the world. If he couldn't bank on Hank Oates, who the hell *could* he count on? You see?"

I nodded. I saw only too well.

"Jim changed. Not outwardly. He looked and acted just the same—except here at home, with me. It frightened me. I didn't know what to do. Maybe his war experiences added to it—reaction from the long strain—I don't know. But he soured. He became bitter against the world. He wouldn't trust anybody. People thought he was happy. Hell, you've never seen such an unhappy man in your life. Of an evening, he'd sit in that leather chair and brood. Saying nothing. Just glowering while it festered inside him. The system was wrong; the world was haywire; he hated everything."

I remembered GI's who, under the pressure and frustration of Army life had crawled into that bitter shell, building up inside until they finally exploded into incorrigibles.

"He had a job, but it was just a job," she said. "He felt life had cheated him. I was afraid he was going to try to take what the world owed him. And—that's what he did. So he had to disappear."

"What did he do?"

"I don't want you to know. Don't get mixed up in it, Hank."

"I'm already mixed up in it. And I feel responsible."

"No, Hank. We all get our kicks in the teeth from life. With Jim it was a combination of several things—battle fatigue, the disillusionment so many GI's had on returning, your betrayal of friendship, smashed dreams, Trudy, the fact he wasn't getting ahead, finding his marriage was a mistake—everything combining. Everything went to pot, and he cracked."

"But I thought he was getting along fine, financially."

"That's how he got into trouble."

I waited for her to add to this. She didn't. I said, "Then you weren't happily married?"

She shrugged. Which she shouldn't have done, with that zipper where it was. "One of those war things. We met one week and were married the next. After he got back the only reason I stuck it out was because he needed help. He was disillusioned with me. He didn't really know me. Overseas, he built me up into something I'm not."

"He was gone for you," I admitted.

"I was a goddess to him. But I'm not a goddess. I'm rather common. I like a good time. I've got to have men admire me. Jim was a homebody. That's not my speed."

No, I reflected, that wasn't Clara's speed.

"I would have divorced him, but I didn't want to add that to the rest of it. He needed me. And, regardless of smashed illusions, he loved me."

I said, "That's a contradiction."

"No; he didn't like me, but he was desperately in love. The two aren't the same. That made it worse for him—the conflict between what he couldn't help feeling toward me and what his common sense told him I was. And"—she hesitated, made another little shrug—"I didn't love Jim. He knew that, too."

I felt that we'd gone into that aspect far enough. "I still don't see why Jim wants to have me killed."

"I'm trying to tell you."

"Being unhappily married just added to his burden."

"No—I mean the big motive for Jim's trying to kill you is that you took me away from him."

This didn't make sense.

"We need another drink," she said, and took the glasses into the kitchen. She had an animal something that just might send a man mad. And she knew it. Well, she wouldn't get anywhere with me. She returned and sat beside me again, too close. She just had to work on any man she was around. But knowing that didn't make it any better.

"Hank, I'm going to tell you something that will sound very silly. You can laugh if you want to. It would be better if you did. Because you won't believe it, and it will be less embarrassing for me."

She took a slow sip of her drink. "Jim was insanely jealous of you."

I wondered if I'd had too much whiskey. I decided I had. But I still knew what was going on. "I'd never even seen you."

"Which made it worse. Jim couldn't fight a shadow. You'd never seen me, but Jim knew I was in love with you."

I gave her the once over. If she was kidding, it certainly was deadpan.

"Go ahead, Hank. Laugh. It's all so silly."

"It doesn't make sense."

"Maybe I used the wrong word. Infatuation would be better. You know—like a bobbysoxer loving Clark Gable or Gary Cooper. It's all very silly and adolescent, I realize. I'm just trying to make you understand what happened. Anyhow, Jim's letters from overseas were full of you. I'd write to him and tell him to say hello to you. You'd add a couple of lines on his letters to me. We did become friends that way."

"Yes."

"But it was more than friendship to me. I can't explain it, Hank. I'm not trying to. I guess it happened when he sent that picture of the two of you by the airplane. After that I knew that I didn't want Jim's letters except for what they said of you. It's all very silly. Certainly I wouldn't be unburdening myself, except that you're looking for a reason. There it is. You threw Jim's sister over, smashed his future, and took away his wife. From his viewpoint, he had every reason to hate your guts."

"Were you fool enough to tell him this silly thing?"

"It came out in a quarrel. I could have bitten my tongue off, but the damage was done."

"This is a hell of a note."

"You represented everything he wanted. You stood for all his frustration. When he saw his chance to grab a lot of money, he took it. Even though it meant murder. It was a chance to be like you. To get even with the world. To win back my love. So he thought. But it backfired and he had to disappear. So in a sense you were responsible. You see? Except for you he wouldn't have been in a jam. Except for you he wouldn't have killed anybody. Except for you he wouldn't have to phony his own suicide and be an outcast. So you are to blame. You follow me?"

I nodded. I followed her, but it wasn't a pretty path.

"Now he can never have what he wanted. His life is smashed. And all because of you. So he figures to even the score by killing you."

I ran a hand across my face. My lips were numb from the liquor. "It's—hard to believe."

"Jim sent Hap and Millie ahead, before he mailed the letter to you. They were to frame you—put you in a spot where you would obey orders. But for some reason of his own, Hap tried to double-cross Jim. Hap warned you, over the phone. He told you you'd be killed if you came out here to help Jim. He tried to stop you by framing you with Millie. Then tonight Hap tried to kill you, since you insisted on getting mixed up in things. We'll never know now what Hap's reasons were, because he's dead. But we do know that Jim will try to kill you. Somebody called Speck is to do it at Jim's orders."

"Maybe it really isn't Jim," I said. "Somebody could have got hold of that typewriter, and forged the signatures."

"You're stubborn. You're loyal to an old friendship. I like that, Hank. And I may be wrong. I hope I am. I'm just putting together what we know, trying to see a reason. Let's hope I'm wrong. But on one thing I know I'm right. Two things."

"What things?" I asked as she hesitated.

She put her head on my shoulder. "One thing is that Jim has already murdered a man. Which makes the second one easier. The other thing—well, when I saw you today, it was just a bobbysoxer meeting Clark Gable in the flesh."

I didn't want to go into that. Particularly with her snuggling against me. That zipper certainly wasn't getting any higher as time went by.

"Who is Hap Arnold—I mean, who was he?"

"He's the reason I've known Jim is alive. I've been paying Hap a hundred dollars a week. Hush money."

"You poor kid."

She said throatily, "Oh, Hank, I'm so glad you're alive."

And then I found myself kissing her. I wasn't sure just how it happened. In fact, I'd been firm in my determination that nothing like that *should* happen. I thought of Caroline and, for some reason, of Trudy. But that was no good while kissing the full and open lips of Clara Daniels.

"Hank …"

"I'd better go."

She made a slow, confident smile. "The iron man."

"Let's wait until we're sober and see how we feel."

"Let's have another drink and see how we feel."

"I've had too much to drink. Anyhow, I'm tired."

"You don't want to drive clear back to that hotel tonight. It's comfortable here."

I stood up. "I'd better go."

The doorbell rang.

"It's Jim!" She sprang up, clutching at me. She seemed a little mad with fear.

"I just hope it is."

"Don't answer it, Hank! It's Jim! He'll kill us both!"

I fought loose of her. "Jim wouldn't ring the bell. He's got a key."

"Yes," she admitted, subsiding. "I guess I'm just upset."

I followed her to the door. Trudy was there.

Trudy said, "Did you see Jim? Is he—" Then her voice died as she looked from Clara to me. Clara's zipper had slipped down almost to her navel. I was mussed up, and there was lipstick on my face.

Clara zipped the housecoat up to the neck. "No, he didn't see Jim," she said. "There was a snafu. Come in, Trudy."

"No, I—don't want to intrude," Trudy said. She turned and went down the steps.

Clara shut the door and turned to me. "I guess it looked bad. I should have known Trudy would be over to see how things turned out. I'll get your coat."

"Get me a drink and let's get acquainted."

She shook her head. "Not on the rebound."

She got my coat, kissed me good night, and I left.

10

I reached the hotel without accident, washed up and got ready for bed. I was dead for sleep, and with the liquor on top of that, I went off as my head hit the pillow.

But not for long. The rat woke me up. Leaping inside my skull, gnawing at my eyeballs, scratching at the nerves of my teeth. I groped for the light switch, got the aspirin bottle from my coat pocket, drew a glass of water and washed down three pills. I was pacing the deck, wondering how long it would take before the gnawing died, when the phone rang. My nerves were raw. I jumped at the ring.

"Hello!"

The voice came quietly. "Hello, Hank. This is Jim."

It was fantasy. My head whirling from the liquor, the dreadful pain churning inside it, and Jim on the phone.

"Hello, Jim."

"I imagine Clara spilled her guts to you."

"That's right."

"I missed twice. But the third time is the charm."

The line clicked dead.

I continued pacing up and down. When the rat went to sleep, so did I.

I woke up to a beautiful sunny day that didn't match at all. Because I felt like hell. My head was full of feathers and there was brown fur on my teeth. My mouth was sore, and I wondered if Cranston's probing had hastened disaster along a notch. I showered, brushed my teeth, shaved. I got dressed and was packing my bags when the rat woke up. But he didn't catch me by surprise this time. He'd hardly begun to twitch when I had those aspirins inside me. But it took a few minutes for them to begin working, and meanwhile the pain was driving me crazy.

I kept on with the packing, being careful to move slowly. To hell with the rat. It couldn't do any more than blind me and split my head wide open. A headache, and the prospect of losing a few teeth, didn't seem so damned important since last night. If I'd taken one more step along the lip of that cliff, the only ones to admire my beautiful teeth would have been the crabs.

The phone rang. It was Clara. "How are you this morning, darling?"

"Horrible. I can't drink."

"You call *that* drinking?" She laughed. "I'll have to teach you things." I didn't doubt that she could. In several ways. "Why I called, we had a cancellation and I shifted a couple of appointments. Leo can see you at ten-thirty and get you all fixed up. Have you had any more headaches?"

"I've decided to wait until I get home."

There was a moment of silence. "Home?"

"I'm all packed. I'm leaving after breakfast."

"But—your teeth. Leo says if you don't get them attended to right away—"

"A few days won't make any difference. Anyhow, I'm going home."

"You're running away!" She said it nastily.

"I've got my war medals," I said, just as nastily. "I can prove intrepid courage in the face of danger. By official mimeograph."

"But he'll follow you, Hank."

"It will be in my backyard, not his. Hell, I'm not afraid of Jim Daniels. Or any bastard who looks like him."

Her voice changed. She did that auditory strip-tease. "We both took a rain check last night, Hank. It won't rain forever."

"That wouldn't work out, Clara."

"I don't ask for much. Just the chance to make you happy."

Tempting as the prospect was, I didn't want to get involved. Such affairs always get complicated. Both she and I were tangled up with Jim, and I wanted no more of that.

"I'll be out this way again, Clara. One of these days. Maybe the sun will be shining then."

"This is goodbye?"

"Yes."

"Hank."

"Yes?"

She whispered, "I'll always love you," and hung up.

I jiggled the phone, got the switchboard, said I was checking out. Then I went down to breakfast. The sight of food gave my stomach a turn, but I forced it down. After a second cup of coffee I thought I might live, and I wondered just what good I was on this earth. Couldn't drink, no good with women, a pampered product of snobbery—what a man! I might have made a good automobile mechanic if I'd been born more fortunately. Anyhow, I liked to tinker with cars. And an automobile mechanic renders a service that people need. I wondered if Oates' Oats were worth a damn. Probably undermining the teeth of the nation's innocent childhood. Business was business. Never knock your competitor. Stab him in the back with a smile. I was on the third cup of coffee when Trudy came in.

"Keep your seat," she said, and took a chair across the table. Her eyes were bright and her cheeks stung rosy by the wind off the ocean. I decided she was a lovely thing, this watch-charm of a girl. She said she'd had breakfast but would take a cup of coffee. I ordered it.

"About last night," I said.

"Your private life is certainly none of my business."

That was true, but somehow I didn't like her to say so. "Nothing happened."

"You don't have to explain to me."

Her coffee came. She began sipping it, black and without sugar. "I thought maybe you'd call."

"I was going to."

"When you didn't, I gave you a ring. The hotel said you had checked out but your luggage was still here. So I came right over." The polite chitchat ended. "Hank, how is he? Is everything all right now? Can Jim come back to us soon?"

"I didn't see Jim. Clara told you so last night."

"I want the truth."

"Don't you believe her?"

"What's wrong? You're avoiding an answer. Did something happen? Is Jim all right?"

I couldn't tell her. I couldn't hit her in the teeth with the truth. "There was a hitch. I didn't contact Jim."

"Maybe you didn't understand the message. I didn't."

"Maybe not."

"We'll just have to wait until he contacts you again."

"Yes."

She cried, "But you've checked out!"

"I'm going home."

Her eyes widened. "But Jim needs you. You've come all the way out to—" Then she smiled knowingly. "You *did* see Jim last night. Now you're going someplace, on an important errand for him. But you can't tell me. I understand." She reached impulsively across the table and took my hand. "If I'm not supposed to know, I won't pry. I'll try not to. What you're doing is for Jim."

I let it go at that. And I realized I wasn't going home because of cowardice, nor from reluctance to get to the bottom of things. It was Trudy and her faith in Jim. I just couldn't spoil that. She was too sweet and lovely a girl to get the bad news through me. The thing to do was to walk away.

I was being paged. I raised a finger and a bellhop brought an envelope. My name was typed on it by the typewriter with the high *E* key. The note inside said:

> The hotel tells me you're checking out. I wouldn't do that, Hank. It just means a long trip home and another one right back again. Pretty soon the police will be wondering what happened to Hap Arnold. I can prove you were the last person to see him alive. Do you want it that way, Hank?
>
> Stick around. Most people don't like California at first. But you'll find it grows on you.

It was unsigned.

I put the note in the envelope, slipped the envelope into my breast pocket. This was something Trudy didn't want to see. What kind of cat and mouse game was this deal? Maybe it was a bluff. If so, it wasn't a bluff I could afford to call.

"Don't let me hold you up," Trudy said. "I'm past due at work anyhow."

"I'll drop you off."

I drove her down California to Montgomery. She worked in a large granite beehive where, she told me, she was secretary for an outfit called Gloster and Cleave, who distributed soft drink syrup.

"When will I see you?" she asked as she got out.

"I'll give you a buzz."

On impulse she slid onto the seat again. "Hank, I don't know how to tell you how grateful I am. For helping Jim. It means so much to me and—" For a moment I thought she was going to kiss me. Then she ducked out, no doubt remembering last night.

She turned into the granite beehive, and I drove away remembering the swing of her miniature body and the straight seams of her stockings. A hell of a note. I'd had that once for the taking and I hadn't taken it. I wondered if this teeth business had started years ago. Some slow poison to the brain that had affected my good judgment. Maybe Edward VIII had something.

I stopped on the way to phone Clara and nail that appointment for ten-thirty and, on the dot, I was in the chair with Clara clipping the bib around my neck. "Yank 'em," I said.

"Good boy, Hank," Cranston said. "I don't want to ruin your dazzling smile before the bridge is made. I'll get everything ready this morning."

Cranston set to work. I'd had no experience with this sort of thing, but I knew immediately that Cranston was a real mechanic. Which is the highest praise you can give a man who works with tools. As an amateur tinker, I admired Cranston's efficiency. By noon the dentist had drilled out eight teeth, cut anchors for a bridge to replace two teeth that had to come out (the other two to be extracted were wisdom teeth which he said I'd never miss), made wax impressions, plugged the holes with temporary fillings.

And it hadn't hurt a bit.

Cranston unclipped the bib. "Come in tomorrow about two-thirty. That will give me time to get the inlays and the bridge ready."

"Okay."

"By the way, I don't want you staying at a miserable hotel."

"It's a good hotel."

"I won't listen to it. I've got a spare room in my apartment. And I want to get to know you better, you son of a gun. No; I insist. Clara's got an extra key in her desk."

I picked up the key from Clara on the way out. She said, "You're staying?"

I nodded. She gave a glad cry, leaped up and kissed me. "Damn it," I said, "why did you have to do that?"

She pulled the handkerchief from my breast pocket and wiped my face. "It doesn't show."

In the lobby downstairs I phoned Irving Kline. Kline invited me to lunch at Number 9, Fisherman's Wharf. Driving there, I decided that fear of the dentist was largely psychological. And that I was whistling in the dark.

11

I waited on the crowded street of Fisherman's Wharf, smelling the boiling crabs and wondering what Irving Kline looked like. I was hungry. Or had been, before smelling the place.

"Hank! Irving Kline!" A roly-poly man, short, bald, with a round face and a wide grin, shook hands with me. As we went upstairs to a table, he explained he knew me from a picture Jim had had. There was nothing on the menu but fish, and fish is not my favorite food. Kline recommended cracked crab and a bowl of chowder. I could still faintly smell the vats outside, but I said okay in the manner of one who is in Rome.

"You're here because of Jim?"

Denying it was too much bother. And to hell with this noise of waiting for Jim's next move. "Yes. I understand he was in business with you."

Kline's grin widened. "He still is. We're doing very well, if I do say so. Hillslope Heights is a honey of a deal."

I tried to be very casual. "How do you do business with Jim?"

"Not with him. For him. It's a partnership. We each have authority to act for the firm."

The chowder arrived. It was surprisingly good. "You kept on a partnership with a dead man? When you thought he was dead?"

"There wasn't much choice. We're in it up to our necks. It's either keep on and make a killing, or take a skinning. I'm keeping on."

"I'm not a lawyer but I had the idea that death terminated a partnership."

"Who says Jim is dead?" he said, grinning.

"You know differently?"

He shrugged. "No body has been found. Legally, Jim Daniels might just as well be away on a trip."

"Jim doesn't have to be on deck to sign things?"

"No, either of us can act for the firm. It's legal."

"And just what is this deal?"

Kline's round face lost its easy grin. For a long moment he studied me. I decided that grin was strictly a business asset. Kline was sharp. The grin came again.

"There's nothing to hide. You could find out anyhow. Did Jim ever tell you about his Uncle Jasper?"

I nodded. Uncle Jasper was a crusty eccentric who lived in a tumble-down mansion on what once was a grand estate, and who resisted all progress. Uncle Jasper's occupation for some thirty years was writing letters to newspapers and public officials denouncing electricity and the internal combustion engine. He had some theory that electrolysis was ruining the good earth and gasoline fumes the atmosphere, as a result of which the world faced doom. Jim had made a good story of Uncle Jasper clogging the traffic on Market Street with his horse and buggy.

"When Uncle Jasper died, Jim inherited the estate," Kline said. "It was a natural—forty-two acres smack in the middle of progress. Jim put up the land, I put in know-how and raised financing. A real estate man's dream. Once in a lifetime."

The crab came. It tasted much better than it had smelled at the vats. I asked, "How did Uncle Jasper die?"

"Classic justice. He was kicked by a horse. Found dead in the stable."

That could have been an accident. Or it could have been something that could be made very easily to appear an accident.

"Give me another year," Kline said. "We're extended now, pyramiding. But give us another year and we'll clear half a million apiece, after taxes."

"It seems you could spare enough so that Clara wouldn't have to work for wages."

Kline shrugged helplessly. "She can't touch it. Jim inherited the estate; it's not community property. Since Jim isn't legally dead, she can't inherit. It puts her in a bad spot. Why did Jim disappear?"

"I wish I knew."

Kline smiled knowingly. "Well, all right. You can tell the son of a gun I'd sure like to see him. He's a great guy. It will take me off the hook when he comes back."

"Why?"

"I'm walking a tightrope on this deal. While I'm technically in the clear, I've got to watch my step. My books had better be right."

And he was handling the books, with Jim gone. Books can be manipulated. "How does Clara feel about it?"

"She hates my guts, of course. I can see her side of it. She doesn't understand why I can't just turn Jim's share over to her."

"Neither can I."

The grin faded and the sharp Kline showed through. Then he made the smile again. "What if Jim was sitting in my office when I got back from lunch, and wanted an accounting? He has given me no authority to turn anything over to Clara. I would be on the spot. Or say that Jim really *had* suicided. No body is found. After seven years the courts declare him legally dead. Then his estate is probated, and, brother, I'm out on a limb if every dime isn't properly accounted for.

I feel sorry for Clara, having to work when she should be wealthy. But I can't do anything about it. I can't afford to. My books have got to be right."

"Has Jim contacted you?"

Kline shook his head. "I thought you might have word from him."

"Why?"

"After all, he must be interested. This is a deal of a lifetime. We'd just got started when he disappeared."

I said, "That was convenient for you."

Kline's round face froze.

"I don't want to be unpleasant," I said. "But let's look at the situation. You've got authority to act in Jim's name for seven years, on a deal involving a million dollars' profit after taxes, by your own estimate."

"I know," he said frankly. "It's a motive for murder."

"I hadn't intended going quite that far."

"But," he said shrewdly, "you thought so. Thank God Jim is alive. We know that, now."

"Do we?"

"It was in the papers."

"Do you believe everything you see in the papers?"

Kline studied me. "Just what do you mean?"

"Nobody has seen Jim alive. There have been some telephone calls. It's easy to fake a voice over the phone. Particularly if the voice hasn't been heard for a while, if suggestion is used, if the person receiving the call wants to believe, if the conversation is limited to a few mysterious sentences. Any actor could do it, and plenty of amateurs. There have been some notes written on a typewriter. Anybody can type. There have been some signatures on the notes. Which could be traced—and there's no way of telling now, for the signed ones have been burned per instructions. The whole thing is as phony as a three-dollar-bill. It's all too elaborate and mysterious. Why hasn't Jim *seen* anybody he knows, if he's close enough to be phoning locally and dropping letters in San Francisco mailboxes? Can't he trust his sister? Can't he trust his wife? Can't he trust you?"

"Then what do you think?"

"I think somebody is in a squeeze," I said. "It might be you. You might be phonying all this to take the pressure off."

Kline said with an easy grin, "We're not going to get along if you keep that up."

"That might have mattered yesterday, but not now. I just don't give a damn. Somebody tried to kill me last night, and that changes things. Being polite and well thought of by people you don't know isn't nearly as important as it used to be."

"Somebody tried to kill you," Kline said slowly, with no expression at all.

"Yes. And there's a lot of smoke boiling up to cover something. I don't buy it. Maybe the smoke screen is to keep me from looking back. But maybe I already know what it is I'm not supposed to see. Maybe I know some little thing about Jim that would nail somebody for murder. Maybe Jim wrote me, or phoned me, or sent me a wire, just before he was killed."

"You're bluffing," Kline said. "Or why would you have waited until now to tell it?"

"Maybe I'm giving somebody enough rope to hang himself."

"You're bluffing, Hank."

"Somebody doesn't think so. Or why was I set up for the kill?"

Kline looked at his wristwatch. "It was nice meeting you, Hank. You'll excuse me? I have an appointment."

As I threaded back through the midday traffic I wondered how close I had come to the truth. The idea had come out of the air, but it still might be a good one. What if Jim actually *were* dead? That real estate deal gave Kline a good motive for murder. With authority to sign, with the books under his control, Kline was in a sweet spot. What Clara had said last night changed nothing. Jim simply was a sharper who ran into somebody who outsmarted him, perhaps. Maybe Jim had planned to do away with Kline, hide the body and play with the money seven years. Maybe Kline had turned the tables on Jim; classic justice.

Now, in the middle of the day with a bright sun and a brisk breeze, the phone call from Jim wasn't so impressive as it had been last night. I hadn't heard Jim's voice in years. And certainly, drunk and with the rat leaping inside my head, I'd been in no condition to judge from a few sentences. It's easy to mistake a voice on the phone. Somebody says hello, this is Fred, and you get the idea it is Fred Bean; you talk with him a couple of minutes before you tumble that it's Fred Pratt. That happens with friends. It hadn't *had* to be Jim on the phone.

Somebody could have gotten hold of Jim's old Corona. The signature could be forged.

Hap Arnold? Well, if I was being hoodwinked, why couldn't he have been? He'd said somebody named Speck was to kill me at Jim's orders. Who was this person called Speck? Was it Kline? Why would Speck be obeying such orders from Jim? What if Speck were hiding his real motives behind a dead man?

Supposing Jim were dead. Supposing he had been murdered. Did I unknowingly have some fact that could pin the murderer? That just might explain everything. But if such were the case, just what *was* that fact?

I mulled it over as I drove to the hotel and picked up my luggage. I was no nearer the goal by the time I had the luggage stowed in Cranston's apartment. You go through a war with a guy. You sit around of an evening tossing the bull with him over a period of years, night after night. Then you try to think back and remember some word he might have dropped that would explain everything. It isn't easy. My brain chased in a circle until I decided to let it lay before I woke up the rat.

From the looks of Cranston's apartment, the dentist was doing quite all right in his profession. The place looked like a movie set, with a process shot of the Golden Gate visible from the big picture window overlooking the bay. All that was missing was the gorgeous gal lying voluptuously on the sofa with as much showing as the Johnson office would allow. I got out my shaving kit, found the bathroom and brushed my teeth. That's something I would have to take care about from now on.

There was a short shelf of books above the towel rack. So Cranston was a bathroom reader, too. He and Father had something in common. A busy man but with a yearning for erudition, Father had, little by little over a period of years, read *The Decline and Fall of the Roman Empire* in the bathroom. The shelf held an odd assortment. I selected *History of the New York Fire Department* and was becoming engrossed when from somewhere within the apartment a door closed. The apartment house was too well made not to be soundproofed between apartments.

I went into the hall from the bathroom. The hall made a T, kitchen on the left, bedrooms on the right, living room straight ahead. "Hello!"

"Hello," a voice said from a bedroom. "Where the hell is your electric meter?"

"I don't know. I'm just a house guest."

"And I'm a new man on the job. Oh, never mind. Here it is."

I went into the living room with the book, took a chair facing the hallway and immediately was fascinated. In 1823 the New York City Fire Department had 46 engines, 4 hook-and-ladder trucks, 16 ladders, 23 hooks, 11,575 feet of hose. That was something to pop up with at a party, when you needed a few such casual facts to squelch one of these boors who try to floor you with learning.

And then two things happened at once. The rat began to stir in my head, and as I looked up it was just in time to see a man moving slowly across the T-intersection of the hallway. At that moment, also, I realized that an apartment like this would come with utilities furnished, or if not, certainly a bedroom was no place for an electric meter.

The man crossing the hall so cautiously had a big nose and was clutching a humpbacked cigar in his teeth. He wore a trench coat.

"White!" I yelled, remembering the name Trudy had called to me as I left the drive-in the previous night. "Hey, you're not—"

He slipped into the kitchen. I ran down the hall and into the kitchen in time to see him disappearing through the swinging door to the living room. I got back into the living room as the front door slammed. I burst out the front door just as the elevator door shut. With the sad thought that I was anything but quick on the uptake, I turned back inside and took my quota of aspirins.

When the severe pain had died into a quiet throb, I phoned Cranston and told him somebody had been trying to rob his apartment. No, nothing was gone that I could see. "It was a guy with a big nose and a trench coat. Trudy said his name was White."

"Oh," Cranston said. "The private detective."

"Oh," I said. "Then we can maybe get his license taken away."

"Have you any witnesses?"

"No."

"We'd better let it drop, if he took nothing."

"What's he snooping around about?"

"He's trying to find Jim. The insurance company hired him. Have any more headaches?"

"No thanks; I just finished one."

"I'll bring some stuff for you to take when I come this afternoon. So you won't be bothered until we get them out tomorrow."

"Why didn't you give me the stuff yesterday?"

"What? And lose the price of four extractions?"

I hung up with the idea that Cranston's sense of humor was of an elementary type. I imagined him with a bunch of his pals at a dental convention killing themselves off with stories about pulling the wrong teeth.

12

That evening Cranston had Trudy and Clara over for canasta. I decided they were all nice people, though my darkest suspicions about Cranston's sense of humor were confirmed. His album of phonograph records was, if possible, on a lower level than his sense of humor.

Trudy, I found again, was particularly nice. As well as cute as a button. In a strapless evening dress she was so exquisite you wanted to touch her to see if she was real. Or, anyhow, touch her. As she sat beside me while I drove her home after the evening, I thought of how casual this might have been. How I might have taken it for granted that she would always be beside me. In fact, there might have been more than the two of us by now. We might have had to arrange for a babysitter before going out in the evening.

"You didn't leave," she said.

"Change of plans."

"I won't pry."

I stood with her at her doorway, saying good night, and I wondered if I could kiss her. Maybe I could, despite what she'd seen last night; but I decided not to try. I was flying false colors. The whole thing would have to come out sooner or later, and then she'd never talk to me again. So I just said good night and drove away feeling that Edward VIII was quite a guy.

Next morning I accidentally drove around until I caught her on the way to a street car, to go to work. So I picked her up. Then she remembered she'd forgotten to leave the key in the mailbox for the cleaning woman, and I drove her back, which made the ride longer. After dropping her at the granite beehive, I followed the signposts of the Forty-nine Mile Drive. It was something to do to keep your mind off a two-thirty dental appointment.

Returning, I let the Union Square Garage swallow the car and decided to take a walk. Probably I needed some lunch but I wasn't hungry. It was another fine, brisk day, and there were forty golden minutes before the dental appointment. Better walking than just brooding.

The walk took me along Grant Avenue through Chinatown, which gave way to an Italian section. I wondered about hiring a private detective. But could I afford to? I'd either have to tell the detective everything, or he could do me no good. And if I told him about Hap's death, he might blackmail me or turn me over to the police. With this happy thought I climbed Telegraph Hill.

The view was practically identical with the one from Cranston's picture window, and I'd seen it on the drive anyhow. I put a dime in a pair of coin-operated binoculars and found myself looking at men behind the grim walls of Alcatraz. I had killed a man. I wondered if someday I would be behind those walls looking at the people on Telegraph Hill.

"Grim, isn't it?" somebody said beside me.

"Yes."

"Nobody ever escaped from Alcatraz. Nobody they'll admit to. Where's Hap Arnold?"

I turned quickly. It was the man with the big nose, trench coat and humpbacked cigar. He grinned, revealing a need of dental work. "Surprised you, huh?"

"I beg your pardon?"

He didn't press the matter. "You didn't call the cops when you found me in your hotel room."

"Nor when I found you in Cranston's apartment."

"Why?" He seemed to think the question pertinent.

"You seemed so shy. Would that be a way to treat a man trying to make friends? I was hoping that in time we'd get acquainted."

White, the private eye, squinted one of his private eyes and considered this. "Got a couple minutes?"

"I have a dental appointment."

"I'll walk back with you." We started down the hill. "What's wrong with your teeth?"

"Nothing that four extractions, a bridge and eight inlays won't fix."

"Just going to hell all at once, huh? Mine done that. Wish I could get 'em fixed."

"Why don't you?"

He gave me a sidewise look that wasn't friendly. "For the same goddamn reason I ain't smoking a four-bit cigar!"

"I'm sorry."

"How is Cranston? Pretty good?"

"The best, from what I hear. Though this is my first experience with dentists. What were you looking for in his apartment and my hotel room?"

He gnawed the humpbacked cigar reflectively, then came to a decision. "I'll lay it on the line. The name's Milford E. White, private detective. I've been retained by an insurance company. Jim Daniels took out a policy for fifty thousand dollars a year ago. On the night of last April seventh, he either did or didn't suicide from Golden Gate Bridge. No body was found; no legal proof of death. As a matter of routine the company mailed out the premium notice for the annual payment on the policy a couple of weeks ago. Mrs. Clara Daniels, the beneficiary and wife of the insured, sent in a check in payment."

He paused, looked at me, chewed on his cigar before he went on. "The company sent a man around to see her. He reported that she was slightly psycho—her place kept just exactly the way it had been when he stepped out. She simply refused to admit her husband was dead. She insisted on paying the premium, even though he pointed out that she couldn't collect on the policy because Jim Daniels had suicided within a year after taking it out. So maybe she's crazy. Or maybe it's something else. It's my job to find out. That's a lot of money, above taxes."

We came off the hill and into Grant Avenue again. I said, "But now we know Jim Daniels is alive?"

"Do we? That's a lot of money. You can buy a hundred thousand four-bit cigars with that dough. Where do you fit in?"

I side-stepped the question. "I don't quite understand about the insurance. Jim went into partnership with Irving Kline. They each took out fifty thousand dollars insurance for the protection of the other partner. A common business arrangement. Yet you said Jim's wife, Clara, paid the premium. And she is the beneficiary."

"That's right."

"That isn't good business practice."

"It isn't," White agreed. "Ordinarily, Kline would pay the premiums on his partner's insurance, and vice versa. A trustee would be the beneficiary. But in this case the insurance salesman was an eager beaver who didn't want to risk losing a fat sale by waiting on red tape. He sold each man the insurance, with the idea that they would transfer it at their convenience into the usual arrangement. And you know how such things are. The partners let it slide. They probably would have fixed it up when the next premium payment came around, but before that Jim Daniels suicided. That part of it don't make much difference as to how it works out, except for tax purposes. And except that, as things stand, Kline couldn't profit by Jim Daniel's death."

"Maybe not by the insurance. But he's handling a fat deal and keeping his own books."

"I've thought of that."

"Are you working on a sliding scale?"

"Sliding scale?"

"Does the amount of your fee depend on whether Jim did or did not suicide?"

"Why should it?"

"If it could be proved suicide, the insurance company saves itself fifty thousand dollars."

"You son of a bitch," he said. "Where's Hap Arnold?"

He had a nice way of throwing that curve; but I was set for it. "The general? He's dead."

"Hap Arnold was a beard-and-sandal boy, a character; San Francisco is fond of its characters. Might run into him anywhere, anytime, wandering about. Had a shack in Sausalito he called a studio. So at three-ten of a foggy morning last April, Hap wandered up to the toll gates of the Golden Gate Bridge and reported an abandoned car with a suicide note on it. Then suddenly he changed. Shaved off his beard, began wearing shoes and Hollywood clothes, bought a Chevy and began drinking whiskey instead of muscatel."

"Coincidence?"

"Maybe. Hap Arnold began paying weekly visits to a dentist. Hap wears false teeth. Clara Daniels works for that dentist. Something to wonder about, huh?"

"Why don't you ask Arnold about it?"

"I have. And his girlfriend. Now I'm asking you. You had a date to meet him, couple nights ago. He hasn't been seen since."

"I don't know what you're talking about."

We left the Italian section and entered Chinatown. White said nothing for a block or so. Then he took the humpbacked cigar from his mouth, smelled it, grimaced and threw it away.

"I came from the wrong side of the tracks. I ought to know better. God knows I've had enough experience. But what's beaten into you as a kid sticks to you. Every damned time, I can't believe it of your sort of people. I just couldn't admit that Henry Chatworth Oates III was mixed up in a dirty, stinking mess of his own free will. So I decided to have a little talk with you and lay it on the line. But you won't talk. You play it cute. Okay. Be cute. But me, I got nothing to lose. I'm out after that four-bit cigar and I don't give a good goddamn who I have to hurt. And a man in your position has plenty to lose. I just hope you've got good reason."

He turned abruptly at the corner and walked away.

I walked to Cranston's office, thinking how dead right White was. Clara appeared at the buzz, as I opened the door of the reception room, and ushered me right through, regardless of four people waiting. Maybe in the next life I would be one of those who waited while others were ushered in ahead. I followed her along the hallway and then stopped dead, with White's warning ringing through my ears like a bell.

Where the hallway widened to form Clara's little office, there were two people. One was Trudy, and the other was a cop. To me the cop seemed eight feet tall and six feet wide. He looked at me, saying nothing, just looking with eyes that had hooks on them that ripped away my false front and exposed the ticking of my brain.

"Where have you been, Hank?" Trudy asked.

So the police were after me. They'd been looking for me. The cop said nothing. He just looked.

"This is Henry Oates," Clara said to the cop.

The cop acknowledged the introduction with a little nod. "You're a hard man to find, Mr. Oates."

So there had been a police dragnet. Calling all cars. Calling all cars. Pick up Henry Chatworth Oates III. Height, five feet ten. Weight, 170 pounds. Hair, medium brown. Eyes, gray. No visible scars or deformities. When last seen, wearing tan worsted double-breasted suit, brown shoes, white shirt, brown-figured tie. This man is wanted for murder. That is all.

"I—went on the Forty-nine Drive Mile," I said. "I mean, the Forty-mile Nine Drive." Guilt, I knew, was written on my face. I couldn't even talk straight.

The cop grinned. "Like it?"

Teasing me, eh?

"Very amusing. I mean funny. I mean interesting."

"Hank doesn't know anything about it," Trudy said. Sweet little Trudy, protecting me. "You certainly can't think—"

"Just out seeing the sights, huh?" the cop said to me.

"That's right," I said firmly. I decided to tell the truth and the whole truth, right up to a certain point.

"You don't think *Hank* had anything to do with it?" Clara said to the cop, coming to my defense.

"Gosh, no, Mrs. Daniels," the cop said. And to me, "I just wondered if you seen anybody hanging around when she put the key in the mailbox."

"Huh?" I said.

"Some vandals tore my apartment to pieces," Trudy said.

"You drove her to the place this morning, Mr. Oates," the cop said, "so she could leave the key in the mailbox for the cleaning woman. And I was wondering if you seen anybody around. Kids in the street, maybe. Anybody at all. Somebody seen her put the key in the mailbox, I figure."

I was weak with relief. "I didn't notice anybody."

"I think somebody had carefully planned it," Clara said. "Somebody knew that Trudy always left the key in the mailbox every Friday for the cleaning woman."

"Maybe," the cop said dubiously. "But why case a job and not take nothing? It looks like punks, to me. Cut open the mattress, slash the upholstery, bust the pictures out of the frames and burn them, rip the sheets, slit the pillows, cut the carpet—but not take nothing. Just punks who seen her put the key in the mailbox. That's how I figure. You don't remember seeing nobody, then, Mr. Oates? Maybe a hot rod going past or something?"

I shook my head. "If I recall anything, I'll let you know."

"Well, much obliged." He went out.

"If I catch those punks I'll wring their necks!" Trudy declared. "Wrecking my place for no reason at all!"

"Thank goodness they didn't destroy your clothes," Clara said.

I asked, "When did it happen?"

"We know the place was all right when the cleaning woman left about eleven," Clara said. "Trudy called me at noon and said she'd have to work straight through to get done in time, so I went over in Leo's car during the lunch period to pick up her bag—and I found the place torn apart. You should see it, Hank. Ankle deep in feathers, everything torn up—"

"I guess there's nothing to be done about it," Trudy said. "Well, I won't even try to straighten things up until we get back Monday."

"Where are you going?" It was none of my business, but I didn't like to think of her being away for the weekend.

"Didn't Leo even mention it to you?" Clara asked me. "That man! We'll all spend the weekend at his lodge. You won't be feeling too well, so we thought Trudy had better drive you up when you're through."

A man came from the dental office, probing at a place in his mouth with his tongue. "You can go in now, Hank," Clara said.

13

When I went in, Cranston was washing his hands. He grinned. "Any more trouble with the rat?"

"The pills you brought home kept him asleep."

"Rat?" Clara said.

Cranston laughed. It was his idea of a joke. I explained to Clara while she clipped on the bib. She began laying out stuff on the tray.

"I had lunch with Kline yesterday," I said. "Since then an idea has been growing. Jim is dead."

Clara dropped something that clattered loudly on the glass of the tray. Cranston stiffened, turning slowly from the wash basin, his hands dripping.

"I didn't mean to drop an A-bomb," I said. "But if you look at it that way, everything fits."

Clara looked at me in a pitying way, then turned to Cranston. "You shouldn't have given him those pills, Leo. He's not himself."

"How many did you take?" Cranston asked me. "I told you a couple at bedtime, one this morning—"

"My head is clear as a bell," I said.

"But Jim talked with me on the phone," Clara said.

"And to me, supposedly. That could easily be faked."

"I could be fooled about the voice," she admitted. "But Jim and I had a little secret language. Words that meant things to us they didn't mean to other people."

"I've heard the same sort of argument from people who were hoodwinked by mind readers at county fairs. You just don't know what Jim might have told somebody about those words. And you wanted to believe he was alive. You were emotionally upset when you got those calls; you were in no condition to judge."

"Aren't you forgetting something, Hank?" Cranston said. "Hap tried to kill you, because of Jim. He told you that somebody called Speck was going to kill you at Jim's orders."

I looked at Clara. She said, "I've told Leo everything."

"Hap had no reason to lie," Cranston said. "He expected to kill you."

"Hap was hoodwinked too," I said. "That's the clever part of the whole thing. Somebody is hiding behind a dead man. Hap didn't tell me he'd actually seen Jim alive. Somebody is using Jim to bring me out here and set me up for the kill. Maybe it's the guy called Speck, whoever he might be. This person's motive has nothing to do with Jim. Jim is just a front to conceal the real motive and to keep me from looking past it. A very clever decoy. As to the actual reason behind it all, that's something I've got to find out. It may be somebody with a gripe against my father. Or just against people like myself in general. A discharged employee of the company. A crackpot. Now that I know what it is, I'll at least be looking the right way."

"Why are you so sure Jim is dead?" Cranston asked. "What did Kline say?"

"It's not one thing, it's an accumulation of little things. The whole thing is too indirect. If Jim were alive, he would have showed himself."

Cranston began working on my teeth. "There's something you don't know, Hank." He glanced at Clara. "I think we should tell him."

She said cautiously, "Everything?"

He nodded. "Hank, this is strictly confidential. Jim disappeared to escape a murder indictment. He killed Uncle Jasper. Hap Arnold had the goods on him."

Clara was mixing some white powder with a liquid to form a paste. "Hank, Trudy must never know of this. Or anyone."

Cranston had removed the temporary fillings. He painted the cavities, held a finger in my mouth to keep it open. "Jim killed Uncle Jasper for the estate. You know what the real estate deal is if you talked with Kline. Hap Arnold just happened to witness the murder. Jim had nailed a horseshoe to a club—"

"Do you have to go into detail?" Clara asked, shuddering.

"We learned of it when Arnold came to us, after Jim had apparently suicided. Since then, Clara has paid Arnold a hundred dollars a week just to keep him pacified. We have the canceled checks if you want to see them. I advanced the money to her. So that, in a sense, we're accomplices to the crime after the fact. Of course you'll say nothing, Hank."

The big white finger was temporarily out of my mouth. I said, "Maybe Hap was lying."

"He wasn't lying. He showed us a photostat of the evidence."

"Why didn't Jim kill Arnold?"

"Arnold has the evidence in an envelope somewhere. Some friend of his knows where it is, and has instructions to deliver it to the police if anything happens to him." Cranston put some of the white paste in a tooth, fitted an inlay into the cavity, held it in tightly with his thumb.

Clara said, "When Hap is found missing, that envelope will go to the police. Poor Trudy."

"I like to think Jim disappeared for Clara's sake," Cranston said. "So she wouldn't lose everything."

"He did it to gain time," Clara said sharply. "To stall Hap off. I'm through making excuses for Jim. He's been after that evidence.... Hank, I didn't tell you about this the other night, because—well, it makes Leo and me accessories or something to murder. I don't like to think about that."

Cranston began fitting another inlay. "This is what happened, Hank. Hap Arnold put the bite on Jim. He wanted a half interest in everything. Jim stalled him off with a story about how much bigger the melon would be when the real estate deal was complete—which was true enough. He played on Hap's avarice to stall him off. But Jim was bright enough to realize there was no end to blackmail. Hap wanted half now, but that wouldn't satisfy him. Too, Hap was getting along in years—particularly for a guy who went on a binge every so often. And Jim's life hung on Hap's whim and good health. If Hap got drunk and had an accident, if he fell dead, Jim was finished. He couldn't face that kind of a future, his life hanging on a thread. So he faked suicide."

"But he hadn't thought it through," Clara said. "Because Hap then came to me with the same proposition, and I had to stall him off with his weekly pension. Hap pointed out that I couldn't inherit what Jim had obtained by murder. Though that isn't why I paid him off. While I love money as much as anybody else, I didn't want that kind of money. It was the mess, the disgrace; I didn't want that. I agreed to give Hap all of Jim's share. I just didn't want that kind of money. But, you see, there was no proof of death. I'd have to wait seven years before getting anything to turn over to Hap. And meanwhile he had to have his weekly payoff."

I found my mouth empty again. "He put you through the wringer."

"Aside from the hundred a week, which I couldn't have raised if Leo hadn't advanced it, now my life was hanging on Hap's whim and good health. I was an accomplice."

"Me, too, since I advanced the money," Cranston said. He began on another inlay. "I worked my way through school—keeping books, waiting on tables, prize fighting, playing football. I came from a trashy family. I'm the only one of nine kids who amounted to a damn. I had to overcome all that, and it took some doing to get where I am. Now I stand to lose everything because of Jim. That son of a bitch."

"I shouldn't have come to you with my troubles, Leo," Clara said.

"Oh, hell. Could I just stand by and let you take it in the neck?"

When my mouth was empty again, I said, "It still doesn't prove that Jim is alive. Nobody has seen him."

"I saw him," Cranston said. "I should have busted his goddamn neck while I had the chance."

"What?" Clara said. "You didn't tell me this, Leo."

"Jim wanted it kept quiet, then." Cranston began on another tooth. "It was the week after we thought he had suicided. He phoned me and I met him at the lodge. He'd found out that Hap was putting the heat on you and that his phony suicide didn't solve anything."

"What did he want to see you about?" she asked.

"He wanted to know what to do next. Hell, how could I advise him? I should have killed the bastard when I had a chance, and be done with it. He knows I will, too, if I get another good chance. That's why he hasn't showed himself since. He's never gotten any closer than a telephone."

This knocked my fine deduction in the head. I had a perfect batting average so far—.000.

"I think I see it now," Clara said. "Why Hap tried to kill you and why Jim—or Speck—hasn't tried it since." She considered a few moments while I waited, then she said, "Hap learned that Jim had written you that letter, asking you to come out here. Hap tried to stop you from coming because he was afraid that the Oates money could clear Jim regardless of the evidence. You ignored his warning phone call, you avoided his badger game scheme at Salt Lake. So Hap lured you to Devil's Slide to kill you. From his viewpoint it was the only thing he could do to protect his own interests. That money he stood to make—and the weekly pension—meant a great deal to Hap."

Cranston had taken his hands out of my mouth for the moment. I said, "But if Hap is dead, why hasn't the evidence against Jim been delivered to the police?"

"Jim must have found that envelope."

"If so, he now can return to life."

Clara shook her head. "No; because he now knows we wouldn't stand behind him. We could convict him of murder."

Cranston said, "I have a photostat of that evidence. Jim knows that if he tries to kill you now, we can nail him for Uncle Jasper's murder."

"He also knows," Clara pointed out, "that Hank was the last person to see Hap Arnold alive."

"Stalemate," I said.

"Nice situation," Cranston agreed. He began cementing in another inlay. "We've got Jim over a barrel, and he's got us. It's a standoff, with just one solution. If he can kill the three of us, he's okay. If we get him first, we're okay."

This was a pleasant prospect, either way. Nobody said anything while Cranston finished putting in the inlays. Then I asked Clara, "Why did you pay the insurance premium?"

"That's what White keeps pestering about," she said. "You must have talked to him. Why shouldn't I keep up the insurance? I knew Jim was alive."

"I insisted that she pay the premium—I advanced the money," Cranston said. "She had to have some protection. It was her only chance of getting an honest dollar out of Jim. She wouldn't touch the Uncle Jasper money, no matter how things turned out."

Clara must have read my eyes. She said, "That was before you got involved, Hank. Now it's a matter of kill or be killed. If we get Jim before he gets us, I'd rather it were never known. Just let it go as it is, that he suicided. I don't want that kind of money."

Cranston polished the inlays. And then I tensed for what was to come. But Cranston was a good mechanic. He eased out two teeth and slipped the bridge into place almost before I knew what was happening. The other two came out just as easily. Cranston told me to sit quiet awhile, keep my tongue from probing, let nature take its course.

"You're a good patient, Hank. We've stopped the damage. The bridge keeps your smile pretty, and you'll never miss the wisdom teeth."

"I've lost three teeth," Clara said helpfully, "and Trudy two."

I found I could speak, after a fashion. "Jim said you had a hell of a time with his wisdom teeth. He'd lost four, as I remember."

"And a couple since the war," Cranston said. "You've been lucky, Hank."

Clara unclipped the bib. "Trudy's waiting."

"Didn't she inherit half of Uncle Jasper's estate?"

"Uncle Jasper was old-fashioned. He felt men were to handle the business and take care of the women," she said.

I had an evil thought about Trudy but immediately put it aside. What kind of a guy was I anyhow, having such thoughts?

"When it starts hurting, take some aspirin," Cranston said. "I'll be on deck tonight if there's any trouble."

Trudy was waiting at Clara's desk when I went out. She asked Clara, "What happened to that picture of Jim and Hank that you always had here?"

"I broke the glass," Clara said. "I'm having it fixed."

As I went down the elevator with Trudy I wondered how long it would be before she had to know everything.

14

Trudy turned off Skyline into a branch highway, presently took a fork to the right onto a dirt road that twisted steeply down through a grove of huge redwoods that looked exactly like the ones on postcards from sunny California. I paid little attention to where we were going. The feeling was returning to my face and it wasn't a pleasant one. The jolting of the car on the rough road didn't help, as Trudy tooled to the bottom of a deep ravine, crossed a narrow bridge and climbed back up the other side of the ravine onto a flat which held a shake lodge. She parked on the flat.

"How do you feel?"

"Rotten."

She murmured soothing words as we crossed to the lodge. She got a key from under the steps, opened the big slab door and we went in. It was a typical mountain lodge, a big main room with the inevitable horrible fireplace of cobblestone, beamed ceiling with the bark on the beams. A fine place for spiders. At the right end as we came in was a balcony with bedrooms leading off it. Below the bedrooms were the kitchen, a bathroom, garage and storeroom.

She insisted I lie down on the big couch before the fireplace. I didn't put up much resistance. She disappeared; there came the sound of running water; she came in with water and two aspirins. I swallowed the pills, drank the water, then relaxed on the couch. She sat beside it on the floor, her neat head with its richly auburn hair near my hand. She watched the black hole of the fireplace, saying nothing, looking no doubt into whatever thoughts lovely girls have. I knew they must be lovely thoughts. She wouldn't have the kind of thoughts I sometimes had. She was born to different things. Better things. I wondered if I could ever be worthy of such a girl.

She lifted back a stray strand of hair, and I took her hand. She glanced sidewise at me, making a little smile. Her other hand came over mine, and she put her cheek atop the three hands while she looked into whatever lovely thoughts she saw in the fireplace.

This, I realized, was what I needed in life. This was what I missed. Somebody to sit with and be with. Somebody to be comfortable with without having to be bright or gay or entertaining or dignified. Somebody you could just sit with and say nothing, and feel warm and comfortable and complete with while doing nothing except being together. This was probably why marriage was so popular. Why people got divorced half a dozen times and still went back to it. It had little to do with passion. Nor was it exactly a matter of comfort. It was not being alone. It was having somebody to count on. Knowing there's somebody you can just sit with and feel happy about it.

"Trudy, will you forgive me?"

"For what?"

"For being a snob."

She kept looking into the dead fireplace. "Everybody is, Hank, one way or another," she said gently. "That's why they have rank in the Army and why we'll always have a Negro problem or a Jewish problem or some other problem. Humans are born with a deep desire for inequality. That's why we have progress, as everybody struggles to be better than somebody else."

"Will you marry me?"

Her eyes came up for just an instant, turned again to the fireplace. I knew I'd hurt her.

"It wouldn't work out, Hank. I understood when your letter came. I knew it would have to come, from the first time I learned who you were. It wouldn't work out."

"There was Edward VIII. He got what he wanted. What more is

there? He paid a price, but nothing worthwhile comes free."

"You made your decision, Hank. It was the wise one."

"I've changed my mind."

"You wouldn't like carrying a lunch bucket."

"I would if you put up the lunch in it."

"It wouldn't work out."

"You used to love me."

"I still do," she said. "I know it's foolish and probably neurotic, but that's how it is. I ought to hate you to pieces. I should have the fury of a woman scorned. But I don't. We said things to one another and they can't be unsaid. We were to be married the next day and when it came and you didn't meet me, I knew you were on the ocean. If you hadn't gone overseas until the following day, somebody would have said some words over us and collected a fee. There would have been a piece of paper. A legal receipt for an emotional state. Lack of the receipt doesn't change the state. What you feel is for richer or for poorer, in sickness and in health, through thick and through thin, until death do you part."

"That's how I want it," I said. "That's how it's been with me. That's why I've been unhappy as hell. But I'm going to quit being unhappy. We'll take it from here on together."

"It wouldn't work out, Hank. We're talking of love. Love and marriage are often very different things with people of your class."

"To hell with my class! We'll get married and Father can do what he damned well pleases about it. It's my life, not his."

"You're upset, Hank. You've been through an ordeal."

"You're right," I admitted. "Henry Chatworth Oates III has discovered that he can die just like anybody else."

Her face came around sharply. "What do you mean?"

"Hap Arnold tried to kill me the other night."

"What? Why?"

"I—don't know. But that isn't the important thing. What matters is that I'm on bedrock. The things that Hank Oates thought happened only to other people can happen to him. He can be bumped off or taken for a ride. He can get mixed up in messes just like the rabble. He's back to fundamentals, the way he was in the Army when it was kill or be killed. And this time he thinks the lesson is going to stick. I doubt if he's ever going to pattern his life to a pretty little plan again. Because nobody can look into the ground any further than the next man, and that goes for him too. He's on bedrock—life and death and love. And he's going to stay on bedrock. Love is elemental. We love each other and that's all that counts."

She said gently, "You're talking too much, Hank."

"I had to get it off my chest."

"There must be a girl of your own class."

"There is. Her name is Caroline. It would be a good marriage. Love is supposed to come later. But that's backwards."

"Your parents would never accept me, Hank. Your father would cut you off and throw you out. He would make me see how selfish I was to keep you from the better things of life. He would never rest until he'd broken up the marriage and you had come back."

"Most young couples start out from scratch anyhow. I'm game for it if you are."

"Try to sleep, Hank," she said softly. "Get some rest." She hadn't said she wouldn't. The world was peaceful and good as I drifted off.

When I woke up it was getting dark. My mouth was exquisitely tender. Trudy had covered me with an Afghan. From the kitchen came the low murmur of women's voices; Clara had arrived, then. I lay half asleep thinking of Trudy as my wife. It would be a blow to Father, a ring-tailed fight— Well, okay and to hell with it. This was my life and I was going to live it. The years since the War had been plain hell. Playing make-believe in the big office with the two secretaries and the Dictaphone. Going through the motions of the big executive while knowing I had less actual authority than a shift boss in the shipping department. From now on, I'd do it my way.

Come to think of it, I hadn't lived my own life except for the years in the Army. That was somehow funny—the discipline of Army life being my only freedom—yet despite the pressure and the fear and the grinding monotony, the War years had been the happiest of my life. Because I'd been a person rather than a symbol. Just a GI, but a GI from choice, and in love with a girl who loved me.

I sat up suddenly, fully awake. What was I doing, proposing to Trudy? Her brother was trying to kill me. To stay alive, I would have to kill him.

My mouth began to throb and I was slightly dizzy as I stood up. Through the front window of the lodge I saw sunlight in the very tops of the tall redwoods. There was deep shadow below; inside the big room it was almost dark. On the flat, parked beside my car, was a battered Nash, a dozen years old or more and sadly neglected for all of them. I crossed to the kitchen door, which showed a line of light at the bottom.

The murmur of voices stopped suddenly as I swung the door open. I saw Trudy and another woman looking at me in stiffly unnatural positions, as if I had startled them in secret conference.

The other woman was Millie Barron, my pal of the badger game in Salt Lake City, her hair the same red color that comes out of a bottle, the lipstick painted in a cupid's bow over a thin mouth, the fake eyelashes curling out an inch; it was all so strictly synthetic that you thought of it as stage make-up that she'd wipe off. She had a shot glass of whiskey in her hand. With a delicate motion she threw it off and said, "Well, he's awake now."

Trudy said, "But, really, Mrs. Barron—"

"He looks all right to me." Millie glared at me. "Can you talk?"

"Hello, Millie."

"He can talk!" Millie said triumphantly.

"Hank, you're too sick," Trudy said. "You shouldn't be up. Lie down. I'll help you back to the couch."

"Just a minute, sister. He's not too sick to answer a simple question. That's all I want to know. What," Millie demanded, "happened to Murray?"

"Murray? I'm sure I don't know."

"I told you," Trudy said to her. "There was no use disturbing him. He knows nothing about it."

"I didn't disturb nobody. He walked in here under his own power," Millie said, pouring another shot from a bottle on the sink. She threw it off, then glared at me. "So you won't talk, huh?"

I shrugged. There was no use arguing with a drunk.

Trudy said, "Hank, perhaps if you'd explain—"

"I'll explain!" Millie cried, with a hard laugh. "I'll explain to the cops! That's who I'll explain to! You'll find out! I'm going straight to the cops!"

"Let's talk this over, Mrs. Barron," Trudy said. "Hank, couldn't you explain enough to her that she would understand?"

"Explain what?"

"Where is Murray?" Millie cried. "That's what I want to know!"

"I'm sure I don't know what you're talking about."

Millie sneered. "So you didn't meet him? He wasn't going to bring you here? You just don't know anything about it?"

"That's right."

"Well!" Millie's lips were thin under the paint. "Somebody's going to do some tall talking to the law. Murray's no fool. He knows how to protect himself." She tossed off another shot, took gloves and handbag from the drainboard, marched past me and out the front door.

"Hank," Trudy said anxiously, "she's going to the police. Can't you tell her something to—"

"She's tight. I don't know what she's talking about."

"But you told me that Murray Arnold tried to kill you."

I did a double-take. "Murray *Arnold?*"

"Yes. You said—"

"*Hap!*" I realized that in my association with Millie, I'd never heard her call Hap Arnold by name. "So his name is Murray Arnold. Why the hell didn't she say who she was talking about?"

"She did, didn't she? I thought—"

I broke for the front door.

The engine of the Nash was very old, very abused, and the victim of cheap oil, neglect and amateur tinkering. It was thundering with a great clatter of slapping pistons, loose tappets and worn bearings, the car almost hidden by the cloud of blue smoke from the broken muffler, when I ran out the door onto the porch. Millie gunned the car in reverse, cutting the wheels sharply.

"Millie!"

My yell coincided with a crash as the rear end of the Nash smashed into the redwood log marking the boundary of the parking area. I yelled again; my voice was swallowed in the thunder of the engine. I ran down the steps, waving. But what with the smoke, the noise, and the shock of backing into the log, Millie didn't see me. Or maybe she didn't want to. Or was just too drunk. The car lurched forward and made a skidding turn into the ravine.

I stood helplessly, the smell of dust and exhaust smoke in my nostrils.

"What can she do?" Trudy called from the porch. "Can you tell me?"

"Nothing to worry about," I said. "Nothing that putting me in the gas chamber won't cure."

This, I felt, was a rather clever remark. Though I doubted if the police would appreciate the repartee.

15

The dust and the blue smoke drifted away as the howl of the old car grew faint. I had a vicious hope that Millie would be going too fast to make the sharp turn over the bridge at the bottom of the ravine. I wondered what I'd come to, to be having hopes like that.

Trudy grabbed my arm. "Come on! She might take any of a dozen roads in the hills. We don't know which town she'll head for!"

We ran to my car. Trudy got under the wheel, backed around, gunned into the ravine. It was getting dark now, the sun was gone from the tops of the redwoods; I snapped on the lights for her. I had a futile mental picture of trying to flag down Millie, being unable to shout from car to car over the noise, while the woman fled in desperate fear of her life. But that thought was better than the one of racing madly among the hills on the wrong roads and never finding her.

"I just woke up; I was groggy," I said. "She hit me with a fast question about *Murray*."

"We'll overtake her," Trudy said.

But I knew we wouldn't, at this rate. My car, with a longer wheelbase than Millie's, couldn't make the sharp turns of the ravine as fast. Nor was Trudy too drunk to care. Now that speed counted, I realized the ravine road was worse than I had supposed on the trip in. It was narrow, eroded, very steep; Trudy had to creep around sharp curves where mere inches stood between the outside tires and the boulders of the creek bed far below. And at the bridge the road made a square turn. There was absolutely no hope of making speed going into or out of the ravine, and meanwhile Millie had done it, drunk, while I stood gawking like an idiot; and now she was grimly speeding to some police station at any one of a dozen surrounding towns on the Peninsula.

As Trudy crossed the bridge and started up the other side, I realized I simply wasn't geared to this sort of thing. Which would have been a fine excuse to walk away from it—if I had been able to.

We came out of the ravine to find a pair of headlights blocking the road. There was no passing here; redwoods stood on either side. I recognized Cranston's yellow Cad. Trudy honked. Cranston honked back.

"Back up!" Trudy yelled.

"Back up yourself!" Cranston called gaily.

What a sense of humor!

I got out, ran to his car. "Back up, Leo. We've got to get through."

"What's the rush?"

"Don't argue. We'll explain later."

"Hank, I told you to stay quiet. And I'm hungry. Don't you two go running off at mealtime."

"For Christ's sake, shut up! Millie Barron was here—Hap Arnold's girlfriend. She's going to the police!"

Cranston chuckled. "What's wrong, Hank? Guilty conscience?"

"Don't you understand? She came up to find out what happened to Hap. She called him Murray. I'd just woke up and I didn't know who she was talking about. Now she's going to the police. We've got to catch her and stall her off!"

"Oh, you mean Millie."

"That's right. Hap's girlfriend."

"Yeah. She's a patient of mine. You wonder what a girl like that sees in Hap Arnold—saw in him. Not that she's any prize, but Hap—"

"Shut up and get off this goddamn road!" I yelled.

"Take it easy, Hank. Don't get excited. Remember that you've just had four extractions. Getting dark now, and it's going to be chilly tonight. You don't want to be chasing around in your condition. You might start bleeding. It could be serious."

I looked steadily at Cranston. The broad pink face had a satisfied grin. Cranston wasn't worried. Cranston didn't have a worry in the world.

"You don't want me to get past," I said quietly. "You don't care if she goes to the police. You can say I told you I killed Hap Arnold. Is that it?"

Cranston nodded, grinning. "It's your neck, Hank." Then he roared with laughter.

Trudy ran up. "Leo, for heaven's sake! Let us past! ... Hank, did you explain?"

"Yeah. Big joke," I said grimly.

"Back there," Cranston gasped between laughter. "We met Millie just as she came out of my road. Clara's with her now. Calming her down. Clara can handle her." He slapped his leg and howled. "Hank, I sure had you worried for a minute or so!"

"Ha, ha," I said sourly. That sense of humor.

By the time Trudy was backing my car between the trunks of two redwoods to turn around, the pale-yellow headlights of Millie's car were waiting behind Cranston's Cad. The three cars went through the ravine and onto the flat before the lodge.

Cranston said, "I'd better check on the pump house. Don't anybody use the bathroom for a while." He disappeared among trees. As Millie got out of the Nash she staggered. Clara took her arm. Millie jerked away.

"I don't know if this is just butter or not," Millie said. She pointed at me. "I'll hear *him* say so. That's the only reason I came back with you. Let him say it."

"Of course, Millie," Clara said soothingly. "Hank, explain to her about Hap."

I didn't know just what story Clara had told, and there was no chance of finding out. "I'm sorry, Millie. I didn't understand. You asked about a man named Murray. I didn't realize—"

Clara broke in with a hearty laugh. "That's wonderful! He didn't know who you were talking about! He didn't know Hap's name was Murray! That's really priceless!"

"Well, he does now," Millie said. "And I don't like people to call Murray, Hap. Murray is a perfectly good name. It's got dignity."

"I'd just woke up," I said. "I was groggy."

"Poor boy; he had four teeth out this afternoon. He's not himself. And you know how careful we have to be, Millie."

"All right, all right," Millie said impatiently. She pointed accusingly at me. "You saw him night before last. Wednesday night. He was to bring you and Jim up here. I was here waiting. You didn't show up, and I haven't seen or heard from Murray since. He told me what to do if anything like this happened. How about it?"

I was conscious of a serious gap in my equipment for this sort of thing. I was no good at a lie. I had always been firmly convinced that the truth, no matter how bad, was always better than falsehood in the long run. I doubted if it would be so in this particular case. Yet if I denied going with Hap Arnold Wednesday night, she would go to the police. If I calmed her down with a fast lie now, it would only complicate the situation later on. Hap was dead, and that would have to come out eventually. Perhaps his car already had been reported to the police.

"Of course he saw Hap Wednesday night," Clara said smoothly. "He just didn't know that it was all right to talk to you, Millie.... It's all right, Hank. She's Hap's girlfriend."

"We're engaged," Millie said. "Practically. And I don't like people to call him Hap."

"Hap—Murray—is all right. Hank told us all about it." Clara took the woman's arm. "Let's have a drink and talk it over."

The prospect of a drink seemed to swing the balance. "If you do have just a little something, dearie," Millie said. "I've been so upset, not hearing from Murray." She and Clara went inside.

Trudy, coming behind with me, whispered, "What happened to Arnold? You said he tried to kill you."

"He's dead."

Her breath came with a gasp. "Jim—is Jim all right?"

"I didn't see Jim the other night."

"You're telling me the truth? You wouldn't lie to me about this? Don't spare me, Hank. I want to know what happened."

"It was an accident. I thought Hap was taking me to Jim. Instead, he tried to kill me at Devil's Slide. He slipped and fell."

"How can we explain this to Millie Barron?"

"We can't."

"What can we tell her?"

"I don't know."

"Then that note really wasn't from Jim. Or else Hap took Jim's place in meeting you."

"We don't know what happened there."

"We've got to protect Jim. I know he can explain."

Now she was a fellow conspirator, ready to cover up Hap's death. I felt a futile and frustrated rage at the circumstances which would involve a girl like Trudy in such a mess. Jim would pay for this. In this world or the next.

Clara was making drinks in the kitchen and had, wisely, given Millie something to do. The doll-like creature was delicately laying a fire, being very careful of her long and violently red fingernails. Trudy began helping, efficiently; I went into the kitchen. Clara glanced at the open door. I shut it.

She said, "We've got to calm that woman down. Let me handle her."

"Should we have told her I saw Hap?"

Clara ran water over an ice tray. "She was on her way to the cops to spill her guts." This wasn't a refined expression, but Clara's salient characteristic wasn't refinement. She was earthy, elemental. I thought, with a sense of discovery, that Clara in life was very similar to a girl on a burlesque stage. She gave the impression that convention be damned and any impulse was possible. "She knows I was paying Hap off. I think she was the one Hap gave the evidence to for safekeeping, about Uncle Jasper's murder. If one photostat was made, there could be another." She put ice cubes in five glasses. "Thank God we met the car just as it came out of the trees, and I recognized her."

"Now I'll be involved in Hap's death. She knows I was with him the last night he was alive."

Clara poured stiff slugs into the glasses from a fifth of bourbon. "We're all in this, Hank. Leo and I are in as deep as you are." She began filling the glasses with water. "We've got to stall her off."

"But for how long? Hap's car might have been reported already. Even if it sits there several days, eventually—"

"Here." She handed me a copper tray, began putting the glasses on it. "The trouble with you, Hank, you've got to see everything to the end. That's why you didn't marry Trudy. You're used to a mental road map with everything neatly laid out and the main highway marked in red. People like me, we meet things as they come up and slap us in the kisser. We've got to meet the emergency tonight regardless of what happens tomorrow." She kissed me on the neck. "Poor dear, you feel terrible, don't you? How's the mouth?"

"Sore."

"Let me handle it, Hank."

She was wonderful. A testimony to the adaptability of the human organism. She was a thing born for satin cushions while men were her willing slaves just because of what she was. Yet from circumstance she had become shrewd and capable, juggling sudden death with casual efficiency. Let me handle it, she said, as if it were sewing on a button or something else which she could do so much better than a mere man. Or, anyhow, this mere man. We went into the big room.

Millie Barron was standing by the fireplace helplessly, a twig held delicately between thumb and forefinger, while Trudy fed the growing fire. Seeing the tray, Millie tossed away the twig and reached for a glass. She downed the highball with a single smooth motion. "Oh, you drowned it, dearie."

Clara took the glass into the kitchen. Trudy tasted her drink and gave me a curious glance. I knew what she meant, having seen the slug poured in those glasses. Clara returned with Millie's refill. Through the open door I'd seen it made; nothing but whiskey and ice.

With exaggerated delicacy Millie threw it off with one swallow, and without even a deep breath said, "Thank you, dearie." Trudy turned politely away; her eyes were popping. "No, thanks, one's enough," Millie said. And added, as Clara took her at her word, "But I'm so upset, dearie. Maybe just a short one. Don't drown it." She settled herself carefully on the couch, and in a baby voice said, "Now tell me about my Murray. Me's so worried about mommie's ittie boy."

I supposed some men would go for that. A man of Arnold's age might eat it up. Which made for horse races.

"Millie, why don't you explain things to Hank?" Clara called from the kitchen. "We don't want another misunderstanding."

"But me did explain," Millie said. "Me waited here, right where me is now, all Wednesday night. But me was so lonely. Murray was supposed to bring Jim and Hank here and we was to have a party. But nobody came. Me was so lonely."

"Then you know Jim?" Trudy said eagerly. "You've seen him lately?"

Millie smiled. She took the glass Clara brought in and with that smooth and delicate gesture emptied it. "I know Jim very well," she said, dropping the baby talk. "I saw him Wednesday afternoon. That's how I know that Murray was to meet you on Skyline Boulevard at nine o'clock that night."

I wondered why Jim would trust this alcoholic. Certainly he had some common sense. Though, I admitted, Jim was in a situation where he couldn't always choose his company.

"Where is he?" Trudy asked.

"I ain't saying," Millie evaded. "But if anything has happened to Murray, the cops will know all about everything."

"Hap is all right," Clara said. "He's in L.A."

"L.A.? Then why didn't he tell me? He's said time and again that he'd get in touch with me every day. If anything happens to him, I'm to turn that envelope over to the cops."

There was another photostat, I decided.

"What's in the envelope?" Trudy asked.

The cupid-bow lips smiled sweetly. "Wouldn't you like to know?"

Clara said, "Hap took you into his confidence?"

"In everything. And don't call him Hap."

"Then you realize, Millie, that things could come up which had to be attended to right away. Hank met Hap—met Murray—on the Skyline the other night, as scheduled. Murray said he had to go to

L.A. but he told Hank to come up here to the lodge and meet you. Hank couldn't find the lodge. He got lost in the fog.... Isn't that so, Hank?"

"You couldn't see ten feet before the car, that night," I said truthfully.

"Hap's all right," Clara said. "He's probably been trying to phone you from L.A. And you've been away. He would phone you at home, not here."

She took Millie's glass to the kitchen for a refill. Evidently the idea was to get Millie thoroughly plastered. Though to me it seemed an extremely temporary expedient. She couldn't be stalled more than a day or so, at most.

Leo Cranston burst in the door. His hair was on end, the dark double-breasted suit covered with dust. "Somebody jumped me! Come on, Hank!"

16

Clara moved swiftly to the big front window and drew the drapes. Cranston said, "Got a gun, Hank?"

"In my car."

"So have I—in my car." He nodded toward the kitchen. "We'll go out this way. Duck under the kitchen window."

I followed into the garage. The place was not used as a garage, being stacked with fireplace wood. There had once been a double door, but half of it was gone. Cranston paused at the opening, looking about. I didn't feel particularly brave. Certainly I was in no mood for a fight, with my mouth. I could see nothing but the silhouette of the treetops against the night sky.

"We'd better wait until your eyes are used to it," he said. "I went to the pump house and oiled things up. Then I checked the tank. I came back to get the luggage from the car and somebody was fooling around your car. I figured it was you, until I stepped up and he jumped me. It was Jim."

"Jim?"

"Yes. He got me by surprise and I went over. I tried to grab him but he kicked loose and beat it. How are your eyes?"

"We'd better wait a little more." I wasn't too anxious.

"We'll get the son of a bitch. How are you with a gun?"

"Only fair."

"I'm pretty good. Don't give the bastard a chance. We'll get our guns and comb the woods for him. Shoot on sight."

It was a chilling prospect, stalking Jim in the night. Regardless of what Jim had done. I couldn't forget the Jim I'd gone through a war with. *That* Jim was a swell guy. The friendship I'd felt for him was something like the kind of love Trudy had talked about, a feeling that went through thick and thin, in sickness and in health, for richer or poorer.

"We can't just shoot Jim down. Maybe he can explain."

"He won't explain to me. Not if I get the first shot."

"Maybe Hap framed him. Maybe Hap really double-crossed him in trying to kill me."

"Don't be a damned fool. How are your eyes?"

The flat, containing the outline of the three cars, now was visible. "I'm all right." We crossed to the cars. The door of mine was open, my overcoat hanging out with one sleeve in the yellow dust. I went through the pockets. "It's gone. The gun."

"Maybe it's on the seat."

I turned on the dash light. The gun wasn't inside.

Cranston asked, "Are you sure it was in your coat? You didn't put it in your luggage?"

"It was in my coat. The right-hand pocket."

"Well, now he's got a gun for sure," Cranston said. "No use sticking our necks out." He turned toward the lodge. "We better get back inside."

"It was Hap's gun."

Cranston turned back slowly. His broad pink face was wooden. "Hap's gun?"

"Yes."

"And now he's got it. He found Hap's gun in your pocket. Now he knows you did it."

"He did anyhow."

"He can nail you now, you fool!"

"How can he prove he found it in my pocket?" I said, a little amazed that I should be talking of such things as the inability of somebody to pin a murder on me.

Cranston began swearing. He smoothed his hair, beat the dust from his suit. "The idea is, get away from it all. Up in God's country. All you get away from is police protection." He indicated the house. "We'd better say nothing about Jim. Just say it was a prowler, and nothing missing. God knows we have enough of them up here."

We went inside. "Somebody snooping around the cars," he said. "I guess just some punk seeing what he could lift."

"I'll call the sheriff's office," Trudy said.

Cranston crossed to her as she turned to the phone; he muttered something. She stiffened as if struck.

"Not Jim!"

Cranston made a shushing gesture. Clara said, "It's all right, Leo. Millie knows about Jim. She's a good friend of his. Jim and Hap are often at her apartment."

"We play a lot of sluff together," Millie said. She made her doll smile as Cranston regarded her steadily. She was fingering an empty glass. I wondered what was holding her up.

"But why would Jim knock you down?" Trudy asked Cranston.

"It was dark. I surprised him. He probably didn't know who I was."

Trudy ran to the door and onto the porch. "Jim! Jim!"

Cranston went after her, took her arm. "He would come in if he could, Trudy. He wants to see us as badly as we want to see him." He drew her inside.

"Why?" Trudy asked. "Why? He knows he can trust me."

Cranston patted her hand, and said to Millie, "Well, have we got it all straightened out?"

"I told her Hap had gone to L.A." Clara explained. "That's why she didn't hear from him. He's probably trying to phone her apartment right now."

"He could be back," Cranston said. "Sitting there waiting for you."

"Maybe he is," Millie admitted. "I think I'd better go. But he told me to turn the envelope over to the police if anything happened to him. If I don't hear from him by tomorrow, I'll know something has."

Cranston said, "You don't want to do anything you might regret."

"And neither do you," Millie said. "I've got my orders."

"Stay for dinner, now you're here."

"Yes," Clara said. "I'll fix something right away."

"No, I'd better go." Millie extended the glass. "Just a short one, dearie. Stirrup cup."

"Don't you think you've had enough?" Trudy asked.

Millie smiled sweetly. "No."

"You'd better eat something."

Millie laughed. "And spoil this edge?"

Clara fixed another slug. Millie inhaled it, pulled on her gloves, took her handbag, stood up, took two steps and keeled over on her face, out cold.

"I wondered what was holding her up," Clara said.

"She was tight when she first came here," Trudy said. "I have never in my life—" She kneeled beside Millie. "We'd ought to put her on the couch."

"And spoil our dinner?" Cranston said. He picked the woman up in his arms. "Never mind, Hank, she doesn't weigh anything," he said as I tried to help. "Go up and open a bedroom door for me."

"You sit down, Hank," Clara said. "You're supposed to be an invalid tonight. I'll open the door." She did so. Cranston carried the woman upstairs and through the bedroom door. Clara came down. "He's fussing over her. He'd ought to have been a doctor. How about something to eat?"

"I'll help you," Trudy said. They went into the kitchen.

"Make yourself useful, Hank," Clara called. "Set the table, why don't you? Dishes are in the cupboard by the door here, and silver in the drawer below."

I had the plates set out and was laying the silver when Cranston came downstairs. His coat was off, shirtsleeves turned up, tie loosened. "I did all I could."

We all looked at him. Trudy said, "She isn't—"

Cranston nodded. "She's dead."

None of us said anything for a bit. Trudy began crying quietly. I wondered what Millie Barron had gotten out of life. What was so hard to bear that she had to drug her consciousness? Or was it that she liked the taste of liquor? I didn't know, but it was the only life she knew. It was hers to live the way she wanted. It was the only one she had. Now it was over, and I wondered if it added up to her total. Everybody has a total.

"Are you sure, Leo?" Clara asked.

"Of course I'm sure."

"I shouldn't have given her that last drink," Clara said. "But she asked for it. She asked for it, didn't she?"

"It's not your fault; snap out of it," he said. "I guess we'd better call a doctor. This will be a case for the sheriff's office."

"Why?" Trudy asked.

"With anything but a normal death there's a routine examination. This was normal for Millie. She's been skirting the brink for a long time. But still there will be an examination."

"What about that envelope?" Clara said. "The police will take charge of her apartment."

"I'll go get it. You'd better call the sheriff's office and let them handle things. When they come, tell them I rushed out, all excited, for a doctor."

"What's in the envelope?" Trudy asked.

"I'll find out."

Cranston went out. I waited until his car drove away, then phoned the sheriff's office.

A doctor came, the coroner, another doctor Cranston had contacted, two deputy sheriffs, and an ambulance. The deputies knew Millie from away back. "She died in bed," one of them said. "I always expected it to be a crackup in that jalopy."

There were some routine questions. Clara tearfully kept saying that Millie had asked for it, and they kept telling her it wasn't her fault. Cranston arrived and answered the routine questions. He said he'd noticed her pulse was very weak. And then she stopped breathing. He'd tried to revive her with artificial respiration. Then he'd got panicky and driven for a doctor. After getting one, in San Mateo, he continued on to the city for a shower and a change of clothes.

Millie was put in the ambulance. The deputies said they'd send somebody for the Nash in the morning, and might drop by for a few more questions. When all the cars but our own and Millie's had gone, Trudy asked in a stage whisper, "Would they leave somebody around to eavesdrop?"

Cranston smiled. "Why? Drunks die every day."

"Did you get the envelope?"

"Yes. I burned it."

"What was in it?"

"I didn't want to know."

"Then how do you know it was the one?"

"It had directions on it—to be delivered to the police in case anything happened to Hap Arnold."

"But how can we help Jim unless we know what he's up against?" Trudy asked in dismay.

Cranston shrugged. "I need a drink."

"But everything will be all right now!" Trudy cried. "They were holding something over Jim. But now they're both dead and you destroyed the envelope. Now Jim can come back to us."

"Yes, dear," Clara said. "Will you finish setting the table?"

I put wood on the fire. The night had turned chilly; probably the teeth business had lowered my vitality. Cranston brought in a tall drink and sat with it before the fire.

I said quietly, "You got the envelope?"

He nodded. "Another photostat."

"Just what kind of evidence is it?"

"It's a confession, signed by Jim. That he killed Uncle Jasper."

"Maybe that was faked. Or gotten out of Jim by some trick. We don't know."

"Face it, Hank. I thought as much of Jim as you did. He was a swell guy. But something happened to him since the war." Cranston snapped his fingers. "What a chump I am!" He remembered Trudy at the end of the room and went on in a low voice, "I shouldn't have burned that photostat. It was our protection. It held Jim at a stalemate."

"But you've got another."

He smiled wryly. "Clara told me after you'd gone, today at the office. I *thought* I had a photostat. But she'd burned it. You know how a woman is. She couldn't bear to have such a thing around." He turned his head to look at Trudy, setting the table near the kitchen door. "She's got to know. We'll have to tell her."

"No. Let's wait until we know the whole thing," I said. "It will break her heart. Let's give Jim the benefit of the doubt."

"Look, Hank. I would as soon lose my right arm as tell her the facts. But we've got to face it. I don't think Jim knew of any photostats. But maybe he's suspicious. Now that Millie and Hap are both dead, he's going to feel safe if no evidence shows up against him. All we've got left is a bluff. We can *tell* him we've got a photostat. If he calls that bluff, we're sunk. He'll nail us for the death of Hap. And unless Trudy knows, she'll spill her guts the next time he phones. She'll tell him I got an envelope at Millie's apartment and burned it. She's got to be told."

"Let's wait awhile," I said.

"I'll talk with Clara."

17

Trudy sat beside me at the fireplace, took my hand. "I'm following orders. I'm to hold your hand until dinner is ready."

"Good."

The firelight flickered on her profile as she looked into whatever lovely thoughts a lovely girl has. "We had a serious discussion this afternoon. Do you really think we could work it out?"

I put my arm around her and her head came onto my shoulder. No man can look into the ground. Take what you can while you can have it. Life is but a series of minutes that come one at a time.

She said, "We've both been unhappy. Maybe if we hadn't seen one another again—but we have. And, Hank, promise me."

"I promise."

"Wait, you don't know what it is. You're giving up everything for me—"

"Nothing that really matters."

"Let me finish. You're giving up everything you've known. Family and friends and position and wealth. You don't know yet what a stiff price that is. You've never been poor. You've never had to depend on a weekly check. You've never had to swallow your pride for money. It's a stiff price, Hank. Promise me that if you ever regret the price, you'll give me up. I don't want to hold you to a bad bargain."

I had something light in mind for a reply, but the kitchen door opened. Trudy drew away from me with a start, then settled back and said, "It's all right. We're engaged." She blushed prettily.

The other two said nothing. Trudy gave a delicious little laugh. "I'm so happy. I couldn't forget Hank so I tried to hate him. Jim will soon be with us again and everything will be wonderful. It's like a dream come true." She snuggled close to me. "We'll all be so happy, darling."

Then presently she realized the tension in the room. She felt it in me, turned to see Clara and Cranston mute and unsmiling.

"What's the matter? Aren't you going to offer congratulations? Why don't you say something?"

"Trudy, dear," Clara said. "Trudy, dear."

"Wait," I said. "I don't want her to know."

"Know what?" Trudy asked. "What's wrong? Why are you all acting so strange?"

"She's got to know," Cranston said.

"Trudy," Clara said, "Jim isn't all you think he is."

I tried to stop it, but once it had begun Trudy insisted on hearing all of it. She pried out every sordid detail about Jim, and when she had it all she sat very small and alone staring at the fire.

Clara touched my sleeve. "We can eat, if anybody wants to."

Nobody wanted to.

I said I was tired. Cranston insisted on getting my luggage from the car. Clara said she'd show me my room; I followed her upstairs, along the balcony to the bedroom on the north.

"Millie died on my bed," she said, with a little shudder. "There's another bathroom upstairs here. Second door. Could you eat a poached egg or something?"

"No, thanks. I'm all right."

She opened the windows, fussed with the curtains. Cranston came in with my luggage. He looked at my mouth and said everything was fine, but I'd better take a couple of sleeping pills. He gave them to me.

"It's a lie!" Trudy's voice shouted from below. "All lies! You're all lying!"

We went out on the balcony. Below, Trudy was standing spread-legged and defiant, face white, eyes wide, at bay, very small and all alone.

"It's a lie! I don't believe any part of it. What kind of people are you, to accept such things against Jim? You all knew him. You're his wife, Clara. You went through a war with him, Hank. Leo, you grew up with Jim. You all know Jim as well as I do. The kindest, sweetest, finest man who ever was born. What kind of friends are you to let him down when he's in trouble? How can you believe he's such a monster? You're lying, all of you. You're conspiring against a man who can't defend himself. Well, I know what I'm going to do. I'm going to the police. They'll get to the bottom of this. Jim never did anything bad in his life. And even if he did, I'd rather see him safe in jail than in the clutches of friends like you."

"Poor kid," Clara said. "Leo, do something to help her."

"Too much for her," Cranston agreed. He slipped downstairs. Trudy charged at him, clawing. He caught her expertly. There was the flash of a needle. He held her until she subsided, then carried her up to her room.

"I'll undress her," Clara said. Cranston and I went onto the balcony. "I expected something like this; I had a hypo ready," he said. "Take those pills, Hank. You need your rest."

"Can I wash my teeth?"

"Better wait until morning. And then go easy."

I lay in bed wondering if every day would be as hectic as the three I'd spent out here. My teeth were jumping and my head seemed bruised inside. I was grateful for those pills.

I woke to see filtered sunlight at the window. A hand was shaking my shoulder. I turned over to see Clara dressed in linen shorts and a halter. The halter was too skimpy for breasts like hers, and it wasn't fastened snugly. I felt again her earthy appeal, and wondered what kind of a heel I was to be feeling it while engaged to Trudy—more properly, to be in love with Trudy, for she would have nothing to do with me from now on. But love and desire can be two different things.

Clara said, "Are you going to sleep all day? It's almost ten."

"Don't you work today?"

"Yesterday was Friday, remember? So today is Saturday. The five-day week. Leo took Trudy to Crystal Springs for some golf. It was something to do, poor kid. Better than just sitting and brooding."

"How is she this morning?"

"Bewildered. But she's beginning to accept it. What else can she do? She idolized Jim as only a sister could. But she will never forgive us, Hank. We shattered her idol."

"Yeah."

She asked about my mouth. I said it was okay. She reached to feel my forehead and the skimpy halter came loose, swinging forward on the cord around her neck. My throat was suddenly tight. She brought her elbows to her sides, drawing the halter over her breasts again. "That damned snap." She sat on the bed with her back to me. "Fasten it, Hank."

One end of the halter was twisted under her left elbow. I had to fish that out, then draw the two ends snug and fasten the catch. It was a hook and eye, and looked perfectly all right to me. Her skin was silky. I wanted to run my hands along it, around her, as she was waiting for me to do.

I said, "If you'll scram, I'll get up."

She looked sidewise over her shoulder. "Still raining?" She stood up. "At least I can cook."

I got my shaving kit and went into the bathroom. I found that with care I could brush my teeth. I washed and shaved. Then in putting the stuff back into the kit I noticed I'd somehow got Cranston's tooth powder; packed it with my stuff in checking out of his apartment. It was the same brand, but my can had been a little scuffed from banging around in the kit while traveling, and this can was brand new. Well, it was no great calamity and I doubted if he'd sue me. I put on shirt and slacks and went down to breakfast.

Clara hadn't been bragging when she said she could cook. I found that with a little care I could eat without difficulty. She watched proudly as I stowed away hot cakes, an omelet, bacon, fruit juice and coffee. Probably in time, as Cranston had said, I'd never miss those teeth. She took a cup of coffee with me. I kept half an eye on that halter, hoping. I decided I was a real heel, and wondered how long I could avoid acting like one.

"Ain't it hell?" she said. "You're in love with Trudy and I'm in love with you. And it's all impossible."

"It's hell."

"But I'm a woman, and a woman never gives up. Do I do anything to you, Hank?"

"You ought to be ashamed of yourself, trying to take advantage of a man in my condition."

"I'll do anything to get what I want."

"You can't get me that way. That snap looked perfectly all right to me."

"I'm utterly shameless. Isn't all fair in love and war?"

"I don't want it to be that way."

"You're a little boy," she said. "Spoon fed on convention. You think it's all right to marry somebody you don't love. That's proper. That's conventional. But what is the essential difference between marrying without love and visiting a girl in a call house? You want me but you tell yourself it's not love. Just what the hell *is* love? It's wanting somebody."

"A roll in the hay isn't love."

She made a slow smile, confident and challenging. "You'll find out."

"Looks like a fine day outside."

"Doesn't it? I'll keep trying."

"I have been warned."

We went outside. It was the sort of day, neither hot nor cold, that makes Californians forget all the other days. Millie's Nash was gone.

Clara said a man had come for it but he'd been afraid to drive it because of the brakes, so a wrecker had taken it away. We sat on a log that bounded the parking area.

"Leo said something I didn't like," she said. "About Trudy. Her mental state."

"We can't expect her to be happy this morning."

"She's drawing into herself again. The way she did when you threw her over. Hank, we were afraid for Trudy, then."

"But—good God—she's not a girl who might—"

"Maybe not suicide. But accident-prone. We watched her carefully, then. We'd better do it now for a while."

I sat with this happy thought. Clara stretched herself on her back along the redwood log. The stretching out process dislodged the halter somewhat and she didn't adjust it.

"Let's go in," I said.

She gave me a slow, wise smile and sat up. "Okay."

We started back across the flat. Something caught my eye. I turned, went back. On the yellow dust were four brownish spots that appeared wet. I stirred a spot with a finger, smelled the finger.

"What are you doing, Hank?"

"Jim tried to murder Millie last night."

"What? How in the world …?"

"Those spots are made by brake fluid. Her car was parked here. Jim buggered her brakes. That's what he was doing at the cars when Cranston surprised him and got knocked down."

"I don't understand."

"With no brakes, she would have killed herself in the ravine. She never could have made the turn onto the bridge even sober."

"How would he do that to the brakes?"

"What does it matter? It's simple."

"I think it does matter. I have a reason for asking."

"There's a nut at each wheel that is used for bleeding air out of the lines. Loosen the nuts and the fluid goes out on the ground—no brakes."

"A nut about this big?" She made a highly inaccurate circle of forefinger and thumb. I had to grin.

"Possibly. Why?"

Clara ran into the lodge. Presently she came out with a wrench and pliers in one hand, a glass vial in the other. "These were in Leo's overcoat pocket. I noticed them when I hung up his coat this morning.

He slipped them there until he had a chance to put the tools away and"—she indicated the vial—"get rid of this."

"What's in it?"

"The label says insulin. Which saves the lives of diabetics and kills normal people. And, except for the tiny puncture of the needle, it leaves no evidence. There is no test for finding it in the system. It's the perfect murder weapon. Don't you see? Leo killed Millie."

I nodded. Yes, I saw. Cranston had murdered Millie to protect the good name of Henry Chatworth Oates III. I sat on the log, feeling a bit sick.

"Don't you *see?*" she cried.

"Yes. It means Cranston did it. He jimmied her brakes so she would wreck. Then when she passed out, he shot her the insulin. All to protect me."

"Protect you—fiddlesticks! He's going to *kill* you! Don't you see?"

I looked at her a long moment. "No, I don't see."

"Don't you *see?*" she cried. Her face was tight. There was a sharp and wolfish something about it. "Look at it! Here's the evidence! It means Jim is dead!"

I looked at it. Just a wrench, a pair of pliers and a vial of insulin. To her it meant that Jim was dead. I didn't see it at all.

18

She said, "I'd better put these back in his coat," and ran inside. I followed more slowly, entering the big room as she was coming downstairs from the balcony.

"Why does it mean that Jim is dead?"

"You men! It's as plain as the nose on your face."

"All right, I have no female intuition. Spell it out and take it slow."

"Leo came dashing in last night and said he surprised Jim fooling with the cars. Why? So poor old Jim would take the rap if there was any kickback about Millie's brakes after the wreck. Because of that wrench and screwdriver, we know it was Leo who tampered with the brakes, not Jim."

"That makes sense. But he could lie about that without Jim being dead."

"He knew a dead man could never contradict the story by proving he was somewhere else at the time. Murder is serious business, remember. He couldn't risk that lie if it could possibly kick back."

"You're forgetting that somebody took Hap's gun from my pocket."

"Maybe somebody did—or maybe it was Leo himself. But regardless of whether or not he saw somebody, he planted Jim in our minds to cover those brakes. When Millie passed out, he had to kill her another way. She knew Jim was dead; she had the evidence. Leo couldn't let her get out of here alive. She would go to the police if Hap didn't contact her."

We sat at the table and I found myself drinking more coffee. It was something to do and supposedly it sharpened the wits. I said, "I tried to tell you yesterday that Jim was dead."

"I didn't suspect Leo yesterday. Now I can see things. He has Jim's typewriter. He could have faked Jim's voice on the phone. He's pretty good at imitations—he does them at parties when he gets a little high. And he knows the little secret words of the language between Jim and me. I had an affair with Leo while Jim was overseas. Maybe it was my conscience—telling Leo those words, pretending to laugh at them."

"Two notes from Jim warned me not to get too close to you," I said.

"Of course. Leo was afraid that this would happen. If we got together we'd figure it out." She took a sip of her coffee, looked over the cup thoughtfully. "Leo is the only one who claims to have seen Jim since the suicide."

"Millie did."

"Millie was Hap's girlfriend. Living his lie. Jim was Hap's meal ticket and—because Millie lived off Hap—hers too."

"Cranston loaned you blackmail money to pay Hap."

"Hap was blackmailing *Leo*, not me. He didn't care who gave him the weekly check." She ran her hands slowly across her face. "Don't ask me too many questions at once, Hank. I don't know everything. But we do know that Jim is dead." She looked around the big room of the lodge. "The typewriter will be here somewhere. Jim's typewriter. If we find it, that will prove that Leo wrote the notes."

"It would be in the city, not here. Cranston wouldn't have had time to dash up here. And some of the notes arrived pretty fast to meet a changing situation."

"Of course—he has it handy wherever it is. He has to, the way things have been happening."

"Then it's in his car."

"With Trudy along? Getting golf bags out of the trunk? He couldn't risk that. He—wait a minute! He said he was going to look at the pump house, the first thing when he got here last night."

From a nail in the kitchen she got three keys fastened to a leather thong which was in turn tied to a stick, and led the way through the redwoods. The earth fell away to a small ravine. At its bottom was a concrete structure, a pipe running uphill from one side of it and a small stream of spring water trickling from beneath the other side and down the ravine. The lock on the pump house was a good one, and when the door swung open I saw it was a solid slab of redwood four inches thick. But there was nothing inside but the pump itself, some oil and grease, a couple of rusty wrenches. Nothing could be hidden in this bare concrete box.

Clara looked about in dismay. "I was sure it would be here."

"What do the other two keys fit?"

"One's the tank house and the other is for the storeroom behind the garage."

We struck out for the tank house. But in the storeroom we found it, more or less by accident. There was an old barrel sprouting an assortment of garden tools. Clara climbed onto it to look on a high shelf and the barrel tipped over, leaving her hanging by the shelf. I lifted her down, pulled the tools out of the barrel to right it, and saw the typewriter. It was Jim's machine—that square black case of the old folding Corona; the fabric of a front flap worn through and repaired by a wide strip of adhesive tape; Jim's name and serial number stenciled on the case.

Clara crouched, huddling the case to her as if it were a baby. "Jim," she said. "Jim."

"I guess this clinches it," I admitted.

She sprang before me as I turned to the door. "What are you going to do?"

"Call the police."

"You silly fool! You have no proof except that you found a typewriter. Trudy and I destroyed the letters, as they told us to. Didn't you?"

"I've still got one. Though it's unsigned."

"You've got a note, unsigned, and you've had access to the typewriter it was written on."

"Our combined testimony—"

"Hank, we know. But let's not warn him until we've got enough to nail him. Jim didn't suicide and he didn't fake suicide. Leo murdered him. We've got to lay low until we have enough evidence to put him in the gas chamber for it."

I righted the barrel, put the typewriter in it, arranged the garden tools as they had been.

"I think," Clara said as she locked the storeroom door, "that I could use a drink."

"I'll try some more coffee. Liquor makes me sleepy."

"Well, all right, sissy."

Clara put the teakettle on the electric stove, dumped the remains of the breakfast coffee into the sink and began washing the drip maker. "Hank, maybe I was a chump. Maybe I was easy to fool. But the way Jim was, always looking for a way to beat the world—I thought a fake suicide was just the sort of thing he might get involved in. Leo hooked me in very well, that bastard. Loaning me money to pay his own blackmail!"

"What about Jim's confession?"

"Faked, like the rest of it. Written on his typewriter, and the name forged. Leo is a fancy penman."

"And how about Uncle Jasper?"

"How do you mean?"

"Cranston wouldn't murder Millie to protect Jim's memory."

"No," Clara admitted, frowning. She measured coffee in the drip maker. "You're right. Uncle Jasper was killed by a horse. Jim's killing him was just a story cooked up by Leo to explain Jim's disappearance to me, and cover Leo's blackmail to Hap."

"Which puts us right back at the beginning."

"Not at all. Leo killed Millie to prevent an investigation of that photostat. It could have hung him. Leo killed Jim."

"That's what I mean—why did he kill Jim? What possible reason?"

"Me," Clara said.

There it was, standing before me in linen shorts and a skimpy halter. As an amateur detective, I decided, I'd better stick to oatmeal.

Clara said, "My affair with Leo while Jim was overseas was just— I'm human and Jim was away. But as I've already told you, Hank, I've got something in the bedroom. Leo went crazy for me and he's never recovered."

"Men have been killed over fatter and uglier women than you," I admitted.

"Thank you, Mr. Oates."

"But what brought it to a head? Jim had been back home for years. Cranston didn't just get up one fine morning and decide, 'Well, today

I guess I'd better murder Jim Daniels.' Something came up."

"It's not what you're thinking," she said sharply. "I had nothing to do with Leo after Jim got home. Hank, I was in love with you at the time. I couldn't bear to think of Leo touching me. Or, hardly, Jim. So I don't know why— But of course! Uncle Jasper dying and leaving the estate!"

"Just money?" I said with some dismay.

"Money is Leo's god. You heard what he said about being born poor and working himself through school. He was pinching pennies until he was almost thirty. He became a dentist simply to make money. He's a good one for the same reason. Though he's doing very well, he can never get enough money. He wanted me, but did nothing about it except make a few passes. Then Uncle Jasper died and left Jim the estate. Jim went into partnership with Kline and stood to clean up half a million or better above taxes. That was too much for Leo. He began making plans. When everything was ready, he went through with them."

Clara took the coffee maker out to the table. "Something in it?"

"Just coffee for me."

"You drink less than anybody I know."

"You know the wrong people." We sat down. "Cranston is trying to establish Jim as alive to get you without waiting, together with Jim's estate when he marries you, including the insurance if Jim can be proved alive a year after the supposed suicide."

"That puts it in a nutshell."

"You think that explains everything?"

She nodded, took the dirty cups out, returned with clean ones and a bottle of whiskey.

"What if Jim *did* suicide," I said, "and the whole thing is an attempt to nail the insurance company for fifty thousand?"

"That doesn't explain Hap Arnold."

"It would if Hap knew that Jim had suicided."

She shook her head. "If Jim jumped off that bridge, how would Leo Cranston be able to produce a body at the proper time? With some phone calls and notes and suggestion he could bring Jim to life, so to speak. Especially if Henry Chatworth Oates III got clipped in a badger game and was willing to bear false testimony about seeing his old pal Jim. All right, so Jim is established as alive, one year after he took out the policy. All right, the next step is to produce Jim's corpse. And he's got to have the right corpse if he wants to collect the money. The insurance company isn't paying out fifty grand for just any stray body."

"Good God! You mean he's got Jim's body hidden away somewhere, ready to produce?"

She shivered. "It's a horrible thought. But what other explanation fits? Now we're getting it straight. That photostat of Jim's so-called confession to murdering Uncle Jasper was cooked up for *my* particular benefit. Hap was really blackmailing Leo for killing Jim. That's why Leo killed Millie last night—to save his own neck. Once he knew it was she who had that envelope, he had to kill her. It wasn't just the insurance, it was his life. By bringing Jim back to life, Leo would clear himself of the murder charge that Hap was holding over him." She concluded triumphantly, "That's how things have to be, Hank."

"Several things don't fit that theory," I said. "That letter from Jim, asking me to come out here to help. If that was written by Leo Cranston, it followed that Cranston and Hap were working together—"

"Of course. Hap and Millie went back to frame you."

"My point is that Hap tried to keep me from coming out here. He warned me with a phone call threatening death and a family scandal. Millie tried to frame me in Salt Lake City, to prevent me coming here."

"Certainly," Clara agreed. "Leo fed Hap a line about getting you out here, proving Jim was alive a year after the insurance was taken out, then finding the body. You were the key to that, because of your friendship with Jim and your family's prominence. Hap was supposed to frame you with Millie, to make you swear that you'd seen Jim alive. Then Jim's body would be found and they wouldn't have to wait seven years to split the insurance and the estate. That was the pitch that Leo gave Hap."

She leaned back, pleased with the way her mind was seeing through Leo's and Hap's plans. "But Hap was smart enough," she went on, "to realize that if Jim were once established as alive, Hap had no hold over Leo for Jim's murder. So Hap tried to stop you from coming here. He made a threatening phone call. Then he tried to frame you with Millie—not for Leo's purposes but for his own, to keep you out of this. That fell through. So the other night he met you on Skyline and was supposed to bring you here, where Millie was waiting again. But by this time he was desperate, because according to plan, Leo was supposed to be the one to discover you and Millie here at the lodge in a compromising position. Hap saw you as a threat to everything. He knew you couldn't be scared away—he'd tried that once. He planned to murder you at Devil's Slide, then tell Leo you didn't meet him at all."

"You're forgetting Speck," I pointed out, "and also what Hap told me at Devil's Slide. Hap told me that Speck was to murder me at Jim's orders."

"No. Hap told you that Speck was to murder you *for* Jim. That's what you told me Hap said."

"It means the same thing."

"Not at all," she said. "Hap was upset and in no position for an exact choice of words. He said that Speck would prove Jim was alive, and then murder you, *because of* Jim. You would of course have to be killed once you had sworn falsely that Jim was alive."

"Then who is Speck? And who was the person who hit me on the head and burned me with a cigarette to find out where Jim was?"

"One and the same—Leo," she said.

"Speck is Leo? Cranston doesn't wear glasses."

"In his football days he was called Special Delivery Cranston. It was a newspaper name, cooked up by reporters. It wasn't a nickname that people called him, except for fans who knew him only through the newspapers and seeing him play. I remember how the fans would yell during a game when Leo had the ball. They'd yell, 'Come on, Speck!' Short for Special Delivery. Hap must have been a football fan in those days."

"You should have remembered this the other night," I said.

"Hank, a person's got to have a place to start. At the time I didn't suspect Leo. He was the last one I would have suspected. 'Speck' is a common nickname for anyone with glasses. It just didn't occur to me. And nobody calls Leo that. It was just a nickname of fans who knew him through the newspapers."

"If Cranston is Speck, and if he was the one who hit me on the head and tied me up and put a cigarette on my neck while whispering in my ear—then why was he trying to find out about Jim? That is, if Jim was dead and he knew it?"

"He asked about Jim for the same reason he whispered—to throw you off the track," she said. "What he actually wanted to know was what Hap had told you. Isn't that what he got out of you, really?"

I admitted that it was.

She said, "He would have killed you then and there if you had understood what Hap had told you. You misinterpreted it, and that saved your life."

"But how would he know where I was? If Hap was supposed to bring me here to the lodge that night?"

"He knew by then that Hap had tried to prevent you from coming to San Francisco. He suspected a double-cross. So he was following behind in the fog with his headlights off when you met Hap at Skyline. When you and Hap suddenly turned into that side road near Devil's Slide he was thrown off the trail. He continued on a way, thinking you were ahead. Then he realized he'd been given the slip. He came back, exploring the side roads. When he found the cars parked, he didn't know where you'd gone. So he waited. When you returned, he thought it was Hap, having killed you. Leo hit you on the head. Then he discovered it was you. So he tied you up and tortured you until he was satisfied that you knew nothing that would implicate him."

"There were two people there," I said. "Cranston was sitting on my back, and somebody else on my legs."

"Leo probably had help in this. When we nail him we'll find out who the other one is. That two-faced hypocrite!" she cried.

"Both Hap and Cranston could have waited," I said.

"A lot can happen in seven years. Hap was an old man. Leo's life hung on Hap's good health. And Leo had to marry me to get anything. What if I fell for somebody else in the meantime?"

As she poured more coffee I gave her the once-over. "That," I admitted, "would worry him."

She poured some whiskey in her coffee. "Sure you don't want yours sweetened?"

I shook my head. "Now I'm in the same position with Cranston as he was with Hap. Cranston knows that I killed Hap. So why is he acting nice to me? If he wants me to swear that I've seen Jim alive, why doesn't he use that?"

Clara took a sip of her coffee and said calmly, "Because he has decided to kill you, instead." She put the cup down, touched her full lips with a napkin. "His plan snafued. There is no immediate pressure on him from Hap, because Hap is dead. The plan for you was to involve you on the way out here in a frame-up with Millie, force you to lie about Jim being alive, and then get rid of you. That failed, Hap got killed, everything snarled up. And he knows now that you wouldn't swear falsely about Jim being alive, anyhow. It was all he could do to keep you from reporting Hap's death to the police. He misjudged you, Hank. He had the idea you were a soft and pampered rich boy who would be putty in his hands. You're not. He's afraid now of what you might be finding out. He knows that you won't leave this until you've got to the bottom of it. For the present, he's holding Hap's death over your head. He'll use that until he has everything ready to kill you."

"I'm not going to sit here waiting for it. We can tell the police everything. If he killed Millie with a needle, the mark will be on her body."

Clara shook her head. "Millie was taking hay fever shots. That needle mark is just one among many."

I decided the coffee was making me jittery. And, possibly, Clara also. "Maybe we've got this all wrong."

"There's no other explanation that fits the facts, Hank."

"I mean, about his planning to kill me."

"He's killed twice, Hank. You're a threat to him. And, too, now he knows he has to kill you or lose everything, even if you don't discover that he killed Jim."

"What do you mean?"

"He knows I love you."

"What?" I said irritably. "How the hell does he know that?"

"Because I told him so last night when he came to my room. I told him everything was over between him and me, because I loved you. He's got to marry me to get any part of Jim's estate. And so long as you are alive, he can't. Whether or not you marry Trudy makes no difference. He knows I'll never give up while you're alive."

I was highly annoyed, among other things. "What the hell am I supposed to do? Sit around being his pal and playing amateur private eye while he cooks up a deal to kill me? Something as cute and easy as a hypo or twisting some nuts on the brakes of a car?"

"You could run away. But you'd never be safe. Or—" She left the thought dangling while she poured more coffee for herself and put whiskey in it. "Or kill him first."

I considered this, somewhat amazed that I could do it calmly. I had killed men during the war. Without remorse. It was a simple matter of kill or be killed. As was this. Knowing Cranston intended to murder me was just the same as having a gun in my ribs. Wasn't it? Regretfully, I decided it wasn't. I was tied up with silly convention, foisted upon my innocent mind when I was a helpless child. I would have to sit and wait until Cranston actually tried to kill me before I could kill him in self-defense. I was tangled in inhibition. And Cranston wasn't.

"Why the hell did he bother with my teeth?" I said irritably. "What the hell does he care, if he's trying to bump me off?"

"Don't think of him as all bad, Hank. Nobody is all bad. Nobody is bad at all. Everybody is justified in what he does. If what he feels has to be done injures you, then to you he's bad. But because you resist, you're bad to him. To Leo, you are a villain of the worst type, a menace to his very life."

Seeing the situation from Cranston's viewpoint was rather startling to me. I was considering it when the phone rang. Clara crossed to it, said hello; then her breath caught and I saw the flutter of her diaphragm at her bare middle.

"We'll be right over." She put the phone down and turned to me. "There's been an accident. Trudy's hurt."

19

As I drove in, a police car was pulling away from the Palo Alto Hospital. I parked beside Cranston's yellow Cad. Clara and I went in to find the big man pacing the lobby. He hurried over. "Oh, my God! I'll never forgive myself!"

I said, "You tried to kill her!" Clara squeezed my arm warningly.

"Yes, it's all my fault," Cranston said.

"How is she?" Clara asked.

"Just shock and bruises. When I think of that truck!"

A doctor appeared. He said they'd keep Trudy overnight for observation. Yes, we could see her. "But don't stay long."

A nurse led us to an upstairs room where Trudy was lying in a high bed. There was a plaster on her forehead. Her right cheek, glistening with salve, was puffed and red. There were plasters on both elbows, a bandage on her right wrist.

"A fine deal," she said. "They won't even let me read." The puffed cheek made her smile one-sided.

"My God!" Cranston said. "I might have killed you!"

"It was my fault. I should know better than to lean against a car door. How's the mouth, Hank?"

I gave her the big grin you put on in hospitals. "Don't worry about—"

Her gasp cut me off. Her eyes widened, face stiffening woodenly.

"She's having a relapse!" Cranston yelled. "Where's the doctor?"

"You'd better go now," the nurse said quietly. We left the room. "She'll be all right. Shock."

"A sudden pain," Clara said. "Poor kid. She's all bunged up."

"If anything happens to her I'll never forgive myself," Cranston said loudly.

"Pipe down," I said. We got into the elevator. "How did it happen?"

"We played nine holes and then took a drive. I was working on her. I didn't like her mental state. We stopped at a highway joint for a coke, then got in the car to go back to the lodge. It was a left turn onto the highway and the traffic was bad." We left the elevator and headed outside. He said, "You never saw such traffic—well, Saturday, you know. I must have waited five minutes. Then I saw an opening and gave her the gun."

He mopped his eyes with a big white hand. "I swear that truck popped right out of the ground. When I saw it, it was too late to stop. So I poured on the coal—the Cad's got a lot of soup—and got in front of it. It was a hard left turn. The door flew open and Trudy was thrown out." We headed down the outside steps toward the cars. "My God, it was a miracle! That big truck ran right over her—she was flat between the wheels. The car following the truck went into the ditch to avoid her. I'll pay damages to fix it up, gladly. I need a drink. My God, I might have killed her!"

"You might have," I admitted.

"I'll drive you home," Clara said. "Hank, you follow us."

I purposely let a half dozen cars get ahead as I followed the yellow Cad past the Stanford campus buildings and onto a back road. Then I turned left into a side road and gave my car the gas. I'd had enough of sitting under Cranston's nose waiting to be killed. From now on I'd run my own war from my own headquarters. I'd get my luggage from the lodge and be gone when Cranston arrived.

Cranston had tried to kill Trudy. That stuff about her being accident-prone was a buildup to murder. Who ever heard of a Cad door flying open by accident? That could be fixed, just like brakes could be fixed.

His motive was obvious. He had killed twice for Clara and her inheritance. Unless Trudy were legally dead before Jim was, Trudy would share that inheritance. He'd been in no rush about Trudy, for without proof of death Jim would be legally alive for seven years. But now things were coming to a head and he'd tried to get her out of the way.

The whole thing, that had seemed utterly beyond all reason, was simple once the basic premise was known. Clara, I decided, had a head on her, as well as something below the head.

How would Cranston engineer Jim's second death? No doubt he had a plan, and a good one.

There was the problem of Jim's body. Where and how? A home deep freeze would hold a body. There was electricity to the lodge. But Clara and I had searched the joint pretty thoroughly, looking for the typewriter. There were no stray wires leading off the power poles. Which ruled out a deep freeze there, unless it was hidden within the lodge itself. But that would be too risky; the noise of the compressor on a quiet night would give it away. Did Hap Arnold have a deep freeze? Millie? That was no good, for they were dead and Cranston would still have to have the body available. I wondered about a commercial cold locker.

The road had developed a series of hairpin turns as it climbed into the brushy hills. What with the traffic, I crawled along at fifteen. The idea of beating Cranston to the lodge went out the window.

Embalming? I'd read some gimmick like that. A corpse had been embalmed, cached for several months, then substituted at the undertaking parlor for the body of a man who had just died. This established the time of the supposed death of the substitute corpse.

I'd forgotten just how the detective of this whodunit found out about the ringer. Had Cranston read the book? Searching for an embalmed corpse was infinitely more complicated than looking for a frozen one. Embalmed, Jim's body could be any of a million places.

I wondered if the frozen corpse, or the embalmed one, was too fantastic. Yet the fact remained that to get the insurance and to avoid waiting seven years, Cranston had to produce a body. And it had to be Jim's.

Cranston had been clever from the beginning, faking Jim's suicide to conceal murder. By establishing the fact that Jim was now "alive," he could clear himself of any possible murder charge. Then Jim's body would be found, in a situation to suggest an accident, or even another suicide. If the authorities did unearth evidence of foul play, how could they trace things to Cranston? The actual murder was several months old. The police wouldn't look back beyond the time when Jim was supposed to be alive.

Yes, Cranston was clever. But he had to have that corpse. Otherwise nothing of what he was doing added up. The one way to nail him was to find Jim's body. It had to be somewhere.

It took me an hour or so, on the twisting road, to reach Skyline Boulevard. I gunned along it toward San Francisco, making up for lost time. There might be something in Cranston's apartment to provide a lead. A body wasn't easy to hide. It would have to be preserved, because identification was essential.

I was clipping along at sixty-five when I rounded a hill and flashed past the road leading off Skyline to the lodge. Cranston's yellow Cad was waiting at the intersection. As I flashed by, it began honking. In the mirror I saw it swing into the road after me, so I pulled up. The Cad came alongside. Clara was driving, Cranston beside her.

"Lost?" he said with a grin.

"I followed the wrong car. What a road it led me through!"

"I saw you turn off," Clara said. "We knew you'd hit Skyline, but it's easy to miss the road to the lodge."

I followed them back to the lodge. We parked on the flat. Cranston got out and began opening and shutting the right-hand front door of his car. "I can't understand it. It works all right. Maybe her coat was caught in it or something."

I figured something had been wedged in the latch. Cranston was too smart to let Trudy fall in the path of a truck from a door whose catch showed signs of tampering.

"Know anything about door latches, Hank?"

"No. Why don't you forget it? Accidents will happen."

"You need a drink, Leo," Clara said.

We crossed the flat and went into the lodge. The big room smelled of cheap cigars. The humpbacked source of the odor was clutched in the mouth of Milford E. White, the private eye, who was taking his ease in the armchair by the radio. Regardless of the balmy day, White was wearing his trench coat. The radio was playing softly and White had helped himself to a highball. He was the picture of contentment. In his lap lay an automatic.

Cranston said, "Well."

"Just make yourself to home," Clara said.

"Thanks," White said. "I am."

Cranston asked, "How did you get in?"

"Locks are for honest men." White set his highball on the radio, took the gun from his lap and gestured with it casually. "Sit down, folks. Let's have a little chat."

"Where's your car?" Cranston asked. He looked through the window as if he might have overlooked it parked on the flat.

"Where's my car?" White laughed shortly. "I got a friend who loans me a bucket of bolts, but he's using it today. There's some people who can't afford a car. They can't afford to get their teeth fixed up by guys like you. But it don't mean that they have to be incompetent, or too dumb to earn a king's ransom driving a truck or laying bricks. Some of them like their work and have principles about picking up dough the easy way."

"Sorry I pressed the wrong button," Cranston said. "I just wondered how you got here."

"Bus." White snapped off the radio. "And hiked from the highway." He motioned with the gun. "Sit down, folks."

Cranston and I took the couch facing the fireplace. White was to our left in the armchair. Clara said, "Can I sweeten your drink?"

"I don't mind. Leave the kitchen door open."

Clara took his glass from the radio and went into the kitchen. Cranston asked, "What do you want?"

White weighed the gun in his hand, gnawing reflectively at his humpbacked cigar. "This gun belongs to Hap Arnold. Maybe I should say it *belonged* to Hap Arnold. I don't know—but he's been missing a couple of days." He looked at me. "How come you had it?"

I realized again what I'd known from the beginning. Lies, evasions and half-truths always entangle you. I should have reported Hap's death at the time it happened. White watched me steadily, waiting for an answer.

"He hasn't got it," Cranston said. "You have."

"So it's that way," White said softly.

"Then it was you, robbing the cars last night," Cranston said. "I thought it was Jim. I'd been in the pump house with the lights on. My eyes weren't used to the dark."

Clara brought in two drinks. She gave one to Cranston, offered the other to White. The detective said, "I'll take the other one." Clara grinned, exchanged glasses. White looked at me. "Hap Arnold had a date with you the other night. He ain't been seen since. You had his gun."

"How do we know it's his gun?" Cranston said. "Or where you got it?"

"A guy with nothing on his conscience is always eager to explain something that looks bad for him. He don't hide behind what can't be proved."

"Dr. Cranston borrowed Hap's gun the other day and loaned it to Hank," Clara said smoothly. "Hank had received some mysterious communications from someone claiming to be my husband. We thought it best if he were armed."

Cranston turned to Clara. "Why explain to this guy?"

"One good reason," White said, "I'm hungry. I can't afford an office. You should see the New Denver Hotel. Walk-up with no lobby. People cook in their rooms and the place smells."

"Oh," Cranston said. "This is the squeeze."

"That's what's wrong with me. I'd sooner go hungry than pry into people's sex life, which is the bread and butter of my trade—movies to the contrary. But that don't mean I hate to eat. I'm after that four-bit cigar. This insurance case just dropped into my lap and I'm not going to muff it. It's my big break."

Cranston said, "A man with ambition."

"I think Hap Arnold had something on you."

"That's right," Cranston admitted frankly. "Jim Daniels did not suicide. He disappeared for reasons we don't know. Hap Arnold was his go-between. Clara gave Hap a hundred dollars a week. She paid the insurance premium because she knew Jim was alive. Meanwhile, Hank received a letter from Jim asking him to come to San Francisco. When he arrived, I borrowed the gun from Hap and loaned it to Hank. Frankly, I was afraid of Jim. A man doesn't fake suicide for nothing. Hank got a message from Jim about a mysterious rendezvous on Skyline Boulevard Wednesday night. Hank was there, but nobody met him. Maybe it was the fog. Or maybe it was something else we don't know about yet."

Cranston was very fast on his feet.

"Then you never met Hap Wednesday night on Skyline?" White asked me.

"No." I realized I was a bad liar, and wished for some of Cranston's gift.

"Hap's girlfriend come up here last night. She died."

"She got plastered. Her heart just wouldn't take it anymore."

"Coincidence."

"What were you doing here?"

White shrugged. "This is a pretty good spot, if Jim Daniels needed a hideout."

"There's something I haven't told you," Cranston said, including me and Clara in the statement. "Jim slipped into the pump house last night while I was there. It was a shock, seeing him."

"Was he all right?" Clara asked eagerly. "What did he say?"

I realized that Clara was a fine actress.

"Jim said he'd disappeared because Hap had something on him. He didn't explain, except to say everything would soon be all right. Just a few words, and then he slipped away. Maybe he'd seen you prowling around, White. When I left the pump house and saw somebody at the cars, naturally I supposed it was Jim. That's why you caught me by surprise."

White finished his drink. He stood up, laid the gun on the radio, then on second thought dropped it into his pocket. He seemed disappointed. "Well, I'll be running along."

Cranston offered to drive him down to El Camino Real, where he could catch a bus every twenty minutes. Clara watched the Cad disappear into the ravine, then slammed the door. "No wonder he lives at the New Denver Hotel! He swallowed it hook, line and sinker!"

"Don't be so sure," I said. "I wouldn't sell a hungry man short."

We expected Cranston right back, so Clara waited lunch on him. But Cranston was gone a couple of hours. I'd had too much coffee during the morning and, hungry, I was jittery. At least I laid the jitters to the coffee.

When Cranston finally got back he was in bad humor and didn't care who knew it. He snapped at Clara when she asked him where he'd been. He got himself a drink and sat by the radio. He snapped it on and sat glowering, sipping his drink. Clara began fixing lunch. "Turn the radio on louder, somebody!" she called. Cranston whirled the volume knob. My scalp began to crawl. I just can't stand that kind of music. After a couple of minutes I felt it would be quite easy to run amok, leap on Cranston and beat him to death with the radio. Justifiable homicide. The only way I can bear such music is after a drink. I went in to fix one.

Clara insisted on helping, getting close as she did so. For once her appeal was lost on me. "Doesn't that music do something for you?" she breathed, wiggling against me. The horrible thought of being married to her, or having her as a mistress, and being forced to listen to such music with her—nothing that she could offer could compensate. Maybe there was something to this class business. Anyhow, you had to have things in common.

"What kind of music does Trudy like?"

"Oh, she puts on. Claims she likes symphonies and stuff. Nobody could like that crap."

I breathed a sigh of relief.

"How about a dance?"

I couldn't avoid it and, holding my drink, I danced with her through the kitchen and into the big room. Clara was definitely close. Embarrassingly so, before Cranston's surly eyes.

"Dance!" Cranston yelled. "Have a good time!" He turned the radio down. "That private eye is on the verge of breaking it. He's not as dumb as he looks. And it's all there ready to break. I dropped him off at El Camino, then took a run out to Devil's Slide. Hap's hat is there on the face of the cliff."

Clara drew away from me. "Is his car still there?"

"Yes, but it won't be forever. Somebody will turn it in. Then the cops will start nosing around. Tomorrow's Sunday; there will be thousands of people at the coast. When somebody spots that hat on the face of the cliff, the cops will know the exact spot that Hap went over. There will be footprints up above, empty shells that fit Hap's gun. If they never find a body now, it will be worse than if they do. It will look like Hap was shot and thrown off the cliff."

Clara turned slowly to the kitchen. I sat on the couch before the fireplace. Why hadn't I thrown that gun over the cliff? But if it hadn't been the gun, it would have been something else. There was always a loose end that began unraveling.

There was a crash. I looked around to see that Clara had dropped the coffee maker. But she was paying no attention to it. She was staring at the radio. I was suddenly conscious of a news broadcast. "… Has Devil's Slide claimed another victim? Washington: On the labor front—"

Cranston snapped it off and began swearing. "Now they've got the car," he said.

Clara said, "But they don't know—"

"They know Hap is missing!" he yelled. "Now they're looking for him. White knows that Hank was supposed to meet him Wednesday night, and Hap hasn't been seen since. White found Hap's gun in Hank's pocket. Somebody will spot that hat on the face of the cliff. They'll find footprints to fit Hank's shoes up above, shells to fit that gun."

The big man paced up and down, swearing. He stopped before me, bringing himself under control with an obvious effort. "We've got to get that evidence before the cops do," he said quietly. "Tonight."

"Okay." I felt a certain relief. Now the play was clear.

20

News of Hap's disappearance had brought the usual crowd of the morbidly curious to Devil's Slide. People were peering over the cliffs, trying to spot a body in the breakers below. On the lesser slopes they were prowling about, poking at the brush.

Clara and I took a position where we could look across a cove at the rock face of the cliff that had held the wartime radar station. Nobody was up on top of that, because of the fence and the sign.

Cranston had left the lodge after lunch, saying he knew a garage that did emergency repairs on Saturdays; he wanted them to look at that door latch. Pretty cute.

The late afternoon sun threw hard shadows onto the yellow face of the sheer cliff below the radar station. I combed it carefully from top to bottom, side to side. What with the shadows, it would be a matter of luck to spot a hat on the enormous surface.

Clara met my eyes. She shrugged, her lips twisting. "There's no hat there."

"Cranston was here before the shadows hit it. We couldn't have come at a worse time."

"How could a hat hang on the face of that slick rock?"

"It could have wedged somewhere."

"Don't you see it, Hank? It's just an excuse to get you out here tonight."

"Maybe the hat is there."

"It doesn't matter. He's going to do it tonight."

"Yes, I know."

"I mean, he's going to kill you."

"I know."

"Well, for Christ's sake," she said, "you don't seem very upset about it!"

"This is the way I want it."

"You're going with him tonight?"

"Of course."

She regarded me steadily. "So you can kill him?"

"I can kill in self-defense." I turned to the car. "Shall we go back?"

Cranston was still gone when we reached the lodge. I remembered I hadn't brushed my teeth after lunch. That was a thing to watch from now on. I found I could do a better job than I'd been able to this morning. I rinsed my mouth, looked at my teeth in the glass, and got a curious shock. It was as if I were looking at somebody else. I wasn't used to the glint of gold in my mouth. Your flashing smile, Hank, I told myself, ain't what it used to be. Too bad the gold had to show. Didn't they have something that didn't? But Cranston would know best. He was a good dentist, whatever else. And better to have gold than plates.

When I came out of the bathroom Clara stood before me with a gun in her hand. It was a Luger, pointed straight at my chest. Her face was expressionless. "It was Jim's," she said.

I said nothing.

"He brought it home from the War. It isn't registered. It can't be traced."

I said nothing.

"Take it, Hank," she said. "Leo will have a gun."

My breath came out slowly. I took the gun. For a brief moment everything had turned upside down and formed into a new pattern where Clara was responsible for everything. But she was just a woman handling a gun, not knowing that a gun is never pointed at anyone unless you mean business.

The Luger was filthy. Evidently it hadn't been cleaned since the war. Clara got a rag and some oil while I stripped it down. I cleaned it, assembled it, tried the action, put in the clip, cocked the weapon with a shell in the chamber, pushed the safety catch on, and tucked it into my waistband. I buttoned my coat over it.

"He'll try to surprise you, Hank," she said. "Don't give him a chance. Don't be a gentleman about this, you fool. It's your life or his." She suddenly was clinging to me. "Hank, I couldn't bear it if anything happened to you!"

Cranston got back a few minutes later. He said the mechanic could find nothing wrong with the door latch. A lesser man than Cranston would have tried to make the latch look like it had been out of whack, which might have been hard to explain.

I thought of Trudy with puffed cheek and bandages. Trudy alive now only because she happened to fall squarely between the wheels of that truck. It wasn't going to be hard to kill Leo Cranston. Once he made his move.

Dinner was a matter of coffee and cigarettes. I was jittery from too much coffee. Or something. Strings seemed to vibrate tautly inside me. We sat around saying little because all of it had been said, while the windows got black outside. Finally Cranston stood up. He nodded at me. "Let's go."

He led the way to the storeroom at the back end of the garage, snapped on the light, climbed onto an old trunk to get a coil of rope from a high peg. "We'll need a crowbar. There's one in that barrel."

As I got the crowbar from the barrel Cranston didn't even glance my way; yet he knew the typewriter was at the bottom of that barrel. The man had nerve. "We'll take my car," he said as we went out.

I made no polite protest. He wouldn't try anything while driving. We stowed the rope and crowbar in the Cad, and drove off.

At Devil's Slide, Cranston turned into the side road and parked at almost the exact spot where Hap's car had stood. I stepped out into a bitter wind.

"You should have brought an overcoat," he said. He put the rope and bar under his own topcoat. "People are nosy."

It was a clear night with a bright moon. We went out of the side road and up the highway. Looming ahead in the moonlight was the high cliff that had held the radar station during the War. From the corner of my eye I kept a watch on Cranston's hands. The left hand was holding the rope under the coat, the right the bar. I slipped open the top button of my jacket. I could reach the Luger with one easy motion.

"You'd think fish weren't worth that much," Cranston said, nodding to a knoll ahead. The knoll split into two narrow ridges reaching out high and sheer above the sea. "There's a beaten path along those ridges. Damned fools creep out to the end, scale down the rocks, and fish. When a big wave comes, that's it."

We passed a warning sign with the ten white crosses. The sign was inaccurate now. And would be more so before the night was over.

At the gate of the deserted radar station Cranston took the rope and crowbar from under his coat, slipped them under the gate. We climbed around the fence, came back for the rope and bar. I carried the bar in my left hand, and made a point of being behind Cranston as we went up that interminable flight of concrete steps that went diagonally up the mountain. On top, we stopped to get our breath. The wind was wild up here, tearing at the stunted brush growing in the cracks of the rock. My left hand was numb from contact with the cold metal of the bar. I slipped the hand inside my coat and warmed the fingers in my armpit.

Cranston asked, "Where did he go over?"

That was my cue to lead. I had no intention of getting in front of him. I pointed. "Over there."

Cranston turned his back on me and started that way, clambering over the rough rock. He could afford to turn his back. He knew that I was brought up wrong. The smart thing, I knew, was to shoot him in the back, or brain him from behind with the bar. But I couldn't do it. I had to wait for him to make the play.

"Wait." I stopped near the edge, where the mountain fell off sheer to the sea far below. "It's somewhere around here."

"Don't you know, for God's sake?"

"The fog was heavy. I remember a flat rock, right at the edge." I pointed. "Maybe that's it."

We went over to the flat rock. Now I could see how it broke away to nothing on the cliff side, like the cornice of a building. Cranston stepped to the sheer edge and leaned forward, looking down. The man had nerve. "I don't see the hat from here." He got out a flashlight, crouched to examine the rock.

"This is the place," I said. "That little crease near the edge—Hap was clinging to that with his left hand. He numbed the fingers of his other hand when he slipped. He was holding the gun, and his fist smacked the rock."

"Here's where the gun hit," Cranston said, indicating a spot where a bit of rock was newly flaked off. "Did it go off then?"

"Yes."

"How was the gun pointing? Show me how it was."

He stepped away from the edge. I eased to the lip of the cliff, crouched on hands and knees. I watched Cranston's hands. "I was standing here and he was about where you are when he pulled the gun on me. I jumped him and it went off right in my face. The gun fell as we went down. He scrambled for it, snatched it up and whirled, jumping backwards, and lit like I am now. Except he jumped too far and went over the edge. His gun hand smacked the rock and he squeezed the trigger off again as his hand went numb. He was holding himself by his left hand, clinging to this crease. I was going to pull him up, but he thought I was going to kill him. He grabbed for the gun with his left hand, and slipped over."

"You were going to pull him up?" he said. "You damned fool."

The light came directly in my eyes. I was dazzled, but I knew the light was in Cranston's right hand. And the outline of the left arm was visible against the night sky, hanging loosely.

He said, "From that position, the ejected shell of the second shot would have gone backwards over the cliff. So we'll only have to look for one. But where that one will be, God only knows. You knocked the gun aside. Well, we'll just have to find it."

We began combing the brush and the cracks of the rock. Though I wasn't much help in the search, for I kept an eye on Cranston's hands. It took an hour or so for Cranston to find the shell, by which time I was shaking in the cold wind, my mouth hurting as the teeth chattered. Cranston decided that the shell, from a .38 automatic, had been fired recently and must have come from Hap's gun. He flipped it over the cliff, then picked up the bar, wedged it in a crack of the rock, and made an end of the rope fast to it.

"I've stepped on every footprint I could find. We'll burn our shoes when we get back. Now for the hat." He pulled at the rope fastened to the bar, testing it. His eyes turned to me. "You're in pretty good shape, Hank."

"Not for that sort of thing."

"But I'm soft."

"I'm afraid of high places."

"Well, okay; it's got to be done."

He took off his topcoat, folded it neatly, set it down. Then he reached into the right-hand pocket of his jacket. I'd seen the bulge there. I slid my hand inside my jacket to the Luger, slipped off the safety. Cranston drew a pair of gloves from the pocket. I slid the safety back on. The big man made a loop around his middle, with a turn of the free end of the rope around the end tied to the bar. He threw the coil over the cliff. Then, gripping the rope with his gloved hands, he began walking backwards, paying out the loop around his middle. His body tilted as he eased over the lip. He paused, leaning out over space, and looked down past his shoulder at the silver breakers far below.

He said quietly, "That's a long ways down."

"Don't do it."

"We've got to get that hat." He eased over the face of the cliff and disappeared below it.

I decided the hat must actually be there.

I was afraid to step close enough to the edge to watch Cranston. I got flat on my belly, wormed to the edge. Cranston was walking slowly down the cliff, paying the rope out to the loop around his middle. Far below and to the left, the headlights of little cars moved along the highway, islands of warmth and security. I wondered what little worries the little people in the little cars were fretting about. Everybody has worries. I wondered what would happen if one of those little people, idly admiring the scenery, should spot a man on the face of the cliff far above. I decided there wasn't much chance of it, in the brief period a car came in view and went past.

Cranston eased over an outcropping. Then the rope shook and he dropped from sight.

The rock I was lying on was bitter cold. Or maybe it was just me who was bitter cold. My loins were knotted. My teeth chattered and were beginning to ache. I wondered if it were the extracted teeth that ached, the way an amputated foot drives a man wild because he can't scratch the itching toes. The rope was still taut.

"Hank!"

"Yo!"

"I got the hat!"

"Good!"

Presently his voice came again, cursing. "I'm in a box. The damned cliff shelves in here. I can't get a purchase for my feet to climb with."

"Let yourself down past that, then walk around the concave place."

"I can't. I'm out of rope. Give me a heave until I can get my feet braced."

I got behind the crowbar, gripped the rope, braced my feet and put my back into the pull. I couldn't budge it; the friction was too great from the rope binding at the edge of the cliff. Cranston was a big man, soft with fat. He would probably run close to two-ninety, dead weight. The only thing to do was to get to the very edge of the cliff and make a straight pull upwards.

I took off shoes and socks, dug my toes in the crack that Hap Arnold had clung to, and put my back into the pull.

The first pull was simple; the rope was tight at both ends. But then as I took another bite the full weight was on me. The wind didn't help any. It was at my back, gusty, trying to upset my balance. I took another bite, another, one more. The rope bit into my cold hands. I should have warmed them before I began. But cold as my hands were, sweat broke out on my body. I began panting. The dead weight of the man got heavier with every bite. Cranston's head appeared, his broad face dead white in the moonlight, taut, expressionless.

The rope jerked as Cranston tried for a foothold. "Wait!" I yelled.

Cranston froze. I was gasping. My hands were going numb, refusing to grip. I released one hand, made a quick snatch behind me to bring the rope in a loop around me; but I missed and didn't have time for another try. The line began sliding through the other hand. I grabbed the loose end and made a loop around the wrist.

"Can you get a foothold now?"

Cranston nodded. "I think so."

"Take it easy."

"Slide your slack back to the bar and make it fast."

"That's what I wanted to do, but now I can't."

"Why can't you?"

"I'm holding by the loop around my wrist. If I take that loop off I couldn't hold you. I can't grip anymore."

"Can you hold me there?"

"Yes. But take it easy."

The rope jerked as he flailed his legs for a foothold.

"Take it easy!" I yelled. "Don't jump around!"

"I'll have to come up hand-over-hand for a ways," he decided. "Past this dish-in."

One hand reached forward, above his head. He hesitated, reluctant to give up that loop around his middle. Then the other hand came up and he began rising in short, jerky movements. His breathing came suddenly loud and harsh, lips drawing back from the teeth in a strained grimace. He kicked out for the cliff. I yelled a warning but there was a desperate urgency in Cranston's movements and he paid no heed. He was wheezing, a gasping half-whistle with each breath. He got his feet braced against the cliff, which added to the pull on the rope. I wondered if the hitch on my wrist would cut my hand off.

"Get the loop around you!" I yelled.

He kept on, walking up the cliff and going hand over hand with the rope. The man was too far gone to stop. He was scrambling with frantic frenzy, the grimacing face somehow faintly green, arms and shoulders shaking from the strain, his breathing now a whistling moan.

"Hank!" With a last lunge he flung up a hand. I caught it with my right hand, fell backwards pulling the big man atop me. He rolled off and lay limply on the flat rock, moaning. Then he was sick; there was the sour smell of vomit.

I rubbed my left hand and wrist, flexed the stiff fingers. Rusty wires pulled inside the wrist. I coiled the rope, untied it from the bar, took the bar from the crack. I realized my bare feet were numb. I put on socks and shoes. Cranston lay gasping. I lighted a cigarette for him and one for myself. We smoked awhile. He got out a handkerchief, wiped his mouth. He sat up.

When the cigarette was finished he flipped it over the edge. "Well, I got it." He drew the hat from beneath his jacket, stuffed it back in. "The slide's a big place. Now they won't have a starting point."

He had certainly proved what he would do to eliminate a menace. I was a menace. Cranston reached for his topcoat, stood up, put it on. "Let's go."

"I'll bring the rope and the bar."

I picked them up, took a step, and slipped in the slick vomit. The end of the bar struck the rock, throwing my right elbow against the stone while the other end of the bar struck my neck. My right arm was numb as I sprawled, clawing at the bare rock with my other hand. Then there was suddenly nothing below me. The clawing hand found purchase as my body swung around and down. And there I was, half numb, sick, dizzy, one arm useless, hanging over the edge of the cliff by one hand. This, I thought, was how it was with Hap. This is how it feels. This is classic justice.

With the noise of the wind, Cranston apparently had heard nothing. Or pretended not to. He was looking off the other way, getting something from a pocket. It proved to be a pack of cigarettes. He put a cigarette into his mouth, slid the pack into the pocket, began feeling for a match.

I wondered how long my left hand could cling to the crack; it was already in bad shape from the rope. I got the numb elbow of the right arm on the rock for support. I tried to flex that hand. The fingers would move just a little.

Cranston found a book of matches in a pocket. He turned away from the wind, facing me, cupped his hands at the cigarette. The first match blew out. The second one stayed alight until the end of the cigarette glowed. He flipped the match away, began turning, then suddenly looked back. He looked one way along the ridge, then the other.

"What the hell?" Then he called, "Hank!"

I said nothing. I could almost close my right hand now.

His eye stopped at the tangle of rope. Then he saw my face and shoulders above the lip of the cliff. "My God!" He ran forward, squatted, got hands under my armpits and fell backwards, pulling me up. I crawled on hands and knees away from that edge.

"What happened?"

"Slipped."

"That was close. Let's get off this place. We've used up our luck."

We went down and drove to the lodge. I was baffled. Cranston not only hadn't tried to kill me, he had saved my life.

21

Clara fixed supper while the hat and shoes burned in the fireplace. We ate and got ready for bed. After brushing my teeth I decided that I was getting used to the glint of gold in my mouth. It wasn't my smile, but I'd get used to whoever it did belong to. A person gets used to anything, the prospect of eventual death or even sudden death. I decided that Cranston hadn't done it tonight because of Clara. She was the key to his desires. He had to marry her. A second accident at Devil's Slide would be too raw. Cranston would be smarter than that. He would cook up something better. I had to admire the sheer nerve of the man.

In bed, I wished I'd asked Cranston for a couple of pills. Then I was glad I hadn't. Maybe I'd better not take any more of Cranston's pills. That would be a way. Accidental overdose. Each time I began drifting off I'd start awake, hanging over that cliff again. I didn't know what time it was when the door opened and Clara slipped inside. It was bright in the room.

She whispered, "Hank."

"Go to bed."

She crossed over and sat beside me. "I'm so happy that you're back safe."

"Why don't you put something on?"

She looked at the nightgown. "I've got something on."

"It wouldn't pass the Johnson office."

"Don't you think it's pretty?"

"You're not making it easy on me."

"I'm not trying to."

"Go to bed."

"Hank, I love you."

"Scram."

"Leo took a couple of pills. He's out."

"That's not what I'm worried about."

She laughed.

"Go on," I said. "Leave me alone."

"What happened tonight, Hank? Didn't you get a good chance?"

"Maybe he's not trying to kill me."

"Don't be a fool. Nobody but Leo has reason for what has happened."

"Nobody we know about," I admitted. "Except you."

She stood up slowly. "Well."

"I'm just thinking out loud. He had plenty of chance. He didn't take it. He saved my life tonight."

"Of course I did it," she said sharply. "I killed Jim. Then I threw his body off the bridge. I fixed Millie's brakes. I made Leo lie three times about seeing Jim. I planted the typewriter in the barrel. I imitated Jim's voice over the phone to you. I killed Millie with insulin."

"It was just a random thought," I said. "I'm sorry. You'd better go."

"If that's what you think about me." She went to the door.

"I apologize."

She turned. "Where's Jim's gun?"

"On the dresser."

She picked it up, swung it onto me. She said, "You son of a bitch."

I said nothing. She crossed to the bed with that gun trained on me. "You son of a bitch, do I have to shoot you to find out if you'll bleed? You *must* be human."

A man will do anything to save his life.

Next morning was another perfect day, neither hot nor cold, with a soft, greenhouse feel to the air. I began to understand how California got people, how they retired and came out to die, and then lived forever because they just couldn't bear to leave the climate. They couldn't die on a bad day because they had to live to see another good one, and just nobody could die on a good California day.

When I went downstairs I saw Cranston stretched on the couch, snoring. Clara was on the porch, working daintily at some needlework. She was dressed this morning in blouse and skirt. The sweet American girl, sedate, reserved; a shy little thing. Damn her. She knew she didn't have to throw herself at me anymore.

She looked up as I came onto the porch and gave me a slow,

confident smile. She knew. From now on I'd be chasing her. She knew. I hated myself, but that didn't help. I had tasted the lotus and nothing else would satisfy. She knew. And it had nothing to do with what I felt for Trudy. This was a fever. A sickness. This was insanity. Obsession. She knew. She'd given me fair warning.

"Sleepyhead," she said. "We had breakfast an hour ago."

That's what she said. But the throaty voice brought back the night before and all the mad desire of it. I said, "Anything left?"

"Maybe." She stuck the needle in the cloth, put it on the deck chair and went into the kitchen. I was right along with her. I had come awake with the determination to ignore her, be casual, offhand, man of the world. This was how I was doing it. Hell, I was acting like a sixteen-year-old kid, after his first lesson by the gay young widow.

"Go out and sit down," she said. "You're underfoot."

And I went out and sat down. She was now telling me. I felt like the graybeard with his chorus girl. But graybeards know they're being fools; they can't help it, either.

When breakfast was ready she rattled the coffee maker and Cranston woke up immediately. He joined us for seconds. After breakfast I phoned the hospital and was told Trudy was staying another day; no, no complications, nothing serious at all, just a matter of complete rest after the shock.

We drove down in my car to see her during visiting hours. Her cheek was down to normal, but a faint blue line was beginning to show around her right eye. She said it was so nice just to lie flat on her back and be waited on. When Cranston began blaming himself she shushed him up. It was all her fault, she said; her coat was caught in the door and like a fool she opened it to get the coat out.

Clara said, "You men wait outside. I want a private word with Trudy. Hen talk."

Cranston and I waited in the car a couple of minutes, then Clara joined us. On the way back, Cranston suggested a round of golf. Golf needs concentration, and I was trying to concentrate on other things. So I dropped them off and said I'd pick them up in a couple of hours. Then I made fast time to the lodge, to see what I could find to add to what I knew.

As I entered the lodge, the phone was ringing. White, the private eye, was on the line. "Can you talk, Hank?"

"Yes; I'm alone."

"Watch your step, Hank. Somebody is building you for the kill."

"Yes; I know."

"Well, for Christ's sake," he said. "I thought I had news."

"I've got it pretty well taped. What's your guess?"

He didn't answer for a while. I said, "Or does it have a price tag?"

"Go goose yourself. I'm getting my fee somewheres else. What's *your* guess?"

"Dr. Leonard Cranston, D.D.S."

"Damn it to hell. It's supposed to be *my* business, coming up with answers like that. You amateurs make me sick. Why the hell don't you stick to your own business and quit horning in on mine? You don't need the money. You can afford a four-bit cigar."

"Let's get together and pool resources."

"Okay, Hank. I'll call you tomorrow."

"Why not today?"

"I'll be busy as a bird dog today. Tomorrow I'm seeing a dentist. I'll call you and let you know."

"Important things first, of course. It doesn't matter that I'm sitting here never knowing when he's going to make his move."

"If I'm right, he won't kill you before tomorrow afternoon," he said. "And I'm damned near sure I'm right."

And with that comforting thought he hung up.

I started upstairs toward Cranston's room, then changed my mind and went out to the car. I could go through Cranston's room in the lodge at my leisure tomorrow; now was my chance to search his apartment. I'd neglected to return his key.

A half hour later I was giving the apartment a toss, in the parlance of detective stories. Just what I expected to stick to the ceiling with the toss, I didn't know. Whatever it was, I didn't find it. After some forty minutes of peeping and prying and tearing apart, I came up with exactly nothing. I should leave this sort of thing, I decided, to men of experience like White.

I left the apartment and went to the automatic elevator. My finger was on the button when I remembered the toothpaste. So I left the mechanical brain of the elevator to be disappointed, and went back in the apartment.

In the bathroom, on the bottom shelf of the linen chest, were nine tubes of toothpaste. A tenth one, half used up, was on the toothbrush holder above the washbasin. No doubt Cranston got some deal on toothpaste and bought it by the dozen. Which was neither here nor there and why I thought nothing about it until I was in the act of pressing the elevator button. Then it came to me that the entire supply was paste and not powder. How, then, had I accidentally carried away from here a brand new, unscuffed can of tooth powder, of the same size and brand as my own? And where was my own can, somewhat battered by travelling, that I'd left behind?

I found it in the wastebasket under the sink. My can of toothpowder, marred a bit by jolting around in contact with the razor, brush, comb, nail clippers, hair goo and other junk in my shaving kit. I put the can in my pocket and got out of the place.

At Crystal Springs, I found Clara and Cranston having a glass of beer in the clubhouse after their game. I had one with them, then drove them to the lodge.

The afternoon and evening passed without event. Cranston went to bed early, after telling me to drop in at the office in the morning for a treatment. I didn't want to be alone with Clara. That is, my mind told me I didn't want to be alone with her. Seeing Trudy in the hospital bed had made me realize what an utter rat I was. I wasn't going to give in to this fever about Clara. That was over. It had to be. I wouldn't get involved. So I said I was sleepy and went to my room. At the door I looked back. Below, in the big room, Clara was lying on the couch before the fireplace, looking up at me, placid and utterly confident.

There was nothing to read in the room except some old movie magazines Cranston evidently had salvaged from his reception room. I looked them over, listening. Then I went to bed, listening. And finally I heard her coming up the stairs. I heard her walk along the balcony to her room. Presently I heard her leave her room and walk along the balcony to the bathroom. The water began running. I got out of bed and locked my door. I went back to bed and listened. The water stopped running, and presently I heard her go back to her room.

I lay there for an hour or so, listening, with no sound in the night but the rustle of the redwoods outside. Then I got up and crept to the door. Very carefully, to make no noise, I unlocked it. I crept back to bed, cursing myself for a weak fool, and lay listening.

But she didn't come that night. The ball was now in my court.

I woke up to another perfect day. Clara and Cranston had gone to work. A note on the table told me there were muffins in the oven, eggs and bacon in the fridge, heat up the coffee, pick up Trudy at ten, come to the office for a treatment, love, Clara.

I made breakfast, then washed and shaved. I had a measure of tooth powder dumped into my palm before I thought of the other can, my own can, in my coat pocket. I got it, and used it to brush my teeth. I wondered if Cranston had substituted that can of toothpowder for mine with some long-range scheme in mind. Maybe the powder contained some slow-acting poison. Something that would build up over a period of time and knock me dead after the can had long since been used up and thrown away. Hadn't I read of that gimmick somewhere? Certainly it was something a dentist would think of.

The morning was so perfect I couldn't ignore it. I decided on a hike in the redwoods. Probably that soft sun was rotting me inside. People stayed in California awhile and something happened to their brains. They lost all judgment and became boosters. I went out and across the parking area. But I didn't go far into the trees before I came hurrying back. The rat had waked up again inside my skull, leaping for a way out, scratching at the base of my brain, gnawing at the back of my eyeballs, clawing the nerves of my teeth.

Back at the lodge I got the bottle of aspirin, washed three down with a glass of water, paced back and forth holding my head while the rat and the aspirin did battle. The rat was going to sleep when the phone rang. It was White.

"Hank? Can you talk?"

"You're damned right I can talk!"

"Getting het up, huh? I figured you was too damned calm yesterday about the idea of being killed."

"That dirty bastard!"

"What's he done now?"

"He buggered my teeth!"

"Oh," White said. "Say, you ought to be in *my* business."

"When can I see you?"

"I've got a dentist lined up to look at you. We've got to be sure. He won't be free until five-thirty. I'll see you then."

"Where?"

"At my joint—the New Denver. See you." He hung up.

I turned to the yellow pages of the San Mateo County phone book and began calling dentists alphabetically. After a half dozen futile calls I decided the dentistry racket was something bright young men seemed to have overlooked as a profession. Apparently the girls in the offices had heard all the stories; the quickest bid I got for an appointment was for three o'clock the following Wednesday, while one girl said she would be happy to book me for the latter part of September.

I switched to the bottom of the list and hit the jackpot on a man named Young. Young's girl said I could come over immediately. I took the luggage to the car wondering if success in life were directly related to the position of a man's name in the alphabet. Somebody once told me that book writers sometimes took pen names near the top of the alphabet to make an early impression on busy and weary book dealers scanning a list.

22

Young, I decided, was not hard up for business, just eager for money. *Your Friend Young*, a big sign atop the modernistic offices proclaimed. *Cut Rate Dentistry*. The sign had neon tubes for night duty. The building was a low, ranch house structure built around a giant live oak. There was a lot of glass trimmed with Carmel stone. It was situated on a beautifully landscaped lot fringed by spotlights peeking from the edges of a bent lawn as tight and smooth as the felt of a billiard table. I went in and was placed on the assembly line.

The receptionist processed me, turned me over to a girl who led me down a long hall. On either side of the hall were tiny cells, each holding a dental engine, a chair, and a waiting patient. A man with a white smock and crooked nose—evidently Your Friend Young— popped from office to office while girls prepared the way ahead and mopped up behind. I wondered if an endless belt couldn't be rigged up to move the patients past the dentist and improve the efficiency.

I was put in an empty cell. The girl clipped a bib on me, said it would be just a few moments and, her duty done, disappeared to convoy the next patient. Another girl came in with a clip board and a ball pen. She asked what the trouble was this morning. I said I'd been under treatment back home but had had to make a trip. She asked treatment for what. I said I didn't know the name of it, but if I didn't have the treatments I would lose all my teeth. She wrote something on a sheet, clipped it to a board on the wall, and went out.

Another girl came in, looked at my teeth, wrote something on the sheet and went out. Another girl came in, got a pair of rubber gloves from a drawer and, bracing for the impact, held them open toward the doorway. I was relieved to see the gloves. I'd been wondering about the sanitary aspect of the assembly line system. The dentist charged in, jammed his hands into the gloves while glancing at the board on the wall, shot a dazzling smile at me, and had a mirror in my mouth before I could reply to his cheery, "Good morning!"

And then something seemed to go a little sour. Your Friend Young maintained that brilliant smile but it seemed slightly fixed. He looked at the sheet on the wall again, then examined my teeth a second time. He asked when the teeth had been extracted. I said Friday. He said healing nicely. I said swell. He asked what I was being treated for. I said I didn't know the name, but it was something that gave me violent headaches and I understood that unless there were treatments I'd lose the rest of my teeth.

"We'll take X-rays," he said, and went out, slowly.

A girl led me to the X-ray room. Another girl led me back to the cell. I waited. It got to be ten o'clock. I thought I'd better phone the hospital and tell them I'd be a little late in picking up Trudy. A girl came in and held the rubber gloves. She seemed frightened. Your Friend Young came in, deliberately. He pushed his hands slowly into the gloves, picked up the mirror and examined my teeth.

The examination took all of eight minutes. Then Your Friend Young held his hands for the girl to pull off the gloves, and turned to me with his brilliant smile. The smile was definitely hard. He said nothing. He watched me, smiling, tapping one of his own teeth thoughtfully with a thumbnail. The second joint of the thumb was enlarged. That and the bent nose suggested that Your Friend Young had worked his way through dental college in the prize ring.

He quit tapping the tooth. The smile disappeared. He seemed to have come to a decision.

"You son of a bitch," he said.

I absorbed this. "You don't get business from your bedside manner. Maybe that's why you have to advertise."

Your Friend Young jerked his chin at the girl. She went out. I was conscious of a strange quietness, as if a gigantic machine had broken down. He said, "You go tell them I wasn't born yesterday."

"Tell who?"

"It's treatments you want. You go tell them I'm not that dumb. I cut rates, but this is no clip joint." He took off the bib. "Get out of here."

At the reception desk I was told brightly that there was no charge. Examinations were free, as advertised.

Trudy was waiting for me at the hospital. She definitely had a shiner. On her, a black eye was cute. I told her she'd ought to do it more often. I drove through Palo Alto to the Bayshore highway and headed for the city.

"Cranston tried to kill you," I said.

"Hank, what are you saying? My coat was caught in the door. I opened the door to get it out just as he made the turn into the highway. It was my own fault. I should have had more sense."

"Then he saw his chance and took it."

"Hank, you're joking."

"It's time you knew everything. For your own protection. Because he'll try to do it again. Trudy, promise me you'll lock yourself in your apartment today. Don't let anybody in. I mean anybody."

"You poor boy," she said. "Are your teeth giving you trouble? Haven't you been able to sleep? You've been under such a strain."

"Trudy, Jim is dead." This was brutal, and I meant it to be. "Leo Cranston murdered him. Cranston faked the suicide to cover the murder. He killed Jim to get Clara, and Jim's property through her. But without proof of death he'd have to wait seven years. Too, Hap Arnold had the goods on him. And because the supposed suicide took place before the insurance policy was a year old—"

She began laughing. "Hank, what in heaven's name are you dreaming up?"

"Damn it, I'm trying to tell you! Cranston faked the letters and phone calls from Jim. He sent Hap and Millie to frame me on a badger game on the way out. Millie put something into my tooth powder to give me headaches."

"I never in my life!" she cried, and laughed again. "Something in your tooth powder!"

"That's right! I got a splitting headache every time I brushed my teeth." I told her about the substituted can of powder. "There's nothing wrong with my teeth and there never has been." I told her about Your Friend Young.

"You'll take his word," she said. "You'll take the word of an advertising dentist. An incompetent who can't make a living by ethical practices. You'll take his word and think the worst of Leo, who is one of the finest dentists on the Coast!"

"That can of tooth powder—"

"What of it? You had another headache this morning. Leo told you there would have to be treatments. You would have had the headache regardless of what tooth powder you used, or if you didn't brush your teeth at all. You've jumped at wild conclusions with no evidence at all. Hank, I hope you haven't been talking around about this. Leo would be terribly hurt."

"Okay, I'm crazy. So's White, I guess. He got the same answer, working independently on his own hook. I'm seeing him this afternoon."

"Oh, dear," she said. "Well, I suppose I'll have to tell you, to keep you from making an ass of yourself."

She didn't say anything for a while. I drove through a railroad underpass. A marshy smell came from the bay to our right. I said, "Tell me what?"

"I saw Jim Saturday."

I looked at her sharply. A car honked angrily, and I pulled back into my own lane. "You saw Jim?"

"Yes. At Crystal Springs, Saturday morning, on the golf course."

"You're sure it was Jim?"

"Don't I know my own brother?"

"How close were you to him?"

"I talked with him."

"Oh," I said.

"I sliced a ball into the rough. I was looking for it in the tall brush when Jim spoke to me. Hank, it was so wonderful to see him again. He told me that everything would soon be all right, and he could come back to us. He and Leo have been working together. Jim said he was going to get in touch with you, soon. He told me not to say anything about seeing him, but— Well, I have to do something to keep you from spoiling everything. And now I hope you can see how utterly ridiculous this whole fantastic web of suspicion against Leo is."

"I see," I muttered. I saw everything. It was all so plain. There was but one reason why she would be lying to protect Leo Cranston. And I thought how fine it would be if somebody started the chain reaction and blew the world to hell. Nothing hurts worse than to find you've been played for a sucker, that the finest emotions of human nature have been used as bait for a trap.

There wasn't much said on either side during the remainder of the trip to the city. I let her off at her apartment and then drove to Cranston's office for a treatment.

The door of the reception room buzzed as I went in. Clara came from the hall and led me in, despite the patient victims waiting ahead of me.

"I want to talk to you," she whispered. "Lunch?" I nodded. We went into the dental office. I took the chair and she clipped on the bib.

Cranston painted my teeth a brilliant purple. He said everything was coming along fine. Just a few more treatments. Took time, you know. "Any more headaches?"

"Yes. I had one this morning."

"Probably just nerves. We've removed the cause."

You bastard, I thought. You fiend. You cold-blooded killer. I'll nail you to the cross. I could curse him silently, but the other thing, the thing that hurt, was something I couldn't even think about.

Clara had her coat on, ready, when I left the chair. She took me to a sandwich shop around the corner. I ordered just a pot of black coffee. I decided to get drunk after lunch. I'd never done that before, deliberately gone on a bender. Now it seemed an excellent idea.

She said, "Irving Kline phoned while you were in the chair. I made an appointment for you at two, at his office."

"Okay."

"How was Trudy?"

I drew a deep breath. "She says she saw Jim on the golf course Saturday."

I looked away from her. We were in a booth. At the counter were people with ulcers, people with debts, girls worrying about their period, men worrying about the same thing, people with wayward kids, people dipping into the till to play the races, people with mortgages, people with bosses who rode them, people who were getting old. What the hell did they have to worry about? They didn't know what trouble was.

"We know that's not true," Clara said.

"Yes; we know it's not true."

"She said it to protect Leo."

I didn't say anything.

She said softly, "I'm sorry, Hank. I was hoping you didn't have to know. About them. The way you felt about her. I didn't want to be the one to tell you that. But when she lied about seeing Jim, you knew."

"Yes, I knew."

I couldn't look at her. I couldn't look anybody in the eye. Not now and maybe never. Because now I'd always be afraid of seeing the maggot. I felt her hands on mine.

"Hank, that's why I was—shameless. I tried to make you love me, Hank. There wasn't much time and I had to work fast. I had to throw myself at you. If I could make you care just a little for me, it wouldn't hurt so bad."

I was twisted and numb inside. "You did everything you could."

"When this is all over, I hope you can remember. I can make you happy. When the other doesn't hurt too bad, I hope you can remember that."

"I can never forget that," I said.

"I love you, Hank. I want to make you happy. That's all I ask."

I made the best smile I could. "You're wonderful, Clara."

"Hank!" she cried. "Do that again!"

"What?"

"Smile. Give me a grin!"

I made a grimace.

"That's why he painted your teeth," she said slowly. Her eyes were wide.

"Huh?"

She seemed stunned. She just stared at me. Her sandwich and the coffee came. I took a gulp of coffee. It burned all the way down.

"That's what has been haunting me. What a fool I've been!"

She opened her purse and I saw the Luger in it. She got out a small leather case with plastic flaps for protecting cards and photographs, and handed it to me, a flap open to a small portrait of Jim. Happy, carefree Jim. Jim was smiling out of the picture, that big smile with the gold showing in his teeth.

"Hank, you have Jim's smile!"

I knew it even as she spoke. I knew what had bothered me about the reflection in the glass, even though it had been reversed in the mirror. There had been that moment of thinking I was looking at somebody else. I'd seen my face, but Jim's grin.

I remembered Trudy's eyes widening with something like terror when I'd smiled at her in the hospital. As if she'd seen a ghost. "He was her brother."

She took my hand again. "It wasn't planned, Hank. Don't think that of her. It just happened. She was having an affair with Leo. Jim walked in on them. There was a fight, and Jim was killed. Then it was a question of being implicated in a scandal and facing a charge of murder. The fake suicide covered that. And then—well, that sort of thing grows. You become involved and the situation brutalizes you. I think Trudy and Leo are secretly married now. Through her, he can get everything by producing Jim's body and establishing the time of death as after one year from the time the insurance was taken out. You are to be Jim's corpse. Your teeth are now his. You will be killed in such a way that the only identification will be through the dental work."

"But you will inherit from Jim."

"Yes—which means I will have to be killed, first."

I said, "There just can't be such people in this world."

"You were the ideal victim. A friend of Jim's, member of a prominent family whose testimony wouldn't be questioned. Trudy knew you had perfect teeth, which were necessary. Any fillings or extractions wouldn't coincide with Jim's. By framing you with Millie, they could blackmail you into swearing that Jim was alive. Trudy would charm you in the meanwhile. And of course you had to be scared into the dental work."

"Millie doped my tooth powder to give me headaches."

"I've been wondering about that. One of the nitrite compounds would give you a violent headache."

"The X-rays were faked."

"Leo had them prepared beforehand. Everything was ready."

"What a fool I am!" I said. "Hap told me, that night at Devil's Slide. He told me in so many words—I was to be killed for Jim. How much plainer could he have put it? That didn't mean at Jim's orders, as I supposed; nor, as you and I figured it out, because of Jim. It meant exactly what he said, *for* Jim—to take Jim's place."

"Of course. There it was, all along. But who would ever think of such a thing, Hank?"

I began swearing thinly. Murder was one thing, mutilation another. The butchery of perfectly good teeth was the work of a fiend. "That bastard! I'll get him if it's the last thing I do!"

Her hands tightened on mine. "Don't do anything rash, Hank. You're safe until your mouth heals. He can't produce a corpse with evidence of recent extractions. You're safe for the present—so long as he doesn't know."

"He does, by now."

"Trudy? Yes, she'd tip him off." Clara rose. "I'd better get back. I'll calm Leo down. I'll tell him you feel like a silly fool about having suspicions. I'll tell him you asked me to say nothing, but it was such a good joke I have to tell him."

"You're wonderful, Clara."

She gave me that calm, confident smile as we went out. She knew what she did to a man. She'd warned me.

I walked to the office building with her. At the elevator she said, "You're seeing Kline at two. Let me know what he says. Maybe he can help us."

"Okay."

I turned away mulling over the idea of getting tight. It seemed an excellent idea.

23

The office was done in knotty pine, given a wash of antique with the knots rubbed. There were two desks, with bronze name plates. The plate on one said, *James Daniels*. It was unoccupied. The plate on the other said, *Irving S. Kline*. The owner of the name sat at it, both of him. Both of him regarded me with less than admiration. Both of him said, "Isn't it a little early in the day?"

"It is never too early in the day to get drunk," I said. I felt like hell. I should have known better. It didn't make me forget. It made it worse. With great effort I focused both Klines into one.

"You're in no condition," he said. "Let's make it tomorrow. Early." Obviously he felt that only an early appointment would find me sober.

"Yah, I didn't think you had anything to say," I sneered.

"I do have something to say."

"Then spit it out."

"I didn't tell you quite everything the other day because you made me sore. Then I got to thinking. You had a right to suspect the worst, seeing it from your viewpoint—"

"Spit it out."

"Please. Well, in brief— My legal standing in this situation is extremely dubious. Ethically, it's worse. I took the stand. I did half to protect my own interests and half as a bluff. The bluff worked."

"What bluff?"

"Clara Daniels never took legal steps to get control of her husband's property. And she could have done it. While Jim was not legally dead, he obviously was in no condition to take care of his own affairs. Yet Clara never called my bluff. Does that mean anything to you?"

"No."

Kline regarded me with even greater distaste. "Bluntly, I think she was afraid to. If I fought her, it might unearth something she wouldn't want to come to light."

"Why should it?"

"You're in no condition—"

"Spit it out, damn it!"

"She was having an affair with that dentist. Cranston. It was common knowledge. Everybody knew about it but poor Jim. Naturally, he would be the last to find out. I think he walked in on them and they knocked him over. I never swallowed that suicide deal. I knew Jim too well."

I began laughing.

"What's funny?"

"You're killing me!"

Kline said testily, "I thought you were his friend."

"I know what you don't."

Kline waited. I wasn't telling him, or anybody, right now. He said, "That's all I know, Hank. I've been hoping she'd call my bluff. I'd force an investigation. The whole deal smells bad. Right now I'm holding a half million dollars that should be hers. And she's afraid to try to get it."

"Thanks for nothing."

I got up from the chair and the floor tilted. The wall came over and smacked me. I climbed to the door and went out. I walked around the block three times wondering why the hell they didn't stake down the hills of San Francisco. You go down a street and the next time around the block you have to climb up it. Each time I passed Kline's office I waved at the window. By the fourth time around the streets were leveling off.

I went into Kline's office, borrowed the phone, called Clara and told her what Kline had said. We both laughed about it. It was very funny. When I hung up, Kline called me a dirty name. I might have made something out of it, but I felt like hell.

At five-thirty that afternoon I felt infinitely worse. I was hanging over from a daytime drunk. Nothing, I decided, could be more horrible. I walked up and down a block of Eddy Street afraid that I might not die after all. There was sand in my knees. Somebody had hung a hundred-pound weight on my chest. Rusty springs creaked every time I turned my eyeballs. I was fairly sober.

Somebody had moved the New Denver Hotel on me. I had walked back and forth on this block where it used to be, according to the address, a half dozen times. And I was in no condition to be walking back and forth. I felt that the city of San Francisco should provide holes for people in my condition to crawl into. Then I saw a narrow hole between two buildings. Stairs led up the hole. I forced my rusty eyeballs upwards and discovered a tiny sign, weathered and peeling, indicating that this was the New Denver Hotel, rooms 50¢ up.

I went up the stairs, wondering if my creaking knees would get me arrested for disturbing the peace. On the landing stood a counter of raw lumber. Nailed to it was a bell to be rung, according to a sign, for service. I tapped it, and cringed at the noise. Somebody had sandpapered my eardrums. Nothing happened, so I tapped again, twice.

"I'm coming," a woman's voice said irritably.

She appeared at a door behind the counter. She was in her late thirties, a full-blown blonde who had been blown too far. She held a dressing gown together with one hand and fluffed the blonde hair with the other. Her lipstick was smeared. She said, "What do you want?" I said I wanted Milford E. White. "He's 207," she said, and went back through the door.

I walked along the corridor looking at the room numbers. The place smelled of rotting carpet, termites, mice, and cooking in the rooms. Number 207 was to the right on a branch hall. I knocked. There was no answer. I knocked again. Then I tried the knob. And instantly I was cold sober. I didn't open the door. I just eased it enough to see that it was unlocked, then pulled it to. I knew what I would find if I opened that door, and I didn't want to find it. Not without a witness.

I wondered if the woman would remember me. And if she did, the time I arrived. That could be important, when Milford E. White was found dead in his room. I went back to the counter and hammered at the bell. The woman yelled that she was coming. She looked out the door. "Oh, it's you."

"Mr. White isn't in. He doesn't answer the door."

"Then he's out."

"But I had an appointment with him at five-thirty. It's five-thirty now by my watch. Do you have five-thirty?"

She looked behind her at some clock in the room. "Yes, I got five-thirty. So what?"

"He doesn't answer the door."

"I don't pry into his affairs. He don't pry into mine." She pulled her head out of the door before slamming it.

With sudden determination I spun on my heel and walked back down the corridor, turned right into the branch hall and flung open the door of 207. It swung back against the flimsy partition and the whole upper floor shook.

There was no dead body.

The room held nothing but a bed and a chair and a rickety table. A rod had been fixed to one bare wall for hanging clothes. I shut the door feeling that Father was right. The reading of murder books gave people crazy ideas. At the desk I hammered the bell several times, then hurried downstairs. Luckily, my knees didn't give way.

I turned into a bar and got a bromo. Then I used the pay phone on the wall to dial Clara's place. There was no answer. So I dialed Trudy's apartment. She answered. "Hank?" she said in a strained voice. "White just called. He's trying to locate you."

"I'm trying to locate White."

"He's at Leo's office. He wants you to call." She hung up.

I dialed Cranston's office. White answered. I said, "What's up?"

"I've got Cranston dead to rights," the private eye said. "Come on over."

"With bells on," I agreed.

I left the bar and began waving at taxis. They were all filled with the afternoon rush. I began walking, keeping an eye out for an empty cab. I was on Sutter, a block from Cranston's office, when an empty came along. I let it go by.

The door buzzed as I entered Cranston's reception room. At this hour there were no victims waiting. But as the door closed I saw that Cranston was waiting behind it. "Hello, Hank," he said cheerfully, taking my arm. "I've been expecting you."

I had expected something quite different. "White?"

"He's resting. You look done up, Hank. How about a bracer?"

He kept that grip on my arm. I allowed myself to be urged along the short hall. I was in no condition to object. At the end, where the hall widened out into Clara's office, I saw through the open door into the dental office. White was in the dental chair, with his neck screwed around in a most unnatural position so he could look back through that door. The reason for the odd position was that his neck was the only thing he could move. He was lashed to the chair.

"Sorry," White said.

I swung at Cranston. For my trouble I got an expert elbow in the neck. That took the fight out of me for the moment. Cranston lifted the phone on Clara's desk, dialed. I heard it ring on the other end, and the connection come open.

"Hello, Trudy," Cranston said. "Put Clara on." He handed the phone to me.

"Hello."

"Hank?" Clara's voice said. "Darling ..." she began, sobbing. "Trudy has me tied hand and foot to a chair. She's holding the phone for me now."

Trudy's voice came: "I'm sorry, Hank, that it had to be this way."

Cranston took the phone from me. "Hello, sweetheart. Keep her on ice. I'll keep calling. Don't take any chances. If I don't call, you know what to do." He put the phone down. "You look bad, Hank. How about a bracer?" He stooped to open a drawer and I jumped him.

He was expecting it, eager for it. He lunged upward from a crouch in a football tackle. His shoulder rammed into my guts. My head smacked back against the wall. I fell heavily to the floor of the hall, with him on top of me. He climbed off, pulled me halfway up and clipped me on the jaw. Then he helped me to my feet. It took all I had just to stand up.

"Take it easy, chum," he advised. "Maybe I should explain things, so you won't get any more funny ideas. We've got Clara at a place you'll never find. Trudy waited at her apartment until you phoned her, then buzzed over there. Trudy and I have a schedule of telephone calls, and it's too late now to be squeamish. I'm to call Trudy every so often. If anything goes wrong so that I don't call, Trudy is to wait two minutes. If I'm two minutes late, it's too bad for Clara."

Cranston stooped again at the desk drawer. White, his neck twisted around in that awkward way, watched impassively through the open door. Cranston handed me a shot glass of whiskey. "Hair of the dog." He got another glass from the drawer and poured it full from the fifth of rye. "If I lose, I'll take Clara with me." He raised the glass. "Here's to crime."

I threw off the shot and it hit me a solid blow. There was one advantage to being a one-drink man; if you needed a jolt you knew where to get it. The liquor steadied me.

Cranston offered a cigarette. "Sit down, Hank."

I took the cigarette and sat down. He was giving the orders. I wondered what chance I'd have with the big guy, without a hangover.

Probably not much. With room to move around in, yes; I could wear him down. In close quarters weight meant more than condition, and he had the edge there by about eighty pounds.

I began getting dizzy. The hair of the dog wasn't what it was cracked up to be.

"Come in the office, Hank."

I got off the chair and keeled forward onto my face. I remembered then that Cranston had brought my glass of liquor from below desk level.

Cranston put the chair against the back wall of the dental office, lifted me easily with one hand on my arm and slammed me onto the chair. The jolt steadied me somewhat. I looked at White with eyes that were trying to cross.

"I'm a chump," he said.

"I'm the chump," I said.

"We stepped into it, Hank."

Cranston went to his usual position as a dentist before the chair. "Let's get on with things."

White called him a fighting name.

Cranston said, "That will get you nowhere."

White called him another name.

Cranston moved suddenly, and with force. When the movement steadied, the shock of what I saw cleared my blurring eyes somewhat. White's mouth was propped open. With one big hand Cranston held the man's head against the back rest and with the other rammed the dental drill into a tooth. The engine whined full speed. White writhed against his bonds. I smelled a faint and acrid scent of smoke. White gave low moans. Then he screamed. Cranston stopped the drill, removed the thing that held White's mouth open. The detective's head rolled back and forth loosely as he moaned.

"How's your memory?" Cranston asked.

"Yes! Christ, yes! But do something, doc!"

Cranston used a hypo. Presently White subsided. He was wet with sweat, breathing heavily. I knew now that I'd never go to sleep, regardless of what had been in that drink. I thought maybe I was going to be sick.

Cranston said, "Well?"

"What do you want to know?" White asked.

"The part you can prove."

"I can prove all of it." White spat at the bowl. "You and Trudy were having fun together. When Jim walked in on you, you brained him with a chair. To cover up, you faked the suicide."

"You've got it taped," Cranston said.

White nodded. "Then things went haywire. A beard-and-sandal character named Hap Arnold just happened to be walking across Golden Gate Bridge at three A.M. in the fog when you threw the weighted body over the rail. You stalled him off at a hundred a week."

"You're a good detective."

White looked down at the bonds and smiled wryly. "Then you saw a way to get Hap off your neck, get everything Jim had, and take a bonus of fifty grand with the insurance. It meant killing Clara and fixing Hank's teeth so he would be a substitute corpse for Jim, but it was worth it."

"Worth it?" Cranston said harshly. "You damned fool, it was my neck! Hap could have put me in the gas chamber!"

"He damned near did when he tried to kill Hank at Devil's Slide and went over himself instead. If Millie had gone to the police with that evidence instead of coming to you, it would have been just too bad."

"How did you tumble?" Cranston asked.

"The teeth. Hank told me he needed four extractions, a bridge, and eight inlays. The first dental work of his life. That woke me out of a sound sleep the other night. I'd seen the police file on the case, including the copy of Jim's dental chart you'd furnished before things got complicated. I checked it and found Jim Daniels had lost four teeth, had a bridge and eight inlays. Curious coincidence. Everything came together."

"How much of this can you prove?"

"I can put you in the gas chamber, Cranston."

"You could have."

"I could have."

"I think I need a drink," Cranston said. "Join me?"

24

I tried to think, but my brain wasn't up to it. I wished I didn't have the complication of the hangover added to the Mickey Finn. It took all my attention just to keep from falling off the chair. If I could only

move around, wear it off. Attacking Cranston wouldn't do any good.
I was in no shape for it. He was bigger, stronger. He had had no
Mickey. He had fought his way up from the gutter while I hadn't
even had a pair of boxing gloves on in my life. Even if I did somehow
get the better of him, tie him to the chair, drill his teeth—what good
would it do? He wouldn't dial that phone at the right time. If he lost
he'd take somebody down with him. He wouldn't lose like a
gentleman.

"Hank?" Cranston asked at the door.

I realized he was asking if I wanted a drink. "No, thanks."

Cranston stooped at Clara's desk. I lunged for his tool cabinet. A
knife, something.... It was a bad idea all around. All the lunge got me
was the floor in the face as my knees crumpled. Cranston came in
with the fifth of whiskey under his arm and three shot glasses
upturned over the ends of his fingers. He lifted me with his free
hand and slammed me onto the chair. "Quit that. Sure you won't
have a bracer?"

"No."

"You mean you're not sure?"

"Quit playing with me."

"But I like to play with you. We're going to play together for a long
time, Hank. Until your jaws heal up to look like old extractions. I'd
rather make it *play* than do it the hard way, wouldn't you? Have a
drink, Hank. You don't have to worry about developing bad habits."

"No, thanks."

His big hand cracked against my face. I fell off the chair. He picked
me up and slammed me onto it again. "You're too nice. You're too
pretty-pretty nice, Henry Chatworth Oates III. You high-class snob.
All my life I've wanted to sock it to people like you. That's why I
became a professional man. I stick it to them and they love it. I'm
going to take you apart and see what makes a snob tick. You're going
to amuse me, Hank. I'm taking you out to my lodge to devote a long
summer to your training. I guess I was just born lucky. This is a
dream come true."

He slapped me again. This time I didn't go off the chair. The slapping
was clearing my head. "You're a fool, Cranston."

"*I'm* a fool!" He laughed.

"You're sunk. Simply because I *am* Henry Chatworth Oates III.
You can't hide *me* out until my jaws heal. You can't even kill me and
throw me off the bridge in a sack, and get away with it. Because I

am what I am, like it or lump it. I'm not a Jim Daniels—just another young man about town. There's power behind me. My family has influence. Drag. Pull. Suction. High up. Up to the top. And money to burn. Henry Chatworth Oates III can't disappear with nothing but a routine police investigation. They'll turn this thing inside out and they'll never leave it. This year, next year, twenty years—they'll never give up. They'll never quit until they dig you out of a crack. You'll never know a day of peace, Cranston, because you'll live under the sword."

He drew back his balled fist.

"Go ahead!" I yelled. "Ruin your dental work, you fool!"

He controlled himself with an effort. He slapped me back and forth, back and forth, back and forth. There was the salt taste of blood in my mouth. But my head was clearing fast. He stepped back, breathing heavily. He was afraid.

"You poor, two-bit guttersnipe!" I laughed. "You can't escape your environment. You think like poor white trash and nothing you can do will change it. That's what's the matter with you. You never thought it through. Like all trash, you just tried to take what you wanted."

"You prissy snob!" He knocked me off the chair. This time I could have gotten up under my own power. He picked me up and slammed me into the chair. Everything helped. I was feeling, considering the circumstances, almost normal.

I indicated White. "Look at him! Have you seen the New Denver Hotel? His room has no bath, no basin, no telephone, not even a closet."

"I'm doing the best I can, Hank," White said. I felt like a heel, but it was for a purpose.

"Let's face it," I said. "Ability is measured by money. What does that make White? And a guy like that broke the case! What do you think will happen, Cranston, when the top brains of the detective profession hit this case with an unlimited expense account? White has been to the police. He talked with a dentist. I went to Your Friend Young this morning. Kline is suspicious. I've talked to people you know nothing about. I've written to my folks about the dental work. No man can walk through a day of life without leaving a trail, if there's enough money and brains to trace it. You're done, Cranston."

"You think so," he muttered. He was shaken. With sudden frenzy born of fear he began slapping me again. I clung to the chair. I'd had enough, and this threatened to reach the point of diminishing returns.

"Don't think I like it!" Cranston yelled. "Jim caught us together. It was kill or be killed. Then Hap popped up. One thing led to another. And a man might as well turn a profit on what he has to do. I can't undo anything. I can't turn back. I'm playing the hand out. And it's my life in the pot."

He suddenly whirled away from me, fighting for control. "I'd better fix those teeth of yours before you start feeling them," he said to White.

"Why bother?" White said.

"We don't want a corpse that points to a dentist. That would narrow the field. In case," Cranston said, "a corpse is ever found."

"I didn't think it was just because you was soft-hearted."

"You're bitter. Why?" Cranston began repairing the damage to the teeth. "*I'm* the one to get sore at the world. How many men play around with a girl and nothing happens? So why do I have to be the one to get a break like this? I didn't want to kill anybody. I was just picking up a little fun on the side like any man. So he walked in and it was either him or me. Does that make me bad? When you're in a thing you can't help it. You do what has to be done."

White said, "You tried to make a profit, Cranston."

"That came later. If I'd had that in mind, do you think I would have been fool enough to have put myself in a spot where I had to have a counterfeit corpse? When things piled up I had to get out from under. And if I could turn an honest dollar on the deal, what the hell? That's human. When this is over I'll be just the same as before. Popular young dentist. Fine fellow. Credit to my profession. I'm not a crook. I just got caught in circumstances."

"I'm not bitching," White said. "You won and I lost." He added wryly. "I'm used to losing."

Cranston said, "Can I do anything for you? Any last little thing?"

"I've always wanted a four-bit cigar. Not that I never had a spare four bits. It's what it stood for. Being on my way. Something ahead. Now there ain't nothing ahead. So I'd like that four-bit cigar."

"You'll have one," Cranston said.

He turned to the cabinet, and that's what I'd been waiting for. After his tirade, the matter of a drink apparently had been forgotten. The whiskey bottle was on the tray by the dental chair. In one leap I could grab that bottle and smash it over his head. It could mean the death of a very nice girl, but that couldn't be helped. White was a human life. And I was through trying to see things to the end. As Cranston turned I gathered myself, and just then the door buzzer sounded. Someone had come into the reception room.

Cranston whirled, his hand going inside his smock. He muttered, "One word," then made his professional smile and slipped into the hall, his hand inside the smock.

I moved to the dental machine, took the fifth of whiskey from the tray, sat down again on the chair, holding the bottle below the chair on the wall side by the neck. White gave me a look of approval. Then a muffled shot sounded.

"Murder always multiplies," White murmured as I rose and cautiously peered past the hall door. I slipped into the hall.

Through the door of the reception room I saw Cranston's big body on the carpet, face down, arms outflung. I eased along the hall, my left side forward, the bottle in my right hand. Then I saw Clara. Her open handbag hung from her left forearm. Her right hand was clenched inside the bag. There was a tiny hole in the end of the leather purse. In the air was the thin bite of burned powder. Clara was looking down steadily at Cranston's limp figure. Then as she caught a movement, her eyes darted to the hallway and she saw me.

She turned and her left arm turned and the bag turned with her right hand inside it. The little hole was pointing directly at my chest. "See if he's dead," she said.

I went through the door, kneeled beside Cranston, turned him over. The bullet had entered his right eye and had come out above his left ear. I stood up. "He's dead."

Then she was against me, clinging, suddenly limp and all feminine. "Hank! Hank! Oh, *Hank!*" She began shaking all over with sobs. "What I've been through!"

I let her cry a bit, until the worst was over. "Tell me all about it, Clara."

"It's too horrible. They—" She stiffened. "The shot. I wonder if anybody heard?" She slipped to the outside door, then paused long enough to wipe her eyes and repair the make-up. She stepped casually into the corridor. After a moment she came back inside. "Nobody around looking curious. The building is pretty well deserted by now; it could have been a backfire on the street below."

"You're wonderful," I said.

"Hank, I—never knew I could do a thing like this." She looked at Cranston's body, shuddered, came against me for shelter. "But it was for you. And for poor Jim ..."

"What about Trudy?"

"I got loose. Oh, Hank, darling! What I've been through!"

"You killed Trudy?"

"No; the law will take care of her, darling. I tied her up. We've got to get Trudy to write out a full confession. Otherwise she may lie to save herself." She wiped the blood from my lips with a handkerchief and put the handkerchief back inside the open purse. "Has he been beating you, darling? You poor thing. Henry, you go, now. Go to the lodge and get some rest. Let me handle this mess. I'll keep you out of it. We don't want your name dragged through the mud. You go to the lodge and get some rest. Let me handle things."

"I want to talk to Trudy. Where is she?"

"Darling, you don't ever want to see Trudy again. Remember her the way she was. I'll get a confession from her. One that doesn't involve you. You go, now; I'll untie White." She turned to the hall.

I said, "How will you explain killing him?"

She paused, looking back over her shoulder. "I killed Leo in self-defense. It will all be plain when we have Trudy's confession."

"I mean killing White."

Her body came around with the slow grace of an alert cat. "What do you mean, darling?"

"I'm to go to the lodge. White just never will be seen again. Just a cheap private eye living in a fourth-rate hotel. Who will bother about it? Who will care? He's got to be killed."

"But he's on our side, Hank."

"He's on our side," I agreed, "but our side isn't your side. You and Cranston were in this from the beginning. Trudy is as innocent as a baby."

"Darling, you've been beaten and drugged. You're so confused. Just this morning Trudy lied to you about seeing Jim alive at the golf course. There's only one possible reason for that lie. To protect herself and Leo."

"There's another reason," I said. "I saw it at the time. I saw the reason for everything. I saw the whole thing, then. You and Cranston were having an affair. Jim walked in on you and Cranston killed him. You covered the murder by a phony suicide—throwing the weighted body off Golden Gate Bridge on a foggy night, and leaving Jim's car on the bridge with a suicide note. But two hitches developed. One was that Hap Arnold just happened to be walking across the bridge late at night in a heavy fog. He saw the two cars stop in the center of the span. He saw Leo Cranston get out of one car, throw a heavy bundle over the rail and get into the other car, which was driven by you. You and Cranston drove away, and Hap investigated the other car and found the suicide note. He knew it was murder. From then on you were paying him blackmail.

"The other hitch," I said, "was with Kline. He wouldn't deliver Jim's share to you. Jim wouldn't be legally dead for seven years. Kline was suspicious, and Hap had the goods on you. To get out from under, and to get the estate, you had to have a corpse. Also, there was the matter of the insurance. So you came up with the idea of a phony corpse that would be identified by the dental work. Which is where I came in."

Clara was smiling, with the tolerant expression of a person listening to a child. "Go ahead, darling. Get it off your chest. Then I'll show you how wrong you are."

I said, "Hap and Millie were supposed to frame me with a badger game, so that I would be forced to swear that Jim was alive. You dangled the insurance before Hap for this. But he was smart enough to see through it. If Jim were established as alive, he would have no hold on you. So he warned me. He tried to frame me to keep me out of it. Then when I was involved he tried to kill me, to protect his own interests.

"The attempt on my life threw your plan out of gear. You and Cranston gave me the cigarette in the neck to find out what Hap told me. You realized that I would no longer be in there pitching for good old Jim. I thought Jim was trying to kill me. So you had to switch your plan and un-sell Jim to me. You did that at your apartment, filling me full of lies about Jim. This was just as good, from your viewpoint, because now you had a hold on me because of Hap's death."

"Oh, you poor thing," Clara said. "You're so upset. If I was in with Leo, why would I kill him? Why would I tell you everything? Why would I do everything I've done to help you? You didn't even suspect Leo before I pointed it out to you. I made you realize that Jim had to be dead. I told you about your teeth being like Jim's. Why would I do that, if I was working with Leo?"

"Because you decided to shake Cranston," I said. "That explains everything. You were toying with the idea that first night in your apartment. That's why you threw yourself at me and pulled the story of having been in love with me for years. You were experimenting with the idea. But you weren't completely sold on it then, because you did let Cranston work on my teeth. And you tore up Trudy's apartment, making it look like the work of vandals, to cover up destroying the pictures of Jim showing his dental work. You were toying with that idea, and playing the original plan, until we went to the lodge. Then you decided to shake Cranston."

"But you know that's not true, darling," Clara said. "Didn't Leo get everything from White? Trudy said—"

"Cranston forced White to lie about Trudy for my benefit. Do you think a detective would be reluctant to talk about what he knew, if he had the goods on Cranston? The whole thing was to make me think the worst of Trudy. Then the supposed danger to you was to keep me in line until my mouth healed—that is how you sold it to Cranston. Cranston bought the idea, not knowing it sealed his own death."

"Trudy lied to you about seeing Jim alive," Clara said. "Why would she do that if she was innocent?"

"Because you told her to, when you had a word alone with her at the hospital. You knew she had recognized my smile as Jim's. You told her I was getting suspicious of Cranston and that I had to be lied to for my own protection, because if Cranston learned of my suspicions he'd kill me immediately. That's why she lied about seeing Jim. I saw it at the time. And I knew you had put it up to her, to make me think the worst of her. I saw it all right then, you bitch!"

"You're so confused, darling," Clara said gently. "If I was involved in such a plan, why would I throw everything away?"

"Because," I said, "you know what you do to a man. If once you could get me into bed, you were willing to gamble on getting me. You told me so. You warned me. You expected me to go wild and forget everything but having you. And then you'd hold out for the ring. This deal with Cranston was peanuts compared to marrying into the Oates family. And you'd get everything but the insurance, anyhow, by waiting seven years. You were willing to gamble fifty thousand dollars on the chance of becoming Mrs. Henry Chatworth Oates III."

This is what had hurt, when everything suddenly had become clear to me while talking with Trudy. I'd thought that Clara was a girl who liked me for myself and not for what my family was.

"Darling," she said, "you're all upset. You poor dear."

Her eyes were tender and her full lips soft as her right hand slipped into the open purse. I swung the bottle. The strap of the purse ripped off her arm and the Luger slithered across the carpet and spun in the center of the reception room. As she sprang for it I knocked her sprawling across a chair. She came up like an animal, teeth and claws. I tried to be a gentleman; but she was after the gentleman's eyes and groin. So I broke the bottle of whiskey over her pretty blonde head.

She looked so beautiful, lying there, so desirable. I hadn't wanted it to be this way. She had everything that called to a man, and she had called to me and I had answered the call. I hadn't wanted it to be this way. I hadn't wanted to think she was just playing me for a chump. Learning about Clara had spoiled my day. It promised to spoil other days. And nights.

I went into the dental office and began untying White.

25

It was a perfect California morning. Trudy and I sat together at the helm of a little sailboat tacking through the Golden Gate. For a couple of weeks we had answered a million questions. The newspapers had had their field day. I was now known from coast to coast as the "Playboy Detective." It was all highly embarrassing. I had had much more trouble with the swarm of high-powered legal advisers Father had thrown to my protection—despite my protests—than with the officials of the law. The family name was at stake. But just this morning I'd received the wire from Mother:

> YOUR FATHER SECRETLY DELIGHTED.
> SALES UP THREE POINT SIX FROM PUBLICITY.

The boat sailed under the bridge high overhead. I let the sail off and Trudy tossed a wreath into the water. A wreath for Jim. It bobbed up and down on the sparkling surface, drifting out toward the open sea. Trudy's eyes were moist. I tried to swallow the lump in my throat. Good old Jim. My best friend. And I'd let a tart like Clara make me believe Jim was little short of a monster. What kind of man, I wondered, am I? Where was my faith? What did friendship mean?

Trudy put her head on my shoulder and cried quietly. I put a guilty arm around her. I wasn't worthy of Jim's sister. Not in a million years. But I'd try to make up.

"Better be getting back," White said. He was lying on his back in the bow of the boat, smoking a four-bit cigar. "Maybe a wind's coming up."

"Maybe not," I said.

He sat up, shoved out his jaw. "We're going back. It's my job to keep you safe on this barbarous West Coast until this is buttoned up and you've testified at Clara's trial and you're back in the bosom of your family. I'm not letting you get drowned on my hands and spoil it. I see a future with the Oates' Oats Company. We're going back."

I brought the boat around. Trudy and I looked back until the wreath was lost in the glitter of the sun.

"You're working for Father," I said to White. "Whose side are you on?"

"He's paying my wages. You're not."

I knew White could never be bribed. But it was worth a try. "How much is it worth not to let him know about me and Trudy until it's all over? I'm willing to abdicate, but I want to give her some of the better things first. How much to keep still until after the trial?"

White sneered. "Trying to buy me! I'm following orders. My orders are to keep you from danger out here." He took a pull on his four-bit cigar. "In my book, Trudy is no danger. So why clutter my reports with stuff about her?"

Trudy said, "Hank, I've thought it over. We can't get married. Planning on that was part of the adventure. But now the adventure is over, and that's over. I couldn't ask you to give up everything for me. It wouldn't work out. Let's face it."

"Yeah," White said, "let's face it."

"You keep out of this," I told him. "This is a private affair."

"That's what you think." He got a picture from his wallet and gave it to me. "How do you like that?"

The picture was of a beautiful girl with almost nothing on. I gave a slow whistle. Then I looked at the face. "Mother!"

"When she was in the chorus," White said.

"Where did you get that?"

"When I investigate, I investigate."

"You're a good man."

"You're damned right," White admitted. "And time somebody appreciated it."

Trudy said, "Hank, I don't think it is going to be as bad as your father made you think. Perhaps he wouldn't have been so violent about his threats if he'd meant it."

"I don't think there's going to be any trouble at all," I agreed. I whispered in her ear, "We'll shake White at the dock and get married in Reno this afternoon."

She nodded, her eyes shining.

White puffed reflectively at his four-bit cigar. "Well, I never thought I'd live to see the perfect crime. But this was it. Jim walked in on Clara and Cranston, and Cranston killed him. The body went off the bridge in a weighted sack, Jim's car was there with a phony suicide note. The perfect crime. And that's what tripped them up. It was *too* perfect. They had to have the corpse back or they were stuck for seven years. Couldn't get a dime of the estate. Couldn't get married. Couldn't get the insurance. So they both got it in the neck because they didn't have sense enough to leave perfect alone."

When we reached the dock I made the boat fast and we went to the car. Trudy and I exchanged glances. I indicated a refreshment stand.

"White, could you get me a pack of cigarettes?" I produced a dollar bill. "And get yourself a four-bit cigar."

"Got one," White said, taking a four-bit cigar from his breast pocket. He took the dollar bill, touched a match to it, and with the flaming bank note got the cigar going. "And don't try that again. You ain't going to shake me while you go to Reno to get married. I'm going with you."

"But—you can't do that," Trudy protested. "You can't go on our honeymoon."

"I got my orders to keep an eye on you," White said. "If you don't try to shake me again, I won't be sleeping under your bed. I'll only be sleeping outside the door."

Trudy regarded the incorruptible White with dismay.

"White," I said, "there's something about me that you *don't* know."

The little eyes blinked in amazement. "What's that?"

"I'm not going home."

"That's what you think." He grunted scornfully. "I got my orders. When you're through testifying at Clara's trial I'll deliver you on the family doorstep. If necessary, sewed in a sack."

I had done a little investigating of my own. "I understand you're a native son of California."

He glowered suspiciously. "Well?"

"I like California. I'm going to stay here."

Agony showed in White's face. Nothing can touch the heart of a native son like praise of California. There is no praise higher than to cut home ties and live there. "What are you trying to do?" he yelled. "Buy me?"

"I'm going to work in the Pacific Coast branch of Oates' Oats. From now on, California is my home."

"Beat it, you two!" White yelled. "But phone me every day so I can fake the reports." He threw his four-bit cigar down and stamped on it. "So I'm the guy who can't be bought! I'm the guy with principles! Beat it, you two, before I change my mind."

I didn't say much for a few miles. I was worried. "Trudy, let's go back and get him."

"A private eye on our honeymoon?"

"We do owe him a lot. And his future is at stake."

"Fiddlesticks," she said. "He was just looking for an out. Why do you suppose he dug up that picture of your mother? Don't you think he's smart enough to realize you'd never forgive him if he went on our honeymoon? Maybe your father is paying his wages now, but White is looking ahead to when you're president of the company."

"With a brain like that," I said, "he ought to go far."

She put her head on my shoulder, and I drove on toward Reno.

THE END

FILM NOIR CLASSICS

THE PITFALL Jay Dratler
"Dratler's novel is darker, sleazier and less forgiving than the film it inspired. A brutal portrait of blind lust and self-destruction... a stellar example of 1940s American noir." —Cullen Gallagher, *Pulp Serenade*. Filmed in 1948 with Dick Powell, Lizabeth Scott, Jane Wyatt and Raymond Burr.

FALLEN ANGEL Marty Holland
"This story, about a small-time grifter who lands in a central California town and hooks up with a femme fatale, is straight out of the James M. Cain playbook."—Bill Ott, *Booklist*. Filmed in 1945 with Dana Andrews, Alice Faye and Linda Darnell.

**THE VELVET FLEECE
Lois Eby & John C. Fleming**
"We guarantee your head will be spinning with double-crosses and you'll be talking out of both sides of your mouth before you finish...."
—*Evening Star*. Filmed as *Larceny* in 1948 starring John Payne, Joan Caulfield and Dan Duryea.

SUDDEN FEAR Edna Sherry
"This is a thoroughly exciting read, with brilliant pacing, which makes you absolutely desperate to know how everything will pan out."
—Kate Jackson. Filmed in 1952 with Joan Crawford, Jack Palance and Gloria Grahame.

HOLLOW TRIUMPH Murray Forbes
"...a disturbed personality done in the noir tradition... an atmospheric and evocative yarn that spans the late 30s to through WWII."—Amazon reader. Filmed in 1948 with Paul Henreid and Joan Bennett as *The Scar*.

**THE DARK CORNER /
SLEEP, MY LOVE Leo Rosten**
"The slang is tangy, the plots magnetic, the suspense sweet, the hilarity edgy... For all lovers of vintage noir."
—Donna Seaman, *Booklist*. Filmed in 1946 and 1948 with Lucille Ball, Clifton Well, Claudette Colbert and Robert Cummings.

**DEADLIER THAN THE MALE
James Gunn**
"The attitude of the book... reels between black comedy and surrealism drenched in a misanthropy that is occasionally stunning."—Ed Gorman. Filmed as *Born to Kill* in 1947 with Lawrence Tierney and Claire Trevor.

In trade paperback from...
Stark House Press, 1315 H Street, Eureka, CA 95501
greg@starkhousepress.com / www.StarkHousePress.com
Available from your local bookstore, or order direct via our website.

Made in the USA
Columbia, SC
07 July 2024

38180434R00176